OPERATION FIREBRAND: DELIVERANCE

JEFFERSON SCOTT

BARBOUR
PUBLISHING

ISBN 1-58660-677-8

Cover image © Lookout Design

Published by Barbour Publishing, Inc., P.O. Box 719, Uhrichsville, Ohio 44683, www.barbourbooks.com

Our mission is to publish and distribute inspirational products offering exceptional value and biblical encouragement to the masses.

ecpa Member of the
Evangelical Christian
Publishers Association

Printed in the United States of America.
5 4 3 2 1

*To the suffering people of North Korea,
especially the Christians—
and to all those who try to help them*

ACKNOWLEDGMENTS

As ALWAYS, I have completed this book only with the help of a host of people who generously (and without compensation, I might add) gave of their time and expertise. I must take a moment to thank them.

My North Korea experts: Pastor Douglas Shin, the Reverend Peter Lee and his assistant, Brother Terry, Eunice Ingermanson, Ronald Boyd-MacMillan, and Jeff Taylor. If I got anything right about North Korean refugees in this book, it's largely thanks to you.

My military advisors: Chuck Holton, Chris Slayman, Steve Watkins, Jeff Bramstedt, and Bruce DeFeyter. What an honor it is to call such men my friends and brothers.

My medical expert: Dr. Clark Gerhart. Once again, Clark, I'm in your debt.

My ChiLibris friends who helped me sort out the "love triangle." More than twenty of you really took the time to help me. A few went above and beyond. Thank you!

My general advisors: Rosalind Skinner, Stu Ehr, Jim Lund, Kirk DouPonce, John Miller, Gordon Golden, and Robin Gerke. Thank you for catching my mistakes! I'd rather look dumb to you guys than to the reading public at large. (Now if I could just figure out how to not look dumb at all!)

Thanks to my editor, Shannon Hill, and my editorial advisor, Mark Littleton, for their incredible insight and loving care in the crafting of this book.

Thanks also to Todd Weitzman and the good people at BirdGard for welcoming me in their halls as I wrote this book.

And my brothers and sisters in the *Battlefield 1942* battalion of the Men of God Christian gaming clan. You guys are awesome prayer warriors and on-line soldiers for Christ.

I always have to thank my Lord Jesus, who grips my heart for people like the ones in this book and then lets me tell the world about them. Thank You, Father.

CAST OF CHARACTERS

KOREAN CHARACTER NAME LIST

KOREAN names can seem strange to Western readers, but they are really quite simple to understand once you learn the pattern. Whereas in the West names are given in this order: first name, middle name, last name; in Korea, the family name comes first. John Wilkes Booth, for instance, would be Booth John-Wilkes in Korean.

Here are the names of the main Korean characters in this book:

CHARACTER NAME—FULL NAME—IDENTIFICATION

* **Chun-Mi**—Kang Chun-Mi—Pregnant woman; wife of Bum-Ji; "Big Sister" to Youn-Chul
* **Bum-Ji**—Song Bum-Ji—Chun-Mi's husband
* **Aunt**—Chun-Mi's aunt; Uncle's wife
* **Uncle**—Kang Ho-Pyong—Chun-Mi's uncle; her father's brother
* **Grandmother**—Chun-Mi's grandmother; Uncle's mother
* **Youn-Chul**—Kang Youn-Chul—Chun-Mi's younger brother
* **Ki-Won**—Son Ki-Won—Chun-Mi's sister's son; Chun-Mi's nephew
* **Chun-Hee**—Kang Chun-Hee—Chun-Mi's sister
* **Gil-Su**—Yi Gil-Su—Missionary
* **Joo-Chan**—No Joo-Chan—Missionary; teenager
* **Myong-Chol**—Kim Myong-Chol—Former NK concentration camp guard
* **Sun-Hye**—Park Sun-Hye—Pretty teenage girl; refugee from North Korea

CAST OF CHARACTERS

The Regulars

THE FIREBRAND team is a squad of specialists who go into the world's hot spots to conduct covert missions of mercy in the name of Christ, armed only with nonlethal weaponry.

Team Firebrand

* **Jason Kromer** Leader of the Firebrand team; former Navy SEAL sniper and point man

* **Rachel Levy** Firebrand's language specialist and con artist; drop-dead gorgeous and knows it; former agent for Israel's Mossad

* **Garth Fisher** Firebrand's explosives and escape-and-evasion specialist; former Green Beret; very tall, very muscular, and very bald

* **Lewis Griswold** Firebrand's computer and electronics expert (i.e., geek); youngest member of the team

* **Trieu Nguyen** Firebrand's sniper and doctor; former Olympic sharpshooter and biathlete for Vietnam and then USA; plays the cello

* **Chris Page** Firebrand's point man; former Marine Force Recon; crazed ornithologist; a model's good looks

THE PROFESSOR AND MARY ANN. . .

* **Eloise Webster** The founder and financier of the Firebrand team; African-American billionaire CEO of defense contractor ABL Corp.

* **Doug "Chimp" Bigelow** Firebrand's operations man; stays behind to monitor the team when they go into the field; former Navy SEAL; paraplegic

* **Jamie Bigelow** Doug's wife and physical therapist

He who saves one life saves the world entire.

TALMUD

PART I

OUT OF THE HERMIT KINGDOM

CHAPTER 1

Paradise

"ALL OF THEM are dead."

My husband, Song Bum-Ji, looked half-asleep when he said it, his wide forehead creased deeply as if straining to hear a voice from a dream. He leaned heavily against the ill-fitting door to Little Sister's house, blocking the rest of us from going in.

"My love," I said, touching his arm, "what are you saying? Move aside. My belly aches. Our baby is restless. I must sit."

Kang Youn-Chul, my little brother, lifted Grandmother down from the wagon and helped her walk. "Bum-Ji, open the door."

Bum-Ji held his arms out. "No, Grandmother, you must not go inside." He spoke in a hush. "We must get away before the police come, or we will all be suspected."

"Suspected of what?" Grandmother said sharply. "What are you babbling about?"

Uncle and Aunt left the wagon and joined us at the door. Bum-Ji blocked us all.

"Get out of the way!" Aunt said. "You will kill Grandmother! The ride has been the death of her. She must get inside and sit."

Bum-Ji squeezed my arm. "Chun-Mi, please. They are all dead. Do not let Grandmother see them."

I couldn't make myself understand him. What was he saying? "How can they all be dead? Bum-Ji, Little Sister is in there."

"I know. Yes, I know."

"Has the famine reached this house, too?" Youn-Chul asked.

"There is no famine!" Aunt said, sounding shrill even to me. "We are living in a socialist paradise! The Dear Leader provides well for us!"

"Enough!" Grandmother snapped, and all chatter ceased. The setting sun glowed kindly on her pale skin. She lifted her head. "I have seen death. I have seen my own son's death and my own husband's death, and many more that I will never speak of." She stepped slowly toward Bum-Ji, tottering only slightly. "If there is death here, I will see it."

Bum-Ji shut his eyes and stepped aside.

Aunt almost knocked Grandmother over in her haste to get inside. Uncle and Little Brother followed more slowly. One by one they entered, and one by one each cried out.

I looked at Bum-Ji, leaning against the crumbling white plaster of Little Sister's home. His eyes blinked quickly, like they did whenever he was trying to think of something to say. My feet were unwilling to move. Then I heard Grandmother groan and the sound of someone collapsing, and suddenly I was inside.

The dying sun only dimly lit the curling floor paper and water-stained walls of Sister's living room. Grandmother sat on the floor, her legs splayed so that the hem of her pants exposed her veined ankles. The curtains were drawn—it was surprising the police hadn't come already to investigate such a certain sign of disloyalty. Kim Il-Sung and Kim Jong-Il presided over the room from their astringently clean framed photos on the wall.

Little Sister was there, along with her husband and his parents. They seemed so peaceful, lying around the room on the frayed bamboo mats. Perhaps they'd celebrated the Great Leader's birthday too hard and were only sleeping off their drunkenness.

Uncle went to them and shook Little Sister's shoulder. Her whole body moved with it, stiff in death. I looked closer and saw the blood. It ran from Sister's eyes and from her nose and from her ears. A pool of bloody vomit lay on the floor paper where her husband lay. Its sharp tang unsettled my stomach as much as what I was seeing. The vomit had mingled with his hair and his blood. His father and mother—emaciated shadows of themselves, really—lay beside him, blood dried in blackened streaks down their faces like tears of ink.

On the low table in the center was a sheet of paper and a pen. And an opened box of rat poison.

Aunt retched on herself and went back outside.

My legs suddenly wouldn't hold me. I sank to my knees, pain piercing my back and belly. Bum-Ji was beside me instantly, easing me to the floor. "Bum-Ji," I said through the pain, "where are the children? Where are Ki-Won and Ji-Hyun?"

Uncle, Grandmother's oldest son and my oldest uncle, picked up the paper. "It is a letter." His eyes jumped to the bottom, then at me. "Written by Kang Chun-Hee." Little Sister. He cleared his throat and read aloud:

All thanks to Kim Il-Sung and Kim Jong-Il, our saviors! This family, Son Il-Sung, Han Kyung-Im, Son Jong-Un, and Kang Chun-Hee, will always be grateful to them for leading us into the revolutionary victory of communism. Please excuse our act today and do not interpret it as disloyalty to the Democratic People's Republic of Korea. Because the food rations are so low, and because of the great tragedy that no one was able to enjoy rations even on the birthday of the Great Leader, the Son family

*has decided to give all future rations to our brothers. We make
this sacrifice to honor the Great Leader and the Dear Leader.*
Signed, Kang Chun-Hee.

We looked at each other. At the cockroaches skittering from
shadow to shadow. At the cobwebs in the corners of rain-stained
walls. Everywhere but at the bodies. Grandmother appeared to be
sleeping. Uncle dropped his hand to his side. The letter spun to the
floor like a cherry blossom falling into the stream. Little Brother
walked to it, careful to step around the blood, and read it. His
young face seemed to shrivel. His eyebrows dropped and his chin
rose like they always did when he was about to cry. Water dripped
slowly in the kitchen basin off to my right.

I could smell the blood now, with the vomit—and something
else, the onset of death-stench—even over the musty odor of the
house and garden.

"The children!" I said, clawing at Bum-Ji to get to my feet. "Did
she send them away?"

"Why should we care, Chun-Mi?" Aunt said, coming back inside, a hand on her forehead. "Why should we care where the children of traitors are?"

"Lower your voice, woman!" Uncle said. "And close the door."

"They are dead, Aunt!" Little Brother said, his voice raw. "How
are they traitors when they are dead?"

"They have shirked their duty to the Great Leader, Youn-Chul!"
Aunt said, pointing at the bodies as if no one had noticed them lying
there. "Now others will have to do their work, too. They have dis-
honored themselves and us!"

Uncle strode across the living room, brushing against Aunt,
and shut the door. "We must wait until dark and then bury their
bodies beside the river. No one knows we are here. We will bury
them and be many kilometers away by daybreak."

"What are you saying!" Aunt said, moving to stand by Uncle.

"Comrade husband, you and I must go to the police this minute! You are wrong. We have been seen! Or do you forget the two children and their mother with the broken wagon? Chun-Mi had to be loudmouthed and show her face to strangers. Now we will be associated with their treachery!" she said, jabbing her finger at the bodies. "Our only choice is to bring the police running and be credited for our loyalty."

Grandmother's eyes flared. "Close your mouth, crazy woman! Do you step over the bodies of good people and speak of them as if their spirits do not linger? Ho-Pyong," she said to Uncle, "you are to blame for her talk. It is as I have always said: A woman will run wild if you do not beat her enough."

"Mother," Uncle said, palms up, "why do we talk of this now?"

I left them behind and walked into the kitchen. Let them argue. I had to find the children.

In my mind I saw Little Sister cradling tiny Ji-Hyun, her newborn daughter, and happy Ki-Won at her knee trying to feed his sister a green strawberry. That had been only six months ago. Sister had looked so thin. She hadn't gained any weight at all with Ji-Hyun, and the baby had been born so tiny. Where were those babies now?

The kitchen was brighter than the living room because there were no curtains. The rusted metal sink was chipped on the edges, like my own, and stained with minerals from the leaky faucet, which spattered lukewarm water on me as I passed. Clotheslines ran back and forth over the sink and counter, dried towels and clothes stiff on them. The faint scent of bleach tickled my nose. Faded, mismatched tiles lined the wall above the sink and around the single window, which was cracked. Little Sister's house was bigger than mine, but she had more people living there, and with the children, I didn't begrudge her the extra space.

I shoved a pile of unwashed towels aside on the peeled white floor paper and walked down the short hallway to the bedroom.

I heard movement, tiny thumping coming from the wall of the

room just to my right. Rats were not so loud, and there hadn't been an uneaten house pet in this part of the country for years. My baby moved inside me, pressing on my bladder. I stopped to wait out the pressure and to listen.

All I could hear was my family arguing in the living room behind me. Aunt was in hysterics. Grandmother was scolding. The men joined in only occasionally.

I looked at the door. My heart was beating fast. I could feel the fullness in my ears and throat. I grasped the handle and pushed the door open quickly.

Instantly the reek of ammonia and human feces struck me. My already queasy stomach threatened to empty itself. I breathed through my mouth.

It was Little Sister's bedroom, where she and her husband and the children slept. Right near the door was a gray mat, askew and untidy. The one window had been covered with blankets held by clothespins, so it was nearly dark inside.

Then I heard the movement again, louder. Something was moving toward me, aimed at my baby. I covered myself and stepped back, accidentally inhaling a full breath of the stench. Eyes glinted in the dim light. Was it some animal, something that killed Little Sister's family, or maybe the vengeful spirit of one of the—

It was a little boy.

It was Ki-Won, my three-year-old nephew. He was disheveled and reeked like a cesspool. His checkered open-bottom pants were sagging and caked with dried excrement. His cheeks—despite near-starvation they still retained some of their baby chubbiness—were smeared with dirt and mucus. But when he stared up at me, his black eyes were afraid and even desperate, and I saw that he was just a frightened little child who had been locked in this room for who knew how long.

I dropped to my knees and reached for him. "Come here, Ki-Won. It's me, Auntie Chun-Mi."

His eyes narrowed and he tilted his head. He stepped backward tentatively, and I was afraid he was going to run. But then he seemed to recognize me. His eyebrows rose, and he broke into a full-mouthed wail and staggered into my arms. I gathered him in, though he was wet and fouled. He clutched handfuls of my blouse and burrowed his face into my shoulder, muffling his cries.

Bum-Ji and Uncle came into the hallway, fear on their faces. I could hear the others behind them, jostling through the kitchen.

Bum-Ji recognized Ki-Won instantly, and for the first time since this nightmare began, I saw my husband's gentle smile. "Ki-Won," he said, kneeling beside me, creases appearing by his eyes in his grin. He tousled the boy's hair and sat against the wall.

"Shut up that noise!" Aunt said, shouldering up to the front. "And what is that horrid smell?" I didn't think her face could turn any more sour, but when she saw Ki-Won it did. "Is it the traitor's kid?"

"There are no traitors here!" Bum-Ji said, then looked pointedly at Aunt. "Are there?"

Aunt blanched. "How dare you?"

Ki-Won peeked over my shoulder, and his crying abated.

Bum-Ji stroked Ki-Won's wild hair. "Ki-Won," he said softly. "Ki-Won? Can you talk to Uncle Bum-Ji? Can you tell me what happened to your mommy and daddy?"

"Mommy?" Ki-Won said, looking between people down the hall. "Mommy? Daddy?"

"Ki-Won," Bum-Ji said, "How long have you been in this room?"

"Ask him why *he* isn't dead, too," Aunt said.

Uncle stepped forward. "Boy, what happened here?"

Their questions continued, each one louder than the last. They crowded forward, towering over me and Ki-Won. He buried his head in my shoulder and cried again. His body shuddered.

"Stop it, all of you!" I said. "Leave him alone. You're scaring him. Go. . .go away for awhile. Let me get him cleaned up. Uncle, Grandmother, find him something to eat. But bring it to him here. I don't want him seeing his parents like that. Little Brother, please can you bring soap and water to clean up this room?"

They dispersed. Bum-Ji helped me to my feet and then went before me into the bedroom. I took Ki-Won's clothes off and wiped him down with a clean part of his shirt. Bum-Ji pulled the curtains aside and light flooded the room. The sun had gone down but it was still bright enough to see.

The room was a mess. A pile of Ki-Won's excrement sat on one of the sleeping mats and had evidently been stepped on. There was no sign of food having been left for the boy, but a steel bowl beneath the window had water at the bottom and all around on the floor. I went to the wooden chest and dug through clothes for something Ki-Won could wear.

"Chun-Mi," Bum-Ji said softly.

My husband's tone stopped me. He was holding a sheet of paper to me. It was a note from Sister. She wrote it to White Heron, her childhood name for me.

White Heron, I know you will find this. I could not force my Ki-Won to make the same sacrifice we all were choosing to make. I hope he can survive until you find him. Ji-Hyun is dead. My milk dried up and she would take nothing else. We buried her in the yard.

Big Sister, what kind of mother lets her baby die? What hope do we have in this land? It is no paradise! There is no victorious revolution. We are suffering and our babies are dying. I don't care if they find what I have said, for I will be dead. I only fear for you.

You must be braver than me. I have lost faith. My heart died with Ji-Hyun, and I will follow her to the grave. But you must carry out our plan. Do you remember? The one we always dreamed of but kept secret? You must do it, White Heron. For your baby.

Take my Ki-Won with you. He is strong and gave me joy.
Make him remember me. Good-bye.

The note had a faded black-and-white photo attached to the back. A photo of Little Sister and her husband on their wedding day, just before the soldiers came. They wouldn't allow the traditional food at the celebration. They came just after this photo was taken and carted the groom's father to prison overnight for "wasting the People's food."

I was aware of people entering the room behind me and of someone asking me a question, but their words were as nonsense to me. I went to the window and looked out upon the ground. At the base of the hedge of bean plants, all dead or dying, was a little mound of fresh earth.

Ji-Hyun.

Little Sister was right. This land was without hope. Its heart had died long ago, just as Little Sister's had. Families were committing suicide to end the slow starvation, the misery. Mothers could not nourish themselves enough to nourish their babies.

I had a baby coming, too. My breasts had hardly grown. I could not even feed myself—how could I feed my own baby?

We had to leave. That was our secret plan, Sister and I. There was rumor of food in China, of plenty! I knew a young man who had fled to China and returned with money and medicine. Little Sister and I had dreamed of going, but the Party told us we had it better here than anywhere else, that in China they robbed you or worse. Certainly we had it better here than in other lands like South Korea or even America—where the people cooked North Koreans and ate them whole. And so we stayed and tried to believe in the Great Leader to usher in the victory we were told had already occurred. But it never came. And now Little Sister was dead. A whole home, dead.

Ki-Won held my leg with both arms. I touched his once-full

cheeks and knew what I must do.

I turned from the window just as the others were entering the room with food and cleaning supplies. I looked at them with new eyes. Could they make this trip I had in mind? Grandmother looked frail beyond belief, but it couldn't be helped. Aunt was a liability, so she had to come along. The men would come.

"Listen to me," I said in a tone I'd never used with them before. "Listen to me. Tonight we must leave this place. We will take Ki-Won but we will leave the rest as they are. We will walk through the night. All of us must come. We will not stop until we have reached the border of our homeland. And when we have reached the river, we will flee to China and never return."

Aunt gave a little squeak and fainted.

CHAPTER 2

THE BORDER

ONE HUNDRED feet from China.

A narrow beach of white rocks washed blue by moonlight. Eighty feet of dark water, gashed like a knife in the center by a white boulder. Swift current. Then a strip of white land on the other bank and a black wall of forest beyond. China.

"This is wrong."

We all looked at Aunt, who was peering across the border from behind the trunk of a changbai larch.

"No, Aunt," I said quietly. "It is the most right thing we have ever done."

The others fidgeted in their hiding places. Uncle rubbed his unshaved jaw and stared thoughtfully across the Tumen River. Little Brother's eyes were open wide, a look I knew well: He was ready to try the crossing. Bum-Ji sat with little Ki-Won in his lap, my husband's kind face showing a calmness I knew he did not feel. Ki-Won had collected a fistful of wooden shapes, puzzle pieces from his home, and was laying them out one by one, over and over, saying their names each time. Grandmother was dozing behind us, her bed the raft the men had constructed from branches, logs, and driftwood.

"We've come so far," I said, making sure they could hear me over the distant roar of the rapids smashing against the boulder. "I never thought we could make it all the way to the border in three days' time. We've done well." I looked across the river at the black unknown. "We will do fine in China," I said, nodding resolutely as if to convince myself. "But we must make our crossing now. Then. . .food, money, a good life. A good place to raise children."

No one but Bum-Ji and Youn-Chul would meet my gaze. I saw a challenge rise in Aunt's eyes, but then she sat back and rubbed her feet.

It was a perfect night for a crossing. There were no clouds. A three-quarter moon hung directly overhead, giving us all the light we could ask for, yet still hiding us from those who would prevent our crossing. Not that there was anyone around here. There were no villages for kilometers, and the nearest guard station was far downstream.

A river breeze bathed my face, promising bliss if only I would cross over. The gnats and mosquitoes couldn't bear up to the wind. They were swept away, and in their place came faint scents of fish, mud, and wild ginseng. Tree frogs and crickets welcomed the moon with raucous celebration. Leafy tree branches swayed and hissed in their nocturnal dance. The summer air was almost chilly here, but oh, it felt sublime! It drew my mind away from my sore back and knees and feet. A brief tremor tickled my belly. My baby had the hiccups.

"I'm concerned about the raft," Bum-Ji said.

We turned to look at it. Grandmother's face shone beautifully under the moon as she slept. What belongings we still had were piled beside the narrow raft. I was worried about it, too. It was two meters wide and three meters long—not big enough for all of us to get on. Uncle had arranged the long pieces side by side and interlaced them with strong thorn vines and his old leather belt.

"What's to worry about?" Uncle said defiantly. "I said it would work, didn't I? I served in the navy, didn't I? Did you, Bum-Ji? Did anyone else here?"

Bum-Ji bowed slightly and lowered his eyes.

Suddenly my saliva tasted like brass. An argument before a venture was bad luck. To me the raft didn't look like it would hold itself together, much less carry all of us across a fast-moving river. But Uncle had been in the navy.

"Besides," he said, "only three of us will ride on it: Grandmother, Chun-Mi, and the boy. The rest will hold on and kick us across."

Aunt's mouth stood open. She looked like she'd popped a tree frog in by mistake. "Comrade husband, must *I* swim in this filthy water, too? I will ride. Let Chun-Mi swim—her shameful weight will doom us all."

"Enough!" Uncle said. "You can swim, or have you forgotten how? You are not old or pregnant or a child. You will swim."

"Perhaps we should make two trips, Uncle," Little Brother said, his head tipping forward slightly to show deference. "I will gladly make the trip twice."

"No, Youn-Chul, it is better if—"

Something heavy rustled in the forest behind us.

Aunt gasped. We all sank lower in the underbrush. Bum-Ji placed his hand over Ki-Won's mouth, but the boy pulled his hand away. Grandmother snored softly, barely audible over the voice of the river.

A quiet footfall. A bush pushed aside then released.

And then we saw it. A Siberian musk deer coming to the water to drink. It saw us at the same instant. Its black eyes, agleam in the moonlight, widened. Its legs stiffened, then flexed. The deer chuffed and pounded away from us, smashing through the undergrowth. Smaller shadows moved on either side. Two fawns, still speckled, bounding away with their mother.

We all breathed out together. Youn-Chul and Bum-Ji laughed nervously.

Grandmother spoke in her sleep. "Two meals a day? What foolishness!" She sat up and seemed to remember where she was. "Well, what are you all sitting around for? If we're going to go to China, let's get on with it."

"Mother, you were sleeping," Aunt said.

"Sleeping? What nonsense." She gave an exasperated sigh. "Well, woman, I'm not sleeping now, am I?"

"No, Mother."

Grandmother looked conspiratorially at me and rolled her eyes. I smiled in spite of myself.

"Are you ready, Mother?" Uncle asked.

"Of course I am, boy. Have you ever known me not to be?"

"No, Mother, of course not."

The men put our belongings on the raft and then carried it to the water. It seemed very heavy to them. Was this raft going to float even with no one on it?

"Ooh!" Little Brother said, as he stepped into the river. He smiled sheepishly. "It's cold!"

Grandmother put her hands on her hips. "Why are we crossing here? It's much too wide. What incompetence! No, we will find an easier spot. A narrower spot." She began hiking downstream.

"Mother!" Uncle said, sloshing out of the water to catch her arm. "We've been through this. The narrow spots are all guarded. If we had money or cigarettes we could bribe the guards to leave their posts. But we have nothing. So we must find an unguarded spot." He swept his arm toward the river. "This is a very good place, Mother. There are no villages nearby and the river is so wide and fast that no one tries to cross here, and so no soldiers guard it.

You see? Your oldest son has Father's good mind."

"Bah!" Grandmother said. "Your father never would've done something so treacherous as leave the Great Leader's care!"

We exchanged confused looks.

"Uh, Grandmother," I said, "don't you want to cross into China?"

"Of course I do, dear child. Why wouldn't I?"

More confused looks.

"Mother," Uncle said, "if we are treacherous to leave the Great Leader's care, we should not cross into China."

Grandmother appeared close to fainting. "Why. . .why do you trouble an old woman? I want to go but I feel I should stay. I don't know! I haven't. . .ordered my thoughts." She pressed her fingers to her temple. Then she dropped them. "But I do believe we must go now. Get me to China and then I can think."

"No, Grandmother!" Aunt said. "You just said it was treacherous, and for once I agree with you! We should turn back immediately and head straight to that last village. The police must be told what—"

"No!" Bum-Ji said, pulling the nose of the raft onto the shore. "No police. No guards. No soldiers. No more Great Leader. No more Dear Leader. No more revolution. No more Communist Party." He challenged us all with his eyes. "We did not walk so hard and so far to turn back now. If we go to the police, they will find us guilty of something. We will all be sent to the death camps."

Aunt huffed. "There are no such places, Song Bum-Ji! And you know it very well. Grandmother is right: We are betraying our homeland! Think long about this, my family. Our whole lives are here. Our ancestors are here. Our way of life, our culture, our great history. Friends. The People! Have we no loyalty to our own country? Are we to become faithless deserters living like thieves in a lesser land? Come, let us go back to our own dear homes."

Stars shone upon us on the moon-swept shore as Aunt's words

burrowed into our minds. The river hurried past, dark lumps of wood and debris carried with it, caught up in something too powerful to resist. A bat fluttered overhead, chirping and darting about as if dangling on a string.

Ki-Won's sweet voice caught my attention: "Triangle. Circle. Rectangle. Square. Pentagon. Hexagon." He was squatting over the white rocks laying out his wooden shapes one by one. Some of his words were very clear. Others I could figure out only by seeing what he laid down when he said them. Pentagon, *o-gak-hyong,* was *o-gyong* and circle, *dong-gu-rah-mi,* was *dun-ga-mi;* but rectangle, *sa-gak-hyong,* was as sharp and well defined as the puzzle piece in his hand.

I shook my head slightly. "No, Aunt. You are wrong. We have no home now. Even if we did go back, the police would come. They would want someone to blame for Chun-Hee's death and the death of her family. They would come to us. Think, Aunt: People have always disappeared around us. It has always been so. They simply vanish. And the soldiers stroll by with something that belonged to the missing person. Either there are labor camps or the soldiers simply kill those who disappear. Either way—" My voice caught as I watched Ki-Won carefully dust the sand off his hexagon. "Either way, it is no longer a place to raise a child. If it ever was."

Bum-Ji came to my side and put his arm around me. His other hand he placed on my belly. Our baby was sleeping now.

Grandmother looked up at the stars and the moon. She blinked in the gentle light, then turned toward the way we'd come, toward the Democratic People's Republic of Korea. We listened to the wind and the water and said not a word. Finally Grandmother looked at me and nodded and stepped onto the raft.

I went toward the water, too. The rocks gave way to fine, wet sand just at the river's edge. I stepped onto the raft and knelt down next to Grandmother. It was an uneven platform, but it didn't collapse. The men eased us out into the water. The raft submerged under our weight. Frigid water spilled over my knees and lap and

I almost leaped off. But the raft bobbed back up. Most of it was at the waterline or below, but it did appear to be floating and it did support Grandmother and me, though we were wet and shivering in the breeze.

Bum-Ji picked up Ki-Won and brought him to me. He clutched his stack of shapes in his small hand as he tried to get out of Bum-Ji's grip. "No! No! Mommy!"

I thought he was scared of the water. "It's all right, Ki-Won," I said, receiving him from Bum-Ji. "Auntie Chun-Mi will keep you safe."

"No! Rectangle! Rectangle! Mommy!"

He squirmed so hard I thought he was going to fall out of my grip. I held him with all my might. He struggled against me terribly. I couldn't believe his strength.

"Rectangle!" He burst into an awful, heartbroken wail.

"He wants his rectangle," Little Brother said. "Maybe he dropped it."

"Never mind, Ki-Won!" Aunt said, testing the water temperature with her foot. "You don't need all your stupid shapes. We'll get you another one. Shut your mouth before the whole world hears you."

Bum-Ji ran across the rocky shore, bending over double to scan the ground. He reached down for something, then trotted back out to us. "Here, Ki-Won!" he said, holding out a four-sided puzzle piece. "Here it is."

"Rectangle!" Ki-Won snatched it out of his hand, and instantly he was calmer. He added the shape to the clutch of others and buried himself into my chest, mumbling contentedly in his secret language.

I smiled incredulously at Bum-Ji. "Thank you, my love. What a father you will be!"

Uncle pushed us away from the shore. "Come on, woman," he said to Aunt. "Get in and push or we leave you behind."

Bum-Ji, Little Brother, and Uncle waded into deeper water. I had a sudden fear that Aunt would not come. I envisioned her running to the nearest guard station and alerting them to what we were doing. Perhaps they would come looking for us by name in China. Could they do such a thing?

Now that we were committed to going, I became terrified. What were we doing? What would we do when we got to the other side? Would China receive us? China had always been North Korea's best ally. Perhaps they would arrest us? Send us back? Shoot us? Chun-Hee and I had never thought about this part. We'd always imagined that China would be a perfect place full of food and freedom and happiness. But what if everything we'd always heard was true and North Korea really was the best place on earth? What if we were headed to a place much worse than what we were fleeing? Were we truly ungrateful?

I tasted vomit in my mouth. The fear and the uncertainty and the flimsy raft combined to form a terror like I'd never felt. Ki-Won was leaning on my baby, and my baby was leaning on my bladder and bowels. I felt I was going to explode in every direction. The smell of our bodies and Ki-Won's soiled pants reached down my throat and threatened to bring up everything in my stomach.

And then I heard a strange voice. *Do not fear, dear one. I have plans for you. I will keep you safe.*

I looked around. No one else appeared to have heard it. Grandmother had her eyes shut. Ki-Won was resting gently against my chest. The others were up to their shoulders in water.

I had no idea what I'd heard. Perhaps it was only what I wished to tell myself. And yet my mind and body flooded with a warm quietness. It wasn't simply the absence of worry: This was an active, charging peace that invaded my heart and overwhelmed my defenses. I felt it would've calmed me even if I'd not wanted to be calmed. But how I did need it. My stomach relaxed, and I found I felt perfectly balanced even though I tottered on a raft in the middle of a mighty river.

And there was Aunt, swimming out to join us.

The raft tilted a bit when she grabbed on. The hair on top of her head was still dry, but the rest of her was soaked. She looked outraged and absurd, like a wet cat.

"You're too far. . .upstream!" she said between gasps. The men were still standing, but she was shorter and so had to hold on and kick. "We should be. . .below the boulder."

"No," Uncle said. "The current will carry us quickly. We'll cross well downstream of the boulder. But I didn't want to start there because then we'd be too far down. We're aiming for that wider beach area just there."

As one, the men pushed off and began kicking. I held Ki-Won close to me, though it felt as though he'd gone to sleep. Our belongings were as soaked as we were, but everything would dry out soon enough.

It was a beautiful moment. The bleached beaches bracketing the black river. The Korean trees waving good-bye, the Chinese trees waving hello. The pure white moon and ten thousand stars. The froth left by our kicking and the rapids' snowy lace tearing across the boulder below us.

As we neared the boulder the river's voice became a low roar, and then finally an unbroken shout.

I heard Uncle saying something, but I couldn't make it out. The swimmers seemed confused. Some were kicking to push us across the river, but Uncle and Bum-Ji were kicking downstream.

The current hadn't taken us as early as Uncle had estimated. We were still upstream of the boulder.

But the current did take us now. We gathered speed. All the swimmers were kicking downstream now, trying to steer us on the near side of the boulder. I could see them shouting at each other, but all I could hear were the rapids.

The boulder was huge, much larger than it had looked from shore. Rapids smashed three meters up its side, slamming against it as if the river were trying to make it tumble over and resist no more.

The swimmers weren't steering, despite all their efforts. They were only hanging on. The river was in charge now.

We were going to hit the boulder.

I screamed at Grandmother to hold on, but I couldn't even hear myself. She was already holding tight anyway.

Just seconds now. So loud! So fast!

I flattened myself on the raft, holding Ki-Won under me, trying not to press too hard on my baby. My hand gripped the side, and immediately I felt a strong hand on mine. It was Bum-Ji. Our eyes met.

And then we hit the boulder.

CHAPTER 3

THE CROSSROADS SIGN

THE RIVER tore Bum-Ji's hand from mine. The raft rose as if lifted by an invisible hand. We hit the boulder with a jolt.

The driftwood pieces shattered. The raft split apart as if the boulder were an axe. Grandmother and part of the raft disappeared on the far side of the boulder.

Ki-Won and I were flipped backward and fell into a hole in the water. I clung to his little arm with a will stronger than any river. We went under.

Silence.

Blackness.

A force holding me down. Squeezing my lungs. Tearing Ki-Won from me.

I held on fiercely. If I died they would find my body with this child's arm still in my grip.

I raged at the force fighting against me. Somehow I knew it was personal. Knew it was evil. *You can have me but you* cannot *have this child!*

And then I felt pushed aside and suddenly I was on the surface. Sweet air.

I pulled Ki-Won's face to the surface. He was not breathing. He seemed asleep.

The river's roar faded now. The current was lessening. Far away I saw someone swimming. I had to get Ki-Won to shore. But. . . which side was China? Where was the boulder?

I looked upstream just in time to see part of the raft speeding straight for m—

* * *

I saw the river again, but it must've been a dream for I was over it somehow and now there were dozens of men standing around in the water and on either bank. They were tall, powerful men. Warriors. I thought at first they must be border guards, but my mind told me these were not enemies. I didn't know how, but I knew in my heart that men like these were at that moment—no, at all times—stationed all along the border between North Korea and China.

There was a presence beside me. I looked, and suddenly I was standing on the boulder in the river. My baby stood beside me. A little girl. She seemed about eighteen months old. Round face, springy pigtail, and a beautiful pink dress. She looked up at me and giggled. My heart almost burst with joy.

Then one of the warriors was standing in the water nearby. The river came only to his knees though his eyes were on a level with mine as I stood atop the boulder. He was flanked by other warriors. There was a slight luminescence around their skin, as if emanating moonlight. I knew I'd never been safer in my life.

There was a peace in those eyes. The same peace I'd felt pouring through me before. I couldn't bear to meet his gaze, but I couldn't make myself look away. I needed that peace. In that moment I knew

I'd craved it my whole life. I wanted to ask him how I could have it, but no words would come.

Then he smiled gently and said, "Dear one, trust the sign of the crossroads."

* * *

"What crossroads?"

"Chun-Mi? Chun-Mi, you are alive?"

I knew that voice. It was my husband, Bum-Ji.

I opened my eyes and found myself staring up at the moon. It watched over me like a peaceful, protective eye.

A head leaned in and blocked my view of the moon. Bum-Ji. He looked so small to me. I'd always thought him large and strong. And his face, always so kind, now looked only emaciated. His eyes did not have the warrior's peace. He needed it, too.

Other people crowded around me, blocking the moon completely. Their faces were dark, as if they had no faces. No souls.

I tried to sit up. Pain shot through my head and neck. I lay back down quickly. I found I was very cold.

"Chun-Mi," Bum-Ji said, "do you know who I am?"

I nodded. "You are my dear husband." I suddenly remembered my baby. I reached to my belly. The pleasant bulge was there. I felt a tiny move. "Our daughter is all right," I said, releasing a breath.

"Daughter?" Bum-Ji said. "You think we will have a girl?"

"I know we will. I have seen her."

The people around me murmured and began to disperse. I heard a woman's voice I recognized: "Her mind is broken. Poor Bum-Ji. We shall have to find him another wife."

"Hush, woman." I recognized the man who said that. It was Uncle.

I turned my head to the side. There was the river. We were still on the bank, right where the sand transitioned to rock. No tall men waded in the water, but the memory of them was so strong it was almost as if I could see them.

"Ki-Won!" I said. I sat up despite the pain. I looked at my family, all of them half-dried. I saw Bum-Ji, Aunt, Uncle, and Little Brother. No little boy and no old woman. "Where are Ki-Won and Grandmother!"

They turned to me slowly. Bum-Ji's high forehead wrinkled.

Little Brother knelt beside me. "Grandmother is all right. She is resting in the trees."

"Youn-Chul saved her," Bum-Ji said. He stepped forward and placed a hand on Little Brother's shoulder. "She would not have made it. He got her to a piece of the raft and then kicked to shore. This shore here—in China. Your brother is a hero, Chun-Mi."

Aunt clucked. "Such disrespect, Bum-Ji. Can you not call her 'comrade wife'?"

"No," Bum-Ji said over his shoulder. "Not on this side of the river."

"No," Little Brother said. "Your husband is the hero. He saw you get hit on the head and go under. I was sure I would never see you again. But he dove down and brought you back up. You spit out so much water I thought a new river would form. But you never woke up—until now."

I grabbed my brother's shirt. "Where is the boy, Youn-Chul? Where is Ki-Won?"

Little Brother looked up at Bum-Ji, who also knelt down.

"I could not find Ki-Won," Bum-Ji said. His voice broke and tears sprang from his eyes. He sat back and wept hard sobs. All his tightly wound composure unraveled on the sand.

I wanted to comfort him, to caress his face and call him my dear, strong, kind, brave husband. But my heart could not. An awful hole opened inside me like the one beside the boulder in the river, and I felt myself flipped backward into it.

"I failed," I said. "Little Ki-Won needed me to hold on, but I let go. I didn't mean to. I tried to hold on. I don't even remember letting go. I wasn't going to let the river have him!" I wiped a tear from my face. "I can see his chubby cheeks and that smart, smart smile. I can feel him sleeping in my arms, his head on my shoulder. Oh, Chun-Hee, Little Sister—I'm so sorry!"

I heard footsteps behind me. "What's all this crying?"

"Grandmother!"

The others went to her side as she approached. Uncle tried to steady her.

"Get away from me!" she said. "I know how to walk. I just wanted to know what these two are bawling about."

"Grandmother, it's Ki-Won," I said, drying my tears. "The little boy. He's gone. He's drowned. I tried to—"

"He's gone, huh?" she said. "Then who's that kid over there?"

We all looked. A hundred feet down the shore walked a little boy just Ki-Won's size. As we watched, the boy squatted down and started meticulously laying something out on the sand, one by one.

"Ki-Won!" I rose to my feet despite the throbbing pain. Bum-Ji helped me and together we ran to him.

I swept Ki-Won up into my arms and spun around. Bum-Ji held us both and I sank to the sand. "Ki-Won!" I cried. "Ki-Won, you are safe!"

The others arrived. "I can't believe it," Aunt said. "Boy, do you know how to swim? How did you make it to shore?"

"Leave him alone," Uncle said. "You know he can't talk well enough to tell you anything like that."

Ki-Won held a square up toward Aunt. "Ney-moh."

"He still has his shapes," Youn-Chul said. "How could he hold onto them through that?"

We watched Ki-Won collect his puzzle pieces and then begin to lay them out again. The hole that had opened inside me now closed. I realized with wonder that somewhere deep down a part of me wasn't at all surprised to find the boy alive. With his shapes.

"Oh, no!" Ki-Won said, becoming agitated. He laid his shapes out again, but that didn't calm him. He pushed my leg aside and shuffled through the sand. "Rectangle! Rectangle!"

"Oh, great," Aunt said. "Here we go again."

Little Brother sifted through the sand with his hands. "Help him find his rectangle, or we'll never hear the end of it."

We all searched. The moon was dropping behind the trees on the North Korean side, and I was beginning to go weak from the stress and relief and pain, but still I felt around for that shape.

Then Ki-Won squealed half words that sounded much like "There it is!" He ran toward the water, his shapes clutched in a neat stack in his fist. He bent down and picked something up from the water's edge. He held it to the night sky, a look of pure joy on his wide face. "Rectangle!"

He came over to me babbling softly in his private language as if welcoming his lost shape back to its loving home.

The family moved back upstream toward where we'd been before.

I turned to follow but first looked back at the river's edge. I noticed a pattern of depressions leading from the water to the spot where the rectangle had been. It looked like a large man's footprints, but of course I knew that was impossible since none of us had been this way. As I watched, the depressions filled with water and disappeared.

*   *   *

Two strangers were on our beach. They were kicking around in the sand, talking quietly to each other. They appeared extremely interested in finding whoever had made these footprints and left these scant belongings. With the moon behind the trees, it was hard to make them out, but they appeared to be men, dressed alike.

"Are they Chinese police?" I asked when I joined the others, who were watching the intruders from hiding.

"No," Uncle hissed. "They're speaking Korean."

"Strange accent, though," Youn-Chul said.

Aunt pulled Bum-Ji's collar. "What are you doing? There are three of you and only two of them. Beat them and take their clothes. Maybe they have food with them."

Bum-Ji pulled away. "And maybe they have helpers with them, too, just there in the trees."

"Yes," Little Brother said, "or dogs."

I looked hard at the two. They appeared to be young and fit, and though they were speaking furtively, the words I overheard— "refugees" and "survivors"—didn't sound threatening to me. They were holding up Uncle's outer shirt, which had been hanging across a driftwood log. It was threadbare, something I'd not noticed before. But even in the dim light I could tell that the intruders' clothing was fine by comparison. And then the taller of the two men stepped into a shaft of moonlight, and I saw something gold embroidered on his shirt pocket.

The sign of the crossroads.

A chill like cold river water iced my arms, though my clothing had dried. "It is safe," I whispered. "They will not harm us."

The others turned to me.

"What are you talking about, Chun-Mi?" Aunt whispered derisively.

"Bum-Ji," I said, taking his hand, "I know this will sound strange, but you must believe me. Before I woke up, I saw. . .I suppose I saw a vision."

They all leaned toward me.

"I. . ." I took a large breath and exhaled. "I heard a voice and the voice said, 'Trust the sign of the crossroads.' And look! That man has the sign of the crossroads on his shirt."

After a moment, Aunt's look of incredulity vanished and she shook her head. "I told you her mind was broken."

"Hush, woman," Uncle said. "All right, here's what we'll do. Bum-Ji and Youn-Chul and I will go talk to them. If they do anything funny, we'll attack."

The two men had left our beach site and were following our footsteps in the sand upstream toward the spot where we'd found Ki-Won.

I looked around. "Where is Ki-Won?" I whispered. I turned in time to see the little boy sprinting away from us right toward the strangers.

"Daddy! Daddy!"

Bum-Ji and the others leaped to their feet and charged after him. "No! Stay away!" Bum-Ji called. "Ki-Won, stay back. You there, stay away from that boy."

The two men whirled around in surprise. One yelped and fell backward into the wet sand. The other stepped into the tae kwon do fighting stance, legs flexed, open hands raised toward the half dozen people suddenly thundering at him from the dark forest.

Ki-Won ran laughing all the way up to the man still standing, then stopped short and stared.

Bum-Ji reached him first. He swept the boy up and carried him back toward the trees. Little Brother and Uncle arrived and stood between the strangers and Bum-Ji. The younger stranger got to his feet, dripping clumps of wet sand, and assumed the ready position, too. The four of them stood twitching and maneuvering, ready to engage.

"Wait!" I said, rushing toward them and holding my belly. "Wait! They are not our enemies."

"He tried to take Ki-Won!" Aunt said from behind me.

"We did no such thing," the younger man said. Another clump of sand fell from his elbow. "You attacked us."

Ki-Won escaped Bum-Ji's arms and ran to me.

I lifted him to my hip. "Did you think he was your daddy, Ki-Won? Poor thing. Your daddy is gone now."

Uncle pointed at the two men. "How do you speak Korean? Are you North Korean agents?"

"No!" the taller man said, his hands still ready. "Are you?"

"No!"

I touched Little Brother's shoulder and he lowered his fists. "We have just come from North Korea," I told the men.

"Chun-Mi!" Uncle said. "Don't tell them anything."

"No, Uncle. I will trust the sign of the crossroads."

The strangers exchanged a wary look.

"We crossed the river tonight," I told them. "We have left our homeland in search of freedom and food and a better life for our children. We made a raft and crossed, but the current pulled us onto a boulder and we fell in. Somehow we all made it here."

Something I'd said seemed to register with them. Both men dropped their hands and stood straight up.

"We found part of your raft," the taller man said. "That's why we are here. We thought someone must've tried a river crossing and met with disaster. We came looking for survivors."

Grandmother stepped forward now, Aunt at her elbow. "Why?" Grandmother asked. "Why did you come looking?"

"Greetings, Grandmother," the taller man said with a bow. At least he knew his manners. "We are Christian missionaries. We help North Koreans flee into China and then on to South Korea or America or wherever they wish to go."

Fear pricked my heart at the mention of America. South Korea was decadent; every North Korean schoolchild knew that. But America was barbaric—inhuman. That these men sent people to either place didn't bode well.

"Why would anyone want to go there?" Aunt asked.

Little Brother appeared puzzled. "You said you're. . .what? Chinese medical workers?"

"No," the younger one said. "We're Christian missionaries. We were watching for refugees trying to cross near the guard station downstream. When we saw the wreckage we came looking. We want to extend to you the love of Christ." He looked at his partner in frustration, then back to us. "We're *Christians.*"

We exchanged confused looks. "We. . .don't know what that is," Bum-Ji said.

"I know," the taller man said. "You couldn't." To his partner he said, "They couldn't know that." He looked at me. "The sign of the crossroads," he said, touching the symbol embroidered on his shirt, "is the sign of God."

Again I recoiled. The word he used—*God*—had been banned in our country. From a child's first years he is taught that there is no god or spirit outside of the superhuman powers of the Great Leader and his son, the Dear Leader. Anyone holding ideas besides this was disloyal to the revolution and was severely punished. Therefore the only people holding such views were considered. . .

"Wrong in the head, then—that's what you are?" Aunt asked. "Wonderful, our rescuers are mad."

"Who cares?" Grandmother said. "If they're here to help us I say we go with them. Anything's better than sitting here in sight of North Korea."

"Good," the taller man said. "Come with us. One of us will lead you to a road and the other will go get our truck. We will take you to a safe house to recover your strength. And then. . . Well, we will speak of that when you have eaten and rested."

We gathered the few items we'd salvaged from the crossing and followed our two possibly insane rescuers away from the river and the Democratic People's Republic of Korea. I hoped to never see it again.

Grandmother took my arm and allowed me to walk with her. "Don't you worry," she said quietly. "I am not so old that I do not remember the words *God* or *Christ.*" She winked and patted my arm.

I didn't know what to think. I'd never done anything so disloyal in my life—fleeing my homeland, allowing banned words to be used in my presence, talking with outsiders about going to forbidden countries—and even questioning things I'd always held to be absolute. Like maybe there were powers beyond, even *greater than,* anything my homeland's leaders could produce. What was I becoming? And what secrets was Grandmother concealing?

This sign of the crossroads intrigued me. This *God*—there, I'd said it—intrigued me even more if it caused young men to search for strangers in need in the middle of the night.

But the thing that affixed my trust to these two strangers more than anything else was that in their eyes I saw absolute peace.

CHAPTER 4

Flipped

Cellodoc (Trieu Nguyen Encrypted) says:
Eloise, you busy? Got a second to chat?

Mamaluv23 (ABL Corporation Headquarters Eloise Webster President Encrypted) says:
Hey, girl. What's on your mind?

Cellodoc says:
I need to talk to somebody, but it involves the Firebrand team so I can't talk to any of them, and I can't exactly just call up my girlfriends and tell them about this top-secret group I'm with, you know?

Mamaluv23 says:
I hear you, my sister. Praise God you thought of me. What's on your heart?

Cellodoc says:

It's about the guys on the team. They can make me crazy, you know? Jason and Chris and Garth used to be in the Special Forces, but sometimes they can act so immature. I know they're amazing at what they do, but sometimes I think they're not paying attention. Sometimes I wonder how these guys who are always joking around can be serious enough to take on dangerous missions, and yet they do so great. Like when we were in Kazakhstan with the orphans or in Sudan with the Dinka. The guys were so brave and professional. Even Lewis. But then they're back to cutting up again. I don't know. They confuse me, I guess.

Mamaluv23 says:

LOL. Yes, I can understand that. Strange creatures, those men.

Cellodoc says:

Your husband was in the military. Was he like this?

Mamaluv23 says:

Lord, have mercy, yes. My Charlie was a radar man, not SpecOps, but he would've fit right in with these pranksters. I don't know what it is about the SEALs, Green Berets, etc., that attract this type of man, but they're full of them. They play as hard as they fight. As for the cutting up, I think they must do it because of all the awful things they've seen. I used to know a medical examiner. He was always making corpse jokes. Ew.

Cellodoc says:

LOL. Gallows humor. It's very common in my field of work.

Mamaluv23 says:

Exactly. Sick is what some of you doctors are. So I think it's a defense mechanism. But don't imagine for one second that such antics mean they aren't paying attention or that they won't be able to handle serious situations. You've seen that already, haven't you?

Cellodoc says:
I suppose you're right.

Mamaluv23 says:
Oh, they're listening. Those boys are paying attention. And when the time comes, they'll be as professional as you could ever want. Every member of this team—including those three special SpecOps men and you and Rachel and Lewis—all of you are the best at what you do. And you love Jesus Christ. What more could a woman ask for? :-P

Cellodoc says:
You're right.

Mamaluv23 says:
Now, tell Auntie Eloise what's really on your heart.

Cellodoc says:
Oh, I don't know. I know you don't want us dating each other, but. . .

Mamaluv23 says:
LOL. Oh, baby, here it comes. Lay it on me, sister. Who do you have a crush on?

Cellodoc says:
:-P

Mamaluv23 says:
;-) Tell me. Dish.

Cellodoc says:
I'd rather not say.

Mamaluv23 says:
You don't have to tell me because I already know! Ha!

Cellodoc says:
Okay, look. I won't lie to you. I am attracted to. . .someone on the team. Don't you dare tell anyone.

Mamaluv23 says:
[zips lips]

Cellodoc says:
It's just whenever I try to imagine me in a long-term relationship with this person, all I see is him cutting up. Oh, that's not all true. I see him being heroic and godly and so amazingly compassionate. That's what I'd rather see all the time. But this image of him goofing off keeps intruding on my little fantasy. And I'm just wondering if that will ever go away or if I have to decide if I could—if the opportunity presented itself—live with such a mixed person.

Mamaluv23 says:
Gotcha, sis. But I don't think you should hold your breath waiting for this man to "grow up." I don't believe he ever will—none of them. And if he did, I think he would lose his edge, that thing that makes him the best at what he does. Trieu, ask yourself why you want to tame this man. Do you really want him to be some sit-around neutered couch potato with only soft edges? Isn't part of what attracts you to him his wildness, his untamedness—even his boyish playfulness? All of us are mixed, my sister. We've all got strange things in us, right along with the good. Maybe some of it needs to go. Maybe some of it is what makes us who we are. Now get on out of here and let an old woman do her work. :)

Cellodoc says:
Okay. I know you're right. I need to let him be who he is. It's only

that just as soon as I see these guys acting like true gentlemen and mature Christian warriors, they always go and do something stupid.

* * *

"Rachel, Trieu, come quick! Chris has gone crazy. He's going to shoot Jason!"

Rachel put her magazine down and looked over her red sunglasses. "What are you talking about, Lewis?"

Trieu snapped her laptop shut and slid it across the glass patio table. "Those two. I was just thinking about them. What are they fighting about now?"

"I don't know," Lewis said. He put his camouflage helmet and computer pack onto the patio furniture table next to Rachel's chaise and pulled from his shirt pocket two tiny electronic devices the size of raisins. "I was testing these, my motes. They're tiny little distributed ant-cams, see? They're really cool. I've put them everywhere around the compound. I even have one inside the dishwasher so we can—"

"Lewis," Trieu said, "you said Chris was going to shoot someone?"

"Oh! Yeah, Chris is totally going to shoot Jason." The young man looked from Trieu to Rachel and back. "I'm serious, you guys! Here, look for yourself."

"Probably paint guns," Rachel said, receiving the helmet from Lewis. She put it on and flipped the eye panel down. The computer pack connected to the helmet dangled over her red Maryann shirt, tied at the bottom to reveal her midriff. She wore white-and-red polka-dotted shorts and white deck shoes with ankle-high white socks.

Lewis pressed a button on the computer pack. "See?"

"Yeah, I can sort of see. Looks like Chris has Jason backed up against some building. I don't recognize it. He's got an assault rifle, all right, but I'm sure it's just got the practice pepperballs in it." She took the helmet off and handed it to Trieu. "Here, tell me what you think."

Trieu put it on.

"Oh," Lewis said, "I forgot your audio." He pushed another button, and the helmet speakers came alive.

Trieu watched for a moment, the summer breeze ruffling her plaid summer blouse. Then she stiffened. "Oh, my." She brought the helmet down and thrust it at Lewis. "Where are they, Lewis? What building is that?"

"I don't know," Lewis said, fumbling to put the helmet on. "I've got these things all over." He brought the eye panel down and found a three-button switch on the thick cables streaming down. He pushed the top and bottom buttons, one eye shut and his mouth in a squint grimace. "Oh, okay, I know where that is. It's the old vehicle shed way out by the creek. I put the mote there because I didn't want to have to go all the way down there just to see if someone had remembered to close the garage door. Man, Chris looks really mad."

"Come on, Rachel," Trieu said. "We've got to get out there. I think Lewis is right!"

She bolted away, taking the steps two at a time and heading out across the dirt courtyard of their training camp. Rachel and Lewis followed.

A beat-up flatbed pickup rolled to a stop at the steps of the lodge. A giant bald man with a bodybuilder's physique and a red goatee got out and lowered the tailgate.

"Garth!" Rachel shouted. "Get back in and drive."

"Huh?"

Lewis jumped in the bed of the truck and helped Trieu up.

Rachel ran to the passenger side. "Chris has gone nuts and says he's going to shoot Jason."

"What?" Garth's forehead wrinkled. "That stupid jarhead. I knew he was going to snap on us one day." He jumped in the truck and headed out the wooden archway.

Rachel slid open the back window. "Trieu," she shouted over the noise of the loud truck speeding over the gravel road, "what did you see? Why do you think he's serious?"

Trieu climbed over a stack of flat bags full of beach sand and shouted back. "It's not what I saw, but what I heard." She leaned closer to the window. "Chris said he was tired of Jason cutting in on him."

"What?" Lewis said, scrambling up next to Trieu. "What does that mean?"

Trieu looked serious. "Chris said he's tired of Jason cutting in on him with you, Rachel."

They rounded the guest cabins and joined the gravel road headed back into their Utah wilderness. It was another hot July afternoon, and it was going to get hotter. Dry trees and brown-green shrubs stretched out to the hills far to their left.

Ahead, mule deer stood on the road. Garth had to hit the brakes. With a little gentle nudging from Garth—and a lot of not so gentle shouting and honking—the deer finally got the picture, and the truck sped off again.

"Here," Lewis said, handing his helmet and computer pack to Trieu. "What's happening now?"

Rachel looked at her feet. "Garth! Your helmet! Can I use it?"

"Sure," Garth said, looking at her strangely. "You think I'm going to crash?"

"No. We can see what's happening with Chris and Jason. Lewis put a camera there." She put the helmet on and activated the eye panel.

She could see Chris clearly. He was brandishing an assault rifle and definitely looking more high-strung than usual. She couldn't see Jason very well. He was just at the right edge of the frame. But he was backed against the vehicle shed, his hands in the air. The vehicle shed was a steel building the size of a barn. It was white and had four blue corrugated garage doors. Both men wore shorts and T-shirts.

"I can't believe he'd really do something stupid," Rachel said, her voice vibrating with the bumpy road. "Gotta be nonlethals."

Chris's voice came over the helmet speakers loud and clear. "You're in my way, Kromer. You've been in my way since the first day you came to us. I had everything the way I wanted it until you came."

"Chris, calm down, dude," Jason said. "We can talk this out."

"No, we can't talk it out!" Chris shouted. A strange, bestial look crossed his face. The rifle quivered in his hands. "It's too late for that! You–you never should've come. Everything was. . .everything was great. Before *you.*"

Rachel pounded Garth's shoulder. "Go faster!"

Garth floored the accelerator. They hit a bump at fifty—which was way too fast on that road—and Lewis actually went airborne. He landed in the truck near the tailgate. Garth slowed down.

"Chris," Jason said over the speakers, "have you been drinking? Maybe you should stick to—"

"So what if I have been drinking?" Chris said. Even with the slightly fish-eye view, his trademark blond curl was visible swishing against his forehead. "All it's done is make me see what I couldn't see before: You've got to go. I see it so clearly now. Before you came, Rachel and I. . .we had something going. We were headed some-where together."

"Sure, Chris," Jason said. "And maybe it will be that way again."

"No, it won't. Not with you around. Now suddenly all she can do is look at you. Trieu's the same way. Everything's ruined. It's not like you're some superstud, either. That's what I don't get. You're shorter than me, uglier than me, and you dress like an old man. I'm *good* for Rachel, Kromer. We're good together. No," he said, suddenly decisive, "you've got to go."

The foliage was getting more lush as they neared a creek valley. They rounded a stand of white pine trees. The silver roof of the vehicle shed came into view. Garth fishtailed around the corner but had to slow as the road became choked with rock outcroppings.

"Wait!" Jason said. "What if I chose?"

The gunpoint dropped a few inches. "What do you mean?" Chris asked. "Chose what?"

"Chose between the girls. I mean, if I chose one then you could go for the other. Does that sound good?"

"Well. . ."

Rachel tore off her helmet. "Why, that egotistical jerk! Who does he think he is?"

"What?" Garth said.

"Jason says he's going to choose between me and Trieu, and Chris will get the leftover! Like we're yesterday's meatloaf."

"Well," Lewis said, now back beside Trieu but holding on very tightly, "that is what this is all about, right? That Jason's being a jerk playing both girls like they're white bread or wheat. Whoa, Garth! A little slower, please! Like I was saying, if Jason chose, then maybe things really would be better. Maybe Chris wouldn't have to shoot him. He could, you know, start hitting on one of you guys again."

"Lewis!" Rachel said. "Shut up."

"Yes, Lewis," Trieu said. "Shut up."

Rachel growled. "It's not up to Jason which one of us he 'gets.' Is it, Trieu?"

"Absolutely not."

"We're not sitting around waiting to be chosen or rejected." Rachel's brown eyes were wide and infuriated. She put the helmet on and spoke to the image on the little screen. "Is that really what you think, Jason?" She *harrumph*ed. "I changed my mind, Chris. Go ahead and shoot him."

As if in answer, the gun barrel rose again. Chris's eyes narrowed. "What if you choose wrong? What if you choose Rachel over Trieu? I couldn't live if she went with you. Since the first time I met Rachel I've wanted no other woman but her." He clenched his jaw. "And she would've been mine, too, if it hadn't have been for you." He lowered his eye to look down the sights. "So what'll it be, Kromer? Choose Trieu or die."

They could see Chris from the truck now. He was around the corner of the shed. He looked terrifyingly lethal, like a terrorist on a hijacking gone wrong. Jason was still out of sight but must've been against the metal wall.

The truck skidded to a stop and everyone jumped out and ran for the shed.

Chris saw them and took aim at Jason.

"No, wait!" Rachel shouted.

POW!

The CAR-15's report was crisp and unmistakable.

"That was a live round!" Trieu said, sprinting with the others.

They finally saw Jason then. He entered their vision when he collapsed onto his knees and fell forward onto his face in the dirt. Chris stood over him, looking dumbfounded.

"No!" Rachel cried.

Garth and Lewis bounded past Jason and struck Chris together. They disarmed him and wrestled him to the ground.

Rachel and Trieu reached Jason at the same time.

Rachel touched Jason's shoulder tentatively then shook it. "Jason? Oh, no," she said, looking at Trieu. "You don't think? . . ."

"Garth," Trieu said, reaching under Jason's shoulder, "you and Lewis help me get him to the truck. We've got to get him back to the compound. My med kit is there."

Rachel knelt beside Jason and smoothed his brown hair. "Oh, Jason, what have you done? Don't leave me, Jason. Please, God, don't let him leave me." She looked at Trieu fiercely. "Fix him! Make him all right!"

Trieu recoiled from her look. "Rachel. . .I–I'll try. Of course I'll try." She appeared about to say more but swallowed the words and turned to Jason. "Wait a minute," she said softly, sweeping her hands across his chest and back. "I can't find any blood." She grabbed the hem of Jason's T-shirt and lifted.

Revealing a muscular chest and washboard belly—but no bullet wound.

"What in the world?"

Jason's eyes flew open. "Woooaahh!" He rose to his feet, hands reaching out like a ghoul rising from the grave.

Rachel shrieked. Even Trieu stepped back.

Then Chris pounced from behind, shrieking like a demon.

Garth raised his arms over the women and laughed maniacally.

Rachel screamed and ran—straight into Lewis, who made a grotesque face at her and howled like a werewolf. She fell back against Trieu.

Then the men laughed. Sidesplitting, stomach-holding bellows that sent a trio of mourning doves flying for cover.

Chris staggered over to a mannequin standing against the shed next to where Jason had been. The mannequin wore steel-plated body armor, which Chris knocked on with his knuckle. "Are you okay, 'Jason'? Sorry I killed you, bro!"

More laughter.

Rachel stamped her foot. "You idiots! I almost passed out."

This sent the men into uncontrolled hysterics. They held their faces and bent their knees. Lewis tripped and fell, then laughed on the ground.

"Ugh!" Rachel said, and stamped away toward the truck.

Trieu lingered a moment, watching them laugh. Her face wasn't angry. More like sad. She turned and strode to the truck, ignoring their calls to come back.

CHAPTER 5

GIRL TALK

"IRRESPONSIBLE!" *Thump.* "Incorrigible!" *Slam.* "Chauvinistic!" *Whack.* "Pigheaded!" *Bam.* "Bigoted!" *Thwack.* "Egotistical self-centered dim-witted maniacs!" *Whump, slam, smack, pow, flap, double bang, CRACK!*

Rachel emerged from her room looking like a wild animal. Her dark brown hair was skewed over her face and down the other side. Her cheeks and neck were flushed. Her knuckles were angry red. She stormed across the sitting room, skirted the coffee table and chair, and burst into Trieu's room on the other side.

"Can you believe those *idiots?* To think I was actually upset when I thought he'd been shot!"

Trieu sat up on her bed and rushed to dry her face. Her eyes were pink, and her mascara was a mess.

"Oh!" Rachel said, suddenly compassionate. She rushed to Trieu's side and put her arms around her. "Oh, honey, I'm sorry! I didn't know you were. . ." She *tsk*ed. "Ugh, those stupid men. Can't they ever get a clue? I hope they enjoy their walk back."

They sat together quietly, Rachel rocking them gently.

Trieu's room, like Rachel's, resembled a small dorm room. White ceiling tiles. Fluorescent lights. A built-in desk with cabinets overhead and a desk light in the bottom. The head of Trieu's bed was against the far wall, an end table and lamp on either side. Yellow-and-white curtains framed the window above the bed. Potted plants sat in the windowsill. A tall fern stood in a green pot in the corner between the closet and the door to the bathroom. A large Asian landscape painting occupied the long wall beside the bed. The comforter was white with yellow pagodas and black Vietnamese script. An octagonal clock hung on the wall beside the door to the sitting room, ticking in a baritone voice. Trieu's cello stood beside a music stand and a straight-backed chair. The room smelled of roses and oranges.

"It's funny, don't you think," Rachel asked, "how the two of us responded? I was over there knocking the stuffing out of my pillows, and you were over here crying." She *harrumph*ed. "Wish I could knock the stuffing out of *them* and leave *them* crying."

Trieu smiled sadly. She disengaged from Rachel's arms and reached for a tissue.

"I don't get it," Rachel said, pulling Trieu's hair behind her ear. "Why *are* you crying? That was a dumb stunt they pulled, but it just made me mad. I want to get them back somehow. But you're. . .like this."

Trieu blew her nose daintily. She dabbed her eyes and looked Rachel in the face. "Are we really going to have this talk? Finally?"

Rachel's brow furrowed. "You mean the why-are-men-such-meatheads talk?"

"No," Trieu said, smiling wryly, "the we're-both-in-love-with-the-same-man talk."

Rachel's head tilted back slowly. "Oohh, that talk. Hmm. Well, I suppose we need to sooner or later. I guess we've had it coming, huh?"

They stared at each other. The clock ticked. A lot.

Trieu sat cross-legged and pulled a pale yellow pillow into her lap. Rachel did the same, facing her.

"Well, where to start?" Rachel said. "I guess I should start by saying that I'm not going to compete with you for Jason or anybody else. Not that it would be much of a competition, Trieu. You're so totally everything a man could ever want! You're beautiful. You're so smart. You play the cello to make my heart melt. You're strong and mature and stable. You don't go flitting around from emotion to emotion like I always do. You're a champion athlete *and* a brilliant physician. Plus you've got that Asian mystique going on."

Rachel squeezed the pillow. "This is going to sound weird, but even though I was so totally disgusted by what happened out there—I was also kind of. . .fascinated. Jason having to choose, you know? I knew he'd shown interest in me, but I'd seen him flirting with you, too. Some sick part of me really wanted to know which of us he would choose." She sighed. "But then I didn't want to know because my heart told me he'd pick you. Didn't you kind of want to know what he'd say?"

Trieu dabbed her nose with the tissue. "Not really."

"No? Well, you're. . .you're more *something* than I am," Rachel said. "Because I did want to know. Still do, actually. Would he have chosen you to save his life, or would he have chosen me knowing he'd take a bullet for it?" She looked at Trieu quickly. "Not that the only reason he'd choose you would be to save his life." She swallowed. "As far as I'm concerned, you can just have him. Right? I mean, who needs the jerk?"

Trieu regarded her thoughtfully. Then she smiled. "You don't really mean that."

"I don't?"

"No."

"Yes, I do."

"No, I can tell. And because of the thing about your father, how Jason makes you feel how you did when you were with your father—safe, able to do anything, beautiful. Don't you remember telling me all this?"

Rachel grimaced. "Yeah, but. . .that was before I knew you liked him, too. I wouldn't have said all that if I'd known."

"Yes, you would've."

Rachel wrinkled her brow and shook her head, but then a smile slipped out. It was an odd expression—her eyes and forehead were saying no but her mouth was saying yes. "Well. . .why would I do a thing like that?"

"To stake out your territory," Trieu said, shrugging. "To tell me to stay away from him."

Rachel's mouth fell open. "I would never do anything like that, Trieu! You make me sound like a stray dog. I said I wouldn't compete with you, not for him, not for anybody. And I meant it!"

Trieu tilted her head and stared.

That freelance smile appeared again on Rachel's face. "Oh, okay, maybe subconsciously I was doing that. A little. But only because I was scared of you. I saw that you liked him and so maybe I. . ." She sighed. "Oh, Trieu, I'm so sorry. What a horrible thing to do. It's just that. . .I'm so competitive. I've been competing with men *and* women for all my life. I guess it's just my first tactic in everything I do now." She bit her lip. "Dude, you can so have him. I'll totally back off. I mean it: Jason's yours. Maybe I'll run off with Lewis."

Trieu smiled and they shared an easy laugh.

"No," Trieu said, "I don't want you to back off from Jason. If you did that, neither one of us would be going after him."

Rachel looked at her sideways. "What are you saying?"

"I'm saying that I don't play games. I'm saying that I'd rather drop out of the competition than run the risk of losing. That would hurt too much. I couldn't be on this team knowing that I'd thrown myself at some man, begging him to choose me and he'd chosen someone else. I respect myself too much to do that." Her black eyebrows narrowed. "If it really is you and me competing for Jason, then I'm throwing the match. I'm handing you the medal. This is the kind of thing that can tear a group apart. I won't allow that to happen, and I won't be part of making it happen."

They stared at each other tentatively, each trying to read the other's eyes. The clock's ticking seemed to crescendo.

"But Trieu," Rachel said, "I thought you liked Jason. I mean, wasn't it you who called this the we're-both-in-love-with-the-same-man conversation?"

"Well, I changed my mind," Trieu said, shifting on the bed. "Come on, Rachel, look at him. He's barely as tall as I am. I could never wear heels with him. He's a new Christian—hardly the spiritual giant I want to marry. He's capable of cruelty, like we just saw a few minutes ago. His history is full of killing and drinking and all the other things sailors do. It's not like I'd be marrying a virgin, you know. And this game he's playing with you and me, considering each one of us like one of us is a Harley-Davidson and one of us is a Kawasaki. Forget it. How can he be a good husband and father if he can't make hard decisions? No, Rachel, he's yours and good luck with him."

Rachel's eyebrows were high. "Trieu Nguyen, are you on medicine? A minute ago you were crying because he hurt you—now he's the Antichrist?"

Trieu shrugged and dropped her gaze.

Rachel's expression shifted from surprise to suspicion. She gasped. "Why, you big fat *liar!* You're lying to me, aren't you?" She pushed Trieu's shoulder with her pillow. "Aren't you? You're just telling me all that because you're trying to be some kind of martyr to save the team. You just made all that up. Why, you big fake. I'll never believe you again!"

Now it was Trieu's turn to smile furtively. "You don't know

what you're talking about. Go away and leave me alone."

"I'm not going anywhere until you tell me how you really feel about him. I know you like him, so don't bother lying again." She tapped Trieu's shoulder. "Come on, girl, dish." Trieu sat up, smashing pillows against the headboard and leaning back. "All right. But if I find out you ever tell anyone else, I'll drug you and surgically remove an organ of my choice."

Rachel beamed. "Deal!"

Trieu drew her knees to her chest and hugged them. "First of all, if we did compete for Jason, Rachel, you would win."

"No, I w—"

"Don't even bother denying it. We both know it's true. Men want a beautiful face with a beautiful body. And if push comes to shove, the beautiful face can go. Rachel, I know I'm attractive; I'm confident in how I look. But nobody beats you."

"But none of it will last!" Rachel protested. "I want a man who will see me for more than that. Like I want to meet a guy on some E-mail thing and have him come to like me without ever seeing a picture. That's a guy I know will love me no matter what I look like. But let's forget about this for a minute. You said you were going to tell me how you felt about him."

Trieu smiled sadly. "All right. Here's the thing, Rachel. I do have strong feelings for Jason Kromer. I remember that moment when he walked into the ABL headquarters and I was posing as the receptionist." She stopped speaking. Her eyes glazed and her head shook slowly from side to side.

"Trieu," Rachel said, snapping in front of Trieu's face, "snap out of it, girlfriend."

"Right. Well, let's just say I *noticed* him right away."

"Huh," Rachel said, "who wouldn't? He's a babe."

"Yes, Rachel, but there are many handsome men in this world. Even on our team. I would venture to say that Chris is by most objective standards more handsome than Jason."

Rachel tilted her head as if to say, *Well, maybe.*

"And Garth is the perfect male specimen. He may not have your 'regular' kind of good looks, but he's so muscular."

"Yeah," Rachel purred, "plus I love bald men. I just love running my fingers over his scalp."

They giggled.

"Even Lewis is starting to look not half bad," Trieu said.

"I know what you mean," Rachel said.

"Which is my point," Trieu said. "Jason is handsome, but so are lots of guys. Handsome isn't enough, not even close."

"Well. . .it might be close."

"No, Rachel, it isn't. After awhile even the most handsome man—or the most beautiful woman—will become just *normal.* Looks, good or bad, fade from importance when you live with someone. After awhile Jason wouldn't be handsome or ugly to me; it would just be how he looked. So good looks don't matter that much to me. What matters to me are the enduring qualities: spiritual maturity, kindness, integrity, commitment."

Trieu tucked a strand of black hair behind her ear. "Of course, I won't complain if the man God has for me is handsome, too."

"That goes without saying!"

"What I love about Jason. . . ," Trieu said, and then stopped.

"Yes?"

She sighed. "What I love about Jason is his heart. He is passionate about protecting people who are being hurt, especially children. It was so amazing to watch him discover this passion just a few months ago in Kazakhstan. Remember him with Damira? Remember him carrying her from the truck? I saw the look in his eyes that night. And since then it's like he's become consumed with it. When we found him there beating the daylights out of that slave trader who'd tried to rape Anei—do you remember Jason's rage?"

Trieu shut her eyes. Her face relaxed and her words came fluidly. "I could get swept up into that passion, Rachel. I could go with him wherever children are hurting. He could get them out of danger, and I could heal them. We could return to Vietnam and we could work there, and in Burma and Laos and Thailand and China—wherever there is need. I've always known God would bring me a man only when we could make each other more effective together than we were alone. And Jason and I make such a great team. I can't think of—"

Her eyes popped open and she looked at Rachel. "But, I mean, there are lots of men I could do that with. And anyway that kind of thing is what this whole team does, isn't it?" She laughed weakly. "It's not like I. . .I mean, Jason's totally right for you, Rachel."

Rachel shook her head. "You are such a liar."

"Well," Trieu said, straightening up against the headboard, "he is a nice man, isn't he? He's kind to children and old women. He's fantastic under pressure. He's strong in body and spirit. And he seems very earnest about his love for the Lord. He'll make you a wonderful husband." She swallowed. "There, I've said it. Will you go now?"

Rachel smiled. "You know something, Trieu? You're a very special lady. Personally, I don't think Jason deserves either one of us. None of these guys do."

"I think you're right, Rachel."

They hugged.

"So. . . ," Rachel said, biting her lip. "Did we solve anything?"

Trieu smiled. "No. But we had our first real girl talk."

"I know. It's so great." Rachel looked away then looked back. "So. . .which one of us gets him?"

"You do."

"No, you do."

"All right," Trieu said, smiling deviously. "I know what we'll do." She reached into a drawer in the bedside table and brought out a quarter, which flashed in the light. "Flip you for him."

Fear and incredulity mixed on Rachel's face. "Are you serious?"

"Well, the Bible says that every casting of the lot is determined by God. Maybe it's no different with a coin. Come on, heads I win, tails you lose."

"Wait!" Rachel said, catching Trieu's wrist. "I know that trick. Heads I win, tails you win. But. . .uh. . .if I don't like the answer, we'll go two out of three. Or four out of seven."

Trieu balanced the quarter on thumb and forefinger and—

Loud sound of radio traffic. Both girls jumped. The quarter slid into Trieu's lap.

"What was that?"

Radio-filtered male voices came to them as if from under something. Squelches of radio noise, then more voices. Laughter.

"Oh," Trieu said, standing and walking to her closet, "I know what that is." She folded open the doors to her closet. Instantly the radio noise got louder. She bent down and pulled up her own camouflaged helmet and computer pack. "Must've forgotten to turn it off after this morning's run. Now my batteries are going to die too early." She reached to turn it off.

"Wait!" Rachel said, leaving the bed. "Let's see what they're doing." She took the helmet from Trieu and put it on, bringing the eye panel down.

"Why, Rachel Levy, I'm surprised at you. A Peeping Tom?"

"I know. Don't tell anyone." She grimaced under the helmet. "They must be by another one of Lewis's mote camera thingies. Ooh, I can totally see them. They're in the lodge by the fireplace." She paused then looked right at Trieu. "They're talking about us! Come here!"

CHAPTER 6

Wouldn't That Be Bigamy?

"Here's your Mountain Dew, Jason."

Jason took the twenty-ounce bottle from Lewis. "Thanks, man."

Lewis stepped over Butch, Garth's old basset hound, and moved along the tan sofa and chairs, handing Garth a SoBe orange carrot elixir and Chris a bottled water, finally dropping into the opposite sofa with a frosty can of Virgil's Root Beer. "Woo," he said. "First a five-mile run with full packs and then a ten-mile cross-country hike. I think we should be excused from tomorrow's run, Jason."

"Ha!" Jason said over his bottle.

They were sitting in the fireside room in the main lodge building. Sunlight shone through the windows along the wall behind the sofa, throwing up a glare on the polished wooden dining table behind them and the polished wooden coffee table in the middle of the sofa and chair ring. The vaulted wood ceilings, normally dark, were actually well lit now. Jason noticed cobwebs up there and knew someone would need to take them down—an ideal job for Lewis. The brick fireplace was dormant now, and military clean. No ashes or soot for the Firebrand training compound. The old clock on the polished wooden mantel chimed 2:15.

"Well," Chris said, "we may've alienated the girls from us forever, but at least we proved that the new steel body armor plates will stop a bullet. I was totally impressed."

"Yeah," Jason said, "but did you see the blunt-force trauma your shot did to that dummy?"

Garth brought his SoBe bottle down and belched. He scratched behind Butch's ears, "Yeah, but it was a lucky shot anyway. Who knew we had the world's only jarhead capable of shooting straight?"

"Oh yeah, Green Bean?" Chris said. "You want to take a trip to the firing range and see who shoots straight?"

"No, no!" Garth said, affecting terror. "I think we need to find you an occupation that doesn't involve firearms, young man. You seem to be a little. . .*whacked* around them right now."

"Yeah, well, that's only because I have to work with Green Berets and SEALs and other lesser humans, like civvies."

"Ouch!" Garth said, holding his heart. He set down his SoBe. "But you know, you guys, that was a pretty mean trick we played on the girls. I don't think we should do anything like that again."

"Yeah, I guess you're right," Jason said. "I think it hit them harder than I thought it would." He winced.

Lewis swallowed a gulp of root beer. "Ahh. Sweet nectar." Then he sighed. "Jason, do we really have to wear those things all the time? Those steel plate things. I feel like King Arthur or something."

"We do, Lewis," Jason said. "You're lucky: These are light. When I was in the Teams, we used these heavy ceramic plates. Six pounds each. When you ran they flapped against your body like cement stepping-stones. These are much better."

Chris leaned conspiratorially toward Lewis. "Don't worry, kid.

We'll ditch 'em when we get in the field."

"I heard that," Jason said.

Chris shook his head. "No, you didn't."

"I didn't?"

"Un-uh."

"Oh."

"You guys," Lewis said, sounding worried, "how long do you think the girls will be mad at us?"

"Could be a very long time," Jason said.

"Are you kidding?" Chris asked. "They'll put on a show of being mad for a day or two, then they'll come running back to us saying, 'Please talk to us, boys,' " he said in falsetto. " 'We need open communication. We need relationship! Let's have a cocoa and talk.' "

They laughed.

Garth pointed a beefy finger at Chris. "You just better be glad they didn't hear you say that, boy."

Jason swallowed a swig of Mountain Dew then lowered the bottle. "Okay, Chris, I have to ask: What was all that stuff about me choosing between Rachel and Trieu? Dude, where did that come from?"

Chris shrugged. "You said to come up with something to be mad about. Something believable." He stared at Jason. "So that's what I came up with."

"Yeah, well," Jason said, chuckling, "I thought you were serious for a minute. Did you guys see that look on his face? I thought you were really going postal, buddy."

Chris didn't blink. "Who said I wasn't serious?"

The room hushed as if someone had vacuumed out all the sound. Jason was intensely aware of eyes on him. He laughed uneasily.

"You know," Garth said, fingertips pressing into one side of his scalp, "Jarhead does raise a good point."

Everyone looked at him.

"You really are being stupid about this, Jason," Garth said.

"Oh, nice. Thanks," Jason said.

"No problem."

"I'm being stupid about *what?*"

"About Rachel and Trieu. They're not items on the buffet, dude. You've got the attentions of two *fantastic* babes. If I didn't like you so much I'd rearrange your facial features just for that. I think up until now it's been okay. You've just been, you know, getting to know them, starting to like them. But now things have gotten serious. It's not fair for those girls that you're keeping them both in suspense. Choose to go after one and let the other go."

"Oh, come on, Garth," Lewis said. "Jason's got it made. He's in ultimate male fantasyland. The two hottest, most dangerous women I've ever seen both want him. Give the guy a break for wanting to ride it out as long as he can."

Jason saw the knowing smiles, the jealous sneers. "Garth, you're right. You're absolutely right. It's not fair to play those girls like this. But I'd be lying if I said I didn't like having both of these gorgeous women wanting to be around me. It's like I get this rush whenever I see them flirt with me. It's amazing to get it from one beautiful woman, but to get it from two? It's unbelievable."

"Yeah," Garth said, "but don't you get it? That rush you're talking about is your flesh. You're feeding your flesh by extracting something from these women. You're like a tick, sucking out their affection. It's sin, bro, and you need to cut it out."

"Besides," Chris said, "we want some of that rush, too."

"Yeah!"

"Oh, baby!"

"You got that right!"

Jason shook his head at them. "Okay, okay. So you guys think I need to choose to go after only one of them?"

"Absolutely," Garth said. "You're disrespecting them if you don't. That's no way to win a girl, Squiddie, not that a SEAL would know anything about it."

"But. . . ," Chris said, a finger raised at Jason, "just be sure you pick the right one."

Jason raised his eyebrows. "By which you mean I should choose Trieu?"

A smile stretched Chris's cheeks. "Choose Trieu or die, baby!"

"Well," Jason said, putting his bottle on the table and leaning back, "Trieu is amazing. I would have no problem settling down with a woman like that."

"Mee-*yow!*" Lewis said. "No kidding."

Jason cocked his head. "Still, Rachel's a total babe, too."

Garth whistled and shook his hand. *"Oo-la-la."*

"Nah," Chris said. "Rachel's fading. Really. Haven't you noticed? She's not for you, Jace. You should definitely go with Trieu."

"Yeah," Jason said, "like I should listen to you."

Lewis almost choked on his root beer. "Oh! I've got it! I know what you can do to decide!"

"What, Lewis?" Chris said. "Flip a coin?"

Everyone laughed.

"No, Chris," Lewis said. "What a dumb idea."

"Okay, Lewis," Jason said, "so what's your idea?"

Lewis sat straight up on the sofa. "Mud wrestling."

No one spoke for three seconds then they all laughed.

"No, Lewis," Jason said.

"Oh," Chris said, tilting his head back, "that's so rich."

Garth shook his head, a wry smile on his face.

"Think about it, you guys," Lewis said. "They go at it in some mud wrestling pit somewhere, and the winner gets Jason. It's beautiful!"

"You are one sick individual," Jason said.

"Lewis, Lewis, Lewis," Garth said.

"Okay, maybe not mud wrestling," Lewis said. "Maybe some

other kind of competition. Maybe they would play Ping-Pong for you."

"What about a target shoot?" Garth said.

"Five-mile run," Jason said.

Chris's eyes glinted. "Wet T-shirt contest."

Pillows and empty soda bottles flew his way. But there were guilty smiles all around.

"No, I've got it," Jason said. "It has to be something balanced. If you do a long run, Trieu will totally win. If you do like a swimsuit contest, it would probably be Rachel, but that's a toss-up. So maybe it's a combination. Like a decathlon or something. You know, like maybe they have to run five miles, then come write an essay, then swim fifty laps, then do some kind of musical performance, then a swimsuit competition, and then finally a written exam."

"You mean like the SAT?" Lewis asked. "High score gets a lifetime Jason scholarship?"

"And we all get to be the judges, right?" Chris asked. "So when Trieu walks by in a swimsuit we hold up a ten, right? And when Rachel walks by we hold up an eleven?"

"Okay, Jarhead," Garth said. "Get past the booby awards, please. You're riding your flesh rush as bad as the squid was. The whole lot of you. The testosterone level in this room is about to blow out the windows." He punched Jason hard in the arm.

"Ow!"

"Now come on down out of that lust-fueled high, you morons," Garth said, "and let's talk this thing over like rational, mature, Christian men."

The others made an effort to calm down. They finished their drinks or bit their cheeks or otherwise settled.

Jason rubbed his arm. "Okay," he said soberly. "So how do we discuss this like mature Christian adults, Garth? What would you suggest?"

Garth looked seriously into each of their eyes. "You're all missing the obvious solution."

"Oh," Chris said, "and what's that?"

"Dudes, this is Utah. Jason, just convert to Mormonism and marry them both!"

They attacked him in a rush, trying to land a noogie or a good solid pinch. Garth kept them at bay with his long arms. Butch barked and ran back and forth, his nails tapping on the wooden floor. Finally Jason and Lewis lunged at the same time, tipping the couch over backwards and sending all four of them rolling across the wood floor.

Eventually they calmed down enough to set the sofa back up and replace the pillows. Chris's right eye was red, and Garth had several angry looking streaks on his bald head.

"Okay," Garth said, pulling Butch into his lap, "I guess that's out. Butch, my friend, these guys just can't take a joke."

"Hey," Jason said. "Wait a minute. If I did marry both, that would sure be nice of me, wouldn't it? I mean, if I took two wives it would totally be big-a-me."

Again the pillows flew.

"Okay, stop it, you idiots," Garth said, sitting on the sofa again. "This time I really am serious. Look, Jason, I can understand the temptation to surf the wave of both girls' affections. But you can't, brother. You just can't. You're wanting to grow as a Christian, right?"

Jason nodded. He hoped what Garth was going to say next really was serious because part of him knew the answer had to come from Christianity. "Yeah, that's right. So what should I do?"

"You've got to fish or cut bait, bro," Garth said. "You've got to choose who you want to pursue, and pursue that one only. And you've got to tell the other one what you're doing. It's probably going to go bad. You may have to sit out our next mission from injuries suffered in the battle. But it's better than disrespecting both women like this. A mature Christian would seek God, maybe even fast over this, and then make a choice."

Jason shook his head. "But how?"

"Easy," Garth said, dropping Butch to the floor. "You pray like this: 'God, which of these two women will I be more useful to You with?' and 'Which of these women will help me reap greater rewards with in thirty million years?' That's what marriage is for, Jason: being more useful to God as a couple than you are as singles. It's not about sex or lust or even companionship. Get it? So, hie thyself to thine prayer closet and seeketh ye the Lord about these things. . .eth."

Jason stared at the fireplace.

Lewis stood to go. "Well, boys, it's been fun, but I hear an hour of *Half-Life 3* calling me and so I shall now retire to mine computer-eth."

The rest mumbled about chores or naps and left, leaving Jason alone with his thoughts.

*　*　*

"Why, those dirty-minded, foul-mouthed, belching, immature perverts!" Rachel handed the computer pack to Trieu. "I'd better go, Trieu. I feel the need to knock the stuffing out of things again, and I don't want to be in your room when I do it."

She stomped out the door and across to her own room. The door slammed and the smashing commenced.

Trieu set the helmet and computer pack back in the closet—turned off this time—and sat on the bed shaking her head. "Oh, Jason." She sighed. "I thought you were going to be different."

She sat in thought for several minutes. Next door, Rachel's domestic violence continued. Finally Trieu went to her desk and brought out paper and pen.

Ten minutes later, Rachel appeared at Trieu's doorway. "Hi."

Trieu looked up from her list. "Feeling better?"

"A little. I'm going to the fridge for some comfort food. Want to come?"

"Sure," Trieu said, capping her pen and standing up.

"What you got there?"

"Oh, it's. . ." Trieu stammered a bit and then shrugged. "It's nothing."

Rachel walked past Trieu and grabbed the paper. "Can't do that now. We're girlfriends. No secrets."

Trieu let her read the paper.

Rachel looked up at her. "Trieu, this is evil."

"I know."

"Girl, are these what I think they are?"

Trieu nodded. "They're my plans for revenge. Petty, huh?"

"Petty? They're beautiful! Trieu, I thought I was the practical joker around here. Obviously I'm not alone. I love this one: 'One of us arrange a date with him and the other show up, since he obviously thinks we're interchangeable.' Ooh, that's devious."

Trieu shrugged. "I try."

"And this one's great: 'Plan a huge argument between all three of us, embarrass him completely, and then reveal that it's all been broadcast live over the Internet to his friends and family and the world.' " Rachel's eyes were wide. "Girl, that's ingenious!"

"No," Trieu said, snatching the paper back. "It's immature. I'm not going to do any of them. I just wanted to write them down to get them out of my system."

"You can have the list," Rachel said. "I already saw the rest. I like the one where we take turns slipping him little notes and Bible verses about Christ honoring the church like a precious bride and about the evils of being a double-minded man. Or the one about getting all these guys to call here asking for us. I'll bet we could find plenty of local guys to ask us out. They'd come up here with bouquets and whisk us away while Jason and those other idiots sat there burping in their Coke bottles. Ooh, yeah, let's stick it to them!"

Trieu ushered them out of her room and shut the door. "No, Rachel, let's not. I told you: I don't want to play games. I wrote those things down to get them off my chest. Now I feel better. It's not my place to teach these guys a lesson."

"It isn't? I think it is. But I understand." She paused as if struck by a thought. A slow smile spread onto her face. Then she chuckled.

"What?" Trieu asked.

"I've just figured out what we're going to do to them."

"You have?"

"Uh-huh. Oh, it's a thing of beauty. But don't worry: It's not too over-the-top. We'll treat them the way we wish they'd treated us. And it does give them credit for the good things they said in their little locker-room talk."

She took Trieu's arm in her own. "Come on, girlfriend, let's go raid the kitchen. We'll be kind to those boys when we've got everything arranged. But right now we're headed to the fridge. And heaven help any man we meet on the way."

CHAPTER 7

UNDERGROUND CHURCH

I will arise and go to Jesus, He will embrace me in His arms;
In the arms of my dear Savior, O there are ten thousand charms.

"TEN THOUSAND CHARMS. That's what we sang, isn't it? My friends, in Jesus Christ we find ten thousand charms."

Yi Gil-Su looked out over his little flock. Emaciated, bent, weatherworn, and so very small, stunted by a lifetime of malnutrition. Gil-Su was a foot-and-a-half taller than every one of them, and he was only five-ten. There were thirteen of them here now, all fresh across the river from North Korea. Eleven of them huddled together meekly in his underground church, wearing the muted color long-sleeved shirts, black pants, and rough leather shoes so prevalent in North Korea.

In this case, the underground church was literally underground. Dug into the hillside like a giant earthworm's burrow. The tan dirt floor was mostly flat, and the walls and ten-foot-high ceiling were arched. At its capacity it could hold thirty people. They'd had fifty in here last winter during the worst of the storms. It smelled forever of mud and unwashed refugees. The little church cavern actually ran parallel to the hillside. The entranceway was shielded from view by a stand of young trees—Korean pine, of course. Eight battery-powered dome lights on the walls bathed the cave in a gentle yellow glow. On the wall at the front of the church, behind Gil-Su, was a marvelous wooden crucifix, complete with Jesus hanging by His hands and feet.

Gil-Su smiled at his congregation. "I know you don't know what I mean. 'What is he saying? Who is this madman who talks about God?' " He noticed them flinch and look at him intensely, though immediately their eyes dropped and they stared forward again. "Ah, you are surprised I use a forbidden word. You see, Kim Jong-Il can forbid the use of a word, but he can do nothing about the One to whom the word refers."

He looked at the elderly woman who came with the Kang family. "Grandmother," he said, using the honorific for an old woman of any family, "you remember when North Korea was a Christian land, do you not?"

She was frail and small, and her white hair was quite thin, but her eyes were bright. She looked at Gil-Su briefly and nodded.

"It is all right, Grandmother," he said. "You may speak. Do you remember what Korea was like before the north became the Hermit Kingdom? Do you remember what Pyongyang was called by Christians all over the world when you were young?"

She looked at him directly, and he felt the force of her sharp intellect. "Of course I do, handsome young man. My mind hasn't left me yet."

Gil-Su smiled. "Yes, I thought you perhaps knew the words to our song. Please, tell us what they used to call Pyongyang."

"They used to call it the Jerusalem of the East."

Her family looked at her in apparent surprise. Gil-Su nodded slightly. So she, too, had gotten good at hiding her faith. How terrible to live in a place where the only thing that can bring true life will certainly bring you punishment and death. He could not condemn her if she had indeed hidden it all these years. And yet he hoped that he himself would choose death rather than keep his light under a bushel.

He could tell the others were getting nervous, though a Westerner would never see it. They still sat shoulder to shoulder in evenly spaced rows, not speaking, hardly moving, and not looking around. But he saw the neck muscles tighten and the jaw muscles clench. A vanishing boot scuff was a message. A slight twitch, a warning.

"Jerusalem," he said in his teacher's voice, "was the city in which Jesus Christ"—he indicated the crucifix—"did much of His work and miracles. It is also where He was killed. Evil men drove heavy nails through His wrists and ankles to affix Him to these crossed planks. He died to pay the debt that we owed. Now that the debt is paid, we can join Him in paradise. That is why we use the cross-pieces as the symbol of our religion." He watched them try to assimilate what he was telling them. Most of them looked politely bored. "People called Pyongyang the Jerusalem of the East because it was a center of study and teaching for those who followed Jesus Christ."

Gil-Su looked at the man sitting on the front row on his left. Myong-Chol had his spindly legs folded underneath him as he sat on the low wooden pew. His normally placid face seemed tight. His knees bounced up and down rapidly.

"In a moment," Gil-Su said to the congregation, "we will have a special speaker who will come up here and talk to us. I think his story will help you understand what I am saying. But first I want to tell you another story."

He placed his hands behind his back and looked at a spot on the back wall. "Long ago, there was a great ruler named King Yahweh.

This king made a law. The punishment for breaking this law was death. Can you imagine such a place?" Gil-Su knew they could imagine it very well. "One day a man broke that law and was brought before King Yahweh. Now, the king had great affection for this man and great regard for his family. He could pardon the man. But what would that do to the law? Perhaps the people would rise up in revolution against a king who did not hold people to the law. He didn't want this man to die, but the law had to be upheld. What could he do?"

No one ventured a guess. Gil-Su smiled ruefully. If they were to stay even one month with him, they would begin to ask questions. But in their first week out of North Korea, Kim Jong-Il's grip on them was still too tight.

"King Yahweh hit upon a brilliant but strange plan. What if someone *else* were to take the punishment in the man's place? What if an innocent man were to be killed in place of the condemned man? The law would be satisfied and the loved one could go free. And then, before anyone in the kingdom knew what was happening, King Yahweh carried out this plan. An innocent man was killed so that a guilty man could go free. Who was the innocent man who died? Why, it was none other than King Yahweh's own son."

Gil-Su watched their reaction. He wondered if they were imagining Kim Il-Sung, the Great Leader, sacrificing his son, Kim Jong-Il, the Dear Leader, to let some lesser person go free. Surely it was a foreign thought.

"This," he said dramatically, hoping for their eyes to turn to him, "is what God did in Jesus Christ. God is King Yahweh. All people are like the man who broke the king's law and were condemned to a death sentence. But all of us have been pardoned because the king sacrificed an innocent man"—he gestured to the crucifix—"so that we could all go free." He held his hands out as if welcoming them into his embrace. "The debt has been paid for you and me, dear friends. Jesus dying on the cross is not the end of the story. Oh, no! He was given life again and lives even today, in heaven. But His death was to purchase our freedom. To obtain this forgiveness, all you must do is run to God and receive it."

No one moved, but Grandmother was nodding almost imperceptibly, and there were tears falling from the pregnant woman's eyes.

This woman, Chun-Mi, was striking and—if given adequate food and grooming—could be beautiful, though he felt no lust for her. She had a wonderful, wide smile, and smile lines by her eyes deeper than he'd seen on anyone coming out of North Korea in a long time. Her hair was short but well kempt, despite her situation. She moved with elegance and grace. How Kim Jong-Il hadn't managed to destroy this woman's bright spirit, Gil-Su didn't know.

He shut his eyes and prayed for the Holy Spirit to move mightily in this place. Then he stepped to his left and placed one hand on Myong-Chol's shoulder. "And now, brother Kim Myong-Chol will come tell us the story of how he found Jesus Christ for himself. Brother Myong-Chol?"

Myong-Chol stood and faced the small crowd. Gil-Su took his place on the pew. For a long moment, Myong-Chol simply stood there, looking petrified. Then he must've met someone's eyes and been encouraged because he lifted his right hand in a small wave and showed a flash of crooked teeth.

"I. . ." He cleared his throat. "I've never done this before." He sighed. "Just begin, Myong-Chol." Then he nodded, as if agreeing with himself. "For twelve years I was a guard at Hoeryong Family Camp Number 22. You will not know this camp exists because it is a secret, as are the other detainment camps for political prisoners. But let me assure you: They are real."

He paused. His lips pursed and unpursed as he appeared to be wrestling with a thought. Then he inhaled deeply. "That is only one of many things you have not been told. Kim Jong-Il is—" He stopped himself and pursed his lips again. "Well, you will understand when you have seen more.

"Anyway, for years I was a guard at this camp. For awhile I was posted near the execution site for Camp 22. We called it Corpse Valley. I saw hundreds of prisoners taken in. None came out. Then I was a driver, which meant I saw the whole camp and all the officers. I saw much death and cruelty. And then I carried out much more. I became. . ."

He stood in silence a moment, staring at nothing, his head shaking slightly as if trying to say *No* in a dream. Then he broke out of his reverie. "I will not say more now because it doesn't matter for the story. But"—and at this, his eyes flared and his voice rose—"you *have to know* that what I am saying is true. You have to know that Kim Jong-Il sends hundreds of thousands of people to these death camps—including innocent children—and they will not come out alive. Even their bones will not escape. They bury the bodies underneath the fruit trees and produce fine fruit for the *People.*" He spat the last word.

"You think I am disrespectful," he said, nodding. "If we were across the river I would be taken to one of these camps for saying this—along with my family and my family's family." He clenched his teeth. "But I *am* disrespectful to that man, that 'ruler,' since I have found a good ruler to give my life to instead. I have found Jesus Christ, and now my life—which I despised when I realized what I'd done—is now good and full of meaning." He sighed a long sigh and his demeanor softened. "Now I will tell you how I found the God who has been banned."

*   *   *

"Why won't you tell me your name?"

Youn-Chul reclined on the grass beside a pretty girl. Dappled sunlight slid over them as a soft wind blew through the pines. In a treetop somewhere across the pine forest, a bird of some kind squawked and screeched. The trees didn't grow all the way up to the spot where the hill sloped up dramatically enough to build a cavern inside it. Instead, grass covered a strip that ran like a green stream between the trees and the almost vertical hillside.

Youn-Chul lay in the grass on one elbow, a knee up. The young woman sat cross-legged beside him, leaning back on her palms. Beyond them, five meters from the cave entrance and with a good view of the approach, stood another teenage boy keeping watch. He was the younger of the two missionaries they'd met by the river.

"She doesn't want to tell you her name," this young man said, risking a look at them over his shoulder, "because she wants you to go away. We all do."

Youn-Chul laughed scornfully. "Shut up, little Joo-Chan. Watch for your squirrels and let a grown man do his business."

"Grown?" Joo-Chan said. "Ha! You're only two years older than me. If I'm not grown, you're not, either."

Youn-Chul looked at his female companion. She was so pretty. And quite tall for a North Korean. She had a narrow nose and a delicate mouth. Her hair was pulled back into a tight string, showing an unblemished fine forehead. She had other charms, too, which Youn-Chul took full note of.

"Our families have been together for a week now, yes? Every day I have watched you, eaten with you, tried to talk to you. But you will not tell me your name. You are a puzzle." He plucked at the grass. "Well, in all that time I have learned a few things about you. I know that you came across the river the day after I did. You came with your family, like I did. You are the youngest in your family, as I am— though we are both very mature," he added quickly for Joo-Chan's benefit. "I know that you are lovely. And I see how you take care of your mother without her knowing you are doing so. See, I am perceptive, yes? Hmm, what else do I know?"

The girl looked at him demurely, with a hint of a smile. "Nothing."

"Not true! I know you are missing your home. I know you are feeling very disloyal to Dear Leader. I know you are scared here.

I know that half of you wants to sneak away from the group and run back to your homeland.

"And yet I also know you are confused. You look around here and already you see people living much better than your family has ever lived. You see people in this barbaric land who eat not two but *three* meals a day. Every day. And not just four grams of rice, either, but meat and juicy vegetables. You see them wearing fine clothes and good shoes, and perhaps they have an extra pair at home—or even two! You see their houses and suddenly you are ashamed of what you were living in. You are glad they can't see your home. The people seem healthier and even happier here. It is as if *this* is the paradise we'd always been told we were living in. And then it makes you wonder—"

The girl looked at him. She waited, watching his eyes, encouraging with her glance. But he did not speak. "It makes you wonder what?" she asked.

Youn-Chul shook his head.

Above them a raven flapped silently by. When it was beyond them, it began cawing mightily as if warning the whole forest that humans were nearby.

"You are right," the young woman said. "How do you know all that about me?"

"Ha," Joo-Chan said, again glancing their way, "that's easy. He's only telling you what he himself is feeling. I've heard it a million times before. Don't listen to him." He stepped closer and knelt on her other side. "If you want my advice, you'll go inside with the others and hear Myong-Chol speak. He used to be a prison guard at the death camps. He's killed lots of people for Kim Jong-Il. But now he's found God."

She looked at him quickly. "I don't believe you. No such thing happens in my country. Dear Leader would not allow it."

Joo-Chan shrugged. "Believe what you want, but at least hear him out. At least Myong-Chol has something *interesting* to talk about, unlike others I could mention who only talk about themselves."

Youn-Chul pointed. "Oh, look, Joo-Chan! I think I saw a rabbit! Go, go, you are not doing your job. If you do not watch carefully, an army of police rabbits will descend upon us and shut down your little God business."

Joo-Chan stood and moved back to his watch position. "You should be more grateful to me since it was I who found you and brought you here." To the woman he said, "They were all soaking and half-drowned until I found them and rescued them."

"As I recall," Youn-Chul said, "we jumped you and you tripped over yourself and fell into the river."

The girl giggled.

"That's not true," Joo-Chan said, stung. "A rock moved under my foot." He turned away from them and folded his arms, staring down the trail.

"Hmph," Youn-Chul said, leaned again on his elbow. "Rescued us. Ha."

The young woman looked at him sweetly. "Aren't you going to finish your story? You were telling me what I was feeling. You said that seeing how good the people have it here made me wonder. . .what?"

Youn-Chul shook his head. "Nothing."

She touched his cheek with a blade of grass. "If you tell me the rest, I will tell you my name."

He looked at her intensely. He felt as though he was seeking something in her eyes, searching for it as if perhaps he had given it to her long ago for safekeeping. "First you tell me your name, then I will finish."

She hesitated. Youn-Chul saw Joo-Chan inching closer, though still facing away.

"All right," she said. "My name is Park Sun-Hye. I came with my father and mother, along with my sister and her husband, and his brother. We fled when it was discovered that my older brother was"—her eyes stared at the grass, and her head dropped—"taking more than his fair share of food from the People. It is so shameful.

He was taken by the police, and we only just escaped."

Joo-Chan touched her shoulder. "Don't believe it."

She wiped a tear away. "Don't believe what?"

"That your brother took more than his fair share. Probably he prevented a party official from taking more than *his* fair share, and the official got his revenge by making up a charge to get your brother condemned. Happens all the time over there."

She looked at him incredulously. "Such things do *not* happen in my homeland! *China* is the land of criminals and lawlessness, not North Korea! The revolution has taught us a better way. The Great Leader is our father. He is generous and forgiving. The Dear Leader does not tolerate corruption of any kind. You are wrong, Joo-Chan!"

Joo-Chan shrugged again. "You'll find out. Stick around here long enough and you'll see that I'm right."

She turned from him, looking sullen and stubborn.

Youn-Chul chuckled. "You're pretty when you're angry, Sun-Hye. In fact, you're pretty all the time."

Her scowl turned into an embarrassed smile. "Oh no."

"You're blushing."

"I'm not."

"Yes, you are. You like me, Sun-Hye."

"Oh, you are impossible! No, I don't."

"Yes, you do."

She folded her arms. "You haven't finished telling me. You owe me the rest of what you were going to say."

Youn-Chul nodded and looked away. "All right, Sun-Hye. What I was going to say was that all of this wealth here in China makes you wonder things. We have always been told that the outside world was barbaric and poor, that people on the outside were wild and dangerous. We were always told that we had it better under Great Leader's care than we would have it in any other country. Other people long to enter North Korea, we were always told, but Dear Leader doesn't let them because they're not worthy. And yet. . ."

He swept the forest with his arm, including the cave entrance, Joo-Chan, and the village on the other side of the pine forest. "And yet look at this place. Look at China. They have it better here, Sun-Hye. They have it better than we ever did in North Korea. Have you ever eaten so much as you have since we've been here? My stomach doesn't know what to do with so much good food. And yet we'd been told that the more revolutionary way was to drop down to two poor meals a day! That was—that was a lie." He met her eyes and breathed through his mouth, almost panting. "If these were lies, then. . .*what else* was a lie?"

They let the question hang before them in the warm sunlight. From inside the cave they could hear sounds of singing. A gust of wind brought the scent of chicken and sweet pineapple cooking in somebody's kitchen.

Youn-Chul saw movement at the hillside at their backs. Uncle and Aunt were first out of the cave, followed by members of Sun-Hye's family and others. Aunt was complaining.

". . .knows only crazy people believe in—well, in what he's talking about." She blinked in the bright sunlight and stepped aside to let others out of the cave. "And besides, everybody knows that if you believe in Jesus you are saying you love America! Ho-Pyong," she said to Uncle, "these people are trying to trick us into disloyalty to our homeland!"

Youn-Chul leaned over to Sun-Hye. "That's my aunt. She says we were better off in North Korea. She is so afraid of secret informers, even here. She must always be heard and seen to be loyal to the Great Leader. I don't think she believes half of it. Who does?"

Sun-Hye looked at him shyly. "I must go to my family now."

Youn-Chul nodded. "Of course."

They stood. Sun-Hye went to the three men and two women of her group. She fell in beside her mother. Her father, a round-faced man with a shaved head, scowled at Youn-Chul. The brother-in-law followed his gaze and added his menacing glare. He was about

Youn-Chul's age and he looked arrogant. His bushy black hair rose in a poor-man's pompadour almost as tall as the one Kim Jong-Il was so fond of. If Youn-Chul and this guy had to spend too much time in close proximity, Youn-Chul was probably going to have to beat him up—if for no other reason than to wipe that cocky look off his face.

Youn-Chul nodded to him, a "watch yourself, pal" attitude in his eyes, and moved toward Uncle.

Grandmother came out of the cave on Bum-Ji's arm. She stopped in the light and seemed to wilt into Bum-Ji's shoulder. "Ah! The sun is too bright in China. Move me to the shade. Hurry."

Bum-Ji eased her to a fallen tree in the shade of the surrounding pines. A breeze whisked the boughs like the sounds of a stream. "Grandmother," he said when she was sitting, "have you always been a— That is, have you always believed in. . ."

"Of course I've always been a Christian, boy!"

She said it so loudly everyone in the clearing heard. Youn-Chul caught Sun-Hye's eye and struck an expression like he was a crazy person. Sun-Hye smiled and hid her face.

"You never told us," Uncle said. "Did Father know?"

"Did Father know? What kind of a question is that to ask your mother? No, your father didn't know. Why would I tell him? Why would I tell you? Did I want you to be sent to the death camps for what I believed? What kind of a mother would I have been? They trick the children, you see. The teachers say, 'Let's play a game. If your parents have a book like this'—and they'd hold up a Bible, the Christian holy book—'bring it to school tomorrow and you will get a prize.' But the prize was that the children would unknowingly betray their own parents. Do you think I wanted that?"

Aunt lowered her voice. "Grandmother, you don't believe in those camps, do you? Not really."

"Ah, woman! Were you not listening to that man? He said he was a guard there. Was he a guard at a no-place? He told you about how they treat Christians, how they single them out for the worst jobs, how they have to always stare at the ground to deny them a look at heaven. Are you deaf now?"

Aunt's face compressed into a furious look. "But he is a traitor! How can you believe anything a traitor says?" She spoke so quietly her voice was barely audible over the wind whisking the pine needles. "Grandmother, you know the North Korean police is here secretly. How do we know that other family is really fleeing? Did you see the men? They have the look of the secret police. They are here marking our names, keeping us here so that we may be more easily caught! Grandmother, we must return to North Korea! We will explain it was a terrible mistake. Perhaps they will be lenient."

"Aunt," Youn-Chul said, "I can tell you that the other family is not working for the police. Sun-Hye's brother was—"

"And we should listen to you?" Aunt said. "You will be the first to be taken because you opened your mouth to that wicked young woman. What did she promise you, Youn-Chul? Sex? Money? An education in Pyongyang? What was the price for selling out your family?"

"Enough, woman!" Uncle said. "Leave him alone. You're the only one seeing danger here. Don't blame him for wanting the affections of a pretty woman. Tell me, Youn-Chul, does she have a tongue like this one?"

Youn-Chul saw Aunt's eyes on him. He scratched his cheek. "She. . .she was very proper, Uncle."

"You see?" Uncle said. "I knew it. Youn-Chul, does she have a sister?"

Aunt elbowed him in the stomach. "Hmph!"

Bum-Ji looked around the clearing. "Where is Chun-Mi?"

"I didn't see her," Youn-Chul said. "Perhaps she passed us by and returned to Ki-Won at the safe house."

"No," Grandmother said, fanning herself, "she's inside the cave."

Bum-Ji looked at her. "Doing what?"

Grandmother looked at him as if he'd just asked why the sky was blue. "Why, praying, I should think."

CHAPTER 8

DEALING WITH ETERNITY

"CHUN-MI, do you have any more questions?"

I looked up at Gil-Su and hesitated. With so few people in the little church, the clay walls echoed in a way that sounded vaguely metallic. I knelt on the damp dirt floor before the crucifix. Gil-Su stood at my left shoulder, Myong-Chol on my right.

A strange terror filled my heart. I was on the verge of the forbidden and the unknown. My body throbbed with energy. At this moment I felt as if I could bound over the treetops to escape any danger. But the fear was strange because it was mixed with a desire like I'd never known, as if I'd stumbled upon Kim Jong-Il's treasury itself at the precise moment I'd discovered my utter poverty. I felt torn, not only in my allegiances but also at the center of my identity.

I nodded at Gil-Su. "Only one more, teacher."

"Yes, Chun-Mi?" Gil-Su said. "What is your question?"

"It is for Myong-Chol." I looked at the former prison guard and tried to imagine that long, likable face locked in a murderous scowl. "Myong-Chol, why did the Christians in the camp not simply give up their faith?"

He tilted his head. "What, Chun-Mi?"

"They were in such torture, as you described. Why did they not change their answer? Like those Christians you say were killed by molten steel poured on them one by one. When the first one was killed in this way, why did the others not say, 'Jesus is not real!' and live? Why would they die rather than say such a simple thing, even if they did not mean it?"

As I watched, Myong-Chol's eyes unfocused, and I imagined he was seeing those Christians drop burning to the ground one by one, their bodies dissolving, their screams of agony mixing with sizzling steel.

"I found," he said, his voice choked, "that they valued their Lord more than their own lives. I found—" He took a breath as if to steady himself. "They believed that if they did not deny Him that perhaps others would follow Him, too. It was so foolish!" At this he broke into sobs. Gil-Su touched his shoulder.

I didn't know what was happening, but my fear was subsiding. I felt that presence in the room now, the presence like in my dream at the river. I knew I was safe in this moment. In a sense, it didn't matter what Myong-Chol or anyone said now. I had already decided what I would do. I would run to the peace!

After a moment, Myong-Chol continued. "It was so foolish because no one there would ever choose to have what they had. No prisoners. No guards. Why should they! Who would choose such an end? Who would choose the worst scorn of the guards and the contempt of the other prisoners? No one! I thought their deaths were foolish and meaningless. But then—" The sobs overtook him again.

Gil-Su rubbed his back. "But then," he said gently, "God found you, didn't He? You heard His voice, didn't you?"

Myong-Chol nodded and sobbed harder. His piteous cries resounded through the underground church.

"Their deaths were not meaningless, Myong-Chol," Gil-Su said. "You are here, full of God's Holy Spirit, away from that horrible life and away from who you were—all because of them. And who knows how many others will come to Jesus Christ because of their witness?"

"I don't think any others will," Myong-Chol said. "I fear that all of them died and I am the only one who was moved. How could so many Christians die only for me? How could God allow such a terrible crime?"

Gil-Su nodded in the glow of the dome lights. "It is a terrible responsibility, Myong-Chol, that God has given you. Even if all of them died only so that God could break through to your soul, then it was because He deemed it a price He was willing to pay. Those precious martyrs, they are in no pain now. They are in the true paradise. They watch you, Myong-Chol, waiting to see what you will do with what they have given you. What will you do, Myong-Chol? What will you do?"

Myong-Chol laughed tearfully. "Poor Chun-Mi! Her little question has caused all this! We should get back to her."

"Myong-Chol," Gil-Su said gently, "what will you do with what has been given to you? Their sacrifice must be honored. You know what it is; I can see it. God has shown you. Come, it will be good for your soul to tell me."

"Yes," Myong-Chol said, his scarred chin quivering. "I know what I must do, but. . ." He breathed raggedly. Tears flashed down his wet cheeks. Then his composure collapsed and he cried like a child. "But I am afraid! God, help me, I'm afraid!" He accepted Gil-Su's embrace and wept on his shoulder. "Oh, Gil-Su!" Myong-Chol said. "He wants me to return! Jesus, please help me, but He wants me to go back and tell them about Him. But I can't. I'm not the one they should've died for. I am foolish and weak and so afraid. Oh, Jesus. . .forgive me! I can't do it!"

Gil-Su held him gently and patted his back. I heard him

speaking comfortingly to Myong-Chol but couldn't make out the words. Finally Gil-Su pulled away and faced me. "I think perhaps you have your answer, Chun-Mi. They did not deny their faith because of those watching. And because Jesus has said that if anyone is ashamed of His name, He will be ashamed of him on the last day. But if anyone stays loyal to Him, even if they face death for it, He will stay loyal to them and save their souls."

I didn't know what "the last day" was, but I trusted Gil-Su. "Yes, I think I understand." I faced the crucifix again, that awful execution scene that reminded me more of Myong-Chol's concentration camps than anything remotely connected to God. Maybe I didn't understand at all. But none of it mattered anymore. My questions, my hesitations, all of it submerged beneath the steady current I felt in my heart. I couldn't see beyond the next corner of the river, but somehow I knew I would be all right. I felt my baby shift, and I rubbed my belly. Perhaps we will both be all right. Then I felt as if I heard again that strange, soothing voice: *Do not fear, dear one. I have plans for you. I will keep you safe.* A God who would speak with *me?* Truly He was a God of ten thousand charms.

I looked up at Gil-Su. "What must I do?"

Gil-Su smiled. He separated from Myong-Chol, who was calmer now, depleted. Gil-Su laid his hand on my shoulder. "If you are ready to become a child of God and a follower of Jesus Christ, you have only to repeat this prayer."

A charge went through my body. "I'm ready."

"Dear Jesus," Gil-Su began.

I stared at the crucifix. "Dear Jesus. . ."

* * *

"Someone's coming."

Joo-Chan pointed through the trees toward the village. The others crowded around him.

Bum-Ji found himself next to the patriarch of the other family. He was about Uncle's age. He'd had his head shaved a few days ago, but it was growing out again and looked prickly. "Can you see who it is?"

"No," the man said, shading his eyes. "Perhaps it is DPRK soldiers coming after us?"

Several of the women gasped.

"I don't think so," Joo-Chan said. "I saw only two, and one was a child."

"Ah," Grandmother said, still sitting on her stump. "There you are."

Bum-Ji turned to look. Chun-Mi stepped out of the cave, followed by Gil-Su and Myong-Chol. Chun-Mi's face was flushed. Bum-Ji went over and touched her shoulder. "My wife, you have been crying. Did those men harm you?" Even as he asked it, he knew they had not. There was something different about her face. She looked less careworn, almost as serene as when she was asleep.

"My love," she said, the gentlest of smiles on her face, "I am now a Christian."

Such a simple sentence, and yet it struck Bum-Ji like a bullet. "I. . .a Christian? I did not know you could do such a thing so quickly. Surely you haven't learned enough yet. Is there a book you could read?"

Gil-Su approached them. "Is she telling you the good news, Song Bum-Ji?"

"She says she has already become a Christian, Gil-Su. Are you sure this is advisable? Everything is so new to us. Perhaps. . .perhaps there are other things she should know before declaring such a thing."

"Do not worry, Bum-Ji," Gil-Su said, smiling broadly. "It has pleased God to cause the largest of decisions to require the smallest of efforts on our part. Perhaps Chun-Mi and I can explain this to you over dinner tonight?"

"Oh yes, Bum-Ji!" Chun-Mi said, almost hopping with

excitement. "You must become a Christian, too! We all must."

At this, the group turned to look.

"What is that loudmouth saying?" Aunt said.

Grandmother laughed on her stump.

Chun-Mi went to her and they hugged. "Oh, Grandmother! Have you known this joy all along? I feel I must burst."

The old woman only laughed and hugged her.

"They are coming!" It was Joo-Chan, the other missionary, calling their attention back. "It is Kora-Lee and the child. Something is wrong."

Kim Kora-Lee was a Korean-Chinese woman who had been Gil-Su's first convert many years ago. She had a wide, pleasant face and short black hair. Today she wore dark purple pants and a pink long-sleeved button-up shirt. She rushed up the trail, dragging Ki-Won with her. The little boy had dried food paste on his cheeks and forehead. He was whining and tugging against her grip—but he still clutched his wooden shapes in his hand. When Kora-Lee reached the group, she let him go. He plopped onto the ground then ran to Chun-Mi.

"Gil-Su, Gil-Su!" Kora-Lee said, out of breath and agitated.

Gil-Su went to her. The others crowded around. "What is it, dear woman? Has the pipe burst again?"

"No, Gil-Su! You must get away! All of you must run, now! Pak Joongbae heard it on the radio. The American television showed our hill."

Gil-Su shook his head. "No, Kora-Lee. They said they would not show where we were. It was only interviews. Our faces were to be hidden. Our voices disguised. Nothing to lead anyone here. It was only to show Americans what we do for refugees."

The others mumbled and shifted nervously.

"I don't think the show has even been shown yet, Kora-Lee," Gil-Su said.

"It has! It has! Only now. And they showed our village! They showed this very cave!" She pointed at the entrance in terror. "They showed North Korea, then they moved the camera right over here to our hill! Oh, Gil-Su, what will we do?"

"Look!" Joo-Chan said, pointing toward the village. "I see trucks coming! Do you hear that hum? It is a whole convoy. The military is here! Soldiers are coming! Everybody run!"

* * *

Youn-Chul found Sun-Hye suddenly in his arms. "Sun-Hye! You have to—"

"Youn-Chul!" she cried, holding him tight as if trying to climb into his skin. "I can't go back to North Korea, Youn-Chul! I can't go back. I hate it there!"

Youn-Chul saw his family trying to get Grandmother to her feet. He saw Sun-Hye's family running into the forest. Through the trees half a meter down the hill, he saw more troop trucks arriving and soldiers jumping out. They wore all green uniforms, with red at their collars and on their hats. "Sun-Hye, what about Dear Leader's protection and your great love for—"

She put both hands on his mouth. "No, Youn-Chul, you were right. It was all a lie. I knew it as soon as you said it. Youn-Chul, if they take us back they will kill us! Even if they don't, I can't go back to the lie. I won't!" She held his face in her hands. "Protect me, Youn-Chul. Please! I want to stay with you. I want to stay with you forever."

Sun-Hye's father hurried up to them, his eyes wild. "Sun-Hye, come! We are making for the road." He tore her from Youn-Chul's grip and led her into the slender pines. To Youn-Chul, he said, "Go to your family, boy. Help them."

Youn-Chul saw Sun-Hye's eyes. They were pleading with him. But she went with her father and her family. They left the trail and stumbled through the undergrowth away from the village.

Youn-Chul looked behind him. His uncle had Grandmother up and walking. Gil-Su, the missionary, was with them, urging them all into the cave entrance. "No!" Youn-Chul called. "Don't go in there. You'll be trapped!"

Chun-Mi reached her hand out to him. With her other hand she held onto Ki-Won. "Come, Little Brother," she said. "There is a secret place. We will be safe."

Gunfire snapped the quiet of the forest. It was a single shot followed by a burst of automatic weapons fire. It seemed to come from the direction of the village, but the echo off the trees and hillside confused the ears. The hum and slam of heavy trucks rose up their hill like flood waters. Youn-Chul thought he could hear distant screams.

Joo-Chan strode to him from the direction of the cave. "You're wanting to go after her."

Youn-Chul looked at him. Despite being his rival for Sun-Hye's attention, he seemed like a friendly person. He was shorter than Youn-Chul and not as broad, but he had bright eyes and smooth skin. He imagined the girls would find him good-looking. He nodded. "Yes."

Joo-Chan's jaw worked as he considered Youn-Chul's family entering the cave, the disturbance in the village, and the direction Sun-Hye had gone. Then he looked at Youn-Chul and raised one eyebrow. "Come on." He loped after Sun-Hye's family.

Youn-Chul turned toward Chun-Mi. "You go on, Big Sister. You will be safe. I'm going with Joo-Chan. We'll be okay. I'll join you later."

Bum-Ji came to stand beside Chun-Mi. "Wife, you must not let him go. He will only be safe with us."

She looked intently at Youn-Chul. "Little Brother, do you have your papers, the ones Gil-Su gave us?"

Youn-Chul felt in his pocket. "Yes."

Sounds of people crashing through the forest reached them.

A man yelled to them authoritatively in Chinese. Youn-Chul could see thirty soldiers running toward them through the underbrush, still eighty meters away. These wore ammunition belts and steel helmets.

"Come on!" Joo-Chan said, pulling at his sleeve.

Youn-Chul looked at his sister and waved. Then he followed Joo-Chan along the hillside at a tangent away from the soldiers and the cave.

CHAPTER 9

THE ROUNDUP

"BE CAREFUL, Little Brother," I whispered, watching Youn-Chul go.

I felt a firm grip on my arm.

"Come, wife," Bum-Ji said. "We must go now." He pulled me into the cave entrance.

Gil-Su waited there. In his hand he held an electrical switch with a black cable leading off into the shadows. "Get all the way back, into the church itself."

"What about Youn-Chul and your assistant?" Bum-Ji said. "They're still out there and the soldiers are coming."

"They are in God's hands," Gil-Su said, backing away from the entrance. The sunlight stabbed deep inside the cavern but finally gave way to the old, cold shade. "Joo-Chan knows this land. I can only help them if they are in here."

I heard men and jingling equipment just outside the cave. I backed into the church proper, where minutes ago I had dealt with eternity. Uncle held Grandmother's shoulders. Aunt stood in the corner, looking terrified. Myong-Chol had found a long wooden peg and wielded it like a club. Kora-Lee had Ki-Won in her lap. The boy seemed fascinated by the battery-powered dome lights and quite unaware of his danger. Bum-Ji pressed into me, placing himself between me and the soldiers.

"Cover your ears!" Gil-Su shouted from the entranceway.

I rushed to Ki-Won and took his head to my breast and tried to plug my own ears, too. Even through my hands, I heard a loud snap, like a walking stick breaking, and then a muffled explosion. *POOM.*

Immediately the sunlight flickered and went out. Sounds of rock and earth collapsing. Gil-Su charged into the room chased by a cannonade of dirt and small rocks. Dust engulfed them, dried their throats. At length the rocks stopped shifting. The church room itself seemed completely intact, though the roof plaster near the entranceway cracked and rained down.

"What have you done to us, madman?" Aunt said, not daring to move more than her eyes.

Gil-Su sighed heavily and dusted himself off. "Do not worry. We planned for this day."

Kora-Lee pulled a dome light off the wall and handed it to Ki-Won. "But we hoped it would never come."

Gil-Su went to the front of the room and pushed the little lectern to the side, revealing a flagstone in the dirt. He lifted this and reached into the cubbyhole beneath. He drew out a flashlight, a still-wrapped package of batteries, a first-aid kit, and several packages of food and bottles of water. These he handed to Myong-Chol, who packed everything into a duffel bag. Gil-Su also withdrew a little black electronic device that he quickly shoved into an inner pocket.

"Gil-Su," I said, releasing Ki-Won, "why did the soldiers come?"

He stood, his back toward them. He seemed to be staring at the crucifix in the pale light of the domes. When he turned toward them, he looked ten years older. "It is because of me, dear sister."

The others stepped nearer. Ki-Won went to the pile of dirt by the entranceway and grabbed fistfuls of it, letting it cascade down his head and front.

Kora-Lee rolled her eyes but let him play. "It is not your fault, Gil-Su," she said, a reprimand in her voice. "It is the Americans. They betrayed you."

Aunt squinted at Gil-Su. "He is in league with the Americans! You see?" she said to Grandmother. "I told you that respecting Jesus means you respect Americans. It is a dishonor!" She spat at Gil-Su's feet. "You brought this upon us, you idiot! And now you have led us to our deaths in this hole!"

"That is not true," Myong-Chol said, shouldering the bag.

Kora-Lee shoved Aunt's shoulder. "Close your mouth, foolish woman!"

"How dare you strike your guest!"

"Yes, a guest. A guest of Gil-Su's hospitality. And yet you dare to insult your host and spit at his feet! This is how you repay his kindness. Foolish woman, do you know how many times Gil-Su has been arrested? How many times his possessions have been taken by police? How many months he has spent in Chinese prison because he helps North Koreans like you?"

Step by step she backed Aunt against the wall of the underground church. "Why does he do it? Why does he stay when he knows that if he is captured again they will surely execute him? 'Go home!' I tell him. 'Go back to America and send others to do this work. Raise money. Welcome them when they come to Seoul.' But does he listen to me? No. And you spit at his feet!"

"Kora-Lee," Gil-Su said, and this time the note of authority was in his voice. "That will do, good sister."

Kora-Lee leaned into Aunt's face a moment longer then sniffed and stepped away.

Gil-Su stepped over a pew and sat on it. "I will agree that the

Americans have apparently done something they promised me they would not. If what Kora-Lee has heard is true and the Americans showed our location in reference to North Korea, and if that is why the soldiers have come, then it is indeed a betrayal. I do not know what is happening out there, but I do know I can do nothing to stop it. I can only try to protect you."

He gazed at his filthy running shoes. "And yet the Americans could not have done this betrayal if I had not given them the ability." He stopped speaking and stared at the fraying toe of one shoe. For a moment the only sound was the gentle drizzle of Ki-Won showering himself with handfuls of dusty pebbles.

"I live in America, you see," Gil-Su said.

Aunt gasped.

He looked at her. "Shocking, isn't it?" He smiled sadly. "I know you will not believe me, but America is not what you have always been told." He examined their faces, his smile deepening. Then he shrugged. "When I am not here, I am a pastor at a church in America."

"I knew it!" Grandmother said, looking very small in the dim light. She pointed a quivering finger at him. "I knew you were trouble."

Gil-Su laughed. "You are right, dear sister!" To the rest of us he said, "My parents live in Seoul, but we have extended family in North Korea. I felt God leading me to come here and try to get my family to come out. They would not. They will have nothing to do with me. And yet God did not release me from this place, and so I come here when I can. I would like to stay permanently but. . . sometimes I have to leave for awhile. You see, there is no better place for a man like me than here, on the Tumen, welcoming people out of the darkness and introducing them to the light. Do I speak truly, sister Chun-Mi? Are you standing in the light?"

I nodded eagerly. "In light and peace, Gil-Su."

"So," Gil-Su said, "the last time I was in America, I was contacted by representatives of a television company. They said they had heard of our work here and the plight of refugees fleeing North Korea. They said—"

"No," Uncle said, astonished. "In America they do not know of us here."

"Yes, yes," Gil-Su said. "Many do not pay attention, but there is much that people on the outside can learn about North Korean refugees if they only look. Television and the Internet spread the infor—"

"The Enter-what?" Grandmother asked.

"It is not important, Grandmother," Gil-Su said. "It is like a great library of information. . .in a way. Anyway, this television company said they wanted to make a show about us. They said they wanted to make more Americans aware of your situation. Since I am always trying to raise awareness about this in America, I agreed to help them with their show. They came here with a camera and some people. They promised me they would disguise everything and everyone so that only good would come out of their efforts, and no bad." His right eye twitched. "I showed them everything. I–I can only assume they made some mistake. But now. . . now it is a disaster." He shook his head and stared again at his feet. "And I brought it about."

Myong-Chol dropped the duffel bag into Gil-Su's lap. "Come on, brother. Get up. You are the only one who can lead us back into the light."

Gil-Su smiled and nodded. "Yes, of course." He stood and shouldered the bag. "I have one flashlight, but the way is long and at times the ceiling is low. Each of you take one of these lights on the wall. They come off easily and are not hot. They will not last forever, but they will help for awhile." He pulled Grandmother to her feet. "Come, dear mother, you must lead your family to freedom."

We stood and gathered our few belongings. Kora-Lee went to Ki-Won and tried to dust him off.

I stood but had to hold onto Bum-Ji's arm a moment. Then I

reached for Gil-Su's elbow. "How far will you take us?"

Gil-Su glanced at Myong-Chol and Kora-Lee before answering. "I will take you all the way, dear sister."

Aunt patted her hair down. "All the way to the end of the tunnel?"

"No," he said, his eyes gleaming in the shifting light, "all the way to Mongolia."

"Mongolia?" Bum-Ji said.

"Yes. There you can go to a special village just for North Korean refugees. They will help you with papers and asylum. From there you can go to South Korea or wherever you choose. You will be refugees, and the world will open its arms to you."

I felt weary already. "But I thought you would hand us off to others who would guide us. That's what you said before."

"Yes," Gil-Su said. "But that was before. Now. . .now there is nothing for me here. I can do nothing for the others out there, the ones I was supposed to be caring for. So I will devote all my energies to getting you few to safety. Then I will find a new place on the border and find new safe houses. It is only a new chapter in God's book, dear sister." He pulled aside a blanket hanging from the wall, revealing a narrow passageway beyond.

"You see," he said, ushering the others into the passage, "it is as someone has wisely said: 'He who saves one life saves the world entire.' "

* * *

"Sun-Hye, wait!"

Youn-Chul and Joo-Chan caught up to Sun-Hye's family easily. Their group was slowed by Sun-Hye's ailing mother. Her sister and the three men had been scraped by low branches and were winded by their flight.

At Youn-Chul's call, Sun-Hye disengaged herself from her

father's arm and ran to him. "Youn-Chul! I am so glad to see you!"

Joo-Chan waved. "Hello. I'm here, too, you know."

Sun-Hye looked only at Youn-Chul. "Why aren't you with your family?"

He held her close, savoring the suppleness of her lean arms. Her family topped a ridge and disappeared over the other side. "You asked me to protect you, Sun-Hye. So here I am."

Her smile was as swift as it was stunning. "Oh." She leaned her head against his chest briefly then looked up. "Come with us! My brother-in-law says we are nearing a road! We will follow it to the next village and then decide what to do." She grabbed his hand and Joo-Chan's, too. "Come on!"

The branches were still swaying from her family's passing. Youn-Chul and the others were about to crest the ridge when they heard angry shouting and the sounds of a scuffle.

Joo-Chan brought Sun-Hye to the ground. "Wait. Youn-Chul, wait!"

Youn-Chul knelt but crept forward to look. There was the dirt road, across ten meters of young pines and heavy bushes. A police Jeep was there. Men were struggling in the bushes. As they watched, a loud diesel military truck pulled up and stopped. Soldiers jumped out and pulled bodies out of the fight. In seconds it was over. Sun-Hye's family was captured.

Youn-Chul felt Sun-Hye about to leap forward to their aid. He covered her mouth, stifling her cry, and pulled her down to the dirt.

Joo-Chan slunk down beside them a moment later. "I think they heard you. Come on!"

There was nowhere to run but toward the village. It took both the young men to bring Sun-Hye. She alternated between fighting against them and just wanting to collapse on the ground.

They ran for ten minutes, stopping occasionally to get their bearings and listen for pursuit. None came. After another five minutes, they spied the outskirts of the village, still half a kilometer away.

"This way," Joo-Chan said, leading them around the village counterclockwise. "We will try to make it to a safe house I know. There is a hiding place."

But it was soon clear that they would never make it through the village. Hundreds of soldiers and police thronged the small village. Vehicles had to pass through multiple checkpoints. Eight-man squads patrolled the streets. German shepherds and their handlers went house to house. The smell of diesel trucks clogged the river-front village's normally clear air.

"Look," Youn-Chul said. He crouched beside Sun-Hye and Joo-Chan in thick brush fifty meters from the edge of town.

The soldiers had cleared the village market of commerce and had herded all the people there. Soldiers with rifles walked the perimeter of an impromptu fence of coiled razor wire. A large green armored vehicle sat at the head of the square. It had six tall wheels and an angular body with twin-hooded windows in the front—like a rolling beetle. A soldier with a black helmet and plastic visor stood in a turret manning a large machine gun atop the steel beast.

Youn-Chul saw in the group other refugees he'd met since being here. "What are they doing? Are they going to kill them all?"

"No," Joo-Chan said. "They don't usually shoot anybody. They're looking for North Koreans. The ones they find, they'll turn over to the North Korean agents. Like that one there, next to the officer. See him?"

Youn-Chul looked where Joo-Chan pointed. He saw a hatless, gray-haired man in a uniform slightly darker green than the Chinese military officer standing beside him. The man had a severe aspect and reflective sunglasses. He looked like an eyeless skull face from a nightmare.

"And then what will happen to them?" he asked.

"And then," Joo-Chan said, "they will be taken to the labor camps you say do not exist. They will of course be tortured—though they'll call it 'interrogation.' If the torture causes them to admit they have consorted with Christians or Americans, they will be executed. If they had been caught trying to leave China, they would be executed. But hopefully these will spend only six months in prison and be allowed to return to their miserable lives in North Korea. And then, two months after that, they will escape again, and we will be here to welcome them."

Vehicles approached from their left. Two troop transports with a Jeep in the middle. They stopped in front of the market, blocking Youn-Chul's view. Soldiers opened the rear gate and brought out Sun-Hye's family. Her father's arms were bound behind him. As he leaned out the back of the truck, the soldiers reached to catch him, then suddenly pulled their hands away, allowing him to fall to the ground. All the soldiers laughed. They pulled him off the ground, though he was having trouble supporting himself now.

"Don't worry, Sun-Hye," Youn-Chul said. "I'm sure your father's—Sun-Hye?"

She wasn't with them. He and Joo-Chan searched the bushes around them. Finally Joo-Chan pointed toward the market.

Sun-Hye was running toward her father. She was more than halfway to the trucks already. The moment Youn-Chul saw her, the soldiers saw her, too.

"Sun-Hye, no!" He called as loud as he dared. Then he called again, louder.

She didn't turn around to look at him, but a soldier in the Jeep did.

Joo-Chan pulled him into the brush. "Quiet! They'll bring the dogs."

When he could bear it no longer, Youn-Chul peeked through the brush. No soldiers or dogs were coming their way. The soldiers who had brought Sun-Hye's family now climbed back into their trucks and drove off, filling the air with black smoke.

A soldier had Sun-Hye by the arm, half lifting her off her feet. He brought her to a man at the wire fence, who wrote on a clipboard.

Youn-Chul watched helplessly, as if seeing newsreel footage of events long over. Sun-Hye reached for her pants pocket, but the soldier slapped her hand away then dug into her pants himself. Youn-Chul felt rage rising in him, scaling the walls of his restraint.

Finally the soldier pulled out Sun-Hye's papers and handed them to the man with the clipboard. These were the falsified identification papers the missionaries had supplied them. Youn-Chul had papers just like them in his own pocket. Would they save him? Would they save her? The North Korean agent took the papers and examined them. Then he said something to the men beside him, and they all laughed. Their laughter carried to them like ravens over the forest. He tucked the papers into his breast pocket and stepped away. The soldiers drew open the razor-wire fence and shoved Sun-Hye inside.

Her family embraced her. Her father sat on the ground. His hands had apparently come untied because he reached up and held her. She sank beside him, her hair falling out of its binding and hanging like a veil over their faces.

How recently it had been she had been tickling Youn-Chul's cheek with a blade of grass. He took a deep breath. "Will she be all right?"

"Um. . .yes," Joo-Chan said.

Youn-Chul looked at him. "You're lying. It was bad that the agent took her papers, wasn't it?"

Joo-Chan only looked at him, his face mirroring what Youn-Chul felt: concern, fear of the worst for their friend, guilty relief that it wasn't them.

When they looked back at the marketplace, a plain-dressed man had appeared. He was in a conversation with the officer and the North Korean agent. A soldier shouted at Sun-Hye, and she stepped forward reluctantly.

"Oh, no," Joo-Chan said. "This is bad."

"Bad?" Youn-Chul said. "How could it be any worse than it is?"

"No, Youn-Chul, this is worse. That man is Kweon Chulsoon. He is a criminal. Chinese mafia."

"Chinese what?"

"Black market. You know, drugs, slavery, people smuggling? Chulsoon is very high up in the underworld in this area. I hope I'm wrong, but it looks to me like he's interested in making a deal for Sun-Hye."

Youn-Chul felt his rage change into dread. "What kind of deal? What are you talking about? What does a criminal want with Sun-Hye? She won't have anything to do with such a man."

Joo-Chan rose to his knees. "She won't have a choice, Youn-Chul."

"Why? Why won't she have a choice?"

In the marketplace, Chulsoon produced a thick wad of paper money visible even across the distance. Sun-Hye retreated to her family and her father rose to his feet. Youn-Chul could hear his shrill protestations. The North Korean agent stood with his arms folded. Chulsoon split his money wad in thirds and offered one third to the agent and another third to the Chinese officer. The agent said something, and Chulsoon went into hysterics. But they were short lived, and with a dramatic sweep of his hands, he thrust all of his money into the hands of the agent and the officer.

The officer counted his half and uttered some command to the gate soldiers, who drew back the fence and went for Sun-Hye.

Her family stood in their way. The lead soldier backhanded her father, and the others fell into a struggle. Other refugees stood and came forward. More soldiers rushed in, rifle butts forward. The officer shouted to the machine gunner in the armored vehicle, and he opened fire with a deafening volley across their heads and into the hillside beyond. The civilians dropped to the ground, allowing the soldiers to easily extract Sun-Hye. They brought her to Chulsoon and threw her at his feet.

Chulsoon said something that made the soldiers laugh; then he and two burly men with him carried Sun-Hye toward a waiting car.

"No!" Youn-Chul said. He stood to run, not knowing what he planned but wanting to help her.

"Youn-Chul, no!" Joo-Chan said, pulling at his shirt.

Across the distance, soldiers spun to face them. They shouted and raised their weapons. The officer peered toward them and issued a command. The nearest soldiers charged toward them, shouting.

Youn-Chul and Joo-Chan ran away. He let Joo-Chan lead as they swerved through the forest, dodging trees and leaping stumps. Vines scratched their skin. Youn-Chul ran through a spiderweb and felt it crackling over his ears.

Behind them, the soldiers opened fire. The shots all missed, but it sent a shock of terror through Youn-Chul. No longer did he care about spiders in his ears or scrapes on his arms.

Joo-Chan led him toward the cave, but fifty meters from it, they could see soldiers there, standing and inching toward the village, perhaps alerted by the gunfire. He swerved to the left, down the hill toward the Tumen River.

More gunfire, and this time someone cried out in pain. The soldiers by the cave took cover and returned fire at their unseen enemy. The soldiers coming from the village dropped to the ground and shot at the ones now shooting at them.

Youn-Chul and Joo-Chan looked at each other, eyes wide. But they didn't stop to enjoy their great luck. They ran deeper into the forest, skirting the riverbank and climbing the back side of the hill, angling far away from the mistaken gun battle.

Joo-Chan burst into a small clearing and stopped, heaving for breath. Youn-Chul collapsed in the wet grass. A fox sped into the trees, making no sound in its escape.

"Are we going anywhere," Youn-Chul asked, "or just running?"

"No," Joo-Chan said, still breathing hard, "we're going to where the cave exit lets out."

"What cave exit?"

"Never mind. We're going back to your family."

Youn-Chul sat up and looked through the dense forest the way they had come. "What about Sun-Hye? We can't just forget her. What did that man want with her, anyway?"

Joo-Chan took a final deep breath. "Do you really want to know?"

"Yes!"

He rubbed his face. "If I had to guess, I'd say she was to be used for prostitution. They will keep her locked away somewhere and rent her out for sex. It happens all the time to women who come here from North Korea. They think they're going to find this great new life here, but they end up in worse abuse than they were in before. That's one of the reasons we do what we do. Even if they don't care one bit about Jesus, we can at least try to keep them from that fate."

Youn-Chul stood, his hands in fists. "Then we'll find her and we'll break her out. We'll find an honest policeman and we'll—"

Joo-Chan scoffed. "Friend, we're in nowhere, China. Far away from civilization. There are about as many honest policemen in this area as there are cars in Pyongyang." He watched Youn-Chul's face. "That's close to none, Youn-Chul. Besides, even if we could find such a policemen, it wouldn't matter. To China, all North Koreans are illegal 'economic migrants,' not refugees." He looked up at the afternoon sun. "No, the only way to save her—if there is a way—is to come in with more hired strong men than Chulsoon has around her. And even then, I don't think there's anything we can do to save her from some of it. Chulsoon's probably 'trying her out' right now."

Youn-Chul dug into his eyes with the heels of his hands. "No!"

Something rustled the bushes and they sprang away.

"Wait!" It was a woman's voice.

Youn-Chul stopped and looked. "Big Sister?"

"Little Brother!"

They ran together and embraced. Gil-Su and Myong-Chol led the rest of Youn-Chul's family into the clearing.

Chun-Mi looked into her brother's face. "Where is the girl? Did you never find her?"

For the first time in ten years, Youn-Chul broke down and cried.

CHAPTER 10

THE EASY PART

IN THE DREAM *men were fighting. Two giants locked in vicious combat. Their steps obliterated low-slung mud homes; their blows shook mountains flat. Their battlefield had become a wasteland. Both were warriors, their bodies hard and trained. Neither could gain the advantage over the other. As I watched them grapple and strike, I had the awful feeling they were fighting over me—and my baby. And though I knew somehow that my champion would never give up and would eventually win, a sharp certainty rose within me that for now he was overpowered.*

I opened my eyes. A dark male form loomed over me, his face black and featureless. "No! I won't let you take my baby! Get back!"

"Chun-Mi! Chun-Mi, wake up, you're having a nightmare." The man sat beside me and some pale light touched his face, revealing a wide forehead and kind eyes.

"Oh, Bum-Ji!" I said, reaching for him. "I had such a terrible dream."

He stroked my hair and simply held me for a moment. Then he pulled back and placed a palm on my belly. "How is our child?"

"You mean our daughter?" I said. "She is fine. Sleeping, I think." I hesitated. "Bum-Ji. . .I have thought of her name. Would you like to hear it?"

Bum-Ji smiled in the almost total darkness. "Does a father not get to name his child?"

"Yes, but listen. I want to call her Shin-Hwa: 'God's peace.' " The chill air finally registered to me, along with the fact that little Shin-Hwa was pressing on my bladder. I tried to read my husband's face. "Do you like it?"

"Song Shin-Hwa," he said thoughtfully. "But 'Shin' is forbidden in North Korea. We cannot give our child a forbidden name."

"Yes, we can," I said, sitting up and leaning against the steel wall of the cargo truck. "Because our daughter will never set foot in that kingdom of lies. My child will bear the name of God in freedom." I softened my tone. "And the peace, Bum-Ji, the peace I saw in the eyes of the warriors in my vision. The peace I saw in Gil-Su's eyes that night on the riverbank. It's the peace I have in my heart now, my husband. You must have it, too. And it will be in our daughter's heart. I will see to it. God has given peace, and so that is what I will name our daughter."

The sound of quiet conversation reached us through the rear door of the truck. I realized belatedly that we had stopped. "Forgive me, husband," I said, touching his cheek. "I see I have overstepped myself. We will name our child whatever you wish."

Bum-Ji chuckled and kissed the top of my head. "My dear wife. How can men say they have authority in their homes with women like you as wives?" He stood and reached for my hand. "Come, Chun-Mi. Gil-Su says we must walk from here."

Bum-Ji swung open the double steel doors at the rear of the truck, letting in a blast of cold wind that penetrated my light jacket and stirred up debris in the cargo space. He hopped down and eased me to the hard-packed dirt at the edge of the semipaved road.

"What a desolate place this is," I said, looking around.

The moon had waxed full in our journey and was now three-quarters again, as it had been the night we crossed the Tumen. It lit a wide, waterless waste untroubled by structures, hills, or trees. Stars above speckled so closely together as to make the sky almost more shimmering white than black. The panel truck sat on the side of the highway, though I could see no other vehicle on any horizon, much less on the arrow-straight strip of a road. The wind whistled steadily, often accelerating into icy gusts. I bit down on sandy grit between my molars.

The others were huddled beside the truck, sheltering from the wind. Uncle sat on the ground against a wheel. Aunt leaned back against him, snoring. Gil-Su looked between the electronic device in his hand and the map held down and illuminated by Myong-Chol's flashlight. Joo-Chan played in the dirt with Ki-Won, Kora-Lee watching them disinterestedly. Grandmother stood leaning against the truck, almost completely covered by a heavy quilt Gil-Su had purchased for her from a trader on the train. Little Brother stood on the other side of the road staring south.

I pulled my jacket shut at the neck and went to him. "Is that the way to Mongolia?"

Little Brother nodded slowly. "So he says. Five or ten kilometers of this barren desert and then a single strand of barbed wire. Who thought it would be so simple?"

I smiled. "I would not call it simple, these two days of train travel, checkpoints almost every hour, Ki-Won's diarrhea, Grandmother's fall, Aunt's constant complaining, and a day of travel in this awful truck and chuckhole-filled roads. Not to mention what happened at the village and before that our crossing from North Korea. No, Little Brother, we have earned a simple walk to freedom, don't you think?"

He smiled slightly.

I pulled my brother's arm around my shoulders. "You are thinking of Sun-Hye."

He didn't answer but rested his cheek on the top of my head.

"I think you should come back for her," I said.

He looked at me sharply. "Go back? Now?"

"No, after we make it to Seoul." I pulled his arm away and gestured. "First, tonight we will get across the border and find the relocation village set up just for North Korean refugees. We will find it easily with Gil-Su's device. Then we will claim refugee status and be flown to Seoul. Gil-Su says the South Korean government will pay us vast riches simply for coming to their country. Can you imagine it, Little Brother? And after all we'd been told about South Korea's corruption and madness! Perhaps they are mad to pay us to leave North Korea, but I don't care. You could use some of this money to travel back to the village and buy Sun-Hye back. You and she can return to Seoul and perhaps get married. If she still wants you, of course."

Little Brother shoved me playfully. "What do you mean 'if'?"

"There," I said, burrowing into his warmth again, "I knew I could cheer you up."

Gil-Su called from beside the truck. "Come and see."

We nine adults gathered around Gil-Su and his map. I kept an eye on Ki-Won, who was leaning into the wind and laughing. Aunt blinked groggily.

Gil-Su laid a dim flashlight on the map, which was now weighted down by rocks. He pointed at lines on the map. "We are right here. This red line is the road coming from Hailar. This blue circle here is Buir Nur, a lake on the Mongolian side. Everything over here," he said, tracing a black line that zigged and zagged very close to where he'd said we were located, "is the China-Mongolia border. Everything on the south side of it is Mongolia. It's that way," he said, pointing across the road. "About seven kilometers according to the GPS."

I didn't know what GPS was, though Gil-Su had explained it to all of us several times. Apparently machines in the sky had some kind of connection with this little device, and all of it helped people know where they were. As long as it worked, he could have had pig entrails hanging from his eyelids and I wouldn't care.

"And the resettlement village," Uncle said. "Where is it?"

Gil-Su traced south-southwest of Buir Nur. "This way, another ten kilometers inside Mongolia." He straightened. "It is a long walk, I know, but it is the last steps of a much longer journey. You have done the hardest part already. Now you have only a little stroll left to do. Come, my friends, gather your things and let's be off. Freedom awaits!"

Little Brother hooted and Grandmother laughed. Even Aunt looked optimistic. Bum-Ji swept Ki-Won up and onto his shoulders. The rest of us had on everything we owned, so Gil-Su led us across the road and into the endless dried grass plain.

Ten steps into our journey, Ki-Won cried out. "Oh! Square! Square!" He all but launched himself off Bum-Ji's shoulders. Bum-Ji tried to hold him but the boy thrashed and squirmed and shrieked. "Square! Mommy, Mommy!" He reared back and walloped Bum-Ji on the face with a fist full of wooden shapes.

Bum-Ji put the boy down and Ki-Won ran back across the road, where he fell into the dirt, picked himself up, and scrabbled around for his square. Joo-Chan trotted over to help him look.

Bum-Ji pressed fingers to his temple and checked for blood. "Chun-Mi, your sister was a great woman. But somebody somewhere forgot to teach this child to control his temper."

"He's a brat," Aunt said, watching Joo-Chan discover the missing puzzle piece and hand it to Ki-Won. "If he doesn't want to lose his stupid toys he shouldn't leave them everywhere."

Joo-Chan picked Ki-Won up and ran back to rejoin the group. Ki-Won held his piece out for the world to see. "Square!"

We set out again, our ankles scraping the brittle scrub grass littering the plain. Sand blew by in handfuls. Grandmother's quilt was getting away from her and the walking was difficult, so Uncle lifted the small woman into his arms and carried her.

Joo-Chan walked beside me. "It's good that Ki-Won is getting out of China. This is the best place to cross because there are no guards for ten kilometers either way."

I had to watch my step carefully, but I glanced at Joo-Chan. "Why do you say it's good that *Ki-Won* is getting out? Isn't it good that we all are?"

"Oh yes, but Ki-Won especially. And you," he said, focusing on my protruding abdomen.

Bum-Ji stepped closer. "Why?"

"Well," Joo-Chan said, shifting Ki-Won's position, "children do not do well if they're captured and sent back to North Korea. Sometimes they pull away too hard and the wire tears them."

Bum-Ji and I exchanged a look. "What wire?"

"The wire they run through your nose when the North Koreans take you from the Chinese. They run a wire through your nose and your wrist to keep you from running. Well, actually, it's not so much to keep you from running as to make a statement—you're an animal now; they are absolute masters over you; submit or die. Sometimes the little ones get frightened and pull it right out of their noses. Soft flesh, you see."

My heart raced. "No. I can't believe that. No government is that cruel to children. No government is that cruel to its own people."

Joo-Chan shrugged. "Anyway, I'm glad we're almost across."

"So," Bum-Ji said, his voice as low as it could be to still be heard over the wind huffing across our ears, "those people in the village, those other refugees, they had this wire strung through them?"

"Possibly, especially if they admitted they'd been talking with Christians. But usually they reserve the wire for people who are try-ing to leave China."

Again my pulse quickened. "But *we're* trying to leave China."

"I know! It's strange," Joo-Chan said, "how they don't really mind that you leave North Korea and go to China. That's all right, I guess. But if you try to leave *China*, then they think you must really be trying to leave North Korea and the whole Communist way of life." He shook his head. "What do you expect? It's a crazy idea from a crazy place ruled by a crazy man."

We walked along in silence for a few hundred meters, concentrating on keeping up with the others. Sand was blowing from behind us in larger swarms now. Occasionally our view of Gil-Su and Myong-Chol was obstructed.

Gil-Su stopped and gathered us. He had to raise his voice. "I don't like the look of this sand." He gestured to Myong-Chol. "We're going to unroll a rope. I want you all to tie it around you. If a sandstorm blows up, it will be very difficult to see. Easy to get separated. But as long as we have this"—he held up his GPS device—"we'll be all right even in a total blackout."

It took fifteen minutes to get everyone roped up. In that time the sand began to really fly. It sizzled into our faces and stung our eyes. I said a silent prayer of thanks to God that the wind was behind us, not in front. Finally we set out again. This time Bum-Ji carried Ki-Won and Little Brother carried Grandmother.

My feet hurt. My back hurt, too. But there was freedom for my baby, for Shin-Hwa, just ahead, so I forced myself to keep a slight droop in the length of rope between me and Joo-Chan just ahead. I touched his shoulder. "Joo-Chan, you said it was good for me, too, that I was leaving China. What did you mean?"

Joo-Chan held his hand to his face to shield his eyes from the blasting sand. "Are you sure you want to know?" He had to almost shout. "It's not pleasant. I shouldn't have brought it up."

I nodded. "Tell me."

"If a North Korean woman is caught in China and is found to be pregnant. . ." He didn't finish, just kept plodding forward. I nearly prompted him when he turned to me again. "If she is found to be pregnant and they believe she became pregnant in China, she will be forced to have an abortion. The North Koreans will kill the baby inside her."

"Oh!" I said. "That is terrible. Why?"

Joo-Chan shrugged. "I suppose they fear you will bring in inferior Chinese blood. Like I said, crazy place."

"But they would never make a woman abort who is as far along as I am. There would be nothing they could do."

Joo-Chan's expression told me I was wrong.

I sniffed. "I don't believe you."

"That's all right," he said. "It doesn't concern you anyway. You'll be free in an hour or two."

I stepped along, conscious of Bum-Ji just behind me. I looked back at him and saw Ki-Won sleeping on his shoulder. Bum-Ji held the boy's precious shapes in his hand.

I tapped Joo-Chan's shoulder again. "They would abort a baby as far along as mine?"

He nodded grimly.

"How do they do it?"

"I don't know. Inject it with something? But sometimes the abortions don't work, and the mothers give birth to live babies in the concentration camps. That's what Myong-Chol says."

I felt my stomach release a bit. "That's good. Then the mother can care for the baby."

"Oh no," Joo-Chan said quickly. "No, they will not let a Chinese baby live."

"But my baby isn't Chinese. If they caught me I would just explain that—"

"It wouldn't matter. To them, you're pregnant and you were leaving China and trying to escape from North Korea. You are a traitor and your baby is a traitor. If the abortion didn't work, they would make you kill your baby as soon as it was born. If you didn't do it, they would twist its neck all the way around. And Myong-Chol says sometimes they throw the babies to the guard dogs."

Suddenly I saw an image of a newborn baby flying toward the open maws of a frenzied attack dog. The sand swirled around me, and I fell to the ground. The rope yanked against my wrist multiple times as everyone up the line was jerked to a stop.

Bum-Ji knelt beside me, balancing Ki-Won on his shoulder. "Chun-Mi, are you all right? Can you get up?"

The others circled me. "What happened?"

Joo-Chan helped me to my feet. "I'm all right," I said. "Let's keep going. Let's go even faster!"

By the time we were moving again, the sandstorm was fully upon us. I could see Joo-Chan ahead of me, though he was dimmed. I could also see Aunt ahead of him and occasional glimpses of Uncle ahead of her, but nothing beyond that. Only yellow sand blowing horizontally and glowing faintly in the invisible moon. Even the stars overhead had been erased. It was as if we were walking through a netherworld. There was no sound besides the storm. The sand shoved me from behind like a jostling crowd. I knew Bum-Ji was taking the worst of it. My fingers were numb from the cold.

I walked along in this two-meter sphere of awareness for what felt like hours. With my wrist tied to the others, I felt like a slave. I thought of Joo-Chan's description of the captives with wire through their wrists. And I'd always been told the *outside* world was barbaric. I felt the image of the attack dog surging to the forefront of my mind, so I shook my head and tried to think of something else. In my mind's eye I saw the crucifix on the wall of Gil-Su's church. Surely He had suffered worse things than this storm for His children. I could endure this for the sake of my own child.

The line stopped. Ghosts of men materialized before me. I thought briefly of the giants from my dream. But as they neared I could see it was Gil-Su and Myong-Chol, followed by Uncle, Aunt, and Little Brother.

Gil-Su held up his GPS device. "It's too cold," he shouted. "Batteries won't work."

We looked at each other, squinting against the merciless sand. "Are we across the border?" Bum-Ji said.

Gil-Su shook his head. "I don't know. I never saw the wire. Maybe it got buried in the sand and we passed it. Maybe we haven't gotten to it yet. But I think we should've reached it by now."

"So you think we're in Mongolia?" Little Brother asked.

For a moment Gil-Su didn't answer. A fierce burst of wind sent us all staggering. Finally he shouted, "I think so."

"Can't we just go with the wind?" I asked. "The wind was blowing south and it was behind us. We should just go with it and it will bring us to safety."

"Good idea," Gil-Su said, "but perhaps the wind has changed."

Aunt moaned, an eerie sound that carried impossibly well on the wind.

I sent a prayer to God. *Master Jesus, can You help us?*

Gil-Su leaned forward. "We could keep going and hope the wind hasn't changed direction. Or we can sit right here and wait out the storm. When it lifts, we'll be able to see the stars again and find our way. While we're waiting I'll try to warm up the batteries."

Aunt yanked the rope. "Can't that stupid thing work in the cold, madman? Did you think it would be nice and warm in Mongolia!"

"Hush, woman," Uncle said.

"It's got two sets of batteries," Gil-Su said. "One for the main functions. That only works if it's not too cold or not too hot. It's got a backup that only works to send an emergency signal. That battery's more tolerant of extreme temperatures."

"Well, you idiot," Aunt said, "this is an emergency! Send the signal."

"I could, but I'd like to—"

"Look!" It was Little Brother's voice. He was pointing into the distance.

"What do you see, Youn-Chul?" Bum-Ji asked.

119

He peered into the murk. "I saw a light."

"A light!"

"We're saved!"

We ran forward together, stumbling over the ropes.

I saw a flash of something. At first I thought it was only a larger clump of bright sand blowing by. But then I saw it again, a shifting light like a guttering candle. "There!" I said. Inwardly, I praised God.

The others saw it, too. In fifty steps we reached a low mud building, the kind we'd passed in the truck as we'd neared Mongolia. I saw a cluster of movement to my right. Sheep.

"It's a nomad's shelter," Gil-Su said. "Shepherds. They'll know where we are." He slipped the rope off his wrist and stepped through the wall of sand.

The wind felt colder now, here with the prospect of warmth and shelter just before us. I found Bum-Ji and nuzzled next to him. Ki-Won was still sound asleep on his shoulder.

Five minutes later, Gil-Su reappeared. With him was a small man in gray animal skins and fur-rimmed hat with short feathers on top. He looked much more prepared for the cold than we were.

"He doesn't speak Chinese or Korean. I think he's speaking Mongolian. There are two other men inside."

"So you don't know if we're in Mongolia or not?" Uncle asked.

"Right," Gil-Su said.

Then the little man spoke rapidly and turned to go. He looked back and gestured for us to follow.

The entrance to the hut was small and short and had been blocked by a heavy wooden door. Inside there was firelight. We hunched over and went inside one by one.

Two men who looked very much like the first man looked up at us from bedding mats inside the low but wide room. The three exchanged a few words, followed by laughter.

As soon as I stepped in, I felt a hundred times better. I was out of the wind and we were evidently *somewhere* because someone else was here. I'd never seen a Mongol before, or even heard of them before this week, but I was sure these must be what Mongols looked like.

We filled the room and immediately lay down. The sweet smelling smoke from the small fire escaped a hole in the middle of the square ceiling. The wind whistled across the top like a boy blowing over a glass bottle.

Grandmother made us all eat something before we slept, but soon everyone was lying down and headed into the slumber of the exhausted. Everyone, that is, except Ki-Won, who awoke and commenced to give each of our hosts a narrated exhibition of all his wooden shapes.

*   *   *

I awoke in the mud chamber to a fire crackling with small sticks. I was struck by the succulent smell of roasting meat. Hunks of what I assumed were sheep stood on sticks over the fire. I felt I could eat the whole thing myself. The others were awake already, sitting around in various stages of readiness for the day. All except for Ki-Won, who was sound asleep under one of our hosts' heavy fur blankets.

At the end of the narrow entrance hall, the door opened, letting in fresh morning sunlight and only the faintest of cool drafts. Gil-Su and Bum-Ji came in.

"Everyone, please get ready," Gil-Su said. "These men are going to take us somewhere. To the nearest village, I think."

"But what about the food?" Little Brother said, rubbing his stomach.

"We'll eat it as we go."

Uncle pulled his coat on. "Your device. Is it working again?"

Gil-Su sighed. "No. I'm afraid the batteries may be dead. But no matter: Now we have guides! Truly the Lord is gracious!"

Ten minutes later, we were all outside. The sheep shifted nervously in the pen. It was a glorious morning, the sun a peach and the sky a ripe blue melon. Birds chirped a welcome to the new day. Every day of freedom should begin like this.

With the sheep to bring along, we made slower progress. But our guides never wavered about their heading and after an hour we spotted a village, smoke rising from dozens of cooking fires. Even our guides seemed to get excited now, for they picked up their pace. One ran ahead into the village.

The village looked like so many of the others we'd seen between Hailar and where we'd left the truck. Mud homes and the sturdy round tents called yurts. Cattle and sheep and small Mongol horses outnumbered the short people three to one.

There was one wooden building. It was taller than the others. One of our guides beckoned us to follow and led us toward that building.

"This is so exciting!" Aunt said, showing a hint of a smile. She walked right at our guide's shoulder. "I know just what I'm going to do when we get to South Korea. I'm going to move to Seoul and open a little flower shop. Won't that be wonderful! Only the freshest flowers. I'm quite a gardener, you know."

We rounded the front of the building.

The guide who had run ahead was there, standing beside two taller men in military uniforms. The uniforms were bright green. They had red insignias at their collars and their green caps bore a bright red star.

"Stop there," one of the soldiers said in Korean. Other soldiers appeared and surrounded my family and me.

"What is this?" I said, overpowered with dread.

"Do not resist," the soldier said, "and you will not be harmed. You are now the prisoner of the People's Republic of China for the crime of trying to leave this country illegally. Please," he said almost kindly, "follow me."

CHAPTER 11

TÊTE-À-TÊTES

"YOU WANT to run that by me again, Billy?"

Eloise Webster sat up in her chair and pressed the cordless slim-line phone tightly to her ear. "You say these babies are in prison? A *Chinese* prison? Including a three-year-old child and an eight-month-pregnant woman?"

"That's right, Eloise." William Mowbray's voice was as clear as if he'd been calling from the next office over.

"And for what—trying to enter Mongolia? What's so special in Mongolia you got to throw folks in jail for?"

"Listen, Eloise," Mowbray said, "these people aren't just in trouble because they tried to cross a border illegally. They're in trouble because they're North Korean citizens. They already crossed into China illegally, which is bad enough, but then they were trying to leave China into a third country, a country that allows North Koreans to claim asylum."

Eloise stood from her cherrywood desk so sharply that her chair rolled back and slammed into the bookshelves behind her. "Maybe you'd better tell me about North Korea, Billy, because I'm drawing a blank here. I knew it was bad, but you're telling me it's worse, aren't you?"

As he explained, Eloise carried the phone to the floor-to-ceiling windows and looked out over a hazy day in Akron.

"So these babies have had a bad time of it already?" she asked when he was done.

"That's right," Mowbray said. "From what the missionary is telling us here in D.C., they were almost to freedom, but a sandstorm came up and they got turned around and ended up walking right up to Chinese border guards. They got sent to the closest city with a jail, Hailar, and that's where they've been ever since."

"Ever since?" Eloise snapped. "How long have they been there, Billy? Tell me how long."

"Coming on two weeks now."

Eloise gasped. "Well, what are you doing to get them out? That little boy's got to get out of there and that pregnant woman needs to be in a hospital, not in no Chinese water torture prison!"

Mowbray chuckled. "I knew you'd be the right person to call about this, Eloise."

"Mmm-hmm," Eloise said, suddenly wary. "Now I know you're putting diplomatic pressure on them. Tell me you're doing that at least, Billy."

"We are, Eloise. We're working all the channels. But so far all we've been able to do is get the two missionaries released. The younger one is a South Korean citizen so he got released after his sending agency paid a fine. The other one, name of Gil-Su Yi— 'course they say it Yi Gil-Su—is a U.S. citizen. We tried to get the others out at the same time, but they wouldn't have it. North Korea's raising a stink over it now, too, which is just what the president needs with everything else going on with North Korea."

"Well, you can't just leave the others there!" Eloise pulled out one of the black chairs from the long conference table and sat down heavily. The wide plasma screen on the wall before her displayed video footage of a snowy mountain stream.

"No," Mowbray said quietly. "No, we can't. That wouldn't be right, would it, Eloise?"

She bounced her fingers quickly on the cool table. "No."

"Eloise," Mowbray said, "our hands may be tied here. China has been embarrassed by this, especially since they didn't know about this until we called and told them about it. That missionary's emergency signal set off pagers and automatic E-mails across two continents. We knew exactly where the man was before China even knew anything had happened. So they think they've lost face in our eyes. And North Korea wants one of the refugees bad. Apparently he was a soldier who'd served in some kind of sensitive installation somewhere. There's no way they're letting him go."

"Mmm-hmm," Eloise said, staring across to the high-backed chairs on the other side of her suite.

"Now Eloise," Mowbray said deliberately, "you are a very smart woman. A deep thinker." He paused for several seconds. "Think now, Eloise. Think very hard. Can you, I wonder, think of anything else that might be done for these refugees? Hmm?"

He knew. Somehow he knew about her Firebrand team. She hadn't told him. She hadn't told anyone except people she was quite sure of. Still, he was with the State Department and she knew he did keep in touch with his old buddies at the Pentagon. But it shook her soul that anyone could've found out.

"Why, I would pray for them, of course," she said.

"Of course."

"Beyond that, I suppose I would have to give it some thought."

"I know you will, Eloise. I know you'll do what's right. I'm sending you some reading material by courier. You should have it this afternoon."

"I'm sure I'll enjoy it." She walked back to her desk. "Question for you, Billy. How long you going to be needing Mr. Yi? Can I have him when you're done?"

Mowbray laughed. "Why, of course you can. We should be done with him tomorrow morning. Let's have our people arrange him a visit to Ohio, shall we?"

"Perfect."

"Oh, and Eloise, don't worry that I know. Oh, *would* that we could do the things you're doing. What I wouldn't give to be part of that." He sighed. "But maybe the closest I can come is to give you the occasional phone call like this. Would that be all right?"

Eloise beamed at him though he wasn't in the room. "That would be lovely, Billy. I would like it very much."

"I thought you would."

"All right then, I guess I've got some phone calls to make, don't I?"

"Yes. I do, too. Nice talking with you, Eloise. Oh, and one more thing."

She shook her head. "You don't have to tell me, Billy. I know what we haven't talked about."

"Okay, good. Good-bye, Eloise."

"Good-bye, Billy."

* * *

". . .ninety-eight. . .ninety-nine. . .one hundred."

Jason carefully set the free weights on the stand above the bench then sat up and wiped his face and neck with his towel. Garth was over on the bench press machine going for five hundred pounds. Chris stood beside him, his Army T-shirt soaked in sweaty Vs down the front and back. Lewis rode a stationary bicycle against the mirrored wall of the weight room. Wires ran from little speakers in his ears, and he surfed the Web on his laptop perched on the handlebars. Trieu was on the other side of the weight machine doing reps with a handlebar she brought down behind her neck.

The survivalists who'd built this lodge had evidently been fitness nuts, too. When the Firebrand team moved in, they'd had to do very little to make this forty-by-forty room just the thing for their needs. The white-and-black multistation weight machine stood in one quadrant of the room, closest to the door to the courtyard. Free weights and sit-up benches stood next to a Jacuzzi. The other half of the room, facing a long wall of mirrors, could be cleared for tumbling or self-defense practice but now had Lewis's bike parked there, along with a treadmill and an assortment of barbells, sparring gear, and empty water bottles. A clear skylight in the center of the room cast a slanted column of morning sunlight at Chris's feet.

"Come on, big guy," Chris said to Garth. "Nail it first time up."

Garth flexed his hands on the grips. He was bare chested—an awesome sight any day of the week. Jason himself was a hard body who had spent the better part of his adult life around warriors of great strength, and yet he could do nothing but stare at the defined, oversized magnificence of Garth's musculature.

Trieu released her bar and came to stand beside Jason. "How is your heart rate, Garth?"

"It's fine," Chris said. "He's fine."

Garth clenched his jaw. "Heart rate's up, but okay."

"See?" Chris said to Trieu.

Lewis noticed them. "Hey, what's— Oh!" He unplugged his ears and hopped off the bike to stand on the other side of Garth's bench. He looked at the weights and counted to where the pin was. "Five hundred pounds? Oh, baby, go for it! Hulk. . .lift!"

Garth dried his hands on a towel across his lap then shifted his shoulders under the load. He gripped the bar and shut his eyes, breathing slowly. Then he opened his eyes and thrust upward with all his strength.

The bar rose three inches and the stack of weight bars lifted.

There it stopped.

"Come on, Garth!" Jason said. "Push!"

"Push!"

"You can do it!"

Garth's face went red. His eyes squinted. Veins bulged in his neck and shoulders. His arms quivered.

Then he groaned hideously and shoved upward, and his elbows locked straight.

"You did it!" Lewis shouted.

"Oh, yeah!"

Garth held it there for a two count then brought it down in a semicontrolled slam that reverberated for ten seconds.

Lewis gave Jason a high five. Chris offered Garth a hand and pulled him to a sitting position. Jason handed him a water bottle.

Trieu knelt beside Garth. "Are you all right? Nothing herniated?"

Garth laughed unsteadily. He wiped his face with a towel and breathed an openmouthed sigh of relief. He looked at Trieu sheepishly. "I don't think I was quite ready for five hundred."

She stood. "Maybe you should go sit in the hot tub for twenty minutes."

"Yeah," he said, not moving, "sounds good."

Rachel opened the door and entered. Like the others she was dressed in her workout attire. Hers were bright pink biker shorts and a matching top that wasn't much more than a sports bra. Bare midriff, of course. Hair back in a bouncy ponytail. She carried a wireless telephone.

"Where's my shirt?" Chris asked her.

"Oops," Rachel said, crossing to Jason. "I forgot."

"You were gone that long and you didn't remember the one thing you went out to get?"

She shrugged. "The phone rang."

"Rachel, dude," Lewis said, "you totally missed it. Garth benched five hundred pounds! That's like half a ton or something, isn't it? You should've seen it. He went all bulgie and—" He hissed out air and spread his hands ever wider, as if trying to contain something that was inflating. "Totally thought he was going super-hero on us."

Rachel ran a finger down the side of Lewis's cheek. "You're cute, you know that, Lewis?"

Lewis's eyes bulged. "Aw, Rachel, don't do that to me."

Chris threw a sweaty towel at him. "Go take a cold shower, kid."

Rachel turned to Jason, one perfect eyebrow raised suggestively. "You big strong men just turn me on. Don't they do the same to you, Trieu?"

Trieu regarded her skeptically. "Um. . ."

"Here you go, Jasie-wasie," Rachel said, handing him the phone. She leaned into his ear and whispered huskily, "It's for you."

Jason took the phone and stepped away. "Uh, thanks."

"Oh, man," Garth said from the bench, "now *I* need a cold shower."

Rachel giggled. "Come on, Trieu, we have some girl talk to discuss."

Trieu grabbed her water bottle and followed Rachel outside.

Chris stood beside Jason. "Jasie-wasie?"

Jason looked at him sharply. "Don't start."

"I don't know, man," Chris said. "Is it just me or are the women acting really whacked lately?"

Garth and Lewis laughed and went back to what they were doing. Jason clicked the hold button on the phone.

"Hello?"

"Jason, it's about time you picked up. You think I got all day to sit on the phone waiting for you?"

"Eloise! I'm sorry, ma'am. I didn't know it was you."

"Never mind. Are you somewhere where you can listen up?"

"Yes, ma'am."

"Good, because I've got a deal o' news to tell you, and then I

129

need you to get that high-priced team of yours out here to see me, copy that?"

Jason smiled. "Roger, Big Mama."

* * *

"All right, people, listen up."

As soon as he said it, Lewis and Chris cracked up.

Jason looked at them. "What'd I say?"

Lewis held his hand out to Chris, who stood from the couch and pulled out a five-dollar bill from his wallet. Garth tried to intercept it. Rachel and Trieu, sitting next to each other on the other couch beside the fireplace, watched tiredly. Finally Chris managed to deliver the five-note to Lewis, who pocketed it greedily.

"You always start that way," Lewis said to Jason. " 'All right, people, listen up.' I bet Christopher Five-Dollars-Poorer Page that you would say it. He said you were not like a bad war movie. I said you were." He patted his pocket. "Money in the bank, baby."

Most of them had changed into blue jeans or cutoffs. Jason was still in his workout gear: blue shorts and white tank top.

"Okay," Jason said carefully, "would you *individuals* please hearken unto the words that are coming out of my mouth?"

They laughed.

"Bravo!" Garth said. "Speech."

"Okay, here's the deal. Eloise called. She's got a job for us. Maybe."

Chris nodded vigorously, then stopped. "Maybe?"

"Well, she's calling us up. You know the drill, Jarhead: on the verge time and again, only given the green light once out of a hundred."

"What's the situation, Jason?" Trieu asked. She wore a yellow T-shirt and white denim shorts.

"I didn't get all of it, but here's the skinny. Eloise has gotten concerned about some North Korean refugees—mostly part of one family, I gather—who made it out of North Korea into China but then got caught trying to sneak out of China into Mongolia. There's a young child in the group," he said, looking at Rachel and Trieu, "and a woman in her last month of pregnancy."

The team exchanged glances. "And Eloise wants us to do what?" Chris asked.

"Well, first she just wants us on site. The State Department is putting pressure on China to let the people go, but for whatever reason, Eloise doesn't think it's going to happen. She wants us there as an option."

Again the glances around the room, but this time with more interest. Garth sat up straighter. Lewis brought his knees under him on the couch.

"Man," Chris said, "finally I get to go to China!"

"It gets better," Jason said. "One of the other refugees used to be in the North Korean military. Some kind of classified position or something. If North Korea gets him back, he's history."

"The others won't have it any better," Trieu said. "North Korea is a terrorist state. If this has become an international incident, they may act. . .unpredictably."

"Huh," Rachel said, "that's a good word for them. I mean, look at what they're doing with their nukes. Half the time you think they're about to start World War III, and the other half of the time you think they're just a bunch of spoiled brats who don't want to play with the other children."

"Where are they being held?" Garth said. "Someplace I can blow up real pretty?"

"How many of them are there?" Lewis asked.

"I wonder what the soldier knows."

"How far along is the woman?"

"Is it a little boy or girl?"

Jason held up his hands. "I know, I know: a ton of questions. They'll have to wait until morning when we meet with Eloise at

ABL headquarters. Here's what I know: We're being sent to China. We're going to be posing as tourists. We're going to take all our gear. And we may or may not get to blow stuff up real pretty."

Garth reared his head back and howled like a wolf.

"So get to it, people," Jason said. "Update your wills, square away your affairs, and pack your gear. I want us at the airport in three hours."

"Three hours?"

"The world needs Team Firebrand again, people. Let's get out there in the power of Christ. 'Hooah' on three. Ready? One, two, three."

"Hooah!"

The team dispersed. As Jason turned to go, Rachel caught his arm. "Jason, can I have a word with you?"

"Sure, Raych. What's up?"

"Well. . . ," she looked at Trieu, who was hanging back, listening, "Trieu and I need you guys for like fifteen minutes before we leave today."

Jason put his hands in his pockets. "Okay. . . Why?"

"It's nothing," Rachel said, with a smile that said it wasn't.

"Hmm," Jason said. "Well, okay, I'll tell the guys. Can you do this right away?"

Rachel grabbed Trieu and they giggled. "Give us five minutes, Jason."

"All right. Where do you want us?"

"How about the sitting room between Trieu's room and mine?"

"Gotcha. Your rooms in five minutes. We'll be there."

*   *   *

"Watch out. Hot stuff coming through."

Rachel carried a silver tray with six steaming coffee cups on it. She walked into the sitting room and stepped over Garth's feet to set the tray on the coffee table between them.

"There you go," she said proudly. "Hot mocha with whipped cream. Bon appetit."

"Mocha?" Chris said. He looked at Jason. "What'd I tell you? 'Let's have a cocoa and talk.' "

Jason squelched a laugh.

Garth and Chris sat on one of the cozy couches in the room. Jason and Lewis sat on the other couch, facing them across the glass-topped coffee table. Trieu sat cross-legged in the plush chair at one end of the table. Rachel curled up into the chair at the other end.

The sitting room was ideal for late night tête-à-têtes between girlfriends. It was small and packed with overstuffed furniture. The drapes over the window behind Trieu were a lovely lavender floral print. The gold-framed art prints on the walls—a sunny day in the park on one wall, a flower-covered gazebo on the other—matched not only the curtains but also the embroidered pillows on the couches. Lace doilies lay out as coasters, like delicate snowflakes on a sheet of clear ice. Jason felt about as comfortable here as if he'd gotten lost in a department store and found himself deep inside in the ladies' underwear section.

"Go on," Rachel said, gesturing to the cups of mocha. "Drink 'em while they're hot."

Jason and the others reached over the table. He despised all manner of hot drinks, but he could at least hold the cup. "Well," he said, pretending to savor the aroma of the mocha, "thanks for inviting us."

"Oh, it was our pleasure," Rachel said, using her tea-party voice. "We simply must do this more often."

"Now," Jason said, resting the cup on his thigh, "you said you two needed to talk to us? We're trying to, you know, get on out of here pretty quick."

"Yes, I know," Rachel said. "This won't take long at all." She took a dainty sip of mocha, then set her cup on a doily. "Trieu, won't you begin?"

Trieu smiled softly. "Yes." She set her cup on the table and cleared her throat. "I'll get right to the point. Gentlemen, you should know that Rachel and I overheard your conversation about us a few days ago."

An icy dread chilled Jason's spine. "Uh, which conversation was that?"

Rachel *tsk*ed. "The one that included mud wrestling, five-mile runs, and wet T-shirt contests. Surely you remember."

Jason's eyes were no doubt as wide as Garth's, Chris's, and Lewis's.

Lewis gulped audibly. "You guys heard *that?*"

"Oh yes," Rachel said. "Lewis, you've got to stop putting those little cameras all over the world and linking them to our helmet computers."

Chris threw a doily at Lewis like a ninja star. "Way to go, Buckwheat."

Jason looked at Rachel, who was grinning, and at Trieu, who was watching him carefully, a complex expression on her face. "So," he said slowly, "you guys heard. . .everything?"

"Oh, we heard everything. Didn't we, Trieu?"

Trieu nodded and looked down.

"So," Garth said, nodding nonchalantly, "you guys know about Jason's love triangle, then, huh?"

Now it was Jason's turn to send a doily slicing across the room. "Would you shut up?"

"What'd I say?"

" 'What'd I say?' " Jason said. "Bro, you're about as subtle as a fragmentation grenade."

"Yes," Rachel said to them, "Trieu and I heard everything. And I have to say that you guys said some pretty insensitive things about us."

Jason winced. That was probably putting it mildly. He kept wanting to say, *But we didn't know you were listening,* but he was pretty sure that wouldn't go over very well.

Rachel folded her arms. "I wanted to teach you guys a lesson that would make sure you never disrespected another woman for as long as you lived. Not only for that, but also for the stunt you pulled on us with the body armor. I had this huge idea of staging some kind of American Gladiator contest where you guys had to compete against each other for our affections. I was going to have hundreds of screaming women judging you on your looks alone. There was going to be mud wrestling and wet T-shirt contests and all the rest—but it would be *you* doing it, all for the pleasure of a bunch of crazed women. Thought you might like a taste of what you made Trieu and me feel like by your talk."

Jason could envision it. A sea of mud. Towers and platforms and zip lines. Rachel in a circus emcee's costume egging on the crowd. It was certainly creative.

"But Trieu wouldn't let me do it," Rachel said. "She kept after me to do to you guys what you should've done to us. And we *did* have to give you credit for some of the things you said that day. Especially you, Mr. Fisher."

Garth lifted his nose at Jason. "Frag grenade, my foot."

Jason rolled his eyes and turned to Trieu. "You didn't want to humiliate us, Trieu?"

"Oh, it did cross my mind," she said. "I'll admit to having some not altogether charitable thoughts toward you four in general, and toward you, Jason, in particular."

"I can imagine."

"I even came up with a list of hateful things we could do to get you back."

Jason's eyebrows went up on their own. "You?"

"Yes, you hurt me that deeply."

"Oh, wow, Trieu. I'm sorry."

Trieu placed her cup on the table with a ceramic *clunk*. "But all I really wanted to do was get away from what all of you were saying. Yes, I was embarrassed by your locker-room talk, but I've heard that and worse many times before. That was nothing compared to the way some Vietnamese men talk. What really hurt was how you were all talking about Rachel and me like we were yours for the choosing. I hated the jealous, petty thoughts that came into my mind toward Rachel. I hated who *I* was in that fantasy world you created with your words. I just wanted to pull away. Better not to compete in that kind of contest than to try my hardest and then be found unworthy and discarded."

Jason tried to judge the other guys' reactions. They seemed pretty stunned, too. "Well. . . ," he said, searching for some halfway decent words. "I guess I. . .I'm glad you didn't go through with that. I think I can speak for the guys when I say we are sorry about the body-armor stunt. That was pretty stupid."

"Even if it was hysterical," Lewis said. "You guys should've seen your faces."

Doilies.

"Also," Jason said, "I'm very sorry our 'locker-room' conversation made you two feel that way. You're sorry, too, aren't you, guys?"

Chris and Lewis mumbled apologies.

Garth looked like he wasn't so sure. "Yeah, I guess. But that Gladiator thing sounded fun. You sure you don't want to do that one, Raych?"

"Okay," Lewis said, "so, like, *this* is your big revenge on us? Mocha and a meaningful heart-to-heart?" He tried to stifle a giggle.

"*Yes,* Lewis," Rachel said, one eyebrow rising dangerously, "we've decided to take the high road. I wanted to knock you all down a few pegs. But Trieu's gentle answers turned away my wrath, and I agreed to handling it this way. As long as you all promise not to talk about Trieu and me like that again."

The guys hesitated.

"Lewis," Chris said, "you think you can find all those mote cameras and disconnect them?"

"Absolutely."

Chris's right hand rose solemnly. "Then I promise."

Jason followed suit, as did Lewis and Garth.

"We all promise not to talk about you girls in that way anymore," Garth said, then muttered, "as far as you know."

Rachel stood and smacked him with a pillow.

"Ow," Garth said. "Why does everybody do that to me?"

Rachel nodded to Trieu. "All right, boys, thank you for our little chat. Now because of those deeply heartfelt promises," she said, walking to the door to her bedroom, "Trieu and I have one last surprise for you. Trieu?"

Trieu went to her bedroom door, too. They both went inside a moment, then stuck their heads out and smiled.

"You won't mind if we leave the dishes for you boys to clean up?" Trieu said.

"Nah," Chris said, "Lewis will get it."

"Hey!"

"Good," Rachel said. "Then we have only one more thing for you."

She and Trieu threw out white blobs. Each guy took one in the face. Then they slammed their doors and turned the locks.

Jason pulled the cold, soggy cloth off his face and held it out in front of him. The others did the same.

Wet T-shirts.

CHAPTER 12

LOVE TRIANGLE

"SIT DOWN, son."

Jason sat in the leather armchair across from Eloise's desk. Outside it was raining.

Eloise, her black hair gathered in the back and dropped from a clip, watched him closely, the dimples never quite vanished from her full brown face.

He tilted his head at her. "What?"

"Oh, Rachel told me about your little mocha party."

"She did?"

"Um-hmm. Rachel and Trieu both." She looked at him as if over reading glasses. "They told me *everything*."

"Oh," Jason said with mock gladness, "isn't that nice?"

"That's not the word I would use. Un-uh." She sat back and rocked in her chair, examining Jason as if trying to decide what to do with him. "Jason, my boy, you have made yourself a mess here. You've told the only two women on my team that you're interested in them both. Lord only knows why, but they're both interested back. All of this after I expressly told y'all I didn't want anybody dating anyone on this team. Or do I misremember?"

"No, ma'am."

She shook her head. "Well, I can't say I'm surprised. I did pull together a pack of good-looking rascals, didn't I? All single, too. I know the marrying impulse same as anybody else. Suppose it was partially my fault for doing it, and my foolishness for expecting you to pretend you didn't notice each other." She opened her hands. "Which is exactly why I'm going to help finish it.

"All right, look. The way I see it, you need to decide which of those two fine women you are going to pursue." She pointed at him. "Hear me right, boy. I said you need to choose who you are going to *pursue,* not who you are going to date. You might pursue one of them and she might send you packing. Ever think of that? Might do you good if she did."

Jason winced.

"You've caused a lot of hurt here, Jason, and I fear you're going to cause more before it's over. Because I'm making you choose one of them. Today. Right now. They're sitting in separate rooms this second waiting for you to come in and tell them what you've decided. And the way I see it, ain't no way both of those talks are going to end well. I've seen *The Bachelor* enough to know that.

"Now," she said, "you go on out and find yourself a quiet spot to pray. You ask the good Lord what you should do. But I want you back in my office in thirty minutes ready to announce your choice, because I promise you, one way or another, this business is going to be over and done with *today."* She sat back in her chair. "The way I see it, you got three options: choose to pursue Rachel, choose to pursue Trieu, or choose to pursue neither one. You do *not* have option four, which is to keep things as they are. Now get out of here and pray, and you'd better hope Jeremiah was right that if you seek the Lord He will be found!"

Jason didn't move. He blew out a breath. "Miss Eloise, ma'am, I don't need to pray about this."

Her eyebrows went up. "You don't?"

"No. See, I. . .I already know what He wants me to do. I just—I guess I've just been putting it off. Like you said, I know it's going to hurt the one I don't choose—choose to *pursue,* I mean. So I guess I've been. . .waiting."

"Yeah, waiting," she said, her head wagging, "waiting and loving it. Waiting and wallowing like a big ol' pig in their love, eating it up that their hearts are breaking and they're both after you. My soul, but you had it fat, didn't you?"

Jason smiled. "I know. I know! You're right. It's gone on long enough."

"All right, then. If you know what you're supposed to do, what are you doing sitting here talking to an old woman for? Get yourself up and obey the Lord your God, my son, before I kick your heinie."

He stood up. "Where are they?"

"Trieu's on the fifth floor. There's a small conference room there. Rachel's on the third floor in the unused office in the corner to your left as you leave the elevator."

He slid his fingers across her desk. "I'm. . .I'm sorry about all this, Eloise. I'll make it right."

"I know you will, boy." She shook her head, a reluctant smile on her face. "You know I love you, son. Now get out of here. And then get yourself back here by two because we really do have a briefing. Believe it or not, the whole world does not stand by waiting for you to solve your little love triangle."

"Yes, ma'am. I'm gone."

* * *

Jason saw her through the glass pane on the office door. Rachel was standing at the window, looking out over rain-drenched Akron. The blinds were up; the lights were off. There was a sturdy wooden U-shaped desk behind her. A computer monitor sat on top and a brown chair sat behind the desk, but otherwise the office was empty. Rachel had a stillness to her that suggested she had been standing there a long time. He almost didn't want to go in.

No, he *really* didn't want to go in.

He went in.

She turned to face him. She was backlit so brightly he could barely see her face. She was gorgeous. It made his insides quiver just to look at her silhouette. Why was a woman like this—as beautiful on the inside as on the outside—interested in him?

"Hi," he said, marveling at his rapier wit.

Her features were all but invisible to him. "Hi."

Jason closed the door behind him. They stood facing each other across the corner office. The distance between them was magnetic.

He blew out a sigh. "Do you know why I'm here?"

"Yes." She stepped closer, then stopped.

Thunder rumbled and raindrops dotted the window behind her.

After a long moment of paralysis, he crossed the distance to her. He took her hands in his. She looked into his eyes with that same vulnerable look she'd shown him months ago.

"I remember the first time I saw you," he said. "Well, the first time I knew it was you. When you were upstairs here, pretending to be Chris's executive assistant, remember?" She only blinked at him. The room seemed to get even darker. The rain *tinked* on the window in narrow teardrops. Low clouds hovered above. The building's air conditioner came on, dropping cool air onto Jason's bare arms.

"I thought I'd seen beautiful women before," he said, "but when I saw you, I had to throw out my whole scale of one to ten. You redefined ten for me, Rachel, and made it that much harder for any other woman to catch my eye. But," he said quickly, "don't get me wrong. You're beautiful, of course, but right away I found out that you're caring and strong and so, so smart. Maybe your incredible beauty caught my eye—that's kind of how guys are wired, I think—but it's your personality that I've come to appreciate even more."

"Oh, Jason."

She fell into his arms.

He took her hands down gently and separated himself from her a few inches.

An ounce of concern weighed on her face. "What's wrong?"

"Just. . .just let me finish, okay?" He held both her hands again. Then he moved her to the chair and knelt in front of her.

"Oh. . . ," she said, her voice quivering. "Oh, Jason, are you? . . ."

He stood up fast. "No. I mean, I wasn't—I was just trying to. . ." He only realized he was backing away from her when he bumped into the wall with his heels and head. He looked at his hands. How could a former Navy SEAL who used to kill bad guys and play with pounds of C4 be this shaky around one woman?

"Okay," he said, his palms forward as if pressing down an explosion, "maybe I shouldn't kneel."

Again her face was troubled. "Jason, you're confusing me. What's going on?"

He rubbed his ear in irritation. Then he sat on the edge of the desk. "Rachel, it's like this: Eloise says I have to make things right between you and me and Trieu. She says I've caused a lot of hurt, and yesterday with your mocha thing, you guys showed me that's true. Eloise says it has to end today. She says I have to choose—not choose which of you I 'get,' but which of you I want to pursue."

Rachel wheeled herself closer to his legs. Now her face was in the beautiful silver light. Her kissable lips, her perfect eyebrows, her angular face, her deep brown eyes. He saw her again in that white gauzy dress she'd worn at the Akron City Club. He saw her in the car as they drove Doug and Jamie Bigelow to their honeymoon hotel. He saw her in her swimsuit in Australia—and then he saw her covering up. Most of all he saw that haunting, needful, innocent look, the look she gave him when she said maybe he was enough like her father that perhaps she could love him for the rest of her life.

He took her hand and brought it to his lips. "Sweet Rachel, I know I could love you forever. You are kind and joyful and fun, and you make me weak in the knees to look at you. I know one day you will be an unbelievable wife and mother."

No more words came. Outside, thunder rumbled softly and the rain raced down the window in winding parallel tracks. The silence in the office grew.

Rachel pulled her hand away. "But."

Jason shut his eyes. And nodded.

"How long have you known?" she asked, her voice edgy.

He looked at her. "I think I've known since Kazakhstan, maybe before. But I didn't know that I knew until that moment when I saw her get shot. When she fell, the blood splashing out, her face so twisted in pain. Something inside me just snapped and. . .I knew. I knew I wanted her as my wife, not just as a woman to flirt with or even as my girlfriend. I knew I wanted to have babies with her and go to PTA meetings with her and grow old with her."

Rachel was staring forward, not moving.

"Rachel, you are such a wonderf—"

Her hand shot up, fingers splayed. "Just–Just go."

"But I want you to know I could love y—"

"Go, Jason! Go, go, go, go!" Her voice was ragged by the end.

Jason went to the door and opened it, but hesitated. What had he just done? How could he look that precious woman in the eye and reject her? Why, if this was right, did it feel so horrible?

Quietly he stepped into the hallway and shut the door behind him.

* * *

Jason found Trieu in the fifth-floor conference room, reading a magazine.

The long table—gray and powder blue—filled the room. Black chairs with wooden armrests ringed it. On one white wall there was a dry-erase board concealed inside a wooden cabinet. Two other walls bore a sequence of framed Western-themed prints advertising various years of the famous Outdoor Quilt Show in Sisters, Oregon. The fourth wall was all windows and one glass door. Beyond the door was a walled balcony with a park bench. Rain pooled on the balcony floor and flowed out a circular drain. The storm was light but steady and showed no signs of slowing.

The door was open, so Jason walked in. "Whatcha reading?"

Trieu flinched. "Oh! Jason, I didn't hear you. Um. . ." She looked at the cover of her magazine as if to remind herself what, indeed, she was reading. "Oh, just *JAMA*. It's a medical journal."

He walked to the chair beside her. "May I?"

"Of course."

"Thank you." He sat. He rubbed his face. He sighed.

She leaned forward. "Jason? Are you feeling all right?"

He shook his head dramatically NO. "Why, yes, of course! Why wouldn't I be?"

Trieu gave a half smile and a half shrug. "I don't know."

"No, actually I'm not all right. But you know, I think I'm going to be. I think this will be better. Just. . .maybe not right away."

He looked at her. She still wore the half smile. "Okay," Jason said. "Why don't I just start?"

"Why don't you?"

"Right. Well, you probably know why I'm here. You probably know that Eloise has me down here trying to solve our little"—he held up his fingers as quotation marks—" 'love triangle.' That's what I called it to Rachel, anyway. Don't know how else to describe it."

Trieu didn't answer. She seemed to be having trouble looking at him.

"What's the matter? Did I say something stupid?"

She shook her head. "So you've talked to Rachel already? You've just come from her? You went to her first?"

Jason smacked his forehead. "Duh. Yeah. Hmm. Sorry, Trieu, that wasn't how I was going to introduce that subject. But. . .as long as it's done, I might as well go for it." He put his hand on hers. "Trieu, I—"

She yanked her hand away.

"What?" he asked.

"Sorry. I'm not— Can we just. . . I'd rather. . ." Her hands disappeared under the table.

"Oh. Okay, I guess." He shook his face to break his thought processes from whatever that was. "Well, yeah, I've been talking to Rachel. I did go to her first. But you shouldn't draw any conclusions from that. Will you please hear me out?"

She nodded minutely. Her jaw was set and her black eyes were narrowed. She appeared ready to chew him out. This wasn't going well. He'd said no to Rachel, and now Trieu was going to refuse him. Yikes.

"Trieu, I know we said we wouldn't talk about this. You said that if God had a future for you and me that He would bring it about Himself. And I know it's hurt you—*I've* hurt you—by dragging you through this, and now it looks like I want to keep dragging. But if we're ever going to get this resolved, we have to talk about it at least this one last time."

Her nod was so tight it seemed her joints had fused solid. "Jason," she said.

Oh, boy, here it came. "Yes?"

"You don't have to tell me."

"Don't have to tell you what?"

"What you're here to tell me. That you've chosen Rachel and

she's accepted your choice." She opened one hand. "I knew from the very first day that you had your sights set on her. And who could blame you? I was foolish to harbor a hope that somehow you would notice me, too. But how could you? Besides, it's not like you're the only nice man I'll ever meet." She shrugged, but now she wasn't looking at him. "God will bring the right one along when He's good and ready. I know how to wait on Him."

"Trieu," he said, wishing her hand would land on the table for more than an instant, "you weren't foolish to think that."

"Yes, I was. It was foolish to put my heart out there. Now you've chosen Rachel and you two will be very happy, and I—"

He waited for her to finish, but she didn't go on. She turned away from him in her chair and appeared to be breathing only rarely.

Jason stood up. He gripped her chair and rolled her away from the table. She held onto the armrests. He spun her around to face him and he knelt before her. He pointed at her right hand. "May I?"

Tears dropped from her eyes. She blinked at them. She made no move to offer her hand.

So he took it, and she did not resist. "Trieu Nguyen, you are a very smart woman. I love that about you. Even beyond your intelligence, you've got that stability, that peaceful wisdom I can sense from a mile away. But smart as you are, you have gotten one thing completely wrong." He looked her full in the eyes, his face inches from hers. "You're right that I talked to Rachel before I talked to you. And you're right that I found her attractive from the very first day I met her. But you're wrong that I 'chose' her and that she chose me. I didn't choose her at all."

He put the contents of his heart into his look. He willed her to understand what he had not said, to see the truth through the windows of his eyes.

She wiped away mascara tears. "Jason, what are you saying?"

"I'm saying, Trieu, that I choose you."

As soon as he said it, his chest seemed to burst into inner flame. Adrenaline shocked his system and excited every extremity. Here it was, right out there in the open. He'd pulled out his heart and laid it before her for the smashing. Everything hinged on this one eternal, petrifying moment.

Trieu's forehead wrinkled. "You—you choose *me?*"

He nodded. "Well, I mean I choose to *pursue* you. I know you're not a—"

She pressed her fingers to his mouth. "Shut up."

"Mmm-hmm."

She tilted her head. "You choose *me? Over her?*"

"Yeah," he said softly. "I choose Trieu Nguyen. That's what I was telling Rachel. I choose to pursue you, Trieu. I choose to ask if I can *date* you. I choose to ask if I can *court* you. Girl, I'm so sure this is right that if you'd let me I'd ask you right now to be my wife."

She blinked at him. "Your. . ."

"But that's too—I mean, come on. I couldn't just. . ." He lifted her chin with his fingers. "Could I?"

She looked at him for five seconds, stunned. Then she laughed—a blubbery, disintegrating kind of laugh.

He laughed, too, but his laughter was tighter. "Could I?"

She wiped her cheeks with both hands. "You could try."

Yikes, this is it. Lord Jesus, help me. He was already on his knees so he just reached up and cradled her face in his hands. "Trieu Nguyen, will you marry me?"

She dropped forward off her chair and knelt with him on the ground. She grasped the back of his head and laid a fierce kiss on his mouth. She kissed and cried and kissed and cried. Jason wrapped his arms around her and squeezed her to himself as if trying to merge her into his body.

"Oh, Jason!" she said breathlessly, kissing his cheek, his ears, his forehead. "Thank you, Jesus. Dear, sweet Jesus, I never thought it would happen. Yes, Jason. Yes, I'll marry you."

CHAPTER 13

FIRST COMES LOVE

CHRIS WAS standing in the rain, binoculars in hand. He looked again at the bird's nest on the ledge of a nearby building but brought the glasses down in frustration. The rain kept marring the image, and now the lenses were fogged. Maybe he could see better from a higher floor of the First National Tower Building, the top and underground floors of which belonged to ABL.

He stepped through the revolving door into the busy lobby, feeling cold water drop down his scalp and back. The glass walls, hanging plants, and two stories of open air gave the lobby an atrium feel. Two steel-sided escalators led to the second floor, where the food court was producing an enticing mixture of culinary aromas.

Chris shook his hair like a wet dog. Then the elevator opened and out walked two women he knew. "Rachel? Jamie?"

Jamie Bigelow, Doug "Chimp" Bigelow's new bride, escorted Rachel into the lobby, holding her protectively under one arm.

Rachel appeared to have been crying.

Chris stopped them beside the escalators. Businesspeople streamed around them, hurrying on their way. It was almost two in the afternoon, though the heavy clouds made it feel much later.

"Rachel," he said, "what's wrong?"

Jamie was a lovely woman with long sandy blond hair and that "babe next door" smile. But today she looked like the angry woman next door whose flower bed had just been dug up by your dog—*again*. She looked at Chris in something close to a sneer. "Back off, cowboy. She's not in the mood."

She pulled Rachel past him, but Chris caught Rachel's arm. "Sweetie, what's happened? Where are you going?"

Jamie jabbed him in the chest with a finger. "Don't you 'sweetie' her today, you—"

"No, Jamie," Rachel said. "It's all right. I can talk to him."

Jamie pulled her arm off Rachel's shoulders and took half a step back.

Rachel looked up at Chris. The skin around her eyes was pink and her eyes were bloodshot. He jutted his chin. "It's Jason, isn't it?"

She looked away quickly, her eyes suddenly glossy. Then she nodded.

"Why, that little— I'll fix him for hurting you. Just tell me how bad to beat him."

Rachel smiled wetly. "No, Chris, you don't need to do that. Jason just. . ." She looked out the tall tinted windows at the falling rain. "Well, anyway, it's over. And I'll be okay. I just kind of need to get away for awhile."

"What about the briefing?"

"Eloise said she'd tape it for me. I'll be back later. I'm just going to the hotel to, I don't know, have a good cry, I guess."

Chris lifted her chin. "So he didn't choose you? Wait a minute. That doesn't make any sense. He chose Trieu?" A joy sprang up inside

Chris, though he really did try to seem sad for her. "That's. . . that's. . .well, it's surprising, isn't it?"

She smiled sadly. "Surprising? Yes, it was. But. . .I don't know, now that I think about it, maybe it's not so much." She stared into space, sometimes nodding absently, sometimes shaking her head.

"So. . . ," Chris said, trying to keep his voice calm, "I guess it's, you know, *over* between you and Jason. Is that right, sweetie?"

Jamie stepped forward. "All right, Chris, that's enough. Can you wait ten minutes for her heart to heal or do you have to make your move now?"

"What'd I do?"

"You know what you did. Now back off."

Chris stepped around to face Rachel again. "I just want to know if you would ever consider seeing me again. You know," he said with a glance at Jamie, "after you've had plenty of time to get over this. Would you ever let me take you to dinner again? Dinner, a movie, maybe dancing? Whatever you want."

Rachel's eyes had dried. She gave him a hard expression that looked a lot like the one his ex-wife had used on him at the end. "I don't know, Chris. You, Jason, Garth, Lewis, somebody else." She threw her hands up. "I don't know if I can take it anymore. Maybe one day we can do those things. Maybe not. But not now. Good-bye, Chris."

Jamie led her to the revolving door. When they got outside, they hunkered under the rain and ran to the right out of his sight. He stood there without moving. People bustled by, immersed in their own troubles. In his mind's eye all he could see was that cold look in Rachel's eyes.

Why, God? Why can't I ever seem to get the things I want?

He stood in that spot for another five minutes. Finally he turned for the elevators. It was almost time for the briefing.

Why don't You ever answer me?

*   *   *

Jason's lips lingered on Trieu's from the seventh floor to the twelfth. Finally he pulled back an inch. "You don't know how long I've wanted to do this with you."

She leaned her forehead against his. "Oh, I think I have some idea."

The elevator stopped on the fourteenth floor and the door opened. Jason moved to Trieu's side, feeling like a teenager caught making out at the mall. A thin woman with black hair and large black eyes stepped in. She wore a smart business dress and jacket and was probably someone's crackerjack executive assistant. She smiled politely at Jason and Trieu, pressed 17, and turned to stare at the numbers.

Jason touched Trieu's hand and this time she offered it eagerly. "So," he said in a soft elevator voice, "do you think we should announce our"—he scratched his head—*"merger* at today's *staff meeting,* or wait?"

She smiled mischievously at him. "Our merger?"

"Mmm-hmm."

The businesswoman's head turned slightly, but she kept her eyes on the ascending numbers.

"Well," Trieu said, "I think we should wait for now. The meeting is not the place. Besides, there's the issue of"—she whispered into his ear—"Rachel."

"I know," Jason said. "Got to be sure the. . .other party doesn't suffer any undue, um, grief."

The elevator dinged at seventeen and the businesswoman stepped off. But not without a wink at Trieu.

When the doors shut, Jason and Trieu giggled like high schoolers, and immediately Jason was after her lips again.

She kissed him back but then pushed him away a bit. "Be serious, Jason. We have to be sure we know how we're going to act in the briefing."

"You mean"—*kiss*—"I can't"—*kiss*—"just keep acting like this?" *Kiss.*

"No! We have to pretend nothing has changed between us. At least until after the briefing. We still have a job to do, even if our worlds have just been turned upside down. You know, you haven't given me a ring, so does that mean we're not technically engaged? And I'm pretty sure you haven't asked my father's approval yet."

Jason stopped caressing her hair. "But isn't he in Vietnam? And I didn't know I was going to do this until it kind of popped out of my mouth."

She smiled. "Relax, I'm only teasing. My father is dead. But I know he would've liked you."

"Good. Maybe tonight after dinner we can go looking for a ring?"

"Oh, Jason! I'd like that."

He stroked her cheek. "Mrs. Trieu Kromer. I don't know, does it sound weird?"

She pressed her lips to his in a long, deep, full kiss. "No, my love, it sounds perfect."

The elevator slowed. The bell dinged at the twenty-eighth floor, and the doors slid open.

Doug "Chimp" Bigelow was there waiting, his wheelchair pointed right at the elevator. His upper body was muscular and he still wore a military haircut, which meant there was nothing to hide his wide, flappy ears. "There you are," he said. "Hurry up, we're about to start. Have you guys seen Chris?" Then he looked at them both more closely. "What?"

Jason followed Trieu off the elevator. "Hmm? What 'what'?"

"Wait a minute." Chimp ran his wheelchair into Jason's legs and grabbed Trieu by the arm. "Jason, bring your face over here." He examined Jason's face from every angle, leaning close to stare intently at something. Then he looked over at Trieu. A look of revelation crossed his face and he nodded deeply. "Ohhh, now

I understand." He released them and wheeled backward. "Trieu, honey, you're looking a bit flushed. And Jason, you'd better go wash your face. You've got Trieu's lipstick all over you, bud."

Jason and Trieu stared at him stupidly. They laughed nervously.

"Don't you worry," Chimp said, wheeling toward the frosted doors leading to the ABL headquarters' reception area. "Your secret's safe with me."

Jason and Trieu blinked at each other as Chimp went through the doors. Trieu licked her thumb and rubbed at a spot on Jason's jaw.

"It's okay," he said. "I'll wash it off. You go on in and keep an eye on Chimp. I don't trust him."

Jason ran to the men's room. He really did have Trieu's lipstick all over him. It wasn't a bright color like Rachel wore, but it was visible all the same. He washed it off. But then he paused, staring at his reflection.

Your life has totally changed today, my friend. You have broken one woman's heart and proposed to another, all in about fifteen minutes' time. It's been a busy day for you. Pay attention now. You're a taken man. You've got the pure and unshared love of the fabulous Trieu Nguyen, way more of a treasure than you deserve. Don't blow it. No more flirting with Rachel or anyone else. Got it? And if you've ever been a champion at anything, you be a champion at treating Trieu right.

Oh, dear Lord, thank You! I can't believe I can love Trieu so much it hurts. Two hours ago I was still doing the two-woman thing. But now it's like a river that was dammed up has busted loose and is finally flowing the way it was supposed to have gone all along. Please make me the man she needs, Lord Jesus. And Lord, take care of Rachel, please. Bring her someone who will make her feel like her daddy made her feel. She's so precious and fragile, too. Amen.

He pushed through the frosted doors of ABL's expansive reception area just as Chris was on the other side of it, entering the door to Eloise's suite. He called for him to wait. Chris waited, but the look he gave Jason was sullen.

"You okay, bro?" Jason asked.

Chris nodded slowly. "I guess."

They went through the magnetically locked doors, then Jason moved them over to the copy machine. He kept his voice low. "I broke it off with Rachel today. You. . .you should know that. I'm out of the way."

"I know," Chris said.

"You know? How?"

"I saw Rachel leaving the building with Jamie. She told me."

"Oh," Jason said, trying to read Chris's expression. "This is what you wanted, isn't it? A clear shot at Rachel."

Again the slow nod. "Yeah. It's what I wanted."

"Okay, then," Jason said, smacking Chris on the arm. "It's a good day for you."

"Sure."

Eloise stuck her head around the corner. "You boys gonna run something off on that machine or are you gonna come over here and join us?"

"Yes, ma'am," Jason said. "We're ready."

Jason, Eloise, and Chris entered Eloise's office suite and stepped toward the long conference table on the left. Garth, Lewis, Trieu, and Chimp were already there.

Chimp looked at Jason then turned to the group. "You guys'll never guess what I saw just a minute ago."

"Chimp!" Jason warned.

"Doug!" Trieu said.

Garth looked at the three of them quickly. "Uh, oh, Dougie's got dirt on somebody. Spill it, baby."

"No," Jason said, "he doesn't need to—"

Chimp smiled devilishly. "I caught Jason and Miss Trieu smooching on the elevator."

The group gasped.

Garth guffawed. "You did not."

Chimp raised his right hand in oath. "I cannot tell a lie. Trieu came out all breathless and red, hair all disheveled. 'Oh, my,' " he said in a high voice and Southern belle accent. " 'I do declare I believe it's a might warm in here. Or is that just li'l ol' me?' "

Trieu folded her arms. "I did not."

"And then Jason comes out strutting his *man* self, you know. And he's totally covered in Trieu's lipstick. All over his head and ears and arms."

Lewis's face was stretched in a soundless laugh. "No way!"

"Don't listen to him," Jason said. "He's delusional."

"Oh, baby," Chimp said, "you guys should've seen it. I thought I was gonna have to call for the jaws of life to pry those two apart."

"Ooh!" Garth said.

"All right, Mr. Bigelow," Eloise said, sounding motherly, "that's quite enough, I believe."

The group quieted down. Jason, Chris, and Eloise found seats around the conference table and sat. The seven of them sat in silence for almost three seconds, but then Garth, Chimp, and Lewis burst out laughing.

Only Chris seemed unamused. He watched their antics with the detachment of a behavioral psychologist.

"Well," Garth said, looking around the room, "I guess that explains why Miss Rachel hasn't joined us yet."

That sobered them all.

Jason shook his head at Garth. "Always so tactful."

"What?"

"Mr. Frag Grenade."

Eloise folded her plump hands on the table. "Rachel will not be joining us for our briefing. I have given her the afternoon off. But Doug will be recording it for her to watch later." She turned to Jason and stared at him for several seconds without speaking. Finally she smiled sadly. "I take it some things have changed, son?"

"Yes, ma'am."

"Do you have anything to tell the class before we start?"

Jason looked from her to Trieu. She gave him a tiny smile. It was the minutest of expressions, but it filled him with confidence. In that moment he felt he could do anything he attempted. And that smile—and its giver—were his, now. Now and for as long as God gave them together. He turned to Eloise. "Yes, ma'am, I would." He stood and cleared his throat.

"Uh-oh," Lewis said.

Jason smiled. "Lady and gentlemen, it is my extreme pleasure to announce that I have asked Trieu to be my wife, and she has accepted."

They gasped again. And judging by Eloise's sharp inhale and her hand to her chest this was something beyond what she was expecting, too.

"Mercy!" she said loudly. "Boy, when you go to end a love triangle you mean to *end* it, don't you?"

Garth stood and shook Jason's hand. Hugs and handshakes and congratulations all around. As Jason shook Lewis's hand and Garth hugged Trieu, Jason and Trieu's eyes met. It was like high voltage. Joy flooded through him. He knew this was all just an emotional high and it would pass, but in that instant he didn't care. He had the love of the woman of his dreams.

He got the strangest feeling that now, this minute, his life had truly begun.

CHAPTER 14

THE HERMIT KINGDOM

"ALL RIGHT, you all, settle down now."

Eloise turned from the others to Trieu. She hugged her firmly. "I'm so happy for you, baby." Then she returned to her seat at the conference table. "Mr. Bigelow, kindly begin recording, please."

"You betcha." Chimp flipped up a panel in the conference table and pressed one of the buttons on it. A small screen set in the panel was split into four quadrants, each showing a different camera's view of the conference room. He uncoiled an earpiece and stuck it in his ear. "Everybody wave and say hello."

"Hello."

Chimp put the earpiece back into its spot. "Sound and video A-OK, Miss Eloise."

"Very good," Eloise said, standing. "Doug, why don't you put the first slide on the screen."

The large flat-panel plasma screen on the wall beside the table popped to life. A multicolored map of Asia appeared. China was a mustard yellow. North Korea was brown. South Korea, tan.

"All right, babies," Eloise said, "if we can all switch gears and start thinking about helping out some people in trouble, I'd appreciate it." She indicated the Korean peninsula on the map. "How much do y'all know about North Korea?"

Chris raised his hand and she called on him. "It's a very bad place."

"Yeah," Garth said, "no kidding. Bad place. Crazy dictator. Million-man army—all starving, so it's use it or lose it. And nuclear weapons." He nodded at Chris. "Very bad place."

Eloise nodded. "Next slide, please."

The screen changed to a map of China and environs. China was tan. North and South Korea were brown, as were Russia and Mongolia. More detail was visible now. Major cities, railroads, and regional borders.

"Actually, Doug, let's go to the next slide for a minute, then we'll come back to this one."

The next slide was of North Korea alone. Bits of China to the north and South Korea to the south were visible, but only in the tan area of North Korea were there city and region names and detailed roads, rivers, and railroad tracks.

"The Hermit Kingdom," Eloise said, staring at the map. "Worst nation on the planet in our day. Most corrupt, most violent, most oppressive, one of the most opposed to Christianity, and certainly *the* worst place to be poor. President Bush did not misspeak when he included North Korea in the Axis of Evil. I've been taking a crash course on the place these last few days and now I'm giving it to you."

She folded her arms. "I've had Doug put together big ol' thick packets on North Korea—the so-called *Democratic* People's Republic of Korea—for you all to read on your trip, but for—"

"You mean we're going to North Korea?" Lewis said, suddenly paying complete attention. "I thought you just said it was the worst place on earth."

"It is," Eloise said. "I'm telling you, Nazi Germany had nothing on this place. Can you think of a place that needs us more?"

Lewis shook his head. "No, but. . ."

"Pshaw, boy," she said, "don't you worry. I never did say I was sending you into North Korea. I'm just saying that's where the story begins."

"Oh!" Lewis said, sighing loudly.

"I don't know," Garth said, scratching his orange goatee, "I'm thinking a sightseeing trip to ol' Pyongyang might be worth doing, though." He looked at Jason. "What do you think, chief?"

"Absolutely."

"Well," Eloise said, "you can just hush about that because it ain't never going to happen. Now, y'all be quiet and let a girl talk."

Garth zipped his lip. "Sorry, Big Mama."

"That's better," she said. "Now, maybe you don't know it, but I'm a big fan of those Complete Idiot's Guide books. You know the ones? *Complete Idiot's Guide to Gardening.* That sort of thing."

"How about the *Complete Idiot's Guide to Breaking Up with One Girl and Proposing to Another in the Same Day*?" Garth said.

"Yeah," Chimp said, "or the *Complete Idiot's Guide to Complete Idiots.*"

Eloise cleared her throat. "You finished?"

Garth looked at the ceiling as if thinking. "Uh. . .yeah. Can't think of any more right now. Go ahead."

"Thank you. As I was saying, those books have a handy feature at the end of every chapter. It's called 'The Least You Need to Know.' It's a quick rundown of the most important facts about what's in that chapter. So if you all will kindly button it, I'll give you *the least you need to know* about North Korea."

For once no one had any smart comments.

"There was no North Korea until the end of World War II," she said. "It was just Korea. When the war ended, the Soviet Union got the top half and the U.S. got the bottom half. Each one established its own kind of government in its part of Korea. Russia set up a Communist state and installed a dictator, a war hero from Korea named Kim Il-Sung.

"Now," she said, interrupting herself, "I need to give you a quick 'least you need to know' course on Korean names. They seem backwards to us because they give the family name first. It's like. . .what's your middle name, Jason?"

"Scott."

Eloise nodded. "Okay—"

"Scott?" Chimp said. "So that makes you. . .JSK?"

They laughed.

"Watch out for the grassy knoll, dude," Lewis said.

"Anyhow!" Eloise said sharply. "If you did Jason Scott Kromer in the Korean style, it would be Kromer Jason-Scott. So Kim Il-Sung, done our way, would be Il-Sung Kim. Got it?"

"Got it," Garth said.

"So," Eloise said, "Kim Il-Sung ran North Korea the way all Communist states are run: the crony system. The top dogs get the best stuff. The 'people' get nothing. Meanwhile, the United States set up a democracy in South Korea. If you look at the two countries today, it's pretty clear which style of government creates healthier people and a better economy. North Korea is starving—except for the leaders. Kim Il-Sung's son, Kim Jong-Il, is the dictator there now, and he's in no danger of starvation. A few years ago he paid to bring real Italian chefs to Pyongyang, the capital, to set up an authentic pizza kitchen just for himself and his top cronies. But the rest of his people have it bad."

She looked at the screen. "Next slide, please."

The image changed to a map of the Korean peninsula during the Korean War. Red arrows moved south; blue arrows moved north. Lots of blue or red cross-hatching here and there across the map.

"Then in the fifties, North Korea invaded South Korea. Both sides got help from other countries to fight that war. The south got help from the U.N., but mostly from us. The north got help from China. The lines moved up and down across the whole place for several years. But the least you need to know is that after it was all over, nothing had really changed. The two countries still existed along roughly the same borders they had before the war began. The line between them, the demilitarized zone, or DMZ, is the most heavily guarded border on the earth. Close to two million soldiers stare at each other along that line, which more or less follows the thirty-eighth parallel. Okay, Doug, next slide, please."

The image changed to a slide with bulleted statistics.

"It's hard to know for sure because of the information blockade imposed by Kim Jong-Il's government," Eloise said, "but most experts believe North Korea has about twenty-one million people in it. I'm just going to read these stats and let them speak for themselves. You'll find more in your packets.

"You might think it's impossible that Christianity could live at all in this place," she said. "After all, all religion is outlawed in North Korea, and Kim Jong-Il and his father both seemed to have it out for Christianity in particular. But before World War II, the part of Korea that is now North Korea was a center of Christianity in the East. When the Soviets took over in 1945, there were still some two thousand Christian churches with over three hundred thousand believers remaining in the north. Kim Il-Sung's own mother was a dear saint of God! But he's not the first boy to turn his back on a godly mother.

"Now, talking about these prison camps: North Korea says it doesn't have any camps at all," Eloise said. "But we know that's a lie. Doug, next slide, please."

The screen now showed satellite photos of brown and green landscape. Red squares and arrows marked out glinting silver structures and gave descriptions in white text: *Guard barracks, Infirmary (human experimentation), Prisoners with families,* and more.

"These ran in a magazine a few years ago and were soon picked up by NBC, CNN, and the rest. A handful of North Koreans who have lived in this camp and made it to freedom—ex-inmates and even a few ex-guards—have identified it as Camp 22, the worst of them all. Now they have visual proof of the story they've been telling for years, and finally people are listening.

"All right, Doug, back to the previous slide, please."

The statistics reappeared.

"The people of North Korea are starving to death. The combination of three things—natural disasters like flood and famine, the man-made idiocy of cronyism, and the loss of Russia as a major ally—have put North Korea in a tight spot. U.N. aid goes in, but all the food gets taken by party officials. Kim Jong-Il eats cheese-crust pizza, but he announces that his people have to go to the 'glorious two-meals-a-day program.' Though his people are deprived of all information from the outside and are brainwashed from birth on the inside, somehow they hear that there is food in China. And so they sneak north across the border into China.

"No one knows how many people have left North Korea since the famine began, but it's probably in the millions. Imagine if millions of Americans were fleeing to other countries. That would say something about America, wouldn't it? Well, I'm here to tell you it says something about North Korea that these folks are leaving. Anywhere from one hundred fifty thousand to three hundred thousand North Koreans are thought to be living illegally in China right now. Ten thousand of them are unaccompanied children. They're called *kotchebi*—fluttering swallows.

"China rounds these folks up periodically and sends them back to North Korea. You see, because China is a signatory to the 1951 Convention Relating to the Status of Refugees and the 1967 Protocol that followed, they refuse to call these North Koreans 'refugees.' If they did, they'd have to grant them official refugee status and take good care of them. But China calls them illegal immigrants and gets to dance around the issue. They want to make nice with North Korea, the only other Communist nation left on the planet and their historical ally. And of course you've got the nuclear issue. If you've got a nuclear power on your doorstep, like China has with North Korea, you do tend to tread more softly, even if you've got nukes of your own.

"When North Korea takes these refugees back from China, they are interrogated, tortured, and either executed on the spot or sent to the concentration camps that supposedly don't exist. Although some, if they have party connections, get off scot-free." She shrugged. "Such is life in the crony system.

"All right, Doug, back to that map of China, please."

The slides cycled backward until the tan-and-brown map appeared.

"As you might expect in such a dark place, there are Christians who have come here to do what they can to help. Lord, bless them. Korean Christians from South Korea and the U.S., mainly, but also from Canada and anywhere else Koreans have settled in freedom and come to Christ. The war separated so many families in Korea, you see. Many of these Christians going in there have extended family members still inside North Korea.

"So these folks go into northeast China, right here north of the China-North Korea border. This easternmost section is called the Yanbian Korean Autonomous Prefecture. Don't fret, babies. The least you need to know is that it's a region of China so filled with ex-Koreans and their descendents that signs written in Korean outnumber signs written in Chinese. Lots of North Koreans find their way to Yanbian because of the common language and because Christians from North America and South Korea go there to help them.

"The problem is, what do these refugees do once they get into China? They can't claim asylum or refugee status. They could try to stay and hide out, and lots of them do, but what kind of life is that? Many of them—helped by the Christians and even by a few sympathetic non-Christians—try to make it to some third country where they *can* claim refugee status." She pointed at brown countries on the map. "Some try to sail to Japan or South Korea. Others try to make it into Russia. Others go all the way across China to reach Vietnam or Burma. But most lately have been trying to get into Mongolia.

"The China-Mongolia border is very lightly guarded. Chinese railroads and highways lead almost to the border with Mongolia. And best of all, Mongolia has proven a welcoming spot for North Korean refugees. South Koreans have built a resettlement village just inside the Mongolian border, kind of an outpost consulate specializing in helping North Korean refugees get the paperwork done to scoot them on their way to South Korea or wherever else they want to go.

"Most of them do go to South Korea because of the language, the extended families, and because it feels like they're not completely leaving their homeland. It also doesn't hurt that South Korea gives each North Korean refugee a healthy money grant and helps them learn skills they can use in a capitalistic society."

Eloise returned to her chair. "In just a minute I'm going to bring a man in here to talk to us. His name"—she consulted a paper on the table in front of her—"is Yi Gil-Su. That's Gil-Su Yi to us Americans. Now Gil-Su is an American citizen, but he's Korean by birth. He's a pastor in L.A., in fact. His life's mission, though, is helping North Korean refugees who come across the border. He spends most of his time living in China, reaching out to these folks, helping them on their way and introducing them to our Savior. I haven't actually met him yet. A little bird told me about his situation, and I've brought him here to tell us his story and to meet you all."

Eloise gestured to the map of China. "He's stateside because he got in trouble with the Chinese. Got captured leading a group of refugees on the underground railroad between North Korea and

Mongolia. U.S. diplomatic pressure got him and another missionary released, but the people they were with—a group that includes a three-year-old child and a woman in late-stage pregnancy—are still there in that Chinese water torture jail. He's been in Washington, D.C., for two days having his brain sucked dry by all manner of State, DOD, and intelligence folk, no doubt."

Jason knew Eloise well enough to know what was coming next. In one sentence she'd told him everything he needed to know: babies in trouble. The Firebrand team was going to get them out. "Eloise," he said, "when do we leave?"

She chuckled. "Now that's what I like to hear. Yes, you'll leave soon enough. I'm doing what I can through diplomatic channels, greasing the wheels of commerce, as they say. But I won't tell you it's going well, because it ain't. I'll not sit here on my rump and do nothing when it's in my power to intervene. So, yes, you're leaving. In the morning."

"Wait a minute," Chris said.

"Yes?"

Chris shifted in his chair. "Hang on here just a second. Am I hearing you right? You want us to go to *China* and assault a prison?"

"Oh, yeah," Garth said, "that'll help international tensions."

"No," Eloise said loftily, "I never did say I wanted you to assault no Chinese prison. I've been *told* that they'll be relatively safe in China. It's when they get shipped back to North Korea that we have to worry."

"So," Jason said, looking around the room and ending on Chimp, "we hit 'em in transit?"

Chimp nodded. "That's what I was thinking. Knock out a truck, pop the guards with a memory-loss cocktail, and be gone before they wake up."

"Ooh!" Lewis said, sitting forward. "We can try out my net mine entangler."

Garth looked at him. "Your what?"

"My net mine entangler. It's a nonlethal vehicle arrest thingie. Kind of like a land mine, but instead of blowing up, it shoots out a heavy net that reaches up and grabs the car like a hand from below."

"Okay, Lewis," Jason said, "we'll think about it. But I'd rather not take something we haven't tested."

"Oh, I've tested it," Lewis said, suddenly turning sheepish. "But. . .I'd rather not talk about it."

Chris turned to Eloise. "When will they be moved?"

She shook her head. "We don't know. That's why I want you on the ground there. I'll arrange for you to be able to get resupplied there if you have to stay longer." She stood. "All right, you all help yourselves to sodas in the fridge, and I'll go see if our guest is here yet."

CHAPTER 15

YOUR TEAM DOES WHAT?

FIVE MINUTES later the team members, minus Rachel and plus Chimp, were back at the table enjoying their soft drinks.

Jason and Trieu hadn't so much as touched each other since coming into the room. She sat on the other side of Garth and Lewis from him. But he could feel her closeness. It was like an invisible tether linked them. He heard every word spoken to her as if it was spoken to him and received every word *she* said to anyone as if it was spoken at least partially for him. Every few minutes a fear would arise in him that maybe all of this was a dream, that he hadn't really proposed to her or that she had changed her mind. But then she would steal a glance at him and their eyes would meet, and along that secret connection would travel volumes of meaning, libraries of affection.

As the others chitchatted, Chris settled into an empty seat beside Jason. "Hey, man," he said, extending his hand again, "congratulations, bro." His voice was low, as if he wanted to keep the conversation between the two of them.

Jason shook his hand and spoke softly. "Thanks, Chris. You feeling any better?"

"I guess. It's just. . . I don't know. I saw Rachel, like I said, and she kind of blew me off. She was like, 'Maybe I'll never date anyone again.' "

"Oh, man!" Jason said. He sighed. "But you gotta know she's just saying that because she's upset. She'll come around. That or leave the team."

"Don't say that!"

"Nah, I don't think she will."

Chris put his elbow on Jason's armrest and looked around as if to be sure no one was listening. "Hey, tell me something. As a Christian, do you ever, you know, feel like you and God aren't on the same page?"

"Are you kidding? All the time."

"Yeah, but I mean like *really* not on the same page."

Jason shook his head. "I'm not getting you, bro."

Chris looked out the windows distractedly. It was still raining steadily. "I don't know. It's something that's been kind of banging around in my head for awhile. Then it hit me again when Rachel said that. I don't know. It's kind of like something's wrong or something. Or missing, or broken, or. . . I don't know. Something."

The sound of the magnetic door lock releasing reached them from down the hallway. Eloise's voice floated to them.

"Hey, man," Jason said, mock punching Chris's shoulder, "let's you and me talk about this later, okay?"

Chris looked worse than before. "Yeah, sure. Okay."

He went back to his seat just as Eloise and a lean Asian man rounded the corner to the conference room. The man was about Jason's height and had a tall, handsome face and thick black hair. He had widely spaced eyes, a broad nose, and nice teeth. He wore a dark suit, perfectly fitted, and a slate gray tie.

"Babies," Eloise said, "this is Yi Gil-Su. Please make him feel welcome."

Even as they rose, Jason saw Gil-Su's eyes jump to Trieu. Of course they would. Hers was the most beautiful face in the room and the only other Asian one. Still, it freaked him out a little. As they stood in line to introduce themselves, Jason came to stand beside Trieu. He put his right hand on the small of her back. It was a simple, possibly only polite gesture, but it sent warmth flowing through his veins. And she leaned into him—just a bit, so subtly no one would notice, but it was a merger of their personal spaces, an acceptance of him into her private sphere, and he delighted in it.

He shook Gil-Su's hand firmly. "I'm Jason Kromer. Very nice to meet you. And this," he said, his hand still on Trieu's back, "is my fiancée, Trieu Nguyen." He imagined he felt everyone in the room react to those words. *You hear that, Asian stud? She's mine!* What a weenie he'd become.

Trieu bowed her head demurely and shook Gil-Su's hand. "Nice to meet you, Mr. Yi."

"My pleasure, Miss Nguyen." His English was flawless.

"All right, y'all," Eloise said, "go on and take your seats. Mr. Yi, why don't you sit here in the middle?"

"Thank you."

"Would you like a pop or a water or anything?" she asked as he sat.

"Yes, a water would be nice. Thank you."

Jason crossed the suite to where the refrigerator was and returned with the bottled water.

"Now," Eloise said, sitting in her spot at the head of the table, to Jason's left, "I'm sure you're wondering what you're doing here, aren't you?"

Gil-Su did look perplexed. "Yes, Mrs. Webster, I am."

"Well, we'll see if we can't clear it all up for you. First, you should know that this group is not part of the United States government.

We're not privy to classified information at any level. So be sure not to tell us anything you heard in Washington that might be considered sensitive information."

Gil-Su nodded. "But if you are not with the government? . . ." He left his question hanging.

"Then why are you here?" Eloise finished.

"Exactly."

"Well," Eloise said, sharing a sly smile with the group, "let's just say we might be in a position to help you with your problem."

Gil-Su looked around the table. "What problem might that be?"

"Oh, you don't have to go that far," Eloise said. "We know that you serve as a missionary in China to North Korean refugees. We know that you were accompanying a group of these people to the Mongolian border when you were captured by the Chinese. We know that one of those people is a pregnant woman and another is a small child. We know that you've been talking with several agencies in Washington. You can talk freely with us about all of that. Just not the content of your conversations in the capital."

Gil-Su's dark eyebrows rose. "For a group that is not cleared for confidential information, you certainly know a great deal!"

They laughed.

"Yes," Eloise said, "I suppose you're right. Now, Mr. Yi, can we assume that you were not completely satisfied with your discussions in Washington?"

Gil-Su closed his eyes wearily, and suddenly Jason glimpsed this man's intense fatigue and worry. *Enough with the stupid competition bit, Jason. This guy's not your enemy. Trieu's yours and this man, your Christian brother, needs help. Those "babies" need help. Grow up.*

"You are correct," Gil-Su said. "While I spoke with several people who were, I believe, in positions of authority in the military and CIA and State Department, people who could've made a phone call and improved these refugees' chances for survival, they did not do so. They all told me how much they sympathized, how much they hate Kim Jong-Il's regime and want it to fall. But none of them raised a finger to help me." He slapped the table, jolting everyone. "Why will they not help me?"

Eloise rocked gently in her chair. "Because, Mr. Yi, international relations between China and the U.S.—especially with North Korea involved—are extremely delicate, as I'm sure you know. I imagine every person you talked to would like nothing more than to send in the marines to get your people out. And while they're at it, why not send in *all* the marines—and the army, air force, navy, coast guard, and junior ROTC—and take down China *and* North Korea? They'd all sleep better at night if they did that. But I don't think any of us are quite ready to go down that road."

Gil-Su nodded wearily. "Yes, yes, I know."

"However," she said, "do not despair, my brother. Allow me to lead us in a short prayer, and then we'll lay out for you what we can maybe do for you."

They bowed their heads.

"Dear God," Eloise said with quick fervor, "I thank Thee that Thou hast brought our brother Yi Gil-Su out of dangers, trials, and snares to be with us here today. We praise Thee, Lord Jesus, for the good work that Thou hast set in our brother's heart to do. And now, our Jehovah Jireh, Jehovah Rapha, we beseech Thee to make straight the paths for our feet and to shine forth Thy will, O Savior, that we may be found servants useful to Thee for service. In the sweet, awesome, *magnificent* name of our blessed Lord Jesus we pray it. Amen."

"Amen."

"Oh, Big Mama," Garth said, "I do love to hear you pray."

"Why, thank you, son. Praise God. All right, Mr. Yi, let's talk turkey."

Gil-Su appeared worried. "I'm sorry. . .turkey?"

Eloise smiled, the dimples deep in her cheeks. "No, I'm sorry. I just mean let's be serious."

"Ah."

She slid her right palm outward across the smooth tabletop as if dealing cards to the gamblers. "What I am about to tell you is something I'd like you to tell no one else. This is why I had to ask you to sign that nondisclosure agreement out in the reception area."

"I understand."

"All right." She pursed her lips. "What would you say, Mr. Yi, if I told you that I had assembled a small team of. . .special people. . . whose job it was to go into foreign countries and conduct military-style activities in order to help people like your imprisoned North Korean refugees get out of dangerous situations, all in the name of Jesus Christ?"

Gil-Su stared at Eloise as if not comprehending. Then he jerked his eyes to Garth, Chris, Jason, Trieu, Lewis, and Chimp. Then back to Garth. He swallowed. "I would say I would be very interested in learning more."

Eloise chortled. "I was hoping you'd say that. Well, our group is fairly new—still less than a year old—but we've already been blessed to help out some people in a couple of tight spots. And we'd like to help you, if you'd have us."

Gil-Su nodded vigorously. "Oh yes."

"Now, Mr. Yi," she said, "I understand part of this problem came about as a result of an American television show? Can you tell us about that?"

"Of course," Gil-Su said. "A few months ago I was approached by someone from ABC. They said they wanted to do a special on our efforts to help North Korean refugees. I agreed, so they sent a cameraman and a reporter. They took lots of video of us and our locations, promising to do something to our faces and voices to make us unrecognizable. They also promised they would do nothing to compromise our work or our safety. But when the show aired a few weeks ago, it was reported to us that they had shown enough of the landscape in our area to clearly identify to the Chinese government where we were operating.

"They moved in with soldiers and police and rounded up many of our workers and North Korean refugees. I had to flee, too, as I am unwelcome in their country, along with a small group of refugees. We ourselves traveled the path I had previously sent other people along. We made it as far as the China-Mongolia border. There we got turned around in a sandstorm and captured by Chinese border guards. Political efforts here and in South Korea got two of us released, but the rest are still in Chinese prisons. Unless they have already been sent back to North Korea." His eyes were desperate. "Tell me, my friends, what can you do? Can you somehow go to China and bring these few refugees to safety? Out of prison, out of China?"

Eloise turned her palms up on the table. "We can sure try."

"Please," Gil-Su said, standing so quickly his chair bumped into the wall behind him, "please, you must help them. Chun-Mi is pregnant. I fear she must have her baby any day; I do not know. If they return her to North Korea, they will make her abort her baby. And Ki-Won is just a child. He is a precious boy who carries always a stack of wooden puzzle pieces in his hand. He can count them and tell you the names of each shape."

Gil-Su circled the table with quick strides. "Youn-Chul is so young. Only a teenager. Already he has suffered tragedy as his young girlfriend was sold into prostitution before his eyes. Bum-Ji is so kind to everyone, and Grandmother and Uncle and Aunt. They all need us. They have suffered so much in North Korea, and now this! And poor Myong-Chol! He is a former concentration camp guard. So far he has escaped their attention, but now they know he is still alive. If he is returned to North Korea, they will surely execute him. Please!" He slammed the table with both hands. "If you can help them, in the name of Jesus, help them! Let us leave immediately. Bring your guns and your bombs and let us leave!"

"All right, my brother, all right," Eloise said. "We will help you."

"Hallelujah!" Gil-Su shouted.

"Amen, brother," she said. "But we can't leave this very second. Now, please sit down and let's us talk about this." She indicated his chair.

He pulled it forward and sat, elbows on the table, eyes afire.

"All right now," Eloise said, "that's good." She turned to Jason. "Jason, why don't you and Doug get out the maps and look at them with Mr. Yi? Come up with a few plans until dinnertime. What do you want the rest of them to do?"

"Sounds good, ma'am," Jason said. "I'd like to include Garth and Chris in the planning because I believe they've both served in South Korea. Lewis and Trieu"—Oh, how he loved to say her name—"and Rachel"—Oh, how saying that name made him sad —"can gather our gear for transit and get us ready to ship out. Lewis can grab his vehicle arrestor device. Then we'll break for dinner and see where we are. I'd like us to fly out tonight, if that's possible." He looked at Gil-Su, then at Eloise. "He's coming with us, isn't he?"

"Of course he's going with you."

"Good. Then we'll need to figure out a way to get him into the country without being picked up at the airport. We'll have to get our gear in, too. And we'll need papers and identities. Maybe after dinner you and Trieu and Rachel and Lewis can figure out good covers for us. Hmm, probably flying out tonight is too early, isn't it?"

Eloise was writing notes on a pad. "Not necessarily. Some of that Doug's already prepared." She set the pencil down. "We'll see. May have to wait until morning."

"Roger that," Jason said. "Anyway, we should be plenty busy until dinner. And deep into the night, I'd say. We can come up with tactical plans when we get there and assess the situation."

Garth stood up. "Excuse me, Mr. Yi, for what I'm about to do." He reared his head back and howled. "Oh, baby, we're gonna hit it again! Man, it's about time!"

The others laughed and bounced around excitedly. In the din

of their celebration, Jason snuck to Trieu and stole a kiss.

"I saw that!" Lewis said.

When they'd calmed and returned to their seats, Garth leaned forward again. "Like I said, Mr. Yi, I apologize."

"Don't apologize," Gil-Su said. "If you can truly help my friends, I don't mind if you cluck like chickens and eat corn off the ground."

That's how it was that the room erupted with barnyard noises.

Eloise shook her head and smiled indulgently. "Just don't nobody lay no egg on my good carpet."

* * *

Trieu found Rachel in bed under the covers. The hotel print drapes were closed, though it was nearly dark outside.

Trieu sat on the edge of Rachel's bed. "Rachel, are you awake?"

"No."

Rachel reached up to turn on the bedside light. She wore no makeup and was already in her sleep shirt. She propped pillows against the headboard and sat up.

They stared at each other for ten seconds.

Trieu's hands opened and shut. "Rachel, I . . ."

Rachel smiled. Then her look shifted to bitter hurt and she moaned.

Trieu hugged her close as Rachel sobbed. Trieu rocked them back and forth and stroked Rachel's hair.

"I remember holding you like this once before," Trieu said. "Do you remember? A hole in the ground somewhere in the middle of Kazakhstan?" Rachel nodded. "You'd just come back from impersonating a Kazakh woman for over an hour. I don't know why you cried, but I was happy to be there for you. I remember being so amazed by you. Here is this woman who speaks so many languages, who is so courageous to walk among the enemy all alone.

Where would this team be without her?" She squeezed Rachel's shoulder. "I was—and am—so proud to be your friend."

That unleashed more tears in Rachel. She sobbed, but finally sobbing gave way to crying, and crying to weeping. She sat up from Trieu and reached for a Kleenex. "The good thing about wearing no makeup," she said, drying her eyes, "is that when you cry your mascara doesn't run."

Rachel leaned back on her pillows. "You know, I really wanted to be mad at you. I tried. I actually sat here and tried to think mean thoughts about Trieu. But then I'd remember your sweet, gentle spirit, how you'd never hurt a fly. Well, unless that fly was the enemy and you were going to shoot it with your sniper rifle."

They shared an easy laugh.

"But I just couldn't stay mad at you." She shook her head incredulously. "Jason is so stinking lucky to have your love. He has no idea what he's got."

Trieu looked down. "Thank you." She sighed. "Rachel, there's something else I need to tell you."

"Oh, you mean about being engaged? I already know."

Trieu looked up. "How?"

"You know Doug. He called Jamie like as soon as you guys went on break. Jamie was actually sitting right there on your bed watching TV when he called. Are you kidding? I'm glad I know. I'm glad I've gotten all the crying out for that, too. You know, get it all over at once."

Trieu heaved a tremendous sigh. "Good! I was dreading having to tell you."

Rachel grabbed her left hand. "What, no ring?"

"We were going to go looking for one tonight, but now I think he's too busy planning our mission. I think we're leaving at something like four in the morning."

Rachel patted her hand. "Well, maybe you and I can go looking. We'll pick out something huge, put him in hock for ten years."

Trieu looked at her askance. "Are you certain you're not bitter about this? Not at all?"

"No, no, not at all." She looked at the ceiling. "Okay, maybe a little." She chuckled. "The worst part is I can't stay bitter because I'm so happy for what's happened to my dear friend."

"Oh!"

They hugged.

Rachel dabbed her eyes. "It's like I'm torn between crying and laughing all the time now. I feel like Elasticwoman."

"Oh, now, Rachel," Trieu said, "that's too much of a stretch."

It took a moment for the joke to register on Rachel's face. "You jerk," she said playfully. "You totally got me." She threw the covers aside and stood. "Have you eaten dinner?"

"No, that's why I came by, to bring you to dinner."

"All right," Rachel said, walking toward the bathroom. "Let me get ready." She stopped by the television and turned back to Trieu. "Only. . ."

"Yes? What is it?"

Rachel bit her lip. "I was just wondering if I— I mean, I know you've got a lot of special people that you'll want in your wedding and all, but. . ." She shook her head. "But you wouldn't want me. Or maybe I could be that cake-cutting girl. I promise I wouldn't make a scene. And I'd cut those slices so—"

"Rachel," Trieu said, coming to stand in front of her, "hush." She took Rachel's hands. "It would be my great joy if you would stand beside me as my maid of honor."

Rachel froze. A vein bulged in her forehead. "Oh, Trieu. . . I don't know. I just— Right now I don't know if I can do that. I mean, I know I brought it up, because I thought I wanted to, but now. . . Can you. . .ask me about it later? Like after the wedding?"

Trieu smiled and nodded. "Of course."

Someone knocked at the door.

"Oh," Trieu said, suddenly nervous, "that'll be Jason. He said

177

he would come by on the way to dinner."

"No problem," Rachel said. "I'll get it."

She walked to the door and opened it. Jason stood there, eyes wide.

"Um, hi, Rachel."

"Hi, Jason." Rachel released the doorknob and whipped her hand across Jason's face in a bone-jarring slap.

"Rachel!" Trieu said.

"Ow!"

"Wow," Rachel said, smiling broadly, "I feel so totally better now." She skipped to the bathroom and shut the door. "Be out in a sec!"

Trieu went to Jason, who was holding his face. "Let me see it. Oh, you poor thing."

He shook his head as if trying to recover from an open-field tackle. He worked his jaw left and right. "What a smack."

She draped her arms around his neck and kissed his wounded cheek. "Well, at least you two have gotten past that awkward moment."

"I guess."

"Oh, look at the bright side," Trieu said, caressing his cheek. "She says she feels better now."

He winced. "I'm glad one of us does."

PART II

CHINA

CHAPTER 16

Mongol Hordes

"Wuoa po hwuCHWEE tyang hyen yeou."

The Chinese flight attendant's eyes narrowed at Lewis only briefly before the smile returned to her face as she thanked the disembarking passengers. *"Au revoir. Auf wiedersehen.* Good-bye. *Tsai teeun."*

Lewis dropped out of the line of Chinese passengers trudging toward the exit and stood beside her. "Yeah, but you didn't answer me." He tapped his PDA emphatically. "Wuoa po hwuCHWEE tyang hyen yeou!"

"Hey," Jason said, standing behind Trieu in the plane's aisle, "give it a rest, why don't you? She doesn't understand, okay?"

Garth grunted from behind Jason. He had to hunch over to stand up in the plane's cabin. "I think she understands just fine," he said to Lewis. "She's just tired of listening to you!"

Jason thought he saw the hint of a smile on the flight attendant's face.

Lewis grimaced. "I'm just trying to tell the girl I don't speak Chinese."

"I think she's got that one pretty well figured out," Garth said.

The airplane was an aging Russian-made twin turboprop passenger plane capable of carrying forty passengers and crew. This flight was about two-thirds full. Chris's blond hair and Garth's red beard represented the only light hair on the plane.

The propellers had just come to a stop and the flight attendant had only now opened the door and dropped the stairs. Beyond, the afternoon was warm and dry. Airport crew and baggage handlers in green Mao caps and bright orange vests busied about on the tarmac. The passengers filed away from the plane toward the main terminal building of Hailar Dongshan Airport.

As the bunched passengers did the disembarkation shuffle, Jason took the opportunity to find Trieu's hand again. He'd held it from Akron to New York, and from there to London Heathrow, to Beijing, and on to here—with only sleep and meals interrupting the bond—and he had no intention of letting go now. For now they agreed to not hold hands or otherwise show romantic affection whenever Rachel might be watching. Both of them wanted to protect Rachel's feelings. But Rachel couldn't see them now.

Holding Trieu's hand like this made Jason feel like a middle-school kid with a bad case of puppy love, but he didn't care. Her hand felt good in his. It felt symbolic, like their personalities were linked when they connected in that way. She squeezed his hand gently.

Finally Jason was beside Lewis and the flight attendant. Lewis had succeeded in drawing her attention to his PDA and was trying to get her to enter something with the stylus. Jason retrieved the stylus from her, thanked her, and pulled Lewis down the steps.

"Come on, Lewis."

The runway was wide enough to serve planes up to the size of small jets, Jason estimated. The control tower looked fairly new, and the terminal building, while not much more than a large square structure, was nevertheless in good repair. The walls were tiled with white reflective ceramic, making it gleam like a pearl in the sun. Here and there tufts of green grass grew through cracks in the white concrete of the runway, and beyond the airport on all sides were beautiful fields of rolling green grass. The Mongol prairie. The grass was a rich green, about shin high, and seemed to carpet the hills, the horizon, the very earth.

"Wow." It was Chris. He, Garth, and Lewis stood beside Jason and Trieu.

Lewis nodded, squinting against the bright sun. "Yeah."

Jason heard a voice he knew coming from behind him, but it wasn't sounding the way it normally did. He turned and spotted Rachel and the flight attendant having a conversation. Rachel said something in Chinese, and the two of them laughed like sorority sisters. The pilot appeared from the cockpit, pulling on his navy blue jacket, and joined in the laughter. Finally the flight attendant pointed toward the left side of the terminal building, chatting speedily. Rachel nodded and thanked the woman, then came down the steps and joined the team on the breezy runway.

"Okay," she said, pointing, "the car rental place is over that way. But Songnu says we'll do better at one of the rental shops in Hailar proper. It's about five miles from here. We can take a couple of taxis or catch the airport shuttle to the Minzu hotel."

Jason and Chris exchanged an amused look. "Rachel," Jason said, "how is it that you know a language in every place we go?"

Rachel shouldered her carry-on bag and they walked toward the terminal. "Oh, that's easy. I pick up languages pretty easily. So back in my consular days, I just decided I was going to learn the language of every country that had nuclear weapons."

They moved across the concrete at a brisk walk. Behind them a private jet accelerated down the runway. A luggage train passed in front of them. A gust of wind brought the sickening smell of aviation gasoline.

"Yeah, but Rachel," Lewis said, hurrying to catch up with her, "that's only five countries, and two of them use English. Don't you speak, like, seventy-five languages or something?"

"Hardly," she said, putting on dark sunglasses. "Just the nine."

Jason looked at Trieu walking beside him. " 'Just the nine,' she says."

"So why all the other ones?" Lewis asked Rachel.

"I don't know. Like I said, they come to me pretty easily. Some, like Spanish or German, were no-brainers. For the others, I just looked at a map and identified which countries were world players, or would be soon, and learned those languages. Never did learn Korean, though. Too bad for us, huh?" Her shoes clopped rapidly on the concrete. "By the way, Lewis, you weren't telling Songnu you didn't speak Chinese."

"I wasn't?"

"No. You were telling her you didn't speak English."

They laughed.

Chris shoved Lewis playfully. "D'oh!"

"Oh no," Lewis said.

Jason stopped them all before they entered the terminal. The whine of nearby turboprops drowned out their voices to any would-be eavesdroppers. "Remember, you guys, we're dumb American tourists. We're here to see the sights, okay?"

"No, we're not," Chris said. He was wearing dark glasses, too. With his gelled hair, glistening skin, and black T-shirt, he looked like a movie star.

"We're not?"

"No. Well, I'm not, anyway," Chris said. "I'm here for the birds. You guys, Hulun Lake and Beier Lake are just to the west and south of us. There are close to *two hundred* species of migratory birds here! Swans, gulls, ducks, more than half the species of cranes in the world. I'm here for that, baby!"

"Okay," Jason said, "whatever. Everybody else is here for the local cuisine or something, okay?"

"Roger that."

"All right," he said quietly, "let's get our bags and get into town. We've got to find a hotel, rent a truck, and scout out some spots in town."

"And eat," Garth said. "I'm starved. Wonder if you can get any good Chinese food around here."

They laughed again.

"Right," Jason said, "and eat. Then we've got to get out of town a hundred miles for our little pickup tonight. So let's move."

*   *   *

"Look at that guy," Garth said.

A man wearing a fine blue shirt and a wristwatch tried to stuff a flapping, squawking goose into a white canvas bag for a customer. Next to him, a man in eyeglasses and a white T-shirt put the finishing touches on a wire birdcage. Behind him stood finished cages, in which pretty songbirds hopped about and sang. Across from him sat a weathered old man with a stringy gray beard. He wore a straw hat, sat next to a wicker basket of straw hats, and had straw hats strewn around his feet like lightweight discuses.

They were in one of Hailar's markets. It was a noisy, smelly, bustling affair on a pavement of square bricks with mud stamped between them. Women shopped for vegetables or new shoes, while toddlers, their pants open to the air at the seat, followed reluctantly. A man smoked a long wooden pipe that looked like it had been formed from a peanut-encrusted chocolate bar. A young man sat straddling a wooden work stool with a hand-operated blade mounted to it. He smiled broadly at them, the skin by his eyes wrinkling under his fur cap with its long earflaps. Everywhere there were merchants sitting surrounded by their wares: vats of nuts, piles of potatoes, bundles of onions. And every Chinese face gaped at the foreigners.

185

The Firebrand team couldn't help but look like tourists here. Trieu could perhaps blend in and Rachel could talk her way through, but there was no hiding the fact that Chris, Jason, Lewis, and especially Garth didn't belong here. The locals—the ones who weren't struck paralyzed by the sight of them, that is—seemed unable to keep their distance. They mobbed the team, smelling them, touching their clothing, trying to read anything in English they wore on them, and thrust into their faces chickens, bread loaves, pots, and wild leeks for sale. It was a warm afternoon, which made the urgent throng smell even more sharply of spoiled fish and unwashed merchant.

Rachel raised her voice to them in Chinese. After a few sentences, the crowd groaned and began to disperse.

"Whew," Jason said, feeling cooler air reach him at last. "What did you say to them, Rachel?"

"I told them the government was holding all our money for customs purposes and wouldn't give it back for four days."

Garth checked his pockets for his belongings. "Ah, good on ya, Sheila."

"Man," Lewis said, looking down the long market aisles, "does everyone in China wear either dark blue or dark green?"

"I think so," Chris said, walking behind him. "Must be what good Communists wear."

"You guys," Lewis said, "what is that awful smell?"

Chris chuckled. "Welcome to Southeast Asia, kid."

Jason had been trying to catalog the smells he detected. First there was the unmistakable smell of open sewage. Human waste smells wafted to them from every side street and alley. Rotting garbage, piled at the curb and everywhere else, added its own putrid odors.

Occasionally he'd detect nicer smells, like jasmine tea, steamed rice, wild onion, cooking eggs, or roasting meat. But then people would crowd around him and he'd smell their body odor, or he'd walk by an open door and smell some dish being prepared, the worst of which was what his mind had decided to call "dirty dog soup," a fetid, rotten-carcass smell that could probably be used as a torture weapon. His nose was running on overload and was on the verge of shutting down for servicing.

Jason caught up to Chris. "Hey, bro, you've been pretty quiet since Akron. You feeling all right about things?"

Chris looked at him, smirking. " 'Things'?"

"Yeah," Jason said, making sure only Chris could hear him. "You know. Rachel and me and Trieu, and what you were saying about feeling kind of disconnected from God."

Chris's smirk faded. They walked silently for several seconds, passing a man leading a pair of goats. Finally Chris looked at him again. "I'm happy for you and Trieu. As for Rachel. . ." He looked at her and shrugged. "Who knows? I don't think I deserve her, you know? And as for God. . . I guess we'll just have to wait and see, huh? I'm feeling a little unbalanced or something. But I'm sure I'll snap out of it, boss."

Jason mock punched his shoulder. "All right, but I still want us to have our 'God talk' conversation. Whenever you want."

"Okay, man, thanks."

The buildings on either side of the cobblestoned street were old wood and brick structures and looked like they might collapse at any moment. Most had an upper story with balconies and wood frame window lattices. Electricity wires crossed and interlaced overhead every ten paces, like a loose net to keep people from flying away. Metal lamps hung from the wires at every intersection. Bicyclists whizzed by without regard to pedestrians. A soldier in blue pants and green jacket with a red rank insignia on his collar and a red star on his green cap strolled past, a dead duck dangling from a stick over his shoulder.

"Rachel," Lewis said quietly, "can't these people afford underwear for their kids? Why are their pants open like that? I can see their. . ."

Rachel shook her head. "I don't know, Lewis. Trieu?"

Trieu smiled. "It's what they do instead of diapers, Lewis. If they need to go, they just squat down and go."

"Ew," Lewis said.

"Check your feet, everybody," Garth said.

It seemed the locals couldn't talk without shouting. Merchants haggled with customers; parents shouted at mischievous children; a man and woman were having a heated marital dispute right in the street. Ducks quacked in cages, pigs shrieked their death screams behind restaurants, and donkeys brayed. Buses and trucks idled on the nearby street, unmuffled motorcycles sped by, and from everywhere came the sound of water buffaloes and bulls clopping on the paving stones, pulling rickety wooden wagons.

Jason looked at Trieu. While it was all the rest of the group could do to keep from holding their noses and plugging their ears, she seemed almost tranquil. He squeezed her hand. "Is it my imagination or are you totally loving this place?"

She smiled serenely. "I grew up in places like this. It feels so alive and natural. Like perhaps the rest of the world is missing out on something in their supermarkets and high-gloss floors."

Hailar was an industrial and agricultural city at the edge of China's northeast frontier. Black smoke from towering brick chimneys made artificial shade over Russian-looking multiapartment units, which all looked vaguely like penitentiary buildings. A thin smog hung over the city and coated even the new structures with a patina of soot and grime.

"Okay," Lewis said, consulting a map on his PDA, "we're here."

They stopped on a corner beside two women wearing surgical masks. Perhaps the three overflowing baskets of red and green onions they were selling from were too much for them to stand. An old Volga, a tiny car that would be laughed off American streets, puttered around the corner a block away. And scores and scores of bicycles.

The only building on the left side of the street was a two-story brick structure with a large antenna tree on top and a bright red flag with golden stars flapping lazily from a pole in front. Good-sized trees flanked the building on both sides and behind. Two armed men in dark blue uniforms stood at the base of the stairs, facing outward.

"Yup," Garth said, "looks like a police station to me."

"Look around, everyone," Jason said quietly. "See if there's a good spot to see into their little backyard. If you see one, get with Lewis to mark it on his PDA. We'll check into them. Maybe we can find a hotel room with a very strategic view."

They walked in front of the police station. Rachel went up to the guards and spoke with them briefly. Chris held up a digital camera and snapped a few intel shots. Jason got a kick out of watching the guards enjoying themselves with Rachel and yet trying to appear disapproving at the same time.

He shook his head. Rachel was hard to ignore. She seemed to come alive when she was on a mission like this. But then he glanced at Trieu, who was chuckling at Rachel's antics, and he knew once again he'd made the right choice.

Ten minutes later they'd completed their surveillance.

"Let's go," Garth said. "My bed is calling me."

They turned toward the market again.

"Good idea," Jason said. "We've got a big night ahead of us. Let's head back to the hotel and try to catch some sleep."

"We'd better check on the truck, too," Chris said. "I'm not so sure that thing's as roadworthy as the guy told Rachel when we bought it."

As they strode again through the crowded marketplace, Jason found Trieu's hand.

*   *   *

"You think he's not coming?"

Jason looked at Chris, who had joined him in front of the

189

truck. "I don't know. He's only twenty minutes late. That's nothing for these guys."

It was 1:30 in the morning, and the temperature was below freezing. They had parked their newly purchased truck literally at the end of the road. The pavement simply stopped and the unbroken prairie began. The wind howled across the open grasslands, making it feel close to zero degrees. Jason and Chris stood at the truck's front bumper, watching light clouds scoot across the familiar stars. The gently rolling plain glowed pale blue in the dim light of the sliver of moon. Aside from that, the plain was absolutely dark. Dark like it had been here every night since creation. No wonder the Chinese called this place "the most unsullied prairie."

The truck was dark green. Indeed, it appeared that all the trucks in China were dark green. The cab was rounded in the style that was popular in America at the close of World War II. With the canvas cover across the frame in the back, it looked like the army truck toys Jason had played with as a kid. The rest of the team huddled in the cab or in the back of the truck, where they could enjoy the dubious shelter of the canvas, which the wind was now pressing against the metal ribbing like skin on an emaciated beast.

Jason consulted the handheld GPS device in his hand. "I've checked our position fifty times. We're in the right place." He pulled his recently purchased wolf-fur-lined parka close around his chin. Somehow uncertainty made the wind bite harder.

"Maybe he got a better deal," Chris said. He wore a shiny black leather jacket he'd brought in his suitcase. The blond curl on his forehead fluttered in the wind under his black knit cap. He looked like James Bond's blond brother.

"A better deal?"

"Yeah, you know these drug runners. Maybe he chickened out or took the gear and found a buyer for it. Who knows? I'll bet he's not coming."

Jason squinted northwest toward Russia, a mere seventy-five

miles away. "Well, I doubt he's found a buyer for that stuff. Who would want it but us? Besides, Eloise only gave him a third of his payment up front. She won't release the rest until she hears from us on our satellite radio—which he's carrying. It's in his own best interest to finish the job."

The truck shifted against their backs. They turned to see Lewis changing position in the cab. He leaned against the driver's door and put his arm around Rachel, who snuggled against his chest.

Jason shook his head. "You've got to give the kid credit. He's not giving up."

Chris turned to the front again without comment.

Ten minutes went by. Though Jason was "wicked cold," as Lewis would say, he had learned as a SEAL what his mind and body could take. This wasn't anywhere close to his breaking point. He knew the same was true for Chris and Garth. He felt bad for the others, but they could take it. Trieu had thought to pack a few of those chemical hot seats in her suitcase. No doubt those were in full use there in the truck.

Jason looked over at Chris, who appeared to be clenching his teeth. "Have you seen any more red-crowned herons?"

Chris looked at him quickly then looked back at the sky to the northwest. "Nah. It was great to see them, though."

Jason blew out a sigh and checked his watch. "No point giving up on him. If he doesn't bring us our toys we might as well go home."

"Maybe we've been ratted out," Chris said. "Smuggler thought he could win some brownie points by turning us in. Maybe the Chinese military is coming to get us right now. Maybe somebody saw our lights on this road nobody takes and they called the army. They'll bring their new Type 98 battle tank with its high-powered laser. *Zap.* It's not like there's a whole lot of places to hide out here. We'll be moo goo gai pan for sure. Or maybe the guy just went to the totally wrong place. He's dropped our stuff in some yurt village and the Mongols are ready to conquer again—nonlethal style."

Jason looked at him over his furry collar. "You're a regular fount of optimism, aren't you?"

Chris shrugged. "Realism, my friend. In the real world, people fail you. They let you down. They do you wrong. They cut you off."

Each sentence was like a block of ice laid around Jason's feet. He cast a last look up before turning.

He saw a light in the sky. "There he is."

Chris followed Jason's pointed arm. "Well, I'll be a buff-breasted sandpiper, you're right."

Between gusts of wind, Jason could make out the faint drone of a single-engine propeller plane. The light they'd seen was not the plane's normal running lights but a front light, perhaps used as a beacon. It flashed on and off.

"He's signaling," Chris said.

"Yeah," Jason said, going to the driver's door of the truck, "but that wasn't part of the plan." He knocked on the window and yanked open the door, almost dropping Lewis and Rachel to the ground.

"Hey!" Lewis said.

"Sorry, you guys." Jason reached under the steering column and pulled the headlight switch forward. He cycled the lights on and off a few times.

"What are you doing?" Rachel asked, hurrying to zip her heavy coat against the cold air outside the cab.

"The plane's here, but it's signaling us with its light. The guy's supposed to just drop the gear out. It'll parachute down, we'll get it, and he'll leave." He cycled the lights again, then turned them off.

The plane swooped toward them. Landing lights blazed on. The engine howled as the small airplane accelerated into a dive.

Chris slapped the hood of the truck and sprinted away into the grass. "Take cover!"

Jason crouched behind the door just as the plane buzzed fifty feet overhead. Instead of a bomb dropping from it, a black plastic garbage bag with an orange glow stick attached fell out and landed in the grass thirty feet to the right of the truck.

Chris got to it first. "It's got a note!" he shouted over the wind. He trotted up to Jason, who brought out a flashlight.

"Cyrillic," Jason said. "We need Rachel."

Overhead the airplane banked and shut off its lights. It seemed to be circling. They took the note to Rachel, who read it under the cab's weak dome light.

"He wants to land," she said.

"What?"

"Perhaps something has changed," Trieu suggested.

The truck lurched as Garth jumped out the back. He came up to the driver's side. "What's up?"

Chris ripped open the garbage bag. "Flares."

"Wait a sec!" Rachel said, reading the note carefully. "He wants us to lay these out on either side of the road so he can see where to land. And he says to hurry because he doesn't have a lot of fuel to spare."

Garth was trying to find the unlit airplane. "What's he up to?"

"I don't know," Jason said, "but we don't have much choice. If he needs to land, he needs to land. Maybe he couldn't get parachutes for the gear. Doesn't matter. If we want our stuff, we'd better do what he says. Lewis, turn the truck around so it faces back down the road, and turn the lights on. The rest of us will break open these road flares and lay 'em out every ten yards, both sides. Let's move, people."

Five minutes later, sparkling white lights edged the road for a quarter of a mile. The plane passed overhead slowly. Then the pilot switched on the landing lights and circled around to get into position for a landing. The team got out of the truck to watch.

"You guys," Jason said as the plane descended toward the road, "go make yourselves scarce. For all I know, ten Chinese commandos are going to jump out of this thing. I'd rather have my team a little away."

"Gotcha, boss," Chris said.

Garth pounded Jason on the back two times, and he and the rest spread out across the dark landscape.

The wind blew at a diagonal across the road. Jason saw the plane's tail pushed sideways and the pilot's efforts to keep it lined up. The wheels touched down, but the plane bounced up. The engine noise fell to virtually nothing, and the plane dropped to the pavement to stay. The pilot revved the engine again and brought the plane close to the truck, where he killed the engine and turned on a dome light inside the cockpit.

Jason could see at least three men inside. That wasn't the plan, either. As the propeller slowed to a stop, he stepped into the open, acutely aware that they could see him illuminated by the truck lights and the plane's landing lights, but he was blinded by them.

A burly Slav with a bushy brown beard hopped out of the pilot's seat onto the ground. *"Dobrie Vecher!"*

Jason shielded his eyes and noticed that the pilot was holding out a hand. He took it. "Hello."

The pilot knocked three times on the fuselage and motioned for Jason to follow him around back. There he reached up to a metal handle and released a cargo door. It dropped open as if in slow surprise.

Which was probably the same look Jason had on his face when he saw what was sitting on top of their pile of gear.

"Gil-Su! What are you doing here?"

The missionary gave a mock salute. "Nice to see you, Jason."

Jason helped him down. "I thought Eloise was going to get you in by boat."

"That. . .didn't work out." Gil-Su wore a heavy black coat and a furry black hat with long furry ears. Jason noticed another Asian man still on the plane. "At the last minute," Gil-Su said, "she got us in with Vasili."

"That's why he had to land," Jason said, nodding.

"Yes, I'm afraid Joo-Chan and I would not have done too well with parachutes."

"Joo-Chan?"

Gil-Su nodded. "My fellow missionary. South Korean citizen. He knows our refugees, too." He spoke in another language to the man in the plane.

Joo-Chan hopped out. He was young. About Lewis's age. He wore a dark green padded coat and a beige scarf across his face. He lowered his scarf, took off his black mitten, and extended his right hand. "Hello, my name No Joo-Chan. I am pleasing to meet me."

Jason returned the handshake. "Jason." Then he added, "Kromer Jason-Scott."

"Ah!" Joo-Chan said, shaking his hand vigorously. "Please to meet. Please to meet."

Gil-Su shrugged one shoulder. "We're working on his English."

"No, it's fine," Jason said. He turned to the open grassland and cupped his hands. "It's okay! You guys come on in!"

The team materialized like apparitions at the edge of the plane's lights. Vasili started in fright, holding his chest. Then he launched into a string of Russian words Jason decided not to have Rachel translate.

Gil-Su began unloading olive-drab duffel bags. "Vasili is anxious to leave."

"Roger that," Jason said. "Okay, guys, let's get this stuff onto the truck. Lewis, find the satellite radio and get us in touch with Chimp. Ol' Vasili here would probably like the rest of his payment okayed."

"Yes, sir."

It turned out their gear was all there. Joo-Chan and Gil-Su had brought one bag each, as well. As the rest of the team checked out their weapons and equipment, Lewis aligned the satellite radio to the proper satellite and gave the handset to Jason, who sat in the cab of the truck, somewhat shielded from the wind.

"Gandalf, Gandalf, this is Strider, do you copy? Over."

Lewis's smile lit the cab of the truck. "It's so *choice* we're using *The Lord of the Rings* for radio protocol this time. So, so choice."

Jason nodded and leaned back in the seat. He looked at each team member trying to remember what character name each person had picked. He tried the radio again. "Gandalf, Gandalf, this is Strider, do you copy? Over."

Lewis pulled out his helmet and computer pack and began checking them out. "You think he's gone again? What time is it there, anyway?"

"No, he's not gone," Jason said. "We covered this last time. When we are deployed, Chimp eats, sleeps, and. . .everything else right there in that room. Maybe he's asleep or—"

"Strider, this is Gandalf." It was Doug "Chimp" Bigelow's voice. "Read you Lima Charlie. Great to hear your voice. Guess you got the gear and found your guests. Over."

Jason smiled at Lewis and gave him a thumbs-up. "Gandalf, this is Strider. Roger that. Have received our gear and our guests. Tell Galadriel she can approve payment to Gwahir the Wind Lord. Over."

They had to wait several seconds for the transmission to reach the operations room in the ABL building and for the reply to bounce back to them across the continents.

"Uh. . .copy that, Strider. I'll tell Ga–Galad— I'll tell *that person* to authorize payment to. . .Gw–to the wind dude. Over."

"Gandalf, this is Strider. Roger that. And Gandalf. . .read a book. Over."

Jason and Lewis traded high fives. In front of the truck Vasili slammed shut the plane's cargo door and came around under the wing.

"Rachel," Jason called.

Rachel zipped a duffel bag closed and came to the driver's side. "Yes?"

"Please tell Vasili his payment's on its way and he can get going."

"Right." She spoke to Vasili.

The big man broke into a toothy smile and gave her a massive hug. Then he spoke to her quickly, gesturing to his plane and pointing down the road. Rachel nodded and called to Garth and the others.

Chimp's voice came through the handset. "Roger that, Strider. I'll put it on my to-do list. In the meantime, can you give a mission update? Over."

"Gandalf, this is Strider. Roger on the mission update. We have made it to Isengard as planned. No incidents. We have purchased suitable transportation, which we will refer to as Bill the pony. Now that we have our goodies, we're fully operational. We have located a good spot with an excellent view of Isengard." Jason looked over at Trieu, who was helping the others push Vasili's airplane to the other end of the makeshift runway. "Lady Arwen will have a clear shot when the time comes. Expect to have full tactical assessment and assault plans within eighteen hours. Standing by for orders. Over."

He waited out the delay. The team and the plane dropped out of the truck's headlights. The plane's landing lights were still on.

"Strider, Gandalf. Copy your good position and mission readiness within eighteen hours. Well done. Copy Bill the pony, too. Be advised that there have been no good developments between Galad-whatever and the other guys. There appears to be no movement on the political side. It looks like you guys may have to. . . retrieve the Ring after all. How copy? Over."

"Copy Lima Charlie, Gandalf. Roger on stealing the Ring ourselves. That suits us fine. Just give us the word and we'll handle it. Any decision yet on how we'd get the Ring to safety once we have it? Over."

As he waited for Chimp's reply, he heard the plane's engine come to life. Judging from how far away the landing lights appeared, there didn't seem to be enough room for the plane to take off before hitting the truck. Anyway, Jason couldn't move without losing the satellite connection. *Hurry up, Chimp.*

"Strider, this is Gandalf," Chimp said over the radio. "We're thinking you guys should take the Ring southwest rather than northwest. It's a little farther for you, but there are likely to be fewer. . .orcs. How copy? Over."

Jason understood him to mean they would take the refugees into Mongolia instead of into Russia because of Mongolia's less guarded border. "Gandalf, Strider. Copy going southwest if we get the Ring. If there's nothing else, I need to sign off, Gandalf. Gwahir needs to take off and I need to get out of the way. Over."

The plane's engine revved, and the lights began to draw closer. *Come on, Chimp.* He started the truck and put it in reverse, but kept his foot on the brake.

"Roger, Strider. Nothing more now. Call again according to our schedule. Gandalf out."

"Strider out."

Jason dropped the handset and released the brake. He rolled backward as the plane rushed directly toward him. It occurred to him that this might disorient Vasili the Wind Lord—or that Jason might back right into a stream or something—but at this point he just wanted out of the way.

The wind shoved the plane to the side just as the tail rose off the pavement. But Vasili adjusted with the rudder and the little craft lifted off the ground right at the end of the road—where the truck had just been.

It roared over Jason's head with not more than ten feet of clearance above the cab.

Immediately the landing lights went out and the airplane became a less and less audible dark spot against the Mongol sky.

CHAPTER 17

THE RING GOES SOUTH

THE CROSSHAIRS rested on the side of Rachel's skull.

She was moving, climbing the stairs. The crosshairs followed steadily. Finally Rachel stopped and the sniper found her head again.

"She's in position," Trieu said over her squad radio. She swerved her Dragunov SVD rifle slightly to the left so the head of the police guard Rachel was speaking to rested under her crosshairs. "He appears to be happy to see her again."

"Roger that."

Jason's voice sounded so confident. How, with just the tone of his voice, could he instill poise in her and the rest of the team?

Trieu lifted her eye from the rubber eyepiece of her sniper scope and glanced at the tree-lined road in front of the police station. She put her face up to the slight opening of the heavy curtains of their new hotel room. She'd been leaning on a table well back from the window so that not even the muzzle of the rifle was visible. From the outside, it simply appeared this was a dark hotel room with the window open and the drapes closed.

Of course Trieu couldn't see Jason, but she knew he was there, somewhere in the dense foliage across from the station and beyond it. She smiled a secret smile. He was hers now.

She looked through the scope again. Rachel and the guard were laughing. Because Trieu knew what to look for, she could see that Rachel was holding something small in her left hand as she spoke with the guard.

Lewis stepped up behind Trieu. "Has she done it yet?"

"Not yet."

She heard Lewis step away from her across the worn carpet of the hotel room. Gil-Su and Joo-Chan were in the room, too. Jason, Chris, and Garth were down in front of the police station, watching, in case something went wrong with Rachel's mission.

Under the crosshairs, Rachel shook the guard's hand. "Stand by," Trieu said. "She's given the signal."

Rachel reached out and shook the other guard's hand.

"Stand by."

Rachel moved as if to step away but then appeared to be overcome by emotion and—seemingly on impulse—ran to the first guard and gave him a quick hug and kiss on the cheek. Her left hand moved deftly to the guard's leather strap that crossed his chest.

"She's done it!" Trieu said. "The item is in place."

The others voiced their hushed approval over the squad radio.

"All right, baby," Lewis said from behind her in the hotel room, "let's see what you've given me."

Through the scope, Trieu watched as the other guard made some remark to Rachel, and Rachel laughed and gave him a hug and kiss, too. Then she waved and walked away down the steps. The guards spoke to each other excitedly, their dumbfounded smiles communicating quite clearly.

Then Trieu realized she could hear their actual conversation—from behind her.

"Bingo!" Lewis said, now speaking into the squad radio. "I've got video and audio. Way to go, Eowyn."

As Trieu watched Rachel go down the steps, a large green form moved in and blocked her view.

"Got a truck," Garth said softly over the radio.

Trieu looked over the top of her rifle. A dark green panel truck pulled up in front of the police station and stopped. Two blue-uniformed policemen hopped out of the cab. The driver ran around to the back and lifted the sliding door. The passenger, who wore a flat-topped officer's hat, strode up the stairs. The two guards saluted smartly. Trieu could just see the officer's head as he spoke to the guards.

"What's he saying, Gil-Su?" Lewis asked.

Gil-Su put headphones on and stared at Lewis's video monitor, which showed the live feed from the mote camera Rachel had placed on the guard's shoulder strap. "I am Captain Xia," he said, translating. "Jilin Province. You are to release to my care your North Korean prisoners."

"What?" Lewis said.

"Jilin is on the border with North Korea!" Gil-Su said.

"Oh no!"

Joo-Chan panicked, all but shrieking at Gil-Su in Korean. Trieu set her rifle down and quietly closed the hotel room window, letting the curtains close again.

"What do we do, boss?" Chris's calm sounded manufactured.

"I'm thinking," Jason said.

"We've got to get mobile," Garth said, the easy slowness gone from his voice. "Or we'll lose them."

"No," Chris said. "We take them here. We're in position and armed. We've got sniper coverage." He paused. "Let's take 'em, Strider."

"Hold, hold!" Jason said. "Arwen, how many bystanders?"

Trieu eased the curtains aside an inch. "About forty on bicycles right now. Two cars. The market around the corner."

Gil-Su managed to pacify Joo-Chan.

Lewis went back to his monitor. "Our guard's on the move. Going inside."

"Give the word, Strider," Chris said over the radio. "We can do this."

Jason didn't answer. Trieu believed he hadn't frozen up. She grabbed her rifle and chambered a sedative-bearing protein bullet. She laid out three more clips ready for fast reloading if the shooting started. She lifted the window slowly and sat behind the table, rifle at the ready.

"Negative," Jason said finally, his voice sure. "We can't do it with this many people around."

"Then we go inside and do it out of sight," Chris said impatiently.

"No," Jason said. "Okay, look, here's what we'll do. Lewis, get on the horn and call Doug. Advise that the Ring is going south. Repeat, the Ring is going south. Find out what happened. Ask for orders. But advise we will be giving chase. Copy that?"

"Copy," Lewis said. "I'm on it."

"The rest of us prepare to travel," Jason said. "Everybody get to the truck. Trieu, help 'em get it together up there."

Trieu set her rifle down. "Roger that."

"Nice and easy, people," Garth said with exaggerated slowness. "Just tourists with funny backpacks headed to their hotel."

Lewis initiated the satellite radio call. As he waited for a response from Chimp, he watched the video monitor. "Gil-Su, is that them?"

Trieu paused from her packing. On the monitor she saw guards leading a group of very small, very hungry looking Asian people down a concrete corridor.

Gil-Su knelt in front of the monitor. "Oh! It is them. Look,

Joo-Chan, they are all right."

The sound of a woman's painful coughing reached them through the monitor's small speakers.

"That sounds like Aunt," Gil-Su said. "Yes, there she is."

Trieu saw an old Korean woman leaning heavily on a Korean man of about the same age. She was coughing deeply and appeared to be having difficulty breathing. Trieu had a suspicion of what that might be.

Behind these two came a very pregnant woman. She was haggard but could've been pretty in another setting. On her left was a man who put an arm around her as she walked. In her arms she carried a young Korean boy whose eyes were open but who appeared listless. A young man walked beside a white-haired old woman. They took two steps together and then the woman collapsed. The young man shoved aside Chinese policemen and lifted the old woman in his arms. Last came two armed guards hauling a man in handcuffs.

"Oh!" Gil-Su said. "Myong-Chol!"

"Who's he?" Lewis asked. "Why's he the only one tied up?"

"He used to be a prison guard and a soldier in North Korea," Gil-Su said. "They consider him the worst kind of traitor." Gil-Su craned his neck as if to see behind people on the flat screen. "Where is Kora-Lee?"

He and Joo-Chan fell into worried chatter.

"Gil-Su," Trieu said, "if we're going to follow them, we need to get down to the truck now. Lewis is on the radio. Can you two carry the video equipment?"

Gil-Su nodded and braced Joo-Chan. "Yes, we will do what we can."

CHAPTER 18

Cannibals

SHIN-HWA, be born now. Hurry! You must try to come early, Shin-Hwa. I will be here to greet you. We will give you to a nice Christian family in China. Or we will find missionaries who will take you to South Korea, and you will be free. But you must be born now. . .before we reach North Korea.

We were being moved in a truck. It squeaked and bounced uncomfortably. To raise my tailbone off the wooden floor, I sat with my heels close under me—as close as they could come without my thighs pressing too hard on my unborn daughter. There must have been an oil-soaked rag somewhere because I could smell the sweet odor with every breath.

There were no lights in the back of this truck, but the rear door would not close all the way and the morning sunlight shone in well enough for me to see. Bum-Ji and I sat at the front of the truck, leaning against the cab. It was so good to finally touch him again after so long in segregated cells. He held me under his arm as if I would float away if he let go. Aunt and Uncle huddled together against the wall of the truck. Perhaps it was because Uncle had not been able to scold his wife in so long that he held her so tenderly. Or perhaps it was because of the dreadful cough she had contracted in prison.

One of the two police guards slept on the raised bench along one wheel well. The other sat cross-legged on the bench across from him, watching us with bored eyes. It was hot in the truck. The gap in the rear door brought in some fresh air, but not enough.

It was amusing to me how the guards at the prison had acted like the little food they gave us was such a torture. They didn't know anything about North Korea. One-quarter prison rations in China were like three feasts a day where I'd come from. Judging from the look of my family, we'd all gained weight in the Hailar prison.

Little Brother stared sullenly out the slit under the rear door. How he had changed in these weeks! If he still had his youthful cheer, I hadn't seen it today. Wispy black hair grew at his jaw line and under his bottom lip. He was a man now. I was proud of him. *We'll get out of this, Youn-Chul. Don't die inside.*

Grandmother's head lay in Little Brother's lap. She slept noisily, her colorless lips hanging open like the mouth of a corpse.

Myong-Chol sat at the rear of the truck, his hands bound in front of him. I hadn't seen him since we'd gotten to the Hailar prison. I thought he'd been held with the men, but Bum-Ji told me he'd been kept somewhere else this whole time. After such an experience, I expected him to look angry or beaten. But instead he simply looked calm, as if willing to accept whatever fate he met. There was no smile in those kind eyes, but neither was there the hatred that must've been there when he'd been so cruel in the death camp. Of any of us, he had the most to fear at this moment: At the end of this journey he would certainly be executed. And yet he seemed most at peace.

Ki-Won lay at my feet. For the sixth day in a row he hadn't played or even smiled. I looked at the policeman sleeping on the bench and the other one sitting up keeping watch. They weren't the ones who had taken Ki-Won's shapes away from him or beaten him savagely when he cried, but they would do as a target for my anger. Prison had not been kind to the child. How would whatever awaited us in North Korea be any better? Perhaps I should pull him close and strangle him right now.

I was shocked by my own thoughts. How could I, a mother to be, consider harming a child? And yet a very tired part of me knew that death at my hands would be far better for the poor child than the living death in a concentration camp. The end would be the same, but if I did it now the suffering would be minimized.

I felt the little Gospel of John booklet in my sleeve. Gil-Su had slipped it to me on the trip between the Mongolia border and Hailar. I'd read it every night by the light of the policemen's card game. I'd seen nothing in there about whether or not a child like Ki-Won who died would be taken to the Lord Jesus Christ's home He was preparing, but I knew He was a gentle man—a good Shepherd—who would surely receive the boy into His arms with love.

Ki-Won's eyes had lost their luster. In my mind I could still hear him calling for his mommy, like he did whenever we'd return to the cell or go into the courtyard. "Mommy? Daddy? Mommy?" He'd look and look, always sure his parents were waiting for him just around the next corner. But that was weeks ago. Now the poor thing seemed to finally understand that his life really was that awful. Only I was left who loved him. Surely I should do the most loving thing.

I reached forward and stroked his hair. But how could I harm this precious boy? How could I not protect him with everything I had in me? I looked swiftly at the guards and the chains and the prison truck. Some protector I'd been.

Oh, Shin-Hwa, be born soon—today. God's peace, my sweet

daughter, come now. If you wait until we get to North Korea, I will not be able to protect you. Do you understand?

Good Shepherd, don't let them abort my Shin-Hwa or let her be killed with a plastic bag or thrown to the dogs. Please let her be born now. Or let her die inside me, inside the only place of love she'll ever know on this earth.

Bum-Ji's cheek dropped onto the top of my head. His body went slowly slack. How had my husband been treated? He wouldn't tell me. But for now it was enough that we were together. He held me and I held Shin-Hwa. For this moment we were a family.

What are You doing, Good Shepherd? Why have You not rescued us? Are we not of Your flock, too? We are being given to the wolves. Will You not drive them away?

I must've fallen asleep, too, because when I looked around next, the sounds had changed. Instead of bicycle bells and constant stops and starts, we seemed to be on a long, straight road going quickly. The truck's wheels went over evenly spaced bumps, like seams in the road. Tu-*tunk*. . .tu-*tunk*. . .tu-*tunk*. The guards had traded off who was sleeping and who was watching.

I knew we'd eventually have to board a train. I couldn't imagine driving across all of China in this truck. I'd never imagined the whole world could be as big as were just the parts of China I'd crossed from North Korea to Mongolia. How could you ride twenty-four hours on a train and not come to a border or an ocean?

Under the rear door I suddenly noticed the wheels of a following vehicle. A moment later I could see a dark green bumper, a license plate, and the front grill of a truck. It was right behind us and still accelerating. Perhaps the driver couldn't tell that this was a police vehicle. The truck swerved to pass us. I saw a glimpse of canvas siding flapping in the wind, but then the truck was past.

A minute later we were slowing down. Then we were braking rapidly. My family and the guards awoke and braced themselves.

The truck stopped completely, even bouncing back a little from the sharp halt. I heard the driver honking his horn again and again. Then the truck shifted slightly and I heard a door slam.

"What's happening?" I said.

Bum-Ji held me tight. "I don't know. Perhaps an accident?"

It could've been my imagination, but I thought I heard a metallic clacking, like links of chain being pulled through a hole in a wall.

Then I heard excited shouting from nearby, perhaps just outside the truck or from inside the cab.

The truck bounced a little. Then the clacking again. Then something like a heavy sack of wheat meal being tossed to the ground.

The guards in the back with us were getting nervous. They whispered to each other in Chinese. They both drew their pistols and faced the rear door.

I heard footsteps around the truck. Soft but unmistakable.

A male voice said something in Chinese. The voice was calm and seemed amused. After hearing the man talk for a few sentences, the guards looked at each other and laughed. They stood up straighter and put their pistols away. I still couldn't see anybody through the rear door, but I could hear at least two people moving around out there. The guards shooed Myong-Chol away from the rear of the truck and together lifted the door to the top.

And were immediately shot.

White smoke exploded off their chests, sending the guards staggering backward.

All of us cried out and lay down.

I saw three of the largest men I'd ever seen in my life sweep around the back of the truck, firing weapons at the guards. These men were not Korean or Chinese. One had brown hair, not black. One had yellow hair. And one, the largest, had no hair at all on his head but wore a beard the color of rust. They were dressed in blue pants and light Western-style shirts. They fired their weapons with precision and confidence.

Our guards fell to their knees, coughing and trying to talk.

Three more attackers—two of them *women*—swept around the back of the truck and shot our guards again, though this time no smoke flew up.

The yellow-haired man and the brown-haired man jumped into our truck. We cried out and tried to appear unthreatening to them so they wouldn't kill us. This had to be a robbery of some kind. But why attack a police truck with no valuables inside?

But the two men didn't appear to be angry with us. They released their weapons, which didn't fall but somehow retracted back to their chests, and rolled the guards over even as they writhed on the floor of the truck. They took the guards' pistols and handed them to the attackers outside.

The brown-haired one spoke to us in an ugly language I'd never heard. Perhaps his tongue was deformed. They showed us their empty hands, backed away, and jumped out of the truck.

And then I saw a face I knew.

"Gil-Su!" I cried. "Is it really you?"

Gil-Su climbed into the back of the truck. His young helper— Little Brother's friend—was with him. When they were both inside, the bald man reached up and pulled the rear door down.

"Chun-Mi! Bum-Ji! Grandmother!" Gil-Su was laughing, trying to touch all of us at once as we crowded around him. "It is so good to see you."

"Gil-Su," Uncle said, "how is this possible? We thought you were sent to America. Did you escape?"

Gil-Su and Joo-Chan laughed. "No," Gil-Su said, "I didn't have to escape. In America I am free."

I shook my head for poor Gil-Su. He had been brainwashed.

The missionary looked around the truck. "But where is Kora-Lee? When I left, she was with you. Did they let her go?"

We all shook our heads. "No, brother Gil-Su," I said. "Sister Kora-Lee got the cough and died in prison a few days after you left." I made myself not look at Aunt, who was coughing in the collar of her prison shirt.

Gil-Su dropped his head into his hand. "Oh, no, Kora-Lee. Dear saint."

The truck's motor came to life and we moved, knocking Gil-Su back onto the bodies of the guards. We rolled forward slowly. From the sound of it, we were pulling off the road. Then the truck stopped and the engine went off.

"Gil-Su," Bum-Ji said, holding Ki-Won on his lap, "who are these people you are with? They must be barbarians to be so big."

"No, they're not barbarians," Gil-Su said with a smile. As he said it, someone rattled the rear door of the truck. "They're not barbarians," he said, "they're Americans!"

Aunt shrieked. "Cannibals!"

The back door roared open, revealing the bald giant on the truck and all the attackers arrayed behind them with their weapons drawn. Americans here to eat us all!

I wet my pants.

CHAPTER 19

TRANSFERRED FREIGHT

"WHAT'D I do?"

Gil-Su walked toward Garth at the back of the police truck. "I should have told you: They're scared of Americans."

Garth released the rear door and looked at the North Korean refugees. "Why?"

"Maybe because we're like twice as tall as they are," Chris said, hopping up into the back of the truck. "Especially you, Green Bean."

The refugees scooted away from them, their eyes wide.

"No," Gil-Su said, standing in front of Garth. "It is because their government has bred them to fear anything outside of North Korea. The more something could be helpful to them, the more they've been taught to fear it. They have been told since they were very small children that Americans are savages. Cannibals." He looked down at the refugees. "They think you've come to cook and eat them."

Chris and Garth looked at each other. "Oh."

Jason stood on the street at the rear of the truck. "Gil-Su, can you try to explain to them that we're here to help?"

"It won't be easy, but I will try."

"Good. In the meantime we need to get some distance between us and the scene of the crime. Can you get them onto our truck? My team will take care of things here."

"Yes."

"Hang on a second," Jason said. He stepped around the truck and cast a look down both ends of the barren highway. It was mid-morning and the temperature was in the upper fifties. It was going to be a beautifully clear, warm day on the fields of grassland. No cars had passed since their little truck stop op had begun. "Lewis, how's it look your way?"

"Clear forward, boss," Lewis said. He was standing on the step at the driver's side of their own truck.

Jason looked backward to where Trieu stood looking down the highway toward Hailar. "Anything?"

"Something on the horizon, but you've got five minutes before they're close enough to see detail."

"Roger that, Trieu." Jason looked at the back of her head, her long black hair rustling in the steady wind. He was going to have to figure out a good term of endearment that fit but didn't make the rest of the team laugh. *Roger that, honey,* just didn't work. He looked back up at Gil-Su. "Okay, let's get them moving. And Chris, find the keys for this guy's handcuffs."

"Roger that."

Gil-Su spoke to the refugees and got them moving out the back of the truck. As Jason helped the oldest woman down, Gil-Su spoke quietly to him. "I have never met men willing to kill in the name of Christ. I have never contemplated such a thing."

"Well," Jason said, handing the old woman off to Rachel, "we haven't killed the guards."

"Excuse me?"

"They're not dead. They're just sleeping. We hit them with tranquilizer bullets that put them to sleep for awhile. That's why we have to get out of here—we need to be long gone before they wake up."

"But won't they just wake up and call for help on their radio? They've seen your truck and your faces."

"Ah," Jason said, helping Gil-Su lower the pregnant woman to the road, "that's something else our little tranquilizer darts do: They make the person forget everything that happened around the time they were injected with it. They're going to wake up, look around, and see an empty truck, but have no clue what happened. That's the way we like it."

When the refugees had cleared out, Chris and Garth arranged the guards in positions that made it look like they were only asleep in the back of the truck. Chris replaced the pistols in their holsters.

While Garth and Gil-Su got the refugees loaded in Bill the pony, Jason and Chris arranged the driver and the officer in the cab of the police truck.

Rachel trotted back to them from their truck, a glass bottle of clear liquid in her hands. "Look what I found in the tool chest of our truck. Vodka!"

"Ah!" Chris said. "The guy who sold us the truck told us he'd made some special modifications himself. I guess this is what he meant!"

"It's perfect, Rachel," Jason said. "Good job." He took the bottle and poured some of the contents on the driver and the officer.

"Car coming!" Trieu called.

Everyone got out of sight. The car turned out to be a bus—blue body and white top. The driver didn't even turn his eyes when he hummed past.

Jason went around to the back of the police truck and poured vodka on the guards. He double-checked them for tranquilizer darts, but they'd all been retrieved. He placed the empty bottle in the hand of one and pulled the door down as far as it would go. He hopped down and put his hand on Trieu's arm. "Okay, future Mrs. Kromer, let's go."

They walked together past the police truck, which was leaning slightly to the right on the shoulder, and climbed into the back of their own truck.

The whole team was there, along with the refugees. Jason's eyes adjusted to the shade under the canvas. "All right, let's get out of here. We'd probably better have Chinese-looking faces in the front. But Gil-Su, I need you back here to translate into Korean and English." He scanned the faces. "Gil-Su, can Joo-Chan drive a truck? It's a stick shift."

Gil-Su asked the teenage missionary. Joo-Chan answered in Korean, but his look of goofy uncertainty needed no translation.

"He says he thinks so."

"Wonderful," Chris said, without enthusiasm.

"Okay," Jason said, "let's do it. Joo-Chan, you drive. Rachel, you'd better ride up there with them, too, to help him with Chinese road signs and to be my eyes. We need to turn around and get back to Hailar to find the road south toward the border. But cover yourself up, okay, Raych? I don't want passing motorists to be able to see you're not Chinese. Keep in touch over squad radio. The rest of us will ride here. Okay, let's move."

Joo-Chan and Rachel moved to leave, but one of the refugees—the teenager—caught Joo-Chan's arm and said something.

Gil-Su turned to Jason. "Youn-Chul would like to ride in the front with Joo-Chan. They are friends."

Jason nodded. "Fine."

"And one more thing," Gil-Su said. He indicated the pregnant woman. "Do you have any dry clothing? Chun-Mi was so frightened of him," he said, looking at Garth, "that she has had an accident."

Chris looked like he'd taken a bite of lime. "Oh, that's what I smell."

"Stow it," Jason said. "You probably smell like bubble bath

Barbie to them, pretty boy." He turned to Trieu. "Can you take care of it?"

"Of course."

Joo-Chan, Youn-Chul, and Rachel went to the cab and started the engine. With much lurching, grinding, and backfiring, they finally got the truck turned around and up to highway speed.

Jason sat cross-legged in the middle of the floor. He looked at each person in turn. Garth leaned on the pile of green duffels at the front of the truck and appeared to drop instantly to sleep. Trieu held a blanket open to shield Chun-Mi as she changed into a loose-fitting dress from Trieu's pack. Chris sat against the wood wall of the truck bed. He seemed pensive, or maybe just bored. Lewis fired up his PDA and handed it to the little Korean boy, who held it tentatively, his eyes wide. The child put the device down but squatted over it, inspecting it closely. He pointed to the screen and uttered a string of toddler words. Lewis nodded.

The white-haired old woman leaned back on the duffel bags beside Garth. She looked like a pygmy next to him. She and the boy were the only ones who seemed to have allowed the cannibalistic Americans into their personal space. The others were huddled together on the opposite wall of the truck. The elderly couple sat cross-legged, watching warily. Every now and then the woman would be wracked with a coughing fit. The pregnant woman's husband watched where his wife was changing clothes.

The one-time death camp guard simply stared straight ahead. Aside from rubbing his wrists when the cuffs had come off, he hadn't expressed much life or even changed his expression since the raid. He had a long face and high cheekbones. What had those black eyes witnessed?

Jason heard a knocking on the window to the cab. Rachel pointed forward. He moved to where he could see through the windshield—just in time to see two military Jeeps pass by on the deserted highway. "Oh, great."

Rachel put her fingers to her cheek as if talking on the phone. Jason nodded and dug out a helmet from the duffels.

"I saw them, Rachel," he said into the helmet microphone.

"Yeah," she answered into her radio. "I'm thinking they're going to see that truck on the side of the road a few miles up."

"Absolutely. I didn't see if anybody in those Jeeps noticed us. You think they did?"

All the English speakers in the back of the truck were suddenly paying attention to Jason's conversation.

"I don't think we can assume they didn't," Rachel said. "Maybe the vodka will fool them into thinking the prisoners are on foot going across country."

Jason blew out a sigh. "Maybe. Well, there's nothing to be done but just keep driving like innocent motorists. Keep Joo-Chan calm. Don't let him speed up or run checkpoints or anything. Just keep me posted."

"Roger that, Jason."

Something about her tone made him look at her through the glass. Since that slap a few nights ago, she'd been all business with him, if she spoke to him at all. But this was a more friendly tone. She was looking at him quietly, her beautiful face partially hidden behind a scarf. But he could see enough to catch her quick, fragile smile. He smiled back warmly, thinking brotherly thoughts.

He put the helmet away and turned to his team. "We just passed a couple of army Jeeps. They're probably going to stop at the truck."

"Maybe not, though," Lewis said wistfully. "Maybe they'll just go on past."

Garth *harrumph*ed.

"Maybe," Jason said, "but we can't count on it. Lewis, fire up the radio."

Gil-Su looked from face to face. "What happens if they find the truck?"

"Well, probably they get on their radio," Jason said.

Chris winced. "Which is bad."

"And they'll report the prisoners are missing," Jason said. "If we're lucky, no one will figure out which prisoners they're talking about, or maybe they'll assume they're just wandering through Genghis Khan-land hiding in some yurts somewhere. Hopefully," Jason said, knowing it was a lame thought even as he spoke it, "they'll chalk it up to the effects of vodka and all go on to more important things."

"Yeah, right," Lewis said. He turned his back to the group and initiated the call over the satellite radio.

Gil-Su leaned toward Jason. "And if they don't?"

"If they don't," Jason said, "if they figure out that these prisoners aren't just shoplifters, they might alert the whole nation, fortify the borders, and call out the dogs. They might begin aerial searches and set up roadblocks. Worst-case scenario, those soldiers we passed will figure out what happened and will remember our little truck. We could pick up a helicopter escort in about ten minutes, and when we get to Hailar we could find lots of guns waiting for us. Maybe we're all tried for spying and assaulting policemen and they execute us on the spot."

"Come on, Jason," Garth said, "don't sugarcoat it. We can take it."

Gil-Su looked at Garth with an expression of such fear that Jason had to hide a smile.

"But," Jason said, trying to sound optimistic, "I don't think that will happen. I think they'll find the truck and discover the missing prisoners, but I think it will be awhile before they figure out what went down. And it will take even longer for them to guess we'd be headed back into Hailar and not any other direction." He nodded resolutely. "We'll be okay."

Garth clapped Gil-Su on the shoulder and gave him a firm thumbs-up. Gil-Su didn't look convinced, but he let it drop for the moment.

Jason heard Chimp's voice on the sat radio. Lewis handed him the handset. "Gandalf, Gandalf, this is Strider. Good to hear your voice. Over."

As they waited out the delay, Trieu knelt beside Jason. "I need to examine Chun-Mi and her baby. Are we going to be stopping soon or should I do it here?"

He sighed. "Not sure yet. Things could get crazy in a minute, or it could be quiet for hours. Do all you can while we're moving."

She touched his hand. "All right. Also, I don't like the sound of that woman's coughing. Aunt. I suspect tuberculosis. I have a skin test I can run on her but it will take forty-eight hours to read."

He nodded and stroked her cheek. "Sounds g—"

Chimp's voice cut him off. "Strider, Gandalf. Good to hear you again, too. Please advise your status. Over."

"Gandalf, Strider. We have retrieved the Ring. Repeat, we have retrieved the Ring. We are heading back toward Isengard and hope to swing down and cross the Misty Mountains—tonight, if possible. The Ring is in good condition. Tired and confused by us and a little sick, but together and glad to be heading toward the Shire." He and Lewis shared a smile. "Be advised that Saruman's forces may soon discover that the Ring is missing. We passed some of them a few minutes ago and they may figure things out pretty quick. Can you be watching and listening? And maybe looking for alternate ways home? Over."

Jason watched Trieu retrieve her medical kit and put a thermometer in Chun-Mi's mouth and a stethoscope to her belly. After listening intently in several spots, Trieu put the stethoscope around her neck and reached into her kit and pulled out a white device that looked like a jumbo-sized PDA with a handle and a coiled cord. The top half was dominated by a rectangular view screen. The bottom half had a small keyboard and a trackball. Trieu powered on the screen and uncoiled the white cable, which terminated at a rounded T-shaped wand.

"Copy that, Strider," Chimp said over the radio. "Copy that you have retrieved the Ring. Well done! Galad—well, um, she told me I could call her 'the White Lady.' Can you believe it? Anyway, the White Lady will flip when she hears it. Copy also that they may be on to you. Will do a little looking around and let you know when I get something figured out. Over."

"Gandalf, Strider. Roger that, thanks. We're not out of this yet. But hopefully in a day or two we'll be sitting in Bag End enjoying a sunset over the South Farthing. Out." Jason handed the handset back to Lewis. "He'll be scratching his head for days over that one."

"No kidding," Lewis said. "For a minute there I thought you were going to ask for prayer from the Valar."

Jason's eyebrows rose. "Okay, you've just gone *Silmarillion* on me, bro, and left me way behind."

"No worries," Lewis said, stowing the phone away. "It happens."

Chris moved closer. "Did he just say you could call Eloise a white lady? Did I miss something? That's about the last thing I'd ever call her."

"Duh, Chris," Lewis said, "it's from *The Lord of the Rings*. Galadriel is the White Lady, a ring bearer, Lady of the Golden Wood."

Chris rolled his eyes. "Whatever, Lewis. 'The White Lady,' what a crock. Next time call me 'The Black Man,' why don't you?"

"Maybe I will."

Jason crawled over to where Trieu was running the wand across Chun-Mi's belly. The small screen showed a gyrating gray scale image that shifted between almost recognizable patterns and a feeling of tunneling downward and upward. "What is this?"

"Ultrasound," Trieu said, concentrating on the screen. She brought the wand down Chun-Mi's left side and pressed it gently into her flesh. "There you are, little one."

Jason saw a perfectly formed baby on the screen in grainy black and white. The child had both its hands near its chin.

"Whoa," he said, shaking his head.

Trieu pressed a key and the image froze briefly, then went live again.

"What'd you do?" Jason asked.

"Took a photo. I'll come back later and do some measurements to see how far along their baby is."

She moved her finger across the trackball, and the image on the screen enlarged. Parts of the baby seemed to go transparent, then reappear as if dropping in and out of dimension. The images scrambled and became incomprehensible to Jason. Then suddenly he was staring at a fluttering oval that leaped and squeezed rhythmically.

"Ew," he said. "What's that?"

Trieu froze the image again. "That, my fiancé, is the baby's heart."

"Whoa."

Trieu looked over Jason's head. "Gil-Su, will you tell Chun-Mi her baby's heart is beating strong?"

Gil-Su brought Chun-Mi's husband close and leaned beside Chun-Mi. He spoke to them in Korean. Relief spread across their faces. They grasped each other's hands.

Trieu showed them the screen. They looked at it in bewilderment. But then Chun-Mi gasped and she pointed at the image, chattering to Bum-Ji. He looked closely, and finally recognition popped onto his face.

Trieu moved the wand across Chun-Mi's belly. "Ask her if she'd like to know the baby's gender."

When Gil-Su had translated, Bum-Ji looked stunned. He said something in Korean.

Gil-Su smiled. "Bum-Ji wants to know how you can know such a thing."

Chun-Mi spoke to Bum-Ji, rubbing her belly with her hands.

"Chun-Mi says you can tell us if you want, but she is positive she's going to have a daughter."

Trieu smiled broadly. "I will look."

Jason watched the screen as if unable not to. The black-and-white images morphed grotesquely, moving through bones and organs as if they were made of liquid. Finally the image settled on two parallel white bones joined into what appeared to be a pelvis, though the whole thing was upside down. He tilted his head. "What am I looking at?"

Trieu looked at Gil-Su. "Do they have a name for their child?"

"Yes," he said, "but only a girl name: Shin-Hwa. It means God's peace. It is a very bold name because *Shin,* the word for 'God,' is outlawed in North Korea."

"Well," Trieu said, snapping another picture, "tell her Shin-Hwa is beautiful."

When Bum-Ji heard it, joyful tears sprang from his eyes. Chun-Mi's smile was more knowing.

Jason heard a knock on the cab window. He went to his duffel and donned his helmet. "Whatcha got?"

Rachel pointed forward. "Coming up on Hailar."

"Roger that. How does it look?"

"So far so good."

Jason watched through the windshield as Joo-Chan drove them into the city. Ahead of them on the highway, a military truck full of soldiers standing in the back approached slowly but turned a corner.

With the team on edge, ready to jump out chunking flashbang grenades, they wove through downtown Hailar. Traffic appeared normal. They passed a billboard advertising, of all things, Coca-Cola. They saw many Chinese soldiers, but no more than they'd seen at any other time. A three-wheeled motorcycle passed them on the right.

"It doesn't look like anybody's sounded the alarm here," Jason said over the radio.

"I agree," Rachel said.

Jason nodded to her through the glass. "You guys be on the lookout for a used car dealership. When you spot one, let's pull over a block or so away."

"Roger that," Rachel said. "You going to get us some new wheels, boss?"

"Our truck's fine," he said. "But I'm thinking of an outrider for our point man." He leaned over to Chris. "You ride a motorcycle?"

Chris blew through his lips. "Duh."

"Hey, chief," Garth said, leaning on one elbow. "I thought you wanted to keep a low profile. You send blondie here out on a motor scooter, and I think you're going to turn a few heads."

"I know," Jason said. "This is for when we get out of town. I'm claustrophobic without eyes over the horizon, you know? Before I get too close to that border, I want to know what's there."

"Gotcha, chief." Garth leaned back, his head resting on his interlaced fingers, and whistled Dixie.

Oh, I wish I was in the land of cotton. Old times there are not forgotten. Look away! Look away! Look away! Dixie Land.

CHAPTER 20

You Shall Not Pass

"I don't like this."

Chris elbowed aside the tall grass to keep the twin-engine airplane in view with his binoculars. "I don't like it one bit."

Rachel lay in the grass five feet to his left. She peered over the ridge toward Mongolia with a second pair of binoculars. "You think it's a military plane?"

"Well," Chris said, sweeping the glasses along the horizon, "it's been by every twenty minutes for the last hour. Either it's really lost or it's flying patrol."

Rachel grimaced. "And that convoy that passed us thirty minutes ago, they probably weren't just a military parade, huh?"

"I'm thinking you're right."

It was late afternoon. They were back on the Mongol grasslands ten miles north of the border with Mongolia. Chris and Rachel had left the others with the truck in a rare stand of trees and had come out here in their newly purchased rider motorcycle to scout the way.

"On the plus side, though," Chris said, zooming in on something ahead and to their right, "I've seen two lifers on our little trip."

"Lifers?"

"Yeah, birds I've never seen in my life. That Siberian crane we saw by the pond and a Pechora pipit just a minute ago. Unbelievable finds. They're worth the trip no matter how you look at it."

Rachel shook her head. "You're weird, Chris."

"Why, thank you. That means a lot coming from you." He crawled backward off the edge of the ridge.

Rachel scooted after him. "What's that supposed to mean?"

"Nothing." He strode to the motorcycle and got on. "Just that—" He shut his mouth with apparent effort. When he spoke again it was obvious this wasn't what he'd been about to say. "Just that I'm glad to have some time alone with you. That's–that hasn't happened in awhile and. . .I like it."

"Hmph," she said, hand on one hip. She stepped into the passenger outrider and put her helmet on. "For what it's worth, Chris," she said softly, "I like it, too."

Chris smiled, an incredible smile that probably broke hearts far and wide, and kicked the motorcycle to life. "Come on, sweetie," he said, "let's go be stupid tourists."

He popped the clutch and sped across the Mongolian highlands like Steve McQueen in *The Great Escape*. He took the ridge at about fifty, sending them airborne. Though she squealed in protest and clung to the sidecar with white knuckles, Rachel couldn't deny she was having fun.

They rejoined the narrow dirt road and rode toward Mongolia, kicking up a plume of ancient brown dust. They crested a hill and almost plowed into the largest flock of sheep Rachel had ever seen. There must've been three hundred unshorn sheep, bleating miserably. They moved more like a swarm than a flock—bunched up here, straggling to catch up there, flowing in a semiaware group consciousness. Three shepherds on hardy brown horses rode into view. Rachel waved and Chris motored on.

Minutes later something glistened on the horizon to the southwest: a lake. Rachel guessed that lake was across the border into Mongolia. They approached a village at a crossroads. Mud homes and thatched roofs standing in a clump like toadstools.

Chris stopped a hundred yards from the village. A dark green military truck stood across the road ahead. Green-clad soldiers with assault rifles manned the roadblock.

"What do you think?" he asked Rachel. "You going to be Chinese or American this time?"

"Uh, Trevor!" she said, rattling her head as if appalled. "Like, I totally can't believe you just asked me that. As *if!*"

Chris smiled and twisted the accelerator.

The soldiers held their hands up for them to stop. Chris complied. There were four soldiers at this checkpoint, though many more milled around beyond it. All wore plain green pants, long-sleeved green shirts, and the green cloth cap with a red star. Two stood in front of the truck. Two others watched from off to the side. One of those two wore a shin-length heavy green jacket with brown fur at the collar. He leaned against a Jeep and watched.

The front two men approached the motorcycle. One with pinched lips and tiny ears pointed back up the road and spoke in Chinese. Rachel could understand him perfectly well: "You can't come this way. Road closed. Turn around and go back."

Chris took his helmet off and handed it to the soldier. "Thanks, dude!" He elongated the word in perfect surfer boy fashion: *dyood.* "Whew, that was rad, huh, babe? No way! How fast you think we were goin' when we caught air? Thought we were gonna be pasted."

The soldier shoved Chris's helmet back toward him and spoke in Chinese with agitation: "You stupid American, I'm not your servant. Get out of here now. Go on, get back to your decadent country before you taint me."

Rachel had to commend the guy for knowing the party line—at least in front of the officers. She noticed, as she was sure Chris did, the line of military vehicles traveling southwest directly toward the distant lake and the border with Mongolia. She also spotted a white command tent flapping just behind the mud homes of the village. She caught a glimpse of officers leaning over a table consulting a map. Overhead she heard the engines of the patrol plane. When it passed over, she could see the red star under the wings. The man in the long coat stood and walked toward them.

She took her helmet off and swished her brown hair around voluptuously for the soldiers. Then she smacked Chris on the arm. "Trevor! Like, can't you see we're not exactly welcome here? Can't you totally even read a map? I swear, I am never going anywhere with you again. 'Come to China with me, Heather. It'll be fun.' You're such a loser." She smiled sweetly to the closest soldier, fluffing her hair. "Hey, army dude, I am like so, so, so, so, so sorry we crashed your war game thingie. Could we just, like, go back to our hotel now?" She waved a tiny wave and lifted one shoulder. "Bye-bye, now." She put her helmet on and smacked Chris again. "Move it, Trevor!"

"All right, all right, Heather. Don't go into one of your 'episodes.' "

As Chris turned the cycle around, Rachel heard one soldier comment to the other: "Lucky stiff. Wish she'd stay with me."

"With you?" the other one said. "Your mother would beat you. Besides, Americans will corrupt you."

"If I was with her, I'd be corrupted gladly!"

Rachel turned to them with a suggestive smile, one eyebrow raised as if in challenge. "Bye-bye, boys." She blew them a kiss and Chris sped away.

* * *

"So you think the whole border is guarded?"

Chris nodded at Jason. "I think maybe. The part here is, at least. My guess is that somebody figured out who got away and where they'd probably head."

They were back at the truck in its spot under a stand of Mongolian Scotch pine trees. In the green distance to the north, thirty horsemen rode left to right across the prairie. Perhaps those were true tourists. The sun was sinking in the west. They had about an hour left until sundown. Jason stood at the front of the truck with a map laid on the hood. Chris, Rachel, Garth, Lewis, and Gil-Su stood around looking at it. Trieu was in the back of the truck doing her exams on Chun-Mi and Aunt. The others sat under the trees or dozed in the back of the truck. The motorcycle sat in the shade beside the truck. The temperature was beginning to drop, but it was still pleasant outside.

Jason folded his arms. With one hand he pinched his bottom lip thoughtfully. "So you think this is a new thing. Those guys at the checkpoint didn't appear to have been there for months?"

"No," Chris said, "their uniforms were clean and creased. The tent we saw was bright white. The trucks had laid over new grass on the roads."

"Plus," Rachel said, "the soldiers seemed a little jumpy. Guys who stay at a post like that for more than a few days get pretty laid back."

"Yeah, and that air patrol," Chris said. "No way they keep that thing up at that rate all the time way out here. I mean, why?"

Jason nodded. "Well, unfortunately that fits with what Chimp's telling me, too. His Icarus satellite is showing large military deployments all through our neck of the woods." He pointed at the map. "Along China's border with Mongolia, with Russia north of here, and along major roadways. Contacts on the ground report new checkpoints on roads plus old checkpoints manned and serious." He sighed. "Yeah, I'm thinking they're on the lookout for us right now. And it would be a major embarrassment for China if these refugees suddenly showed up on Seoul TV."

Trieu hopped out of the truck. She walked to them, stripping off rubber gloves. She looked fatigued.

"How are they doing?" Jason asked.

"I believe Aunt has tuberculosis," Trieu said. "Probably contracted it in prison. I've given her a purified protein derivative test. In forty-eight hours we'll know for sure. I'm going to test all of them to be safe."

"Ew," Lewis said. "Tuberculosis. That's like consumption, isn't it? Doesn't it usually kill you?"

She gave a tired smile. "You've been watching too many old Westerns, Lewis. Today we have something called antibiotics. It is a common disease in such places, so I brought plenty of isoniazid."

"And what about Chun-Mi?" Jason asked. "Weren't you going to do a better exam once we got stable?"

"Yes, I examined her. She is complaining of occasional contractions, but I believe them to be Braxton Hicks contractions. False labor. She is not dilated. The cervix is not effaced. And the baby has not dropped, but it has turned. Measurements on the ultrasound show a baby at thirty-eight weeks of development. This baby could come at any time."

"Whoa," Lewis said. "You mean she could have a baby now? Today?"

"Yes," Trieu said, brushing her hair aside, "she could go into labor today, I suppose."

Lewis looked worried. "Wouldn't we have to get her to a hospital then?"

Garth slapped him upside the head. "Relax, kid. Women have been squattin' to have their babies for thousands of years. Plus, we've got Trieu!"

"Well," Trieu said, her hand finding Jason's out of sight from the others, "let's just get her to South Korea in the next two days and let a hospital there handle it."

Everyone looked at Jason.

Trieu noticed. "What?"

"Well," Jason said hesitantly, "we may not be able to get out as quickly as we thought."

"Why not?"

"It seems the Chinese dragon has decided to rouse itself and curl around its borders to protect its treasure."

"Ooh, Jason," Rachel said, "going poetic."

"Hmph," Jason said. "Anyway, Trieu, Chris and Rachel found increased military presence at the border where we were hoping to cross tonight. Plus aerial patrols. And Chimp says the same thing is happening all along China's border up here."

"But can't we just go at night?" Trieu said. "We'll turn off our lights or buy a wagon and go across country away from any roads."

Garth bobbed his head. "Not a bad idea."

"There's a lake that straddles the border, isn't there?" Chris said. "We saw it. Why don't we rig a raft and cross that way?"

"Don't listen to him, Jason," Rachel said. "He just wants to go to that lake for the birding."

Chris looked at her, astonished. She mirrored his look with mock astonishment. Lewis laughed.

"Okay, you guys," Jason said. "I know we all want to get out of here and get these people safe. But I'm thinking maybe it would be better if we just lie low for awhile."

They considered it in silence. A bird flitted into the treetops and Chris's gaze went there instantly. The thirty horsemen had ridden far off to the right.

"Well," Trieu said, "how long would you want to wait?"

Jason looked across the darkening horizon to the southwest. "I don't know. Three days maybe. Just long enough for these new guards to get bored at their posts and become convinced that they missed whatever action there was to have. Then we use one of your ideas and sneak across at night."

Nobody looked happy with that plan.

"Look," Jason said, "we'll call Chimp and ask for advice. But if he asks my opinion, I'm going to say I'd rather wait three days and get them there safely than rush it now and maybe get them *and us* captured."

Chris and Garth nodded grimly. The others were at least listening.

"We'll have to find a place to lie low," Jason said. "You guys think this stand of trees is enough to hide us from prying eyes?"

Garth looked around dubiously. "Nope."

"What about that big barn we passed coming into Hailar?" Lewis said. "Maybe we could get the truck inside it."

Gil-Su lifted his hand. "Jason, if I might suggest something."

"Sure."

"I maintain two safe houses around Hailar. One inside the city with a Korean family, and the other a farmhouse on the far outskirts owned by a Chinese brother. We use them when refugees must rest before making the final journey into Mongolia. Would one of those be helpful?"

Jason's eyebrows rose. "That would be fantastic, Gil-Su!" He thought about it. "I'd rather not go back into town if we don't have to. Can you take us to the one on the outskirts?"

"Of course."

"Great," Jason said. "Let's do it."

CHAPTER 21

SAFE HOUSE

"How's it look?"

Trieu lowered her binoculars and sank back into the wheat. "All clear."

Jason knelt in the moist earth beside Trieu's sniper rifle and helmet. He and Trieu were at the top of the low hill above the mud-walled farmhouse that was their safe house. From here they could see for miles in every direction.

To the southwest the horizon was hazy from the industrial pollution over Hailar proper, fifteen miles away. In every other direction there was open farmland in which wheat, rape, potatoes, and corn grew. Misty low hills rose here and there in the distance, and lines of birch crossed narrow irrigation canals. It was late morning and the sun was finally beginning to burn off the overnight chill. Birds chattered and bugs droned. Sounds of workers hacking and plowing the fields floated on the musty breeze. If it weren't for the brown farmers in their conical straw hats spotting the landscape, it could've been a Kansas farm bottom.

Trieu glanced at Jason before resuming her vigilant watch of the horizons. "Are you checking on me, Jason? Did you think I'd fallen asleep?"

"No way." He smiled warmly. "I never worry about you. You're the most reliable member of the team."

She raised a scolding finger at him. "No fair sweet-talking the person on watch."

"Oh, yeah? Then what about this?" He took her face in his hands and kissed her deeply.

She returned it for a long moment before pushing away. "Jason Kromer, I'm surprised at you. If you caught any of the others doing this on watch, you'd have them running fifty laps of the Great Wall of China. Now leave me alone and let me do my job."

Jason backed away. "I never argue with a woman with a gun." He winked. "I've got my radio on my belt, so just call if there's trouble."

"Jason." She had her back to him.

"Yes?"

"I love you."

He felt himself smiling like a donkey. "I love you, too, Trieu." Just saying it sent a cold shock down his back. He wanted another kiss. Instead, he stood and headed back toward the farmhouse.

The homesite was a brown spot in a sea of green crops. The house was rectangular and had a peaked roof of tan thatch. There was one doorway, though no door. The "yard" just outside this portal was packed earth within which stood four poles holding a light pallet platform six feet off the ground. Here new thatch was drying in the sun. The pallet also appeared to be a general storage area for the farmer's junk. A two-wheeled wagon sat out here, standing diagonally like a mobile seesaw.

Garth and Ki-Won, the little Korean boy, were playing around the wagon. Ki-Won chased Garth, who fell to the ground whenever the boy touched him. Gil-Su watched them from the doorway, laughing and urging Ki-Won on.

Jason spotted three men making their way through the wheat field toward him on his right. It was the two teenagers, Joo-Chan and Youn-Chul, and the old farmer, Han Huaiju, whose home this was. Joo-Chan wore blue jeans, Nike sneakers, and a black long-sleeved T-shirt. Youn-Chul wore tan pants and a brown button-up shirt. Huaniju wore loose beige pants and a white cotton shirt, pleated all around. On his head he wore a wide-brimmed straw hat and carried a thick walking stick Jason would not want to be hit with. Though Huaniju was shorter even than some of the North Koreans, he'd already shown them he knew how to bust a move, Kenpo karate style.

Youn-Chul spoke Korean to Jason in a plaintive voice. It sounded like a request. Joo-Chan added something in a more urgent tone. Jason looked over at Gil-Su, who walked toward him to translate.

This was a good thing, since in the time they'd been staying here, Jason's Korean vocabulary had grown to all of four phrases: *ahnnyong haseyo* (good morning), *gamsa hamnida* (thank you), *ahndwae* (no—mostly used for Ki-Won), and *juseyo* (give that back, please—also used for Ki-Won, as when he had found Rachel's rucksack and had run around the house clutching a flashbang grenade).

Gil-Su asked Youn-Chul what he'd said, but Huaniju interrupted him, speaking sharply in Chinese and gripping his stout staff with both hands. The staff vibrated as if it wanted to fly into a world-class whuppin' on the boys and Huaniju was struggling to hold it back. The teenagers backed away. Then Huaniju lowered his staff and laughed in gap-toothed joy. He raised a finger like Confucius and proceeded to give Jason a profound lesson on. . . something. Jason turned to Gil-Su helplessly.

"He says these boys don't know the first thing about farming,"

Gil-Su said. "He says they'd rather be fishing in the creek than helping him in the field." Huaniju continued and then Gil-Su translated. "He says he'd be glad to offer his 'rod of discipline' to help drive the foolishness from their hearts."

Huaniju laughed with evil glee.

"Um. . . ," Jason said. "Can we tell him no thanks?"

Gil-Su shrugged. "It *is* biblical. Might do the boys some good."

"Yeah, I'm sure it would. But I'm thinking Miss Eloise wouldn't take kindly to us getting our refugees beaten up." Jason smiled warily at Huaniju. "Maybe another time."

Huaniju nodded and raised his staff at Youn-Chul.

"Wait!" Gil-Su intervened, quickly explaining to the farmer.

Huaniju's face fell dramatically. He leveled a "you'll regret this" finger at Jason and tore off through the wheat field, muttering in Chinese.

Youn-Chul and Joo-Chan said something in Korean that sounded like "Whew, thanks!" Then they restated their case to Jason.

"Ah," Gil-Su said when they had finished. He stared into space.

"What is it?" Jason asked.

Gil-Su sighed. "They want your help."

"Okay."

"No, it is not that simple," Gil-Su said. "They want your team to use your weapons to rescue a friend of theirs."

"Oh," Jason said, folding his arms. "Who is this friend and where is he?"

The teenagers stood by nervously, trying to read Jason's reply in his tone and body language. Down in the yard, Garth tossed Ki-Won into the air again and again. The boy laughed as if he'd never laughed before.

"It is not a he," Gil-Su said, "but a she. Her name is Sun-Hye, Park Sun-Hye. She is a teenage girl of some beauty. She and her family fled North Korea the day before Youn-Chul's family. The boys befriended her in their short time together. Unfortunately," he said, staring at the waving wheat, "she and her family were captured in the raid that caused us to flee. The boys feel sure they saw Sun-Hye sold into prostitution. They wish for you to go back to that place and free her so she can come to South Korea with them."

Jason whistled. "Hoo-boy. They don't ask much, do they? And I don't suppose this girl is being held anywhere around here, is she?"

"No," Gil-Su said, looking grim. "She is probably still in a village very near the North Korean border. Probably kept in a cell. Possibly chained there."

The teenagers could tell things weren't going well. Joo-Chan said something to Gil-Su, but he shook his head.

Jason was just glad Eloise wasn't around to hear their plea. An innocent girl held as someone's sex slave, hired out to anyone who wanted her, separated from her family—all because she wanted to escape the horrors of North Korea? Oh, yeah, Eloise would be all over that. She'd want to send the whole team to the edge of North Korea for this girl—possibly endangering not only the team but also the refugees they'd already rescued.

"Look, Gil-Su," he said with a sigh, "I don't think we can do this. I feel for this poor girl, you have to believe me. But we just can't this time. We can't rescue every abused person in the world, though all of us would like to. We don't even know where this girl is or how we'd get there or get her out. Then she probably wouldn't want to leave without her family, so would we have to go find them, too?"

It felt wrong to say this, even though he knew he was talking sense. "Look, maybe when we get you and the others safely into a third country we can talk to Eloise about it and see what she says. We can get reprovisioned and could reinsert somewhere closer to the action. I just can't see us taking a two-day train trip across China with our weapons and gear." He shook his head. "I'm sorry, Gil-Su, I really am. Maybe in a week or two. We'll just have to see what Eloise says."

Gil-Su put his hand on Jason's shoulder. "I understand, my brother. Don't let it burden you. We will continue to pray for the Lord to protect her. Let us first concentrate on getting these to safety. I agree."

Jason nodded but didn't feel any better.

Gil-Su explained to the teenagers. They didn't take it well. Youn-Chul got in Jason's face and complained bitterly. His voice rose from anger to frustration, and finally to desperation. He pushed Jason in the chest, then pushed him again.

"What's wrong with him?" Jason asked, not taking his eyes off Youn-Chul. "I thought he just met this girl, so why's he trying to fight me over her?"

"I've seen it before," Gil-Su said. "Refugees meeting and linking up romantically or in strong friendships even after knowing each other only briefly. I think it has to do with them being in similar situations and in great distress. I will try to calm him down."

Gil-Su put a hand on Youn-Chul's arm, but Youn-Chul knocked it off and spat angry words.

Garth set Ki-Won down and walked toward the disturbance. Members of Youn-Chul's family came out of the farmhouse at the commotion.

Joo-Chan and Gil-Su tugged at Youn-Chul's arms, but he pulled free, screaming at Jason.

Jason stood ready, one foot in front of the other, legs shoulder width apart, hands resting lightly on his thighs.

Chris and Myong-Chol exited the house. When they saw what was happening, both strode forward.

Youn-Chul swung between angry cries and crying anger, and back again. Gil-Su spoke calm words to him, but they weren't penetrating. Youn-Chul's fists clenched and unclenched. He scuffled in the dirt, flattening wheat and nearly stumbling.

Over Youn-Chul's shoulder, Jason saw Huaniju running toward them, his staff held above his shoulder like a javelin. Things were going to get serious in about fifteen seconds.

Youn-Chul finally summoned the courage to launch an attack at Jason. He punched at Jason's face.

The punch was halfhearted and off target, but it gave Jason what he'd been waiting for. He turned the punch aside with an inward block then grabbed Youn-Chul's wrist and swept his leg behind the boy's legs. He went down with a solid thump. Jason followed him down and pinned Youn-Chul's arm behind his body—just as Huaniju arrived.

"It's okay!" Jason said to Gil-Su. "Tell him it's under control."

Gil-Su translated. Huaniju's bottom lip jutted. *Another opportunity lost! What's a guy got to do around here to get some action?*

By now the whole group had gathered around Jason and Youn-Chul.

"Jason!" Rachel said, pushing through the crowd. "What did you do to him?"

"It wasn't him," Garth said. "The kid got mad about something, and Jason took him down nice and easy. Ish."

Grandmother bore a hole through the group with her voice. She was ticked in any language. Everybody let her pass. She stood over Youn-Chul and demanded something of him. He answered petulantly. That sent her off. She harangued him with a force Jason never would've suspected her capable of. She turned to Jason and he thought he was in for it, too. But her tone changed and she bowed to him three times. She grabbed Youn-Chul's ear—another universal sign—and Jason released his arm. Grandmother pulled Youn-Chul "out back," her face hard and the teenager stumbling behind her, lobe first.

Chris was at Jason's shoulder. "What was that all about?"

"Oh, it's all right," Jason said, brushing himself off. "He's got a friend being held back at the North Korea border, and he wants us to go get her."

"Oh," Chris said.

"Yeah," Jason said. "When I told him we needed to think about him and his family first, he kind of lost it. Poor guy. I can totally understand."

The crowd was dispersing.

"Wait a sec, you guys," Jason said. "Firebrand team and Gil-Su, stick around a minute, please."

They turned back toward him.

"Lewis," Jason said, "would you please go ask Trieu to put her helmet on? I've got my radio. She can listen in while she keeps watch."

"Okay." Lewis took off up the hill.

While they waited for his return, they could hear Grandmother's voice as she lectured Youn-Chul.

Lewis bounded down the hillside. "She's on."

"Thanks, Lewis." Jason clipped his microphone to his T-shirt. "Okay, here's what I'm thinking. We've been here three days. Chimp says the Chinese aren't flying the aerial patrol on our border anymore and that the military buildup on the borders has ceased and in some places they're standing down and going back to base. Radio traffic has lessened, and there seems to be a general relaxing going on. I'm thinking we could try a crossing into Mongolia as early as tonight."

That excited the group.

"However," he said quickly, "the more I think about it, the less I like the idea of crossing that way. We'd have to ditch the truck and walk something like fifteen miles to the nearest town where we could find transportation. No way Chun-Mi could walk that far— or Grandmother or Ki-Won or Aunt, in her condition. Maybe we could carry them. Maybe we could take some carts like Huaniju's here. But there's still the increased military presence on this border and the real chance of capture if we go that way."

Ki-Won ran to Garth. "Hey there, little buddy," Garth said. "Want to ride on papa bear's shoulders?" The boy smiled and up he went. When he was seated on high, he patted Garth's scalp like a skin drum. "So," Garth said, not even wincing, "what do you suggest, chief?"

"Okay, look." Jason pulled out a map from his pants pocket. "We're here, northeast of Hailar. We could go south to Mongolia. Or. . ."—he slid his finger north—"we could go into Russia. The Trans-Siberian railway goes through Hailar. We get on in separate groups and just take the train all the way to Moscow if we want."

"Hmm," Chris said.

"Gil-Su," Rachel said, "are the false papers you got for the refugees good enough to get them by if we get stopped?"

"I believe they are," Gil-Su said slowly. "We have used the same person for visas and passports for years. Many others have safely carried them out of China. But," he said, his hands spreading, "most of them have never had to show their papers. We sneak across the border, remember? The false papers are only in case something goes wrong."

"Plus now they're looking for people on the borders," Rachel said. "I don't know, Jason."

Chris chewed his cheek. "What would we do with our guns? Just hold them in our laps?"

"We'd have to stash our gear somewhere," Jason said. "Maybe Huaniju could arrange to have it smuggled out to us in Russia in a few days."

They pawed the soil uneasily.

"Look, guys," Jason said, "it's a risk, I admit it. I hate the idea of leaving our weapons behind. But what's our first goal here? Isn't it to get these people out of China? They can't walk out; we've already established that. We could try to drive out, but how would we explain a truckload of Koreans in the back? Seems to me an elegant way out of this is just to let the Chinese drive us across the border in a train."

Jason's radio squelched. "What about the plane?" It was Trieu's voice.

239

"Say again, Trieu," Jason said.

"What about the plane that brought Gil-Su and Joo-Chan and our gear? Couldn't we just send them out a few at a time that way?"

Ki-Won wanted off Garth's shoulders. The boy touched down and immediately ran to Jason. He touched the radio pack on Jason's belt and turned the knobs. Jason moved the boy's hands away, an action that made Ki-Won mad. He squealed and ran toward Garth, his head lowered like a battering ram. He hit Garth just above the left knee.

"Ow!" Garth grabbed Ki-Won off his feet and held him to his chest. "Little buddy, we've got to work on that temper. Papa bear's leg doesn't like collisions, okay?"

Ki-Won's anger appeared to have dissipated. He looked at Jason's radio and spoke earnestly in his private language. It seemed like he was saying, "That's a very important thing over there, and I would like it for myself because I could do amazing things with it, so I'll just have to wait until none of them are watching. Heh-heh."

Jason chuckled in spite of himself. He tried to speak seriously into his microphone. "Good idea, Trieu. That might work. The only reason I can think of why it might not is that there is still all that military presence at the borders now. I'm thinking they might be suspicious of a private plane making multiple trips across the border."

The others nodded thoughtfully.

"Here's what let's do," Jason said. "Let's pray about this. Now, and then over the next few hours. Lewis, let's you and me call home and see what they suggest. At dinner we'll make our decision. Brother Gil-Su, would you lead us in prayer?"

"Of course." They held hands. "Mighty Savior, Lord of Creation, holder of lifetimes, thank You for Your blessings on our journey so far. Thank You again for helping these men and women rescue Your dear children who have come from North Korea. We ask for guidance just now. We ask for protection and supernatural aid.

Show us which path to take, then be our foot lamp as we go. All this we ask in the tremendous, wonder-working name of Jesus Christ, in whom there are ten thousand charms. Amen."

As they headed back toward the house, Lewis pulled something out of his pocket. He knelt before Ki-Won. "Come here, little guy. Look, look what Uncle Lewis has."

Jason looked in Lewis's hands. He held forward six pieces of flat pale wood, neatly cut and sanded down. Geometric shapes.

"Ney-moh!" Ki-Won said, snapping up the wooden square. *"Sey-moh! O-gyong! Dun-ga-mi!"* He clutched the square, the triangle, the pentagon, and the circle in his left fist and stared with consternation at the final shape.

"It's a trapezoid," Lewis said. "It was supposed to be a rectangle but I got a little off, so I decided to make it a trapezoid."

Ki-Won took it. *"Sa-gak-hyong?"* Then he said something in toddler talk that sounded like "What is this strange thing?"

"Trapezoid," Lewis said carefully. "Trapezoid."

"Traps?" Ki-Won said. His chubby cheeks spread in a smile of pure joy. "Traps!" He ran to Garth and laid the shapes down in the dirt, naming each one formally. Then he picked them up and began the process all over again.

Jason put an arm around Lewis. "You, my friend, have done a very good thing."

"Thanks, Jason. I saw the wood and the tools and just went for it."

"I didn't know you were such a carpenter," Jason said, releasing him.

"I'm not. But I thought, I can build computers and write the code that runs them; no way I can't handle wood shop. Besides," he said, watching Ki-Won play with the shapes, "the kid's been through a lot. The least I could do is give him some toys."

Jason nodded. "He's looking better now, isn't he? Those multivitamins Trieu's been giving him have done him some good. I thought he was really sick the first time I saw him. But now look at him."

"Yeah," Lewis said. "I guess prison's pretty hard on kids, huh?"

Chris came away from the entrance to the house, his ear cocked and his eyes scanning the sky, a severe look on his face.

"Chris, man," Jason said, "you've got to stop doing that. I always think you've heard a tank or attack helicopter coming. But then you always say, 'I think I heard a spotted nosefinch' or something. Come on, now, 'fess up: You heard a bird, didn't you?"

Chris's expression was smug. "Jason, one day a bird I spot will provide a clue that saves us all. You watch."

"Okay, buddy, I'll do that."

As the group moved toward the door, Chris caught Gil-Su's arm. "Word with you a minute, bro?"

CHAPTER 22

GOING BACK

"COULD YOU tell him what we're doing, Rev.?"

Gil-Su nodded at Chris and spoke to Myong-Chol, who was seated on a low wooden stool beneath the farmhouse's lone window.

Chris and Gil-Su sat on the dirt floor beside the stool, facing Myong-Chol. The one-room home was dark and cool, like a mud-walled refrigerator. The refugees and the Firebrand team lazed around in ones and twos. Lewis sat down in a corner and unfolded the arms of his "banshee" flying robot. Aunt lay sleeping on a pallet nearby. Most of the others were there, too. Everyone seemed about as intellectually stimulated at the moment as a person could ever be in any kind of waiting room.

Rachel noticed Chris, Gil-Su, and Myong-Chol sitting together and stepped closer. "Is this a private party or can anyone join?"

Chris patted his thighs. "There's always a seat for you here, sweetie."

Rachel sat next to him instead. "Thanks. This is fine."

Gil-Su turned to Chris. "He says he'll tell you whatever you want to know."

"Great," Chris said. "Can I just talk to him and you tell him what I've said?"

"Of course."

"Okay," he sighed. "Myong-Chol, I understand you were a soldier for North Korea. A guard of some kind?"

Gil-Su translated and Myong-Chol answered. "That's right," Gil-Su said in English. "I was a guard at Hoeryong Family Camp Number 22, a political prisoner camp. For eight years."

"Can you describe what the camp was like?"

Gil-Su kept the dialogue going with his translation. Chris asked about Myong-Chol's responsibilities, the prisoners, the punishments, the slave labor, and the practice surgeries performed by North Korea's budding military doctors. Myong-Chol answered every question, his tone flat.

Rachel followed the conversation with fascination. It went on for over an hour but never got boring. It was one thing to hear about the horrors of these supposedly nonexistent death camps from Eloise or to read about them in an information packet. But it was something else entirely to hear about them from someone who had seen it and been part of it.

"Christians are not allowed to look up," Gil-Su said, translating for Myong-Chol. "Because they believe in the existence of God in heaven, they are prohibited from looking up to the sky. From the moment they enter the camp they are forced to bow their necks. They must only look at the ground. This changes their posture so that they become disfigured and hunchbacked, with their necks at a ninety-degree angle from their back. When they die, their necks are broken and they are buried facedown so that even then they cannot look up to heaven."

Chris looked at Rachel, his handsome forehead creased. "Is it people of all religions who are treated like this," he asked Gil-Su, "or just Christians?"

"Mainly only Christians," Myong-Chol said, through Gil-Su.

"Why only Christians?"

"Because they are so defiant. The propaganda officers say it is because people who believe in Jesus favor America. That is enough to make people fear and despise it. But none of the Christians I ever saw in the camp were fond of America. Most had never heard of the place. The truth is that Christians are singled out because their spirits are strong and unbroken. This is not tolerated in the camps."

"It's unbelievable," Chris said.

"Christians in the camp are under constant pressure to renounce their faith. We guards were promoted if we could get a Christian to renounce Christianity. So we tortured them and singled them out for the hardest and most dangerous work. And not only the guards did this; their fellow prisoners did, too. Everyone informs on everyone else in the hope of getting favor with the guards.

"Many times we would call out all the prisoners," Myong-Chol continued, via Gil-Su. "We would line them up around the Christians and demand that they denounce Christ. If they did not, we would lay them on the ground, and all the prisoners would step on them until they died. Another time I heard of Christian prisoners being sent into an exhausted coal mine and the shaft exploded on top of them."

Chris dropped his face into his hands.

"One time," Myong-Chol said, "the officers told me and another guard to throw a Christian woman into a tall vat of fouled water—four meters deep. She could not swim and she could not reach the edge of the vat. The other prisoners stood around to let her die, but we had separated out eight Christians to see what they would do. One of them climbed into the vat to try to save her. He fell in and began to drown. One by one all the Christians tried to save the others, and one by one they fell in and died. We buried their bodies under our prize-winning fruit trees. Excellent fertilizer."

Gil-Su fell silent. Rachel noticed that the refugees had been listening to Myong-Chol's story. Chun-Mi and her husband, Bum-Ji, sat nearby. Chun-Mi caressed her belly and wept softly. Bum-Ji sheltered her under his arm.

Chris looked pained. He squeezed the skin of his forehead between his thumb and forefinger. "See," he said to Rachel and Gil-Su, "this is what I don't get. People dying for their religion. I just. . ." He scratched his scalp irritably. "I mean, how hard would it be just to *say* they'd renounced their faith but just *not?* You know? Just say it but not mean it. That way they could go on living but have an easier time of it. God's not going to mind. He understands."

Gil-Su smiled gently. "My brother, you of all people should see why they do not renounce the faith. You are a soldier, yes? You serve your country with honor?"

"I was in the military, yes."

"And what if you were captured? Would you betray your fellow soldiers? Would you betray your nation?"

Chris dropped his head. "No, and I know what you're trying to say, but this is different."

"No, no different. What if you were captured and they tortured you? What if they told you you would have an easy time of it if only you betrayed your nation? Surely you could be forgiven for doing so. Perhaps many others would die because of your betrayal. Perhaps your family would hear of your betrayal and lose face. Perhaps your fellow prisoners of war would lose hope. But they would understand. All who you betrayed would understand. Your officer, he would surely understand, would he not? After all, you can be expected to endure only so much. They will all understand that you had to betray them to make it a little easier on yourself."

"All right, preacher. I get it," Chris said, his eyes hard.

Myong-Chol asked Gil-Su something. As they conversed, Rachel tried to read Chris. Something was up in his heart. What they'd heard was disturbing, certainly, but it was how Chris had reacted to parts of it that had caught Rachel by surprise. Myong-Chol nodded his head deeply and looked at Chris. He touched Chris's knee and said something that sounded like an encouragement.

"He wants you to know he understands your questions," Gil-Su said to Chris. "He says he had the same ones himself. Why were these Christians so stubborn?"

Myong-Chol began to speak with passion, gesturing with both hands. Gone was the flat tone from before. Gil-Su translated on the fly.

"I began as a simple guard and driver. But I earned my rank and my reputation because of my treatment of these Christians. I decided I would make them my own little experiment. How much could they take before they cracked? Where was their breaking point? What was their trigger? Could I discover the secret to making them renounce their faith? I told myself I was doing this for the promotions. If I did especially well, I would be transferred to Pyongyang and sent to college! My career would be assured.

"But the truth was, I was doing it because they intrigued me. As for me, I had nothing I would die for. I would do things to *avoid* punishment, perhaps even die in combat for my country. But that was built on fear of what would happen to me if I did not. What was it these Christians had that would make them *accept* punishment rather than renounce their religion?

"I devised many tricks to fool them. I told a husband I would save his wife from execution if only he would renounce Jesus. He would not, so I executed them both. I told a mother I would send her child to a good party family if she renounced Christianity. She would not, so I executed her—but not before disemboweling her child before her eyes. I subjected Christians to intense torture and pain. To amputations, electric shocks, water torture, psychological stresses, pain, and deprivations of all kinds.

"I had some successes. Some did renounce Christ. With each one, I rose in rank. My reputation grew. Soon every Christian in the prison system was sent to me. I gathered around me the most ruthless guards. They called me Headhunter because I preferred to kill by decapitation with a sword. But my successes disgusted me. The ones who renounced their faith I killed in disappointment. Only the ones who would not recant interested me. I remember one—"

Gil-Su fell silent, waiting for Myong-Chol to continue. The former guard stared straight ahead, but even in the dim light Rachel could see his face flush. His eyes shone and finally tears dripped out. Gil-Su touched his shoulder, and Myong-Chol burst into violent sobs. Myong-Chol the Headhunter cried horrible tears for five minutes. Ki-Won walked up to Myong-Chol's face and wiped away a tear. Myong-Chol stroked the boy's hair clumsily and slowly the tears dried up.

"There was this one woman," Myong-Chol said through Gil-Su. "She reminded me of my sister. I tortured her severely to make her recant. Sixteen days I hung her from the ceiling on wrist rings. Another time I struck her on the back of the head with a club—so hard her right eye fell out of its socket. She stuffed it back in and kept talking to me about Jesus. 'You need Jesus. Jesus loves you. You are His child.' On and on she went. I tortured her family before her eyes. I amputated her feet without pain medicine. 'Run into His arms. Call on Jesus. He will save you. You can find peace.' She was driving me mad. Nothing I could do would stop her. Finally I bashed in her teeth with a stone. She choked on her own teeth, and I strangled her with my bare hands. I impaled her body on a pole and left it for the birds. I made all the prisoners and guards parade by.

"And yet even then I couldn't escape her. Her voice haunted my mind. 'You can be saved. He will receive you.' Her dead eyes followed me. Wherever I was in the camp I could feel her staring at me! Through walls; across miles. I burned her body and buried the ashes, but she pursued me in my dreams. 'Come to Jesus. You are not too far gone. Come to Him and find forgiveness.' *Forgiveness! Peace! Absolution!* How I craved them! But how could one like me ever deserve it? She had convinced me, you see. They all had. Here was a force greater than man, greater than anyone's ability to silence. Though I was in control, they held the true power.

"Rumor spread that the Headhunter had lost his mind. And," he said, rubbing his face, "I suppose I had. I executed the rest of the Christians without torture. Without even giving them the chance to renounce their faith. Partially because I was lost in madness, partially because I was afraid they *would* renounce Him. I couldn't let them do that. As soon as a new Christian came to me, I had him executed.

"I had to get away. That woman's voice pursued me. Her eyes were everywhere I went. I finally understood that she had been right and I had been wrong. I was killing the people I knew were standing in the truth. I was killing truth and preserving lies. It tore me apart.

"I found out that orders were coming down to remove me, to send me to DMZ duty. So I used my privileges as an officer to simply drive to the nearest train station and buy a ticket for Hyesan. There I used my rank to commandeer a boat, which I rode to China. And I have never returned.

"It took me a month, but I finally bribed enough people to track down a Christian missionary." He smiled at Gil-Su. "When I found him he thought I was going to take him prisoner in North Korea. He was quite surprised when I told him I knew Jesus Christ was the greatest power in the universe and I wanted him to help me find the forgiveness that. . .someone. . .had told me about. And," he smiled wanly, "here I am."

Chris hadn't looked up in ten minutes. Rachel had heard him sniffling, just as she and most of the others in the house had been.

Now he raised his face out of his arms. "Amazing." He wiped his cheeks. "You've finally found something worth dying for. I'm glad for you."

Gil-Su translated. Myong-Chol answered.

"Yes, worth dying for. But also worth living for. How many people know the power of Jesus Christ like I do? I have seen it. I have tested it. I have tried to break it. So who better than me to tell others about it? That's why I work with Gil-Su and Joo-Chan. That's why I stay in China near the border with North Korea. And that's why. . ." He paused in a stillness so complete he appeared catatonic. Finally he blinked. "And that's why I have to go back."

Chris stared in confusion at Gil-Su, who had translated. "Go back? Go back where?"

"Back to North Korea. Gil-Su, I'm going north when I should be going south."

Rachel felt her heart squeeze at the thought.

"Go back? No, Myong-Chol," Chris said, "you can't go back there. That's crazy. They'll kill you as soon as they see you. Look at the great work you're doing with Gil-Su. You can keep doing that for years. Think of all the people you can tell about Jesus. You go back and they'll kill you on the spot."

"Perhaps," Myong-Chol said, "but not before I can tell the guards that they can find forgiveness in Jesus, that He will welcome them, that He is truly God and greater than Kim Jong-Il and even Kim Il-Sung. And perhaps, if I am very lucky, they will send me to the concentration camp where I can tell many more people about Jesus Christ. Every day I live I will tell them. I will slice a gash from the edge of North Korea to as deep as my Lord wants me to tear. A gash of truth."

Gil-Su and Myong-Chol shared a tearful hug.

Chris sat back, his hands over his face. Rachel could see his chest heaving. He stood and rushed from the house. Rachel went after him.

He walked past Jason, Garth, and Lewis, who were eating MREs for lunch, and headed through the wheat up the hill toward Trieu.

"Chris, wait!" Rachel called. She caught up with him halfway up the hill. "Chris, honey, stop."

He stopped so abruptly she passed him. He held a firm look for a moment, but then his mouth opened and he breathed heavily. He blinked and a tear spattered onto Rachel's cheek. She took both his hands.

"What is it?" she asked. "Please tell me."

He looked at the light clouds, then at her, then back at the clouds. "A minute ago Myung-Chol said—" He stopped. His breath came sharply, irregularly. He seemed to be riding the edge of a breakdown. "He said if he was *lucky* they would send him to the concentration camp. Did you hear him, Rachel? 'If I'm very lucky they won't kill me right away and I'll get sent to a concentration camp.' "

She squeezed his hands. "I heard him."

"What kind of—" He brought his knuckles to his forehead. "I mean, I don't have—" The tears came again.

"Oh," she said soothingly. "Come here." She brought him into an embrace.

He rested his cheek on her head and stood there. They rocked side to side slowly. In the yard below, the guys were talking quietly.

"Rachel," Chris said, more calm now. "What does it mean that I wouldn't do that? That I wouldn't go somewhere hoping to be executed or hoping to be sent to a death camp just so I can tell maybe only one person about God?" He pulled away from her. "I wouldn't, Rachel. I know I wouldn't."

"Oh, Chris, yes, you would."

"No, Rachel, I wouldn't. I know myself." He stared at Rachel, but to her it felt more like he was staring through her. "I'm Marine Force Recon," he said. "I've been in combat in seven countries. I've gone into situations that would make enlisted men mess their pants. I've been shot at. I've been hit. And I've shot back and hit. I know I'm no coward. I know how to look at the situation and do a gut check, even way back at base, and know whether or not I can do it. And I'm telling you I wouldn't do what Myong-Chol says he wants to do."

"Chris," Rachel said, taking one hand, "that's crazy talk. You're one of the bravest men I know. I'm sure that if the—"

"But that's just it, don't you see, Rachel? It's not that I'm not brave. I was willing to die every time I went out. It's that I wouldn't die *for the same reason* Myong-Chol is willing to die." His eyes were wild. "Don't you get it, Raych? I wouldn't die for Christ! I wouldn't. Dear God, help me, I wouldn't die for Christ."

He broke from her grip and streaked across the wheat fields as if chased by the dogs of hell.

Jason, Garth, and Lewis came to stand beside Rachel. "What happened?" Jason asked.

She watched him go. He disappeared over a low ridge, then reappeared seconds later still running strong. "I think," she said softly, "he needs to be alone with God for awhile. But he'll be okay."

I hope.

CHAPTER 23

MANZHOULI

WAIT A FEW more days, Shin-Hwa. I know your mother is confusing you. But now please stay where you are until we reach Moscow or somewhere even better. Soon, God's Peace, you will see what the sun looks like in a free land. Be born in a free land, my daughter.

I felt Shin-Hwa moving. Her elbow stretched my belly on the right side. I took Bum-Ji's hand from the armrest and placed it on his daughter's movement. He smiled. The morning sun shone through the window behind him so his face was almost invisible to me, but I saw his cheeks widen. I leaned in to his chest and watched China slide by. The roar of the rail didn't sound as loud to me anymore, and the jostling of the cars, which before had seemed so unnerving, now felt like a mother's gentle rocking.

Judging from the reactions of the passengers around me, this was not the most luxurious part of the train. People complained about the seats where the padding was torn or the upholstery soiled. But to me it was opulence such as I had never experienced on a train or anywhere else. We had padded seats, curtains tied back on the window, and a Russian man who came by with blankets and little pillows every once in awhile. Bum-Ji had room for his legs to stretch out. Ki-Won snored lightly on the seat beside me—a seat all to himself. The windows were clean and unbroken on both sides of the car. Grandmother and Aunt and Uncle even had a sleeping berth!

But that was three cars back, and we weren't supposed to be with them. It was just. . .Kim Yong-Jin; his pregnant wife, Paek Ae-Sook; and their son, Kim In-Tak, visiting China and Russia and then returning to their home in Yangpyong, South Korea.

What else had the Americans told us? We're traveling alone. We don't know anyone else on the train. They would be watching, but since they had left their weapons with Huaniju, there would be nothing they could do if something went wrong. What else? Oh, and as soon as we crossed into Russia, we would be free.

The Americans were nothing like what I'd always been told. I had imagined all Americans to be as tall as the one called Garth and as savage as he looked. But he was so gentle with Ki-Won. Children are the best judges of character, and Ki-Won adored Garth. And the funny one, Lewis, had made Ki-Won new wooden shapes—the shapes Ki-Won held now even in sleep. I never would've imagined an American capable of such kindness. The women surprised me, too. So strong and forceful, yet beautiful and kind. They took my breath away. My Shin-Hwa would be like them. I hadn't gotten to know the one called Chris. He seemed impatient at times, but polite. And certainly troubled.

And Jason, their leader. Confident, sure, decisive. But it was his obvious infatuation with the Vietnamese woman, Trieu, that endeared him to me. I caught him bringing her flowers after every patrol. I saw him watching her over every meal. And I saw the special smile she revealed only when he was nearby. If Americans could treat children with gentleness and flirt with each other like young lovers, perhaps they weren't as strange as I'd always been told.

I looked at the "tennis shoes" on my feet and the Western-style maternity dress over my knees. Bum-Ji wore "blue jeans" and a "baseball cap." Such affluence! If we were supposed to be South Korean tourists, we couldn't very well be dressed like North Korean peasants or escapees from a Chinese prison. But the clothes felt as foreign on me as costumes in Kim Jong-Il's birthday celebration. Still, I felt perfectly decadent in them, so brave and free—I could quickly get used to them.

"Chun-Mi," Bum-Ji said, shaking me softly. "Chun-Mi, the train is slowing. I think we're coming into Manzhouli."

The terrain changed. It was still flat and dry, but low trees increased into the distance and farms reappeared. We passed huts not unlike what we had left in North Korea, but now I saw them as where the poorest of the poor lived, whereas in North Korea everyone lived in such places. These gave way to stone homes, squat warehouses, and finally four- and five-story buildings with no Asian flavor whatsoever. I wondered if this was what Russia would look like. Manzhouli was smaller than Hailar but still was home to probably a hundred thousand Chinese. I still hadn't gotten used to such large cities.

No matter. This was the last Chinese city I would ever see, so I didn't care if it was home to nine million rabbits living in crystal cages, so long as I got into Russia now.

"It's so exciting," I said, squeezing Bum-Ji's arm.

He nodded, but his forehead was creased. "Remember, we are from Yangpyong. Yangpyong, my dear *Ae-Sook.*"

"Yes, of course, Yong-Jin." I leaned on his shoulder and squeezed his arm even tighter.

Dear Jesus, thank You for bringing us to this place. Thank You for the Americans who have come, who love You and have come only for us. This is like what You did, Good Shepherd, when You came to gather Your flock. Bring us to safety. Amen.

The train continued to slow. Elevated cables now ran alongside the rail on both sides, stretching between metal poles and, as we got closer to the station, metal towers. I saw a large parking lot full of cars. As many of these as I'd seen in China, I still hadn't gotten used to them. By comparison North Korea had so few cars it was almost laughable. Only the army and cadre officials had working vehicles there.

New tracks ran on either side of ours now. Ten rows of cables stretched overhead. Low buildings with signs in Chinese and Russian faced us as we passed. We reached the part of the station where a raised concrete landing stood between each of the three tracks and a huge metal roof stood overhead.

Another train was parked at the station, facing the other way. Passengers walked around on the landing. I saw a Chinese woman pushing a baby buggy. She had two long braids and wore a white long-sleeved shirt and a red skirt. A tiny hand with a baby rattle waved from the buggy.

The train lurched to a stop, momentarily rousing Ki-Won. In-Tak, I mean. He wiped his nose and fell asleep again.

"What do we do now?" I asked. "Should we go somewhere? Should we stay in our seats? Where is my passport? Bum-Ji, where are our passports?"

"Chun-Mi," he said, ducking his head. "Ae-Sook, calm down. I have our passports here."

I tried to relax, but my heart was thumping so. I wanted to jump up and run off the train. I felt I could run all the way to Moscow. I sat in my chair forcing myself to breathe slowly. There was much clanging and bouncing, and many Chinese police around every car, but so far ours was still shut. Some of the passengers on our car collected their belongings and stood in an impatient line in the aisle.

Finally the crew came to the outside of the door and opened our car. The passengers filed out slowly. Ki-Won woke up. When he saw people getting off, he wanted off, too. He pushed into the line and would've run off if the people had been moving any faster. I grabbed his arm and pulled him back to our row. He squealed and yanked and struck me with his hand. I spanked his hand, which made him cry. Bum-Ji lifted him into his lap and held him down.

The final passengers disembarked, and the passport police stepped on. There were three of them, all around the age of nineteen. They wore navy blue wool coats, with their badge and rank displayed in silver embroidery, navy blue pants, and navy blue Mao hats with the red star. There were only two other passengers in our car riding through to Russia. They sat forward of us. The first policeman spoke with them. Ki-Won's cries were less hurt and more angry now.

The second passport policeman, a nice-looking boy with a clean-shaven face and brown eyeglasses, stepped toward us. He reminded me of Little Brother. He said something in Chinese. I did not avert my eyes as a North Korean woman would, but instead smiled how I thought a free South Korean woman would smile. Bum-Ji offered up our passports and included Ki-Won, me, and himself in a gesture that said, "We're together."

The policeman nodded, seemingly bored, and took the passports. He opened the first one and spoke again in Chinese. Bum-Ji smiled and shrugged. The policeman then spoke in Korean: "How is the weather in Seoul this time of year?"

It thrilled and frightened me to hear my native tongue. Was this a trick? Was he a friend?

"I'm sure it's quite nice," Bum-Ji said. "But we spend most of our time in Yangpyong." He handed Ki-Won to me and stood to look at the passport the policeman had open. "There, you see? We live in Yangpyong." He sat, nodding as if he couldn't stop.

Good, Bum-Ji. But don't overdo it.

The policeman opened the next passport. He looked at it, then at me, then back down at the passport. Then he looked at Ki-Won, who was whining and trying to slink down out of my grasp. "Hey, boy. What's his name?"

"Ki—" I said. "In-Tak."

"Hey, In-Tak," the policeman said, bending down. "You want a badge, huh?" He pulled a plastic train pin out of his coat pocket and offered it to Ki-Won. "You see? Choo-choo!"

Ki-Won calmed instantly and took the pin. He turned it over in his hand and spoke in his private language.

I sighed. "Thank you."

"My pleasure." He straightened. "Are you three traveling alone?"

Bum-Ji was still nodding. "Yes. Yes, we're quite alone. All alone. Yes. Quite."

"Anything to declare to customs?"

I looked at Bum-Ji, who seemed as confused as I was. "Pardon?"

"Anything to declare. Did you purchase anything in China that you want to take into Russia?"

"Oh!" I said. "No, no. Nothing like that." I felt like the new clothes we were wearing were screaming *We're new, we're new!* I knew Jesus called liars children of the devil, but I hoped He would let me ask forgiveness once we got into Russia.

The policeman looked at me. His gaze rested as heavily on me as if he were standing on my shoulders. I felt a scream building up inside me. The urge to blurt out the whole truth. We're North Korean refugees trying to flee this awful country! We escaped Hailar prison. American soldiers are with us. The rest of my family is spread out all through this train. Please, please, let us go!

He pointed at my belly. "When is your baby due?"

I almost fainted from the relief. He didn't know! And I hadn't told him anything. I touched my abdomen. "Any day now. But perhaps as late as three weeks from now."

His eyebrows drew together. "A strange time to go on vacation."

I looked at Bum-Ji.

His eyes widened slightly. "Uh. . . ," he said. "I. . .made arrangements for this trip before we knew she was pregnant. And then it was too late to change the tickets." He smiled innocently.

"Yes," I said, rubbing my belly, "and the train's movements feel nice. Perhaps it will make our baby come now. I'm so ready for her to come."

"Her?" the policeman asked. "You know it is to be a girl?"

Was that a mistake? "Well. . .yes. I believe it will be a girl, anyway." And then, just to prove how un-North Korean I was, I told him one more thing. "Her name, if it's a girl, will be Shin-Hwa. It means God's peace."

"Yes," he said quickly. "I understand the meaning." He shut our passports and handed them back to Bum-Ji. "Enjoy your vacation."

"Thank you," I said. "We will!"

The three policemen stepped out onto the concrete and moved to the next car.

I melted into Bum-Ji's shoulder. "What a terrifying thing!"

"Yes," he said brightly, "but we did well, I think. Perhaps you and I should go into spying, eh?"

I shushed him. "Yong-Jin, don't joke like that. Not until we're across. I couldn't take this kind of life. No thank you."

New passengers were coming onto the car now, stowing luggage in shelves overhead and plopping down in seats. Most were not Asian. White faces. Brown hair. These were Russians, perhaps? Outside, yet another train was pulling into the station. It was pulled by a loud locomotive that seemed to do little else besides blow black smoke into the late morning sky. The concrete landing was thronged with bustling passengers and their luggage.

"Yong-Jin," I said softly, "would you hold In-Tak while I pray?"

"Pray?"

"Yes, to thank God we got through that and to apologize to Him for lying."

"Aah, Ae-Sook, you take that stuff too seriously." He took

Ki-Won, who was laying his shapes and his new pin in his lap one by one.

"No, dear husband, I don't take it seriously enough or perhaps I would not have said what I did."

"Aah," he said with a dismissive wave. "If you had not, things would have gone badly for us."

"Tell me, Yong-Jin, what do you think of. . ."—I whispered in his ear—"Jesus?"

A look of consternation came over Bum-Ji's face. "I. . . I see that He means much to you. And I have seen you soften since. . .since we left. But is that because of Him or because we left that place?"

I felt a gap between us. I felt farther away from him right now than I had since we'd been married. "So you're still not convinced you need Him?"

He smiled sadly and looked down at Ki-Won. When he looked back at me his expression was tired. "I am trying, my wife."

I nodded and leaned on his shoulder. I did pray for forgiveness for my lying, but somehow I knew my prayers for my husband concerned God more.

Twenty minutes later the passengers were getting restless. No one had come on for fifteen minutes, and it was getting hot in the car. The train that had been here longest had pulled out. Now only crew members and the occasional late arrivals busied the concrete landings.

A family of tall, white-faced Slavs stepped onto our car and made for the rear seats. A large Chinese man who smelled of tobacco smoke squeezed past us. The train jolted forward briefly and I could hear the locomotive revving up.

And suddenly, there was Aunt! She and Uncle and Grandmother stood in the aisle beside us. Grandmother looked spry and Uncle's hair suggested he might have been napping until recently.

"We did it!" Aunt said, her voice still raspy. "We answered all their questions and now we will go into Russia! Since we are done, we wanted to see if there were seats in your car. But I don't see any."

She clapped her hands, but had to pause to allow a coughing fit to pass. "Oh, Chun-Mi, I'm so excited!" She bent down and gave me a hug. The train jolted again. "Well," Aunt said, "see you on the other side!" Then she and Uncle got Grandmother turned around and headed toward the door.

The smile wouldn't leave my face. "Oh, this is so wonderful!" I said to Bum-Ji, looking again out the window. "In five minutes we'll be—"

The passport policeman was staring at me through the window. "Oh, no."

Bum-Ji looked at me. "What?"

I didn't answer. I sunk behind Bum-Ji's shoulder. The policeman looked from me to where Grandmother, Aunt, and Uncle were stepping out of our car.

"Oh, no."

"What?"

The policeman called to his two associates. He spoke to them, jutting his chin at my family and then at me. They pulled out a clipboard and flipped back the pages. Something they saw there sent them into a higher level of intensity. Two of them called to Aunt's group and stopped them as they were climbing aboard the next car. Our policeman stepped onto our car and walked back slowly, his eyes never leaving me. Ten excruciating seconds later, he stood in the aisle beside us.

"I thought you were traveling alone."

My mouth dropped open. "Oh, yes. . . Well, what a surprise to see someone here we know!"

His jaw clenched. "Please come with me."

*　　*　　*

Oh, dear Jesus, no.

Jason watched through the window as Chun-Mi, Bum-Ji, and

Ki-Won were pulled from the train and grouped with Grandmother, Aunt, and Uncle.

In the seat beside him, Trieu was praying softly but urgently. Twenty rows back, Garth and Lewis glanced up at him, a look of helpless terror in their eyes. Dozens of Chinese and Russian passengers pressed their faces to the window, watching as more and more policemen and then soldiers ran toward the group on the landing.

Dear Jesus, please protect them. Please hide the others. Please hide us. Deliver them, Lord Jesus. Lord, we can't do anything here. You have to intervene. Please!

A Chinese army officer arrived at the landing. He talked to the passport policeman with the glasses. The policeman showed the officer his clipboard and seemed to be telling him what had happened. The officer's expression grew angry, a look Jason had seen in warriors before. Things were about to get ugly. The officer shouted orders to his men, who shouted back and fanned out toward every train car.

Not good.

Two soldiers stomped into their car, their assault rifles in both hands. Jason sat back in his chair, his poker face firmly affixed. The soldiers yelled something in Chinese and passengers reached for their passports.

Jason pulled his out and took Trieu's from her. He rested his hand on hers, and she gripped it tightly. "God's in control," he whispered, more for his own benefit than for hers.

The soldiers didn't appear interested in the inside of the passports. If passengers held theirs open toward them, they twisted them around to look at the front covers. Two rows in front of Jason and Trieu, one of the soldiers saw passports he liked and snatched them away. He spoke sternly to the Asian couple and gestured for them to stand and precede him up the aisle and out the door.

"South Korean passports," Trieu said. "They're pulling everyone off the train with South Korean passports."

Jason rubbed his face. Even if they'd had their weapons and been in perfect position, what could they have done? Too many witnesses. Couldn't shoot them all with Versed. And now there were too many guns. He whipped himself for not just trying the nighttime crossing into Mongolia. What an idiot! He kicked the bottom of the chair in front of him.

The other soldier looked at him sharply.

"Sorry," Jason said.

The soldier said something and reached forward. Jason handed him the passports. He glanced at both covers and handed them back, a wary look on his face as he moved on down the aisle.

By the time the search was completed, twenty Koreans stood on the landing, surrounded by armed soldiers. Joo-Chan was there, along with Myong-Chol, Youn-Chul, all of Chun-Mi's family, and ten other innocent South Koreans on business or vacation. Meanwhile soldiers threw the Koreans' luggage from the baggage cars.

The passport policeman's boss had arrived and was working with the army officer. A soldier reported to them with a message. The officer nodded and gestured to the nearest Korean in the group: an old man in a loud Hawaiian shirt. Two soldiers escorted the man to a low building just off the landing, the army and police officers right behind.

"What should we do?" Trieu asked quietly. "They'll interrogate them one by one. These people can't hold up to it."

"I don't know, Trieu." Jason opened his mouth, willing a great idea to come out. But nothing did. "I just don't know."

The Chinese army solved it for him. A lower-ranking officer walked forward with the train's engineer. The officer spoke and swept his arm at the train. The engineer nodded and trotted forward, yelling to his crew. Two minutes later the whistle blew and the train crawled forward. Diesel fumes came through the open windows.

Jason looked backward down the car. Garth and Lewis were ready to bolt for the door. They looked at him with question marks in their eyes. Were Chris and Rachel about to jump off their car, too? Had they already? What about Gil-Su? Where was he? Jason shook his head *No* to Garth and Lewis. They sat down reluctantly, Garth with his upper lip curling in a snarl.

But what could they do? A pack of Americans jumping off the train right now would look just a little suspicious—and even if they did, then what? No, they'd have to cross into Russia and cross back. They could retrieve their gear and be back in the game in six hours. With any luck, the prisoners would be sent back to Hailar prison, and maybe this time they'd take it down hot. And if they were very, very lucky, or if God had chosen to answer their prayers the way he wanted, the refugees would stand up to the interrogation and be put aboard the next train to Russia.

And so Jason and Trieu watched the North Korean refugees—pregnant Chun-Mi and her doting husband, little Ki-Won and those shapes held protectively against his chest, Grandmother that spark plug, passionate Youn-Chul, Aunt who was showing the first signs of recovering from TB, silent Uncle, and the true South Korean: Joo-Chan—their friends and their responsibility—slide silently by as the Trans-Siberian railway train pulled away from the People's Republic of China and rolled into freedom.

* * *

"Gandalf, this is Strider, good to hear your voice, too."

Jason lowered the handset and rubbed his mouth with the back of his hand. He blinked at the Firebrand team in the dawn gloom of Huaniju's farmhouse, lit primarily by one orange glow stick.

"Gandalf," Jason said into the satellite radio, "we have to report that the Ring has fallen into enemy hands. Repeat, the Ring has fallen into enemy hands. How copy? Over."

That was not the message he'd been hoping to send today. He imagined Chimp in the operations room, the Icarus satellite feed on the big screen, perhaps sitting beside Eloise, as his words arrived. The mood here in the farmhouse wasn't any better. Joo-Chan was here, speaking with Gil-Su and Rachel, but he didn't have much information to offer.

"Strider, Gandalf," Chimp's voice said evenly. "Copy the Ring in enemy hands." There was a long pause. At length he continued. "You. . .want to tell us what happened? Over."

"Roger that, Gandalf," Jason said. "We were following the extraction plan, but something went wrong and all components of the Ring were taken off and interrogated. There was nothing we could do but watch, Gandalf. It stunk. Our young missionary friend from the South Farthing was released and put on the next train north. We were hoping to find the Ring with him at the first stop north of the border, but he was alone. He says the soldiers interviewed them all individually and kept them isolated after that.

"We spent the day there and took the train back across the border last night. Nothing visible at the station. A nice soldier told Lady Eowyn the Ring has been taken south and is headed for Mordor. We rode the train to the town where the Ring had been previously held then made it back to Farmer Maggot's home. We've retrieved our things and Bill the pony. We intend to ride him south to interdict before the Ring goes through the Black Gate. Please advise. Over."

Chris and Garth zipped up the last duffel bags and carried them out into the pink dawn to load them on the truck. Trieu sat on a bamboo mat, finishing her inventory of her medical supplies. Lewis checked the banshee's battery level, then folded away the banshee flying robot—a glass-domed contraption with four long arms bearing wide plastic rotors at the tips—into its case. Rachel brought Joo-Chan a third energy bar, which he attacked.

Chimp's voice arrived in the handset. "Strider, this is Gandalf. The White Lady is disappointed, as you could've guessed. She says she's glad the Fellowship is all right. She wants you to consider stashing the stuff again and just riding right back out of that country.

Come on home. You've done great work. There will be others to help later. But she says she's going to leave it up to you how to respond. If you decide to interdict, we will support you if we can. The White Lady has been working on a crazy scheme that might just work if you can get possession of the Ring again. So, Strider, the choice is up to you and the group. What do you want to do? Over."

"Roger that, Gandalf. Stand by."

Jason put the handset down. He found he was alone in the farmhouse. He stepped outside onto the packed earth in front of Huaniju's house. The sun was cresting the horizon in the east, and birds streaked through the morning chill. The Firebrand team was arrayed around the truck facing him, waiting for him grimly.

"Eloise wants us to get back on the train and ride into Russia," he said. "She says it's up to us, but that we ought to at least consider cutting our losses and trying again next time."

They looked at him as if he hadn't spoken at all. Gil-Su and Joo-Chan watched nervously, but no one in the team moved. From a neighboring farm, a rooster crowed.

"Kromer," Chris said from beside the driver's door, "get your butt on the truck."

Jason smiled in spite of himself. "Roger that. You guys get aboard. I'll be right out." He trotted inside the farmhouse and picked up the handset. "Gandalf, this is Strider. We have decided to go after the Ring. Repeat, the Fellowship is going after the Ring. Out."

PART III

DELIVERANCE

CHAPTER 24

SUN-HYE

MEN LAUGHED outside Sun-Hye's door. Footsteps approached. Another man who would pay to have her. She thought he was the fifth today—or maybe sixth. It didn't matter anymore.

Kim Jong-Il was right, she had decided. North Korea was the only civilized nation in the world. Why did she listen to her brother and father and come to China? Here perhaps *they* had freedoms, but for her it was better back in her homeland.

Her brother and father, her sister and her husband and his brother—where were they? Had they been wise and decided to return home, or were they making their way in China? Men had the power, she had concluded. Men could come and go. Men could purchase women for an hour or a night. Women were weak. They were like ducks sold in the market.

The footsteps stopped. The customer was haggling for a better price. She was to be discounted like a loaf of old bread. And Dolkun would beat her for "robbing" him of the extra money.

Perhaps this time he would just kill her. Perhaps she could provoke him. He would kill her or throw her out. Either way she would be free.

She arrayed the sheer silks over her body on the mat. She struck the pose Dolkun had taught her but modified it to hide the bruises on her thighs. Once again she would do everything Dolkun had taught her for this customer. She had learned how to shut her mind off. Sometimes when the men were with her she felt like she was outside her body, as if she were a little moth watching from the corner of the ceiling. She didn't know why she obeyed Dolkun. To avoid the beatings, she guessed. But they were unavoidable.

She had been funny once. Her mother used to say she could turn hemp into gold with her happiness. She was smart and strong and had the attentions of young men wherever she went. Even in China it was true. What was that boy's name? The handsome one who had come from North Korea, too. Youn-something. Youn-Chul. He and the other boy competed for her. Where was Youn-Chul now? Probably making money like crazy in China.

She still had the attentions of men. Just not in the way she had imagined. Instead of competing for her, they haggled for her. None of it had gone as she had imagined. Kim Jong-Il was right.

She looked around her room, her cell. Dirt floor. Cinder-block walls. Plaster ceiling with brown water stains all across it like a map of Asia. Her mat. The small lamp and its lampshade with a faded red dragon on both sides. Her shameful dress in the corner for when she had to stand outside to draw customers in. Everything that had truly belonged to her had been taken that first day. Everything.

The men agreed on a price, and the door opened. Dolkun entered first, his expression angry. He saw Sun-Hye's pose and grunted then let the customer through and left.

The customer was tall and stood up straight. He was clean. He dressed well. He had thick hair and a narrow, handsome face. A man like that didn't need to pay for a woman. But she'd had all kinds. Perhaps he liked to hit, and his wife wouldn't allow it.

He stood at the door looking at her. The red scarf over the table lamp dimmed the light, but it was still bright enough for her to see the indecision in his eyes.

"Come," she said in Chinese, reaching her hand out to him, letting the silks fall from her. "Let me take off your clothes."

That seemed to snap him into action. It usually did. He put his finger to his lips and stepped across the room away from her. "Sun-Hye?" he said.

She knew that name. It was her name. She hadn't heard it in weeks. Or months, or years. From the first day she'd been *Josun Rose,* Korean Rose. "I. . . How do you know that name?"

"Shh," he said. "I've come to help you." She must've looked at him in deep confusion because he smiled. "Sun-Hye, don't you remember me? I am Yi Gil-Su. I welcomed you and your family when you'd come across the river. I told you about Jesus Christ. Do you remember?"

Now that he said it, he *did* look familiar. That realization was chased by the awareness that he'd switched to Korean, something else Sun-Hye hadn't heard in a long time. A sudden mental image appeared to her: Gil-Su leading her family into that cave in the side of the earth. That's when she'd met Youn-Chul. A sudden thrill shot through her. He was here to help her?

But then her hopes sank. He was *here*—in a brothel. That couldn't be good. She had heard him haggle for her. He'd wanted her for the whole night.

"I guess your Jesus doesn't make good company at night, eh?" she said. "So you've come to Josun Rose to keep you warm. Fine. Let's get on with it." She lay on her mat. "How do you want it?"

"No," Gil-Su said, taking off his overcoat. "You don't under-stand. I'm here to take you from here." He handed her his coat. "Put this around you, my child."

"What?" The coat did feel nice. She was always so cold.

He went to the lamp and took the scarf off. "Do you have anything you want to take with you?"

She looked at the coat. "Are you going to take me outside and kill me? Or am I to be your slave now?"

Gil-Su pulled aside the heavy drapes across the small window. "No, no, Sun-Hye. I'm going to set you free."

"Ha," she said. "I hear that a lot."

He turned the lamp off, then back on, then off and on again. He set it down and faced her. "Come, my child. It is because of Jesus Christ that we have come for you."

* * *

"There's the signal."

Jason knelt at the corner of the warehouse next door to the brothel, his CAR-15 ready to pepper anyone who came his way. Finally they were in full battle gear—green camouflage uniforms, Kevlar helmets, sophisticated electronics, steel armor plates, plastic shields on elbows and knees, and weapons of nonlethal destruction. The harness on his chest tugged gently on the gun, ready to pull it snugly to his body if he needed his hands free.

He faced the direction they would go. Garth, Chris, and Rachel knelt, facing the other directions. From where they were, they couldn't directly see the light in the window, but the village's nighttime darkness was so complete—helped to be so by a few strategically removed lightbulbs—and their night-vision gear so sensitive that they could see the glow cycle off and on from around the corner.

"Roger that," Jason whispered into his helmet mic. "What do you know? For once a local informant was right. How's the street look?"

"Clear," Trieu said. "No cars, bikes, or pedestrians. Only the two heavies out front smoking."

"Roger that." He glanced at his team—glowing monochrome green in their infrared night-vision gear—and spoke again over the squad radio. "Lewis, you guys in place?"

"Affirmative, Jason. Bring her in and we're out of here."

"Roger that. Stand by, Trieu. Okay, fireteam, let's move into position Bravo. Go, go, go."

He led them in the classic assault advance position: legs flexed, torso bent slightly forward, weapons at the shoulder ready to fire. They moved silently and gracefully, a martial ballet. On Jason's left was the long wall of the brothel. The cinder blocks had gaps between them in places, through which came sounds of the oldest profession. By now he almost didn't even notice the smells of the open toilets and decaying garbage.

Fifty slow paces later, Jason knelt at the front corner of the brothel. His team knelt behind him, covering all approaches. He nodded to Rachel, who brought out a large Ziploc bag with folded cloths inside.

Tired laughter came to them from around the front of the U-shaped brothel. The guards, bored and sleepy. Perfect. Jason and Garth took out the cloths from Rachel's Ziploc and folded them in their left hands. He found the three-button mouse box on the straps across his chest and keyed the go button.

Jason never heard the shots, but he heard the guards yelp in surprise. That was their cue. He and Garth hurried around the corner, weapons forward, breath held, cloths ready.

The guards were looking at their shoulders, where they'd been hit. They were sitting on the wide wooden steps leading to the front doors at the middle of the U. A bright lightbulb illuminated the whole area. Jason picked the guard on the right, leaving Garth the one on the left.

Jason's guard looked up at him in pain and confusion just as he reached him and shoved the chloroform-soaked cloth over his mouth and nose. Garth's guard didn't even look up.

The guards struggled violently. They would've yelled, too, if they'd been able.

The scuffle ended abruptly. Both guards passed out—first from the chloroform and second from the Versed cocktail Trieu had given them. Trieu's concoction would've knocked them out in thirteen seconds, but that was a long time to scream for help. They would sleep soundly, and when they awoke, they wouldn't remember a thing.

Jason and Garth tossed their cloths to Rachel, who now knelt in the shadow just around the lip of the building. She closed them back in the bag and trained her MP-5 on the front door. Jason and Chris lifted the larger guard. Garth picked the other one up by himself. While Rachel watched from the corner and Trieu covered them from her hiding spot across the street, they carried the guards around back and hid them under a bush. They came forward again in their forced-slow tactical advance.

Three doorways opened onto the courtyard. One in the middle and one each from the two wings. A fourth door opened through the back, their alternate exit route. Sun-Hye's room was on the left prong of the U as they faced the middle doors.

Rachel and Garth knelt on either side of the door on the left wing. Jason stood at the door itself. Chris stood right behind him. They were bunched at the door as if all trying to listen to sounds on the other side.

Shadows passed over one of the two windows flanking the middle door. Garth turned to face that door. They paused.

But no one came out. Moths fluttered around the bulb—clinking into it and sending it swaying. Shadows tilted eerily.

Jason keyed the go button again.

He shoved the wooden door open and barged in, heading right. Chris followed immediately behind, heading left. Rachel and Garth came in behind them.

A prostitute and her customer were on the mat in the middle of the floor. The woman saw the soldiers running in and started to scream, but Rachel was there with the chloroform. The sound she did get out was nothing odd for this place. Chris took care of the man, using Garth's chloroform cloth.

Rachel put the cloths away again and switched off the room's only light. Garth shut the door to the courtyard and slid the couple's mat out of the way.

Chris and Jason took positions by the door leading to Sun-Hye's room. Jason nodded to Chris, who pushed the door open. They went in and swept all corners with their weapons.

There stood Gil-Su by the lamp. A woman Jason presumed to be Sun-Hye sat on the mat, a dark overcoat wrapped around her.

"Turn off the light," Jason hissed.

Gil-Su, who knew they were coming yet still looked shocked solid, broke out of his trance and turned out the lamp.

"Is this the girl?" Jason asked him.

"Y–yes, this is Sun-Hye."

"Okay, let's go."

The girl didn't seem willing or able to move. Gil-Su spoke reassuringly to her in Korean and got her to her feet.

Rachel stood guard at the door to the courtyard, propping it open slightly with her tranquilizer-filled submachine gun. It was cramped in the little room with so many bodies and their gear. Jason put his hand on Rachel's shoulder to tell her he was there and they were almost ready. Chris led Gil-Su and Sun-Hye close to the door, ready to run.

"Trieu," Jason said, "we have what we came for and are ready to exfil. How's it look out there?"

"Stand by, Jason," Trieu said over the squad radio. "Stand by. Someone's coming in from the street."

Jason looked over Rachel's head and saw a portly Chinese man in a dirty undershirt walk up the front steps, looking around him guiltily.

"Looks like a customer," Trieu said.

The man entered the front door. A man challenged him from inside. The customer answered testily and gestured to the empty steps.

"Uh-oh," Jason whispered. He pulled Rachel away from the door and signaled to the others to stand ready. Chris took Gil-Su and Sun-Hye back into her room.

"He's coming out," Trieu said. "He's looking for his guards."

Jason heard the man call out in irritation.

"Where are you, lazy fools?" Rachel whispered, translating. "If I catch you dicing again, I'll have your ears."

"He's coming to your door!" Trieu said. "I'll take him down."

"Negative," Jason hissed. "Wait."

Trieu's voice rose in pitch. "Jason, he's—" A beat. "No, wait. The customer's coming out."

Jason heard the man complain. He could understand "How about some service here?" just from the guy's tone.

"He's going in," Trieu said.

Jason heard the main door shut.

"They're inside," Trieu said. "The street is clear."

Jason patted Rachel's shoulder. "Go, go, go."

Rachel pushed open the door and went into the courtyard. She cleared the doorway and knelt, her MP-5 trained on the main door.

Jason went to her right and knelt down, covering the door on the other wing.

Chris came next. He peeled off to Jason's right and knelt in the shadow at the lip of the building. He made the A-OK sign and motioned to Garth in the doorway.

Gil-Su led Sun-Hye down the steps and around to Chris. Garth came down the steps, the unconscious prostitute in his arms covered with a blanket.

"Garth," Jason said softly, "what are you doing?"

"I'm not leaving her."

Jason ground his teeth. "Right. Wish we could take 'em all.

Okay, Chris, lead us out of here. Rachel, escort the civvies. I'll pull rear guard. Move!"

Chris led them the way they'd come, through the darkness beside the brothel. Rachel tugged Gil-Su and Sun-Hye, who couldn't see in the black night. Garth came next with the woman. Jason backed first into the shadow, then into the full dark behind them.

"Trieu," he said, "we are leaving. Exfil now."

"Roger."

"Lewis, fire it up. We're headed your way."

"Copy that, boss."

They had a full village block to cross to where the truck was waiting. But they'd been this way already and knew the obstacles. They crossed the distance as quickly as Rachel could move Gil-Su and Sun-Hye. Twice, dogs complained about their passing. But as before, nobody paid them any heed.

Finally the truck's dull canvas siding came into view. Lewis was there, covering their retreat with his MP-5. Joo-Chan stood on the step at the driver's door, watching them arrive.

Chris got Sun-Hye and Gil-Su into the truck then fell back with Jason to watch for witnesses.

Trieu trotted lightly across the street, her Dragunov rifle slung over her shoulder on its strap. She hopped into the back of the truck with the others.

"Okay, chief," Garth said over the radio, "we're all in."

"Roger that," Jason said. He nodded to Chris for him to peel off, which he did.

Headlights appeared down the street the way they'd come. Truck headlights, if Jason had to guess. Narrowly spaced but high.

"Car coming," he said.

"Forget it," Chris said. "Let's go now."

Jason stepped backward, still watching the lights. The vehicle stopped a block and a half away and the lights went out. Jason turned and ran to the truck. He jumped in and keyed his helmet mic. "I'm in, Lewis. Get us out of here."

"Roger that."

Lewis bounded into the cab beside Joo-Chan and told him to drive.

Bill the pony, who had brought them halfway across China, proved reliable one more time. They pulled away into the night.

* * *

"I don't understand. Who are these people?"

Sun-Hye couldn't see any of them in the back of the truck. They were soldiers. She'd seen that much in her room. And they weren't Chinese, that was obvious. They frightened her. But they *had* taken her away from Dolkun, and they were with Gil-Su, who hadn't touched her. So perhaps they were to be trusted.

But she'd gone from bad to worse before.

"It's. . .hard to explain," Gil-Su said. Sun-Hye could faintly make out the line of his cheekbone as he sat across from her in the bed of the truck. "Let me say that they are friends of mine. They love Jesus Christ, just as I do. And they are friends of Joo-Chan and Youn-Chul. That's why we—"

"*Youn-Chul?*" she said. "Joo-Chan? Where are they? Where is Youn-Chul?"

"Joo-Chan is here," Gil-Su said. "He is driving this truck. As for Youn-Chul. . ." He didn't speak for several seconds. "Youn-Chul was with us until a few days ago. His whole family was. We were trying to get them out of China. But they were captured. They're on their way back here to be given over to North Korea. That's why we're here. To try to catch them before they're given over. They won't arrive for another day. Since Youn-Chul had wanted so badly to come rescue you, we decided to—"

"Youn-Chul—he wanted to rescue me? He–he even remembered me?"

"Yes, my child. Joo-Chan, as well. They came to these soldiers here and tried to convince them to come here for you. But they refused because we were so close to getting Youn-Chul's family to freedom. Youn-Chul became so enraged that they would not help you that he attacked the lead soldier." He chuckled. "He didn't last very long, of course, but his concern for you is great, my dear."

She was chilled but it wasn't from the cold. Youn-Chul had wanted to come after her? Joo-Chan, too? When there were so many other women Youn-Chul could choose from? And when he was so near to his own safety he wanted to come back for her? Wanted it bad enough to attack a warrior for her honor?

She found herself weeping. Something hard inside her began to crack loose. And she discovered that beneath it waited a thousand tears.

The truck slowed and turned a corner. Through her blurry vision, Sun-Hye saw Jilin Jade—the woman from the cell next to hers—sleeping beside her under a blanket. The giant had carried her out. At first she'd thought it was to increase the number of their sex slaves, but now she knew it was a rescue. A lovely, brilliant rescue. She felt ashamed that they would risk themselves for her, and yet it made her feel so wonderful that they considered the risk to be worth taking to save her. She'd never been that important to anyone.

She wiped her tears. "Gil-Su, what will you do with me? With us?"

"We are taking you to my last safe house in this region. All the others were shut down in the raid when you were captured. You two will stay there for now. One of the soldiers is a doctor. She will make sure you are healthy and will help if you are not."

She cocked her head. "One of the soldiers is a woman? Ha. Women are weak."

"Two of these soldiers are women, Sun-Hye. And when you see them, you will know they are anything but weak."

She looked around the back of the bumpy, squeaky truck. Her

eyes had adjusted well enough to make out faces. Most of the soldiers had taken off their helmets. Two of them had long hair and soft, feminine faces. How incredible. For some reason she felt stronger, too. She had been freed from Dolkun's grip and from the power of men. These women were showing her that they could be strong in a man's world. From now on *she* wanted to be strong, as they were.

"Can I come with them?" she asked. "Can I be a soldier, too?"

"What?" Gil-Su said. "Sun-Hye, maybe one day, but not yet. You have been through too much. You and this other dear child must go to the safe house and recover your strength. If all goes well, tomorrow we will have Youn-Chul and his family and we will be leaving the country together."

She shook her head in disbelief. It all sounded too incredible. This day had gone exactly as every other had for she didn't know how long. Until half an hour ago, she was one of Dolkun's prostitutes. He had owned her like a person owns a goat. Surely this was only a dream, she thought, and in an hour she would wake up to her nightmare.

Still, it was such a pleasant dream.

CHAPTER 25

TUMEN

CHRIS WOULD know what kind of bird it was that made such an ugly screech right over Jason's head. It sounded like a blue jay that had screamed itself hoarse at the Super Bowl.

Jason knelt in the dense woods at the edge of the wide street, behind a low white stone wall decorated in a V-shaped pattern. Thick willows swayed overhead. Dark green shrubs behind him sealed him from view. If anyone did look his way, his camouflage uniform would take care of the rest.

The street in front of him had the layered tarmac finish they'd seen throughout China. It looked pretty much like small-town America in that respect. Across the street was another wall, with trees and bushes behind. The perfect spot for an ambush. The team was arrayed on either side of the road, each in his or her own cover. A makeshift roadblock—an old door balanced on two sawhorses—stood across the road, manned by two familiar-looking men in ill-fitting army uniforms: Gil-Su and Joo-Chan. High above it all, only a speck to eyes that knew what to look for, hovered Lewis's banshee.

"What do you see, Lewis?" Jason said over the squad radio. "Talk to me, baby."

"Well," Lewis said, "I see a really squatty town. Tumor, or something."

"Tumen, Lewis," Rachel said.

"Oh, right. Tumen. I see a train at the station. I see. . .a river spangling in the hot, hot sun. I see a pretty pink building that looks like it came from the Barbie aisle. I see guys in a backhoe digging up a perfectly good street because Rachel showed her bare shoulders."

"I did not! I only flirted with them a little. But *no* bare anything. Just lots of pretty Chinese paper money."

"Hmph," Lewis said. "Well, they're making a serious hole, whatever you did. And I see two silly persons standing in the middle of the street pretending to be soldiers."

Jason nodded. "Okay, good. Keep an eye on that train. Let us know when a big truck moves out from the station. That'll probably be our guys."

And please, Lord, let the impromptu construction work divert that truck down our little street.

Jason felt eyes on him. He forced himself to look around slowly. It wasn't Gil-Su or Joo-Chan. The last bicyclists they'd seen were long gone. He focused his eyes on each position he knew his team members were in. Then he saw who it was.

Trieu was watching him from her spot directly across the street beneath willows whose leafy branches swayed in the gentle breeze as gracefully as Trieu's hair did. Jason waved. She waved back. He wished he had a private channel to talk with her on the radio.

Jason had a mental flash of Trieu and him sitting side by side at the reflecting pool in front of the Lincoln Memorial, their children playing on the lawn. After this mission, maybe they should take a few months off. Plan the wedding, get married, go on their honeymoon. Maybe they should take a year off: six months before the wedding and six months after. It wouldn't do for either of them to get shot before the wedding.

His stomach tensed. He hadn't wanted to think about this, but now he realized it was a strong fear inside him. Surely one of them would die before the wedding. Or one of them would die within a few months after the wedding. It would be one of those tragic stories that made women cry, the movie version of which would star Mel Gibson. He was trying to be humorous about it even in his own thoughts, but that clamp on his gut told him some part of himself thought it was deadly serious.

Maybe they should retire from the group altogether. Pull out. Get married. Have some kids. Maybe by the time the kids were in college, they could come back to it. Of course then they'd be old and feeble and about as much use on a mission as square wheels on a pushcart.

Certainly as soon as they had kids he couldn't be dragging Mommy *and* Daddy out to get shot at. Man, marrying Trieu might be the best thing that had ever happened to the two of them, but it sure could mess the team up—big-time.

Still, as he'd seen in the SEALs over and over, it wasn't exactly as if he and Trieu were irreplaceable. Eloise would find another sniper and doctor. Chris could take over the team. He was always itching to do that, anyway. Jason and Trieu could go off and be old married lumps and get fat together.

He smiled at his thoughts. Trieu wouldn't find them especially romantic. What a dolt. Why was she marrying *him?* He looked across at her. Even from thirty yards the glint of her eyes, the bright flash of her face, made him go all wobbly inside. The team was great, but if he had to choose he was going with Trieu.

"Uh-oh." It was Lewis's voice over the radio.

"What, 'uh-oh'?" Jason said. "I don't like 'uh-oh.' "

"Take a look at your camera," Lewis said.

Jason dropped his eye panel down and used the three-button mouse to cycle through the available views. He saw the gun cams from each team member, the mote camera's view on the roadblock, and finally a fish-eye view from high over the border town of Tumen, China. "Whatcha got, Lewis?"

"Hang on," Lewis said. "I'll zoom in."

The view, which rocked back and forth as if it were on a hammock, zoomed in to an open-topped military truck pulling away from the train station. A group of familiar-looking Asian civilians rode in the back with three soldiers.

"That's it, Lewis," Jason said. "Good job."

"No, not so great. Look."

The image zoomed out shakily, then panned left. The truck they'd seen fell in line behind another open-topped truck—filled with soldiers in dark green uniforms. Then another. And in front of that, a six-wheeled armored vehicle with a nasty looking antiaircraft machine gun on top. The image zoomed right, where two military Jeeps pulled in behind the truck.

"This is bad," Jason said.

He heard his team's muttered disbelief and frustration over the radio.

"Yeah," Lewis said. "No kidding."

The convoy took the anticipated road away from the station. It turned left on the main thoroughfare, traveling slowly and staying together. Two sidecar motorcycles went ahead, clearing the way and stopping traffic.

Jason looked at Gil-Su and Joo-Chan. They had no clue what was coming their way. "Okay, everybody, listen u—"

"Oh no!" Lewis said.

"What, Lewis?"

"Look!"

Jason focused on his eye panel. The column had stopped beside a minor intersection. Policemen on the street held traffic back and motioned for something else to come from the side street.

It was a tank.

It looked like a Soviet T-80, which meant it was probably a Chinese Type 98, based on the Russian tank. Fifty tons of reactive armored mayhem adding its fifteen-hundred horsepower to the parade. Its boxy turret looked sleek and deadly. The 125mm main gun rode forward—in battle position. This was the big stick, Chinese style. He couldn't see more than a dark green protrusion at the commander's cupola, but he knew that's where the laser self-defense array was. The beast pulled into position at the head of the column then accelerated to forty miles an hour, momentarily leaving the trucks behind.

"Okay, boys," Jason said, "party's over. Let's pack up and go home."

"What!"

"But, Jason," Lewis said. "Our friends are in—"

"Our friends are quite safe from the likes of us right now," Jason said. "We took on some tanks last time, and as I recall the experience didn't agree with us. Garth?"

"Yeah. Let's go."

"I'm guessing the Chinese have lost enough face with these refugees and don't want to take any more chances," Jason said, "so they're making sure they really do get handed off this time."

The column paused briefly where the construction crew was digging the hole for Rachel. Then they turned down the road, headed toward the ambush position.

"Get them off the street, Chris!" Jason said. "Get them out of here. Lewis, bring the banshee down now."

Garth and Chris hopped over the low wall, running at Gil-Su and Joo-Chan full speed. "Get off the road!" Chris said. "They've sent the whole stinkin' Chinese army."

Garth swept up the door and the sawhorses and hurdled the wall.

Chris dragged Gil-Su and Joo-Chan off the road and pulled them into the bushes. Trieu ran across the road and hopped the low wall.

The motorcycles appeared at the head of the street, and behind them, the tank. It dwarfed the motorcycles, though they were much closer.

"Fade into the woods, people," Jason said. "Away from the road!"

Jason found himself running with Trieu. They were well hidden from the street, where the convoy was passing just now. They knelt down together and looked back.

The truck carrying the refugees rolled by. Jason could see them through the wooden rails on the side. Uncle and Myong-Chol were standing. The rest were sitting down. Jason thought he spotted Ki-Won's hair flying in the wind. The column was half a mile from the prison.

"What are we going to do?" Trieu asked.

Jason just shook his head. What *could* they do?

* * *

"Are they inside?"

Trieu leaned into the rubber eyepiece on her sniper scope. "I believe so. I saw Youn-Chul hop down but couldn't see any others. The truck bounced several times as if people were getting off one by one. And now the soldiers have gone inside."

Jason looked with his binoculars. The Tumen prison building was cosmetic pink. Somebody's idea of a joke or maybe just the only color the People's Republic had sitting around. It was a small, windowless building, probably able to contain only twenty prisoners at the maximum. A high fence topped by coiled razor wire surrounded the prison. Four armed guards watched the front gate, and another four watched the rear gate. The armored column had bypassed the prison and was now lined up on the bridge over the Tumen River, ready to escort the prisoners across into North Korea.

The Type 98 tank idled in a position guarding the highway bridge across the river.

The Firebrand team plus Gil-Su and Joo-Chan, still in their "borrowed" Chinese uniforms, lay flat on rocks overlooking the prison far below. Low trees blanketed the hill except right there at the top. A small stone pagoda with a metal spire stood at the crest like an ancient antenna tower. It was a beautiful viewpoint to overlook the town of Tumen, the sparkling Tumen River, and hazy North Korea beyond. On any other day, Jason might've appreciated the vista. The team was out of breath from the run and the climb, but they would live.

"This is so bad," Lewis said, looking toward the prison and shaking his head. "This is really, really bad. Jason, what are we going to do?"

Jason almost threw his binoculars. "I don't know, Lewis, okay? They're going to drive them right across the river. What are we supposed to do, assault an armored column?"

"We could blow the bridge!" Lewis said. "Remember in Sudan we—"

"No," Garth said. He was guarding the approaches behind them. "That was in the middle of nowhere, and we had plenty of time to prepare. And we had tons of C-4. Here, we're late, we're surrounded by bad guys and civilians, and I didn't bring enough C-4 for *that.*"

Rachel squinted down at the prison. "It looks like they'll have to walk out that back courtyard and through the rear gate before they reach the truck. Maybe Trieu could take out the guards when they're walking. Could you hit them from here, Trieu?"

"Possibly," Trieu said. "But then what?"

"Yeah," Chris said, "she's right. Maybe she could drop them, but then what do we do? There's like seventy-five soldiers down there."

"And a tank," Jason said.

"And a tank. And that APC with the big gun on top," Chris said. "No," he said, his expression bitter, "they win another round. We lose."

Jason bellied up over the crest of the rock. "Gil-Su," he said, "can you tell us what's happening in there right now?"

Gil-Su and Joo-Chan moved nearer. "They're being processed," Gil-Su said. "Paperwork, fingerprints, etc. Their clothing and belongings are being taken from them. There will be North Korean agents inside. Perhaps the Chinese police will interrogate the refugees; perhaps they will simply turn them over to the North Koreans."

"Then what?" Lewis asked. "They'll just drive them across and slap their hands and let them go, right? It's not like they've committed murder or anything."

"No, Lewis," Gil-Su said. "They have committed a crime far worse in the eyes of the North Korean government: disloyalty. They fled North Korea, but many do that. What proves their disloyalty is that they were caught trying to leave China—not once, but twice. That is enough to earn any North Korean the death sentence."

Garth whistled softly. "Hikers coming."

"Drop out of sight, people," Jason said.

They crossed over the stone hilltop and slid down into the trees ten yards below.

Gil-Su whispered, drawing the team close to hear. "It is worse for our friends. They have come into contact with Christians, something Kim Jong-Il finds abhorrent. They won't be able to hide this fact, and they may not want to. Chun-Mi and Grandmother and Myong-Chol, and perhaps more in their group, will be hard-pressed to denounce their faith. We have to pray for them right now. They are possibly living that moment we all pray we never come to, when they must deny Christ or risk death."

Jason redoubled his prayers for their faith to hold. He burst into God's throne room shouting for help, begging for help. *Lord, please, can't You send a miracle? Can't you send an angel? Send an earthquake. Send me!*

He looked at Chris, who was trying to glimpse the prison through the trees.

"Gil-Su," Chris said. "What about Myong-Chol? What will happen to him?"

Gil-Su squeezed his eyes shut and shook his head. "Myong-Chol will certainly be executed. He is doomed three times over. He will not denounce Christ, and for that he will die. He tried to leave China, and for that he will die. And, worst of all, he was a concentration camp guard—a high-ranking one—who deserted his responsibilities and has, for all they know, told the world about these camps that Kim Jong-Il continues to deny. I hid him as long as I could, hoping North Korea would forget about him. But now that he has emerged. . ." He looked down. "I fear our brother is getting his chance to be a blessed martyr."

Oh, sweet Jesus, help him. Help them all.

Garth whistled to them from the crest of the hill. "All clear."

When they reached the top, Trieu again trained her Dragunov's scope on the prison. "Something's happening," she said.

All in the group who had binoculars raised them to their eyes.

The area behind the prison was a white concrete exercise yard the size of an inner-city basketball court. Five prison guards lined up with their backs to the rear fence gate, rifles pointed inward. North Korean agents, all in black, stood at the edges. Two Chinese guards opened the back door to the prison and led out seven adults in gray prison clothes, all shackled at the ankles and wrists. Little Ki-Won was naked except for the chain around his neck by which a guard led him out.

"They're all there," Chris said. He counted again. "Yeah, I think they are. And Myong-Chol's not dead yet.

"Oh!" Rachel said. "Look at poor Ki-Won! Oh!"

Garth rushed back to them. "What about Ki-Won?" He grabbed

Chris's binoculars. "Take security," he said, pulling the glasses to his eyes. He found the prison courtyard and let out a sound like an enraged bull. He shoved the binoculars at Gil-Su and paced around the hilltop, grunting and growling. When he turned to Jason his eyes were wild. "I'm going." He dropped his pack and headed down the hill, his CAR-15 in his hands.

"No, you're not!" Jason said, rushing after him. "Guys, help me."

There was no way Jason and the others could stop Garth in his fury—not on the side of a hill and with him already ahead. But they had to try. Lewis, Rachel, Trieu, Joo-Chan, and Gil-Su—everybody but Chris, who was pulling security duty—ran after Garth.

"Stop, Garth," Jason said. "This is crazy. You won't save anybody, and you'll get yourself and all of us killed or caught." He grabbed Garth's legs to tackle him. Better a broken arm from the fall than death or capture.

A cry of pain floated to them across the distance. Everybody stopped, listening.

"Guys!" Chris called over their helmet radios. "Come back. They're hurting them. They've hurt Aunt."

Jason stood in front of Garth, their height difference that much more apparent with Jason below him. But he jutted a finger at Garth just the same. "You're smarter than this, Green Beret. Think for a minute." He walked around behind Garth, following the others back up the hill. "Go down if you want, but you know you put us all in danger if you do." Jason walked away from him, praying he would make the right decision. More screams reached his ears.

At the top, he found the courtyard with his binoculars. Aunt and Uncle were kneeling on the ground as if in pain. North Korean agents stood over them uncoiling a long strand of something.

The rest of the refugees stood watching in fear. They tried to move away from the Chinese guard as he came toward them, but the shackles held them fast.

The guard pulled Youn-Chul to his knees. He unlocked his

wrists and ankles as two more guards held him in place. A North Korean agent approached, the black strand in his hands. He tugged on the strand, which caused Uncle and Aunt's heads to swivel in unison and their bloody right arms to rise. The guard tugged again and urged the Chinese guards to pull Youn-Chul closer.

"It's the wire," Gil-Su said, looking through binoculars. "They're running a wire through their wrists and noses."

"Say *what?*" Garth said, approaching the hilltop from below.

"The North Koreans wire such prisoners together. Sometimes they only pierce the skin. Other times. . . You see, to them, these people are animals now."

They heard a scream. It was Youn-Chul. The North Korean agent leaned over a wooden block and drove a thick needle through Youn-Chul's wrist with a hammer. It took three or four hits before it went all the way through. Youn-Chul writhed so hard it knocked back the two guards holding him. The men all laughed and more guards held him down. The agent pulled the wire through Youn-Chul's wrist as if sewing. Sewing people together.

The guards held Youn-Chul's head on the pavement, facing sideways. It took only a single blow to thread the wire through his nose.

They left him kneeling beside Uncle and Aunt, moaning and bleeding. The agent drew the wire through all of them, unrolling it off a spool held by another North Korean agent standing beside Aunt.

Chun-Mi was next. She was balled on the ground. Bum-Ji stood in front of her, interposing himself between his pregnant wife and the horror coming for her.

"This is terrible!" Lewis said. He was weeping.

Rachel and Trieu were crying, too.

Jason had to wipe his eyes to see. "This is wrong." Whether he said it aloud or to himself he didn't know. "This is all wrong. We came here to prevent this from happening. It's the only reason we're even here. We've got weapons and training. We should be *doing something,* not watching it like some kind of sick voyeurs. This is like watching the crucifixion and not being able to do anything about it. Oh, Jesus, can't we please help them?"

In the prison courtyard Bum-Ji was pleading with the North Korean agent. The man tried to push him aside to get at Chun-Mi, but Bum-Ji held his ground, leaning against the chains so hard he dragged the others over. Grandmother stumbled. Ki-Won wailed and wailed as if the world were ending.

A Chinese guard pulled Ki-Won's chain, yanking the child off his feet and onto the pavement. He wailed even louder. His cries were thin and disembodied, like a lost soul.

Bum-Ji pulled the whole group toward Ki-Won. He reached for the child but couldn't touch him.

The guards grew agitated. The North Korean agents yanked the wire, drawing wails from those already threaded.

Men ran forward, pulled the prisoners back. Myong-Chol fended them away from Grandmother.

Guards pulled Bum-Ji back. He shouted and fought. Others unlocked Chun-Mi and dragged her over to Youn-Chul.

The agent grabbed her wrist and set it on the block. He raised his hammer.

Chun-Mi screamed.

Bum-Ji threw off his guards.

Slashed the agent's arm with his shackles.

The hammer clattered to the pavement.

The courtyard erupted. An alarm clanged deafeningly. The prisoners ran at the guards. The guards fought them back, grabbing their ankle chains and dropping them to the cement. The gate guards advanced, shouting and shaking their assault rifles. North Korean agents pummeled Bum-Ji with rifle butts. In the face. Sternum. Neck. They lifted him up. He struggled against them, dragging them toward Chun-Mi. The agent grabbed a rifle.

CRACK!

Bum-Ji's head snapped back. A pink spray spat out the rear of his head. The guards fell backward. They kicked Bum-Ji's body off their legs and rolled away in terror and pain.

"No!" the team shouted.

Chun-Mi screamed. She ran to Bum-Ji and threw her body over him. She rolled his head to look at his face and gave a heart-rending cry.

The guards pulled her off him, though she fought to stay beside him. They dragged her to the block and drove the needle through her wrist and nose. Her cries submerged beneath the clanging alarm bell.

Chinese officers gave orders. Soldiers subdued the other prisoners. A soldier ran off and shortly the alarm bell fell silent. No sounds escaped the prison yard now.

Guards unchained Bum-Ji's body and kicked it out of the way. They carried Ki-Won forward next. The boy had either been killed or rendered unconscious in the fight. They punched the wire through him as he lay still on the pavement. Next they threaded the wire through Grandmother's frail body.

Myong-Chol raised his voice and addressed the assembled guards. The listeners appeared stunned.

"He is telling them about Jesus," Gil-Su said, his voice awed. " 'I love Jesus Christ,' he's saying. 'You can ban the word for God but God still exists. He loves you and will receive you. You can find forgiveness for the things you have done! Come to Him by calling on the name of His Son, Jesus Christ!' "

The North Korean agent struck Myong-Chol in the stomach with the rifle butt. He snapped orders and a soldier went to Bum-Ji's body and tore off a strip of his prison clothes. He brought it to Myong-Chol, who was still testifying, and stuffed it in his mouth. A soldier brought tape, which they wrapped over Myong-Chol's mouth and around the back of his head.

When the agent drove the needle through Myong-Chol's wrist,

he could not cry out. Jason heard the thump of the hammer on the block. It was a curiously domestic sound, like someone working on a project in his garage down the street. It made the moment that much more grotesque.

Now they were all connected, looped together by metal wire through their soft flesh. The guards and agents led, pushed, and carried the refugees out the metal fence and toward the trucks that would take them across to North Korea.

They were loaded onto a flatbed truck and the military convoy rolled out. Jason and the team had to move to a new spot on their hilltop to watch their progress. On the North Korea side, more military vehicles awaited. The lead Chinese vehicles rolled across the highway bridge. Once the refugees' truck was across, the following Chinese vehicles turned around and drove back across the Tumen. The tank backed out of its position and moved off the way it had come.

The Firebrand team assembled without being told to. They walked down the hilltop to a spot of complete concealment under the low trees. For several minutes they squatted in a circle, not speaking. It was late afternoon now. The day was warm. The sky was spotless. If they'd been only tourists, it would've been a fantastic moment in a beautiful spot.

"I'm thinking about Bum-Ji," Jason said into the silence. "There was the language thing, so I never really got to know him. But he was so gentle with Chun-Mi, did you notice? So protective and tender. He had that kind face. His smile brightened a room, you know?" He shook his head. "That man is what a real hero looks like. He gave his life trying to protect his wife and little Ki-Won. His life! Man. . . Would I have done the same thing? I just don't know."

Garth cracked every knuckle in his hands. Slowly. With a simmering violence. "We're going to just leave, then? 'Well, we tried. Sorry, Chun-Mi, but your husband died for nothing. Sorry,

Grandmother, you're a statistic now. Sorry, Ki-Won, you're—' " He stopped. His nostrils flared and his cheeks flushed. He sprang to his feet and paced away.

Then he spun and stomped back, glaring at Jason. "We *know* these people, Kromer! We've spent time with them. We've been through stuff with them. Hard times and good times. They're our friends. Jason, they're our brothers and sisters. Man, this is why we came. For *them!* How can we just let them go?"

Jason flung his arms forward. "Well, what do you suggest, Fisher? Huh? You wanted us to take on that tank? Us against that tank and all those guns? Is that what you wanted?"

"No."

"Look," Jason said, "I hear you, buddy, I do. But what do you want to do, just walk across that bridge, ask 'Pretty please, may we come through?' And then. . .what? Take on the North Korean army, too?"

The idea coalesced in the air between them. Jason looked at it hard in his mind, and he could tell the others were doing the same.

"We're low on food," Rachel said.

"We should be eating the local diet anyway," Chris said, "so we don't smell like Americans if dogs are ever after us."

"Eloise wouldn't go for it," Lewis said.

"No," Jason said, "I'm afraid she would."

"You guys," Rachel said, "marching into North Korea is like walking into Stalin's Russia, okay? This isn't Sudan or Kazakhstan. This is Hades, okay? Sheol. The place of the dead. We go in there and there's a very real chance we're not coming out."

Jason nodded. He scanned their faces, dappled in the leaf shadows. Most of them had their helmets off. His eyes came to rest on Trieu. She looked fabulous sitting there in green camouflage and a sniper rifle across her knees. He realized he did know how he would've acted if he'd been in Bum-Ji's shoes. "Trieu, you're the only one I haven't heard from yet. What's your thought?"

She tucked a strand of hair behind her ear. "I think," she said slowly, "that we have come to care a great deal about these people in a short time. Five days ago they were names on a list to us. Now we know them, we've seen them laugh and bicker and share meals. We've seen them love each other as a family. We've seen husbands and wives devoted to each other. We've seen them play with Ki-Won as we would play with our own child or nephew. I think we have come to understand that they are very much like us. If God had arranged things a little differently, they could *be* us, and we could be them. And when we see that, I think we can only treat them the way we'd like to be treated if we were them."

As she spoke it was as if God's own voice was echoing each word inside Jason's heart. They resonated in his soul. So convincing were they that before she was done, his mind had turned to how in the world they were going to pull this thing off.

He looked at Trieu, then at the group. "Okay, can I just say that my fiancée is a remarkable woman? Would that be crass or something?"

They chuckled.

"So." Jason clapped his hands together and rubbed. "How are we going to get them out of North Korea?"

Chris's eyes snapped to him. "So we're really going to do it?"

"I think so. Unless someone can give me a reason that trumps what Trieu just said."

Some of them looked relieved. Others looked concerned. Some cycled back and forth between the two.

"Lewis, fire up the radio. I want to tell Eloise what we're up to."

"Roger that."

"Chris and Garth, see what kind of mappage we've got for North Korea."

Garth threw his pack off and dug into it. "You got it, chief."

"Gil-Su," Jason said, "do you understand what we've decided?"

Gil-Su and Joo-Chan, who had been sitting outside their circle, came to kneel beside Jason. "Yes. But I have to say I'm stunned. I don't think *I* would go into North Korea, and I've been working with refugees for years. Yet you come in and decide to do it in one week, all because of your faith. I am. . .humbled."

Jason touched his shoulder. "Well, you've humbled us with your faith, brother, so we're even. Now, about that part about you not going into North Korea. . .I, uh, think I'm going to have to ask you to pray about coming with us. None of us speaks Korean and you speak Korean, Chinese, and English. We need you, if you can see your way clear to coming."

"Yes, of course. I will. . .pray about it." Then his muscles tensed and he shook his head. "No, I will go. My heart knows I am to go. God told me as soon as you said it. The only reason I would hesitate is out of fear. I will go."

"You're a good man, Gil-Su," Jason said.

"What about Joo-Chan?" Gil-Su said, slapping the teenager on the back. "He is young and courageous, as well."

"I know he is," Jason said, smiling at Joo-Chan. "But I don't think he should come. He doesn't speak English, so he can't help us that way. And, frankly, having one extra person along is a liability. Having two would be too much for us, especially if we do manage to release some refugees. Have him stay in the safe house with Sun-Hye and the other girl. He can take care of them."

"Yes," Gil-Su said. "He could do that."

Jason looked at Joo-Chan, who didn't have a clue what they were talking about. But he was a red-blooded young man about to be staying alone with two former prostitutes who weren't sure which side was up right now. "Just, uh, you know, make sure he behaves himself, okay?"

Gil-Su smirked. "I understand."

CHAPTER 26

WHERE THE SHADOWS LIE

"GO FARTHER, LEWIS. Push its limits. I don't want to be surprised this time."

Jason watched Lewis tromping through the field of tall dead grass beside the wide dirt road. The banshee was already out of sight to the north. Two hundred yards away, Lewis stopped and turned around.

"How's this?" he asked.

"That's good, Lewis. I don't want you any farther away than that. Now have the banshee show me how far up the road it can see."

"Okay, just a sec." A moment later he said, "Boss, next time can we leave the plate mail armor behind? Or at least secure them to my body better? These things bounce up and smack down when I run."

"Roger that, Lewis. Why don't you be in charge of that when we get home?"

"You got that right."

They were in the Democratic People's Republic of Korea. Only

298

about eight miles southeast of Tumen and the same distance southwest of Onsong, North Korea. The team hid in the unmowed hay field on either side of the brown dirt road that passed for a superhighway here. It was the main route from Onsong, where the refugees had spent the night, to the rest of North Korea. It was also—they hoped and prayed—the road the refugees would be sent along, perhaps any minute.

Jason scanned the road. It was 8:00 in the morning—but no rush-hour traffic. No traffic at all. No farm equipment headed into the fields. Not even a line of rice paddy workers or maybe a farm boy with a cow. In their whole overnight crossing, they'd seen not a single other human being or domesticated animal. Why was Kim Jong-Il so adamant about protecting this place? There was nothing here. But the birds that liked deep thicket seemed to appreciate the place, so at least Chris was happy.

"Hey," Jason said into his helmet mic, "who's awake here? Sound off." He looked around the yellow hay but couldn't see anyone.

"Rachel's awake. Gil-Su's snoozing, though."

"Chris Page, ready for action, sir."

"I'm here!" Lewis said.

"Trieu is asleep," Trieu said. "Or wishes she were."

Jason waited. "Garth?"

"Hang on," Rachel said.

To Jason's left across the street, he saw the top of Rachel's helmet appear over the hay. She trotted toward the road and turned right.

"I thought he was right here som— Whoa!" She went down with a thud. "Uh," she said, groaning, "I found him. He was asleep, but he's awake now."

Garth yawned. "What'd I miss?"

"Nothing," Chris said over the radio. "Unless you count the exotic ornithology going on all around you."

"I missed the exotic dancers?"

"No, you big Neanderthal," Chris said. "Birds."

"Oh. Like I care."

Jason dropped the eye panel down on his helmet. The default view was what he called the dot race: a map schematic with electronic blue dots representing his team members' up-to-the-second precise locations. He saw five clumped together on either side of the road and one by itself a good distance away. "You got a good view for me yet, Lewis?"

"Take a look."

Jason cycled through the gun cam views, headed to the banshee's feed. But he stopped when he came to Trieu's gun cam. The camera feed actually worked through the optics of her sniper scope, so he saw a zoomed image looking directly up the dirt road. Nothing but slight morning fog at the edge of her vision.

"You okay, Trieu? Your grass blanket keeping you warm?"

"Very."

Jason checked both directions then stepped out into the road. Twenty yards to his right he spotted Lewis's net mine entangler land mines in the middle of the road. A few paces to Jason's left, Trieu was lying in a slight recession just at the side of the road, covered by a low mound of chopped-up hay. She was the most exposed, but a person could step right over her and never know she was there. He could see where her rifle barrel and scope were only because he knew they must be under there. "You're looking good, Trieu," he said, then stepped back to his hiding spot.

"Now, now," Rachel said. "You two cut that out."

"No, I just meant—"

"Yeah, uh-huh. What?"

Jason sank into his place. "Never mind."

He cycled to the banshee's camera feed. It was a great view of the road, which ran mostly straight for twenty miles. "That's perfect, Lewis. How much battery does the banshee have left?"

"Another hour or so," Lewis said. "Conditions are pretty much perfect for maximum battery life."

"Jason?" Rachel said.

"Yeah?"

"Gil-Su's awake now. He's worried about crossing back to China in the daytime."

"I know," Jason said. "Tell him we'll try to hide out here and cross at night. That's *if* the North Koreans cooperate and bring our friends right to us. If they wait for whatever reason, it might be night before we get them anyway."

"Roger that," she said. A minute later she called him again. "He's also concerned the safe house won't be big enough to house all the refugees plus the ones staying there now, plus us."

"Understood," Jason said, "but it will have to do for at least a night. Chimp says Eloise has worked something out that will be ready for us right there in Kaishantun in a day or two. We just have to hide out until then. We can sleep in the woods if we have to."

"Roger. I'll tell him."

The climate here was warm and humid. Jason was already sweating, and he had a feeling it was only going to get worse as the day wore on.

"Uh. . .Jason?"

"Whatcha got, Lewis?" Jason focused again on the banshee's camera feed.

"It's a car," Lewis said, something like wonder in his voice.

Jason looked hard at the aerial shot. A small gleam as from a passenger car windshield moved along the road, kicking up a cloud of dust like brown sugar. "Can you zoom in, Lewis?"

The image centered on the white vehicle and zoomed in.

"It's a Toyota," Chris said. "A stinkin' Toyota Camry. What's that thing doing here?"

"Tourists, you think?" Jason said.

"Rachel here. Gil-Su says it must be a party official. They're the only ones authorized to have private cars and allocated the gasoline. It must be somebody important."

"And he's headed right into our ambush," Garth pointed out.

"Roger that," Jason said. "Garth, Chris, hop out there and retrieve those land mines. While I'm sure our country wouldn't mind us capturing a North Korean big boy, it's not what we're here to do."

"Roger that."

Garth's torso rose out of the grass like a pirate scarecrow. He and Chris swept off the hay that had been hiding the disc-shaped arrestor land mines and gently carried the mines back into the hay.

"You're sure these things can stop a truck?" Chris said. "It's nothing but net, right? I think the truck will drive right through it or drive off with it glommed onto its belly."

"No way," Lewis said. "We only need one to do the job anyway. All I have to do is deploy the thing and *whap-snap-bam,* the axle is fouled and the truck stops. Works the same way if it gets rolled over, too, but only on one wheel."

"Lewis," Jason said, "how far away is the car?"

"About three miles now, boss. Woo, that boy's going to need to wash his car when he gets home. Now *that's* a dusty road."

"Roger," Jason said. "Trieu, why don't you go ahead and pull off into the grass? No need to risk you being seen if we're just going to let the guy pass."

"All right," she said. "Moving."

Lewis's gasp broadcast to the whole squad. "Uh oh."

"What is it, Lewis?" Jason said.

"Oh no. Look at your monitor. I must've missed it in the dust cloud."

Jason watched as the banshee's view zoomed back out. In the midst of the dense plume of dust kicked up by the passenger car he thought he saw a flash of sunlight reflecting off something. The image zoomed in. There, plodding forward as if in an Iraqi sand-storm, was a military truck.

"It's them!" Rachel said. "They're here!"

"Oh no!"

"Great."

"Get the land mines back out there!" Chris said.

"No!" Jason said. "Wait. Everybody stay cool. Lewis, how far behind the car is the truck?"

"Hard to say. Half a mile maybe."

"Okay," Jason said. "Then we let the car go and we stop the truck. We drop the land mines out after the car goes by, or maybe we just shoot the tires out. That dust cloud's so bad that if we're lucky, Mr. Party Line will be in Pyongyang before he realizes he's lost his truck."

"Roger that, chief," Garth said.

"Lewis," Jason said, "check for more vehicles in the cloud. Look hard, bro. Then get yourself back here as quick as you can, and bring the banshee."

"Yes, sir."

"Jason," Trieu said, her voice perfectly placid.

"Yes, ma'am," Jason said.

"How do we know the refugees are in this truck? It could be empty. It could be full of soldiers."

"I know!" he snapped. "I know. But I don't know what else to do. We can stop the truck and see what's inside. We'll Versed the drivers and whoever else we don't want. If we're wrong, we'll bug out into China and try again tomorrow. But the sat photo Chimp sent showed just one panel truck at the Onsong prison complex overnight. And this thing has gotten so big I can't see them letting high-profile deserters sit in tiny Onsong for any time at all. I know it's not a sure thing that this truck has our friends in it, but I think there's a good chance." He blew out a sigh. "What do you guys think?"

"I think," Garth said, "that we'd better make sure we're out of sight. Car in view at the corner. Half a mile."

"Roger that," Jason said.

"Jason," Chris said, "let's stop the truck. If there's a chance

Myong-Chol and the others are there, I say we take it. These guys are dead if we don't save them."

"I agree," Rachel said. "Let's take the truck."

"Roger that," Jason said. "All right, team, here's the plan. We let the car go by, but we hit the truck. Rachel, take some footage of the car with your gun cam. Maybe it'll be intel our guys can use back home."

"Roger."

"Everybody be aware that it's about to get very dusty. Let's use the black masks we brought for the party, copy that?"

The team answered in the affirmative.

Jason pulled his own black knit ski mask over his face then replaced his helmet. "As soon as the car passes and the dust cloud is over us, Garth and Chris drop the land mines on the road. Then get out of sight and prepare to assault the truck."

"Roger that."

"You got it, chief."

"Lewis, you pull the plug on the mines, okay?"

Lewis arrived behind Jason, out of breath but composed. "No problem."

"Trieu," Jason said, dropping a tear-gas canister into the grenade launcher slung under his CAR-15, "stand by to shoot the tires out if the land mines don't work. It'll be a shot worth a medal if you make it, but I know you can do it."

"I'll try."

"You'll be great," Jason said. "And. . .I'm sorry about snapping at you."

"Don't worry about it, Jason."

"Here it comes!" Garth said.

The white Toyota made a low roar as it advanced. It was fifty yards away now. The road was like powder. A cone of dust billowed up from the car's rear tires like brown rocket exhaust.

Jason hunkered down. He pushed aside the hay with his rifle

to have a brief but clear glimpse at the occupants when they passed.

"Truck at the far corner," Lewis said.

"Roger that," Jason said. "Everybody down!"

The Camry rolled close. The wind of its coming rustled the hay by the road in a rolling cascade of air. The car passed Jason's gap at fifty miles an hour.

But halfway past it seemed to shift into extreme slow motion. The driver was a soldier. The passenger a man in a black suit.

But in the back seat. . .

Recognition chilled Jason's chest.

He saw her only in profile and partially concealed by the window frame, but there was no mistaking who it was. Or who was the little boy standing up looking out the back window.

"That was Chun-Mi!" he shouted. "And Ki-Won! They were in the car! Trieu, shoot out the tires!"

"The car's gone, Kromer!" Chris said. "We get the truck!"

The dust cloud struck him with the wind of the car's passing. Suddenly his visibility was down to twenty feet of brown fog. He knew Trieu couldn't see the car in this. He saw ghostly figures running on the road—Garth and Chris planting the nonlethal land mines. Through the dust beyond them he saw twin yellow eyes—the truck's headlights.

"Off the road!" he called. "The truck's here."

They could've all been standing in the middle of the street for all anyone could see. The dust cloud was the perfect camouflage. But already it was thinning. And Chun-Mi and Ki-Won were getting farther away.

"Lewis," Jason said, sinking into the hay, "you ready to blow it?"

"I'm on it, boss. Finger on the button."

"We've only got one shot at this."

"I'm *on* it."

The truck was twice as loud as the car had been. Its twenty-year-old diesel engine clattered like a school bus. The driver, a young North Korean soldier with no hat, leaned up to the windshield trying to see through the dust. He was traveling no more than thirty-five miles an hour.

Fifty feet. Forty. Thirty.

The driver's window was open.

Twenty feet.

Should he pepper him as he passed?

Ten. Five.

"Now, Lewis!"

Jason didn't hear anything. The truck rolled on. "It didn't work! Take out the tires. Everybody shoot!" A new dust cloud walloped him from the side. He stood and ran beside the road on the left, staying clear of where the others would shoot, hoping to catch the truck on foot by—

The truck seized up and lurched left. It ground to a stop with its nose in the hay field just in front of Jason.

His training clicked in and he went into battle-ready posture: knees flexed, weapon shouldered, safety off. "Come on-line," he whispered into his mic. "Take 'em down hot."

The dust cloud thickened around them, again giving the Firebrand team the advantage.

The driver's door opened and the young soldier hopped out, complaining acerbically to his companion. He shut the door and looked down at the front left wheel.

SNAP-SNAP-SNAP!

Puffs of white oleoresin capsicum powder irritant exploded on the soldier's back, mixing with the dust like flour in a cake mix. Jason knew from experience those pepperballs stung.

The soldier flinched violently and reached for his back. He turned to see what had bitten him—and received three more rapid-fire pelts on the upper chest.

He saw Jason and his eyes widened, but the pepper powder took effect and he coughed and dropped to his knees.

Jason felt a teammate circling around to his left. He heard the distinctive *phhtt* of an MP-5 firing the tranquilizer cocktail dart. It hit the soldier in the left hip. Jason turned to see who was with him. It was Lewis, looking like a terrorist in his black mask.

Another CAR-15 fired on the other side of the truck, followed by the *pyew* sound that could've been a laser gun from a movie, but which Jason knew to be Trieu's Dragunov SVD. The passenger dropped to the road.

Jason and Lewis fell into position outside the back door beside Garth and Rachel. Chris and Trieu joined them an instant later. Garth approached the handle at the bottom of the sliding door.

"Wait," Jason said. "Trieu, Chris, pull security front and back."

"Roger that."

Trieu trotted forward of the truck; Chris went the other way. Lewis and Jason got into better position behind the truck.

Jason nodded at Garth. "Do it."

The big man released his CAR-15, and the harness pulled it snug to his chest. He climbed onto the rear step of the dark green panel truck. He grasped the handle, then paused. He mouthed and pointed to the right: *I'm going that way.* The team nodded. Garth yanked the handle upward.

It roared up, creaking rusty rollers.

Garth leaped out of the way.

The Firebrand team squeezed on triggers.

Then lowered their muzzles.

There were the refugees. Their friends. Grandmother, Aunt, Uncle, Myong-Chol, and Youn-Chul. Their faces and clothes were dark with dried blood. But they were alive and, when Jason pulled his mask off, suddenly very happy.

* * *

"We're sure we got everything from the truck?" Jason asked.

"Nothing left that would make anyone suspect anything? No darts on the ground, no pieces of those land mines, no candy bar wrappers, right?"

"Relax, Squiddie," Chris said. "We got it all."

Jason sighed. "I still can't understand why they put Chun-Mi and the boy in the car. Why'd they have to do that?"

"Who knows?" Chris said. "Maybe they were being taken somewhere different? Maybe the fat cat thought he could rape her? Maybe she asked to ride in the car and he said okay. Doesn't matter why."

Jason felt himself clenching his jaw. "It matters to me."

Garth put his hand on Jason's shoulder. "Come on, bro, let's be about our business."

Jason, Chris, and Garth stood by the truck, which now idled in the middle of the road. The two North Korean soldiers were sleeping it off in separate parts of the hay field. The rest of the team and the refugees were half a mile to the west, waiting.

"Okay," Jason said, nodding reluctantly, "let's blow it."

"I love it when you talk that way," Garth said. He slapped Jason on the back and flipped open his little detonator keypad.

Chris climbed into the driver's seat but kept the door open. He put the truck in gear. "You'd better move back. I'm jumping at ten m-p-h."

"Roger that," Jason said.

"You girls ready for some fireworks?" Garth said.

"If it will make the bad guys think all the refugees died inside it," Jason said, "I'm ready."

"Well," Garth said, smiling dangerously, "they're not going to think anything survived this."

"Okay, Chris," Jason said, "get it moving."

Chris saluted and ducked inside the cab. He gunned the engine and accelerated up the road. Despite his promise, he got the truck up to around twenty miles an hour. Finally the door opened and he jumped out. He rolled to his feet and bounded away across the hay field. The truck coasted on, easing slightly to the right.

Garth held his finger over the detonator button, watching Chris and the truck. "Right. . .about. . .*now!*"

BAA-*OOM!*

They hit the deck as shrapnel and bits of panel truck erupted into the sky, followed by a rolling fireball like a scoop of orange sherbet. The heat wave washed over them like the blast from a kiln. The truck rolled on, then listed into a ditch and fell over onto its right side. A secondary explosion burst the windshield.

Garth tucked his detonator away. "I love doing that."

The fire devoured the truck. The side panel facing the sky caved inward. A flaming tire spun in the heat. Burning chunks rained into the dry hay field, spouting ominous plumes of gray smoke to mix with the black smoke roiling from the fully involved truck. Chris ran up to them, laughing insanely.

"A–th–th–th–that's all, folks," Garth said in a poor imitation of Porky Pig.

Jason stood. "Let's get out of here."

CHAPTER 27

NOT YET RELEASED

"KROMER JASON-SCOTT, come."

Uncle beckoned to Jason in the fading light of dusk. They were inside the safe house in Kaishantun, China. It was a two-story building, a fabric merchant shop below and living quarters above. Large photos of Mao Tse-tung and Hua Guofeng presided over the proceedings. Family photos and certificates of achievement stood over a simple wood table and bamboo chairs against the white plaster walls. Most of the Firebrand team, back in tourist clothes, sat around a low table studying maps and Lewis's PDA, on which were the satellite images they'd looked at in their briefing back in Akron. Jason shrugged at the team and followed Uncle into the next room.

This was the hosts' bedroom. But they had given their home to the refugees and gone to stay with family in the next village over. It reeked of unwashed refugees, but Jason was growing accustomed to the smell. Grandmother, Myong-Chol, Aunt, Youn-Chul, Gil-Su, Joo-Chan, Sun-Hye, and the other former prostitute lay on the wooden floor around the edges of the room, which was lit by thick white candles in the middle of the floor. Trieu knelt beside Aunt, taking her pulse. Uncle moved to his wife and sat beside her.

Jason felt the rest of the team pushing into the room behind him, so he stepped forward to let them in.

"Jason," Gil-Su said, leaning against the plank wall, "Aunt wants to talk to you."

"Aunt?" Jason went to his knees beside Trieu. "How is she?"

"She definitely has tuberculosis. I've got her on isoniazid. If she can just take it for the full course she should be fine."

Jason eyed the bloody scab at the bottom of Aunt's nose. "And where the wire went?"

"I've given them all tetanus immunoglobulin shots," Trieu said. "Their wounds should heal fine now that I've treated them. They'll carry the scars forever, though."

"In more ways than one, I'm sure." Jason's eyes went to Aunt's wrist. It was bandaged, as were several other wrists in the room, but he could see the dark bruises spreading wider than the gauze. "Okay," he said to Gil-Su. "What would she like to say to me?"

Gil-Su spoke to Aunt, who answered but immediately had to stop to cough. She finally regained her voice, and Gil-Su translated.

"I want to thank you all for coming to rescue us. All of us want to thank you."

The refugees and the team members touched hands and gave hugs for the hundredth time since they'd left the truck. Jason noticed that Sun-Hye stuck closely to Youn-Chul's side. They held hands all the way up to the shoulder. Youn-Chul was bruised and scabbed, but his spirits had definitely been lifted since his reunion with pretty Sun-Hye.

"But," Gil-Su continued his translation, "I beg you to save Chun-Mi and Ki-Won. And Chun-Mi's baby, if it can be saved now."

Aunt's voice rose with emotion, doubling the intensity of her coughs.

"It is my fault they are in danger." Gil-Su said, translating. "We all would have gotten away if it hadn't have been for me. I've been a problem to my family from the beginning of our trip. I picked on Chun-Mi and Ki-Won especially. But now that they're in danger and the rest of my family is safe, I feel terrible. Please! Please, you—" He waited out her coughing. "You must save poor Chun-Mi and little Ki-Won. Please!"

The coughing took her. Trieu laid her back on her mat. Uncle touched his wife's shoulder and Aunt squeezed his hand.

Jason stood. "Gil-Su, please tell them we are discussing right now if there is any way we can locate Chun-Mi and Ki-Won."

Gil-Su translated.

"Come on," Jason said, herding people toward the door, "let's go, team."

"Good," Lewis said, standing in line behind Garth. "I'm getting a little claustrophobic. I need air."

Before they could exit, Grandmother got to her feet and strode to the middle of the room, speaking energetically. Jason turned to Gil-Su.

"Uh. . . ," he said, flustered. "She says you *will* go rescue Chun-Mi. She is not ordering you; she says God has told her this."

Jason turned. "Oh?"

As Grandmother continued, Gil-Su translated on the fly.

"You are the mighty osprey over the sea. The hand of Jesus God is upon you. You swoop to pluck the fish from the water. The rabbit from the snare. The branch from the fire. You bear it to safety. Creator God is your shield, your mighty wall. You are not free to turn from this course. He has not released you."

A warm wave spread down Jason's arms. Either this woman was cracked or he was hearing the word of God through a prophetess.

"You are the net in the fisher's hand. He scoops"—she did so with her hand—"until He is finished. You have done well, mighty warriors, but some of My children you came for are yet to be plucked. The task appointed you is yet to be completed. And one must surrender to Me still. I will guide. I will protect. Ten thousand will fall at your side, but you shall not."

Then, as suddenly as she began, Grandmother stopped. She returned to her mat and lay down, her eyes snapping shut.

"Well. . . ," Jason said. "I, uh, guess we have some thinking to do. Come on, team, let's. . .go look at a map or something."

He was last to arrive in the living room. The team sat around the low, square table. Then he felt someone behind him. It was Myong-Chol.

The wire had torn through Myong-Chol's nose. Trieu had stitched the septum together again, and he wore a tuft of blood-tinged bandage over the spot. He took Jason's arm and looked in his eye. It was a man-to-man look, one Christian warrior to another. Jason felt stronger just meeting Myong-Chol's steady gaze.

Myong-Chol looked back into the bedroom and called to Gil-Su. Gil-Su translated as Myong-Chol spoke to Jason.

"I am the one Grandmother spoke of. The one who must surrender to God. You see, I know where Chun-Mi and the boy were taken. We were all going to the same place. I heard the guards talking. They didn't name it, but I spent many years of my life there and I knew what they were describing. They are being taken to Hoeryong Family Camp Number 22, where I was a guard. It is one hundred kilometers south of where you intercepted our truck."

Jason raised his eyebrows. "That's fantastic, Myong-Chol. Thank you! Can you show us on the map?"

As Gil-Su translated, Jason knelt beside the low table with the map of North Korea spread over it. Myong-Chol traced his hand down the road from the ambush, following a line hugging the border with China, and came to rest on a spot. The Firebrand team leaned across the table to watch.

Garth looked at the name under Myong-Chol's finger. "Haengyong? I thought you said *Hoeryong.*"

Gil-Su translated and received Myong-Chol's answer. "It is the same."

"Well," Jason said, "this is great. Gil-Su, please tell him we'd like him to help us plan our visit to this camp. Anything he can tell us. I guess we'll need you, too. Sorry, brother."

Gil-Su smiled wearily. "It is no problem. It is one way I serve my Lord."

He translated to Myong-Chol. But then Myong-Chol said something that seemed to upset Gil-Su. They exchanged spirited volleys. The team watched with interest.

Finally, Gil-Su turned to Jason. "He says he will help you any way he can."

Jason looked at Trieu, who appeared as confused as the rest. "Is that all he said?" he asked Gil-Su.

Myong-Chol's expression was resolute. He sat cross-legged at the table and rested his arms heavily on it as if no force on earth could remove him.

"No," Gil-Su said, letting out a slow breath of air. "That is not all he said. He says he will do more than help you with information. He says he will take you there himself."

"What?" Chris said sharply, as if slapped awake. "What? No, no, no, no, no." He pointed at Myong-Chol. "You're not going back there. Tell him, Gil-Su. Tell him he's not going back there."

Gil-Su translated as Chris spoke.

"You've had your little martyr thing, okay?" Chris said. "You've proven your courage and your faith. You stood up for what you believed in. You shouted it out. God's got to be doing backflips over it. Okay? But you're done now. That woman in there says we plucked you out of the fire, right? You're out. You're safe. You did your Christian thing, but you're sitting the rest of this one out."

"Chris," Jason said.

"I'm not finished."

"Chris!"

"No, Jason, look. If we pluck them out of the fire but they go crawling back into it on their own, well, that's just stupid. And I'm not going to let him do it."

Gil-Su finished translating and fell silent. No one spoke. Wax sizzled in one of the candles on the table. Garth rubbed his scalp and face. Myong-Chol stared at the map.

"Okay, look," Jason said. "Let's pretend you're in the marines again, Chris. Your squad's been tasked with a rescue op inside an enemy-held prison. You've got less than six hours to plan and execute the mission. All you have is the location of the prison and some sat photos. You have no clue where the person you're supposed to rescue is being held. And along comes a local who says he can get you in and out of there easy and he knows right where your hostage is being held. What are you going to do?"

"I'm going to tie him up and leave him behind," Chris said, "because he's probably a spy."

"Yeah, okay," Jason said, irritation tingeing his voice. "But what if you knew he was legit? You're not going to turn him down. No way. You're going to bring him into your planning and you're going to take him with you. That's what you're going to do. And that's what *we're* going to do, too."

"Yeah, but he's—"

"No, Mr. Page, that's it," Jason said. "Maybe he's captured and killed on this mission. Maybe we are, too. Maybe we're too late and Chun-Mi and Ki-Won are already dead. But that's the risk we all signed up for when we joined. Myong-Chol knows the dangers of this camp better than any of us. If he's willing to go, then I'm willing to take him. Besides, you heard the woman in there. I don't know about everything she said, but there's one thing I think she got right: God has not released us from this yet. I say we see it through to the end. And Myong-Chol is our only chance for pulling it off."

Again they sat in silence. From the next room over came the sounds of people snoring. Jason's stomach rumbled, but the thought of more *kimchi*—pickled cabbage on pepper override—stifled that idea right away.

Myong-Chol picked up Lewis's PDA from the table and looked at the small color display. He brought it close to his face as if seeing something he recognized. He asked Gil-Su a question.

"He wants to know if this is Camp 22," Gil-Su said.

Lewis nodded. "Sure is." He rounded the table to sit by Myong-Chol and show him how to navigate the image.

"All right," Jason said to the team, "it looks like we've got one last decision to make. Do we go back into North Korea—*with* Myong-Chol—infiltrate a death camp the likes of Auschwitz, try to find our two needles in the haystack, and try to get out with our lives—or do we cut our losses and sit here waiting on whatever plan Eloise has figured out? What do you guys think?"

"Oh," Rachel said, as if he'd asked if she would like a million dollars, "we definitely go. I mean, there are two innocents out there about to be hurt by evil men. If that's not what this group is all about, I don't know what is."

"Yeah," Garth said, "we go. Little buddy needs his papa bear."

Lewis pulled from his pocket a wooden rectangle puzzle piece. "I finally got Ki-Won's *sa-gak-hyong* right. I'd better take it to him."

"If Chun-Mi is still alive," Trieu said, "she will need medical care. If they abort the baby with a hypertonic saline injection, as Myong-Chol says they often do, it will basically burn the baby to death in her womb. She will need medical help at the least and intense psychological intervention. If we can get her to safety, Eloise will provide for her mental health. I know she will."

She lifted her eyes to Jason's, and in one electric exchange her gaze conveyed an intimate message: *We are risking our future, you and I, if we go on this. Yet because you ask it of me and because of the need, I will join you.*

Jason shut his eyes against the grief that rose inside him. He swiped his hand down his face and looked back at Trieu. He gave her what he hoped was a loving smile but feared it probably looked a lot like a frown.

"Chris," Jason said, "what about you?"

Chris sat with the fingers of one hand rubbing his forehead. "I think," he said, his eyes shut, "that you're all right. I just hate it that Myong-Chol is going back to that place. I'm afraid he's not coming back."

Jason nodded. "Yeah, I know. I wonder if any of us will."

"Hey, now," Rachel said, "don't let's talk like that. Grandmother said God was protecting us. I don't know about the rest of you, but I believe that none of us can die until God is done with us. If He's done with one of us or more than one of us on this mission, then we get to go straight to Paradise. Sounds pretty good to me. If He's not done with us, it means we'll live because He's got more for us to do. Either way, we win."

"Yeah, that sounds real good, Raych," Lewis said, "except if they, like, capture us and cut out our tongues or something, or they put us in a coma but keep us alive. Then we wouldn't be serving God at all, but we couldn't go to heaven, either."

"Oh," Garth said, "now that's an encouraging thought. Thanks, kid."

"I'm just *saying*. . . ," Lewis said. "That's one of my fears, is all."

Chris dropped his hands to the table. "Well, if we're going to do this, let's do it. If we're a hundred klicks from our location, we'd better get moving."

"Right," Jason said, leaning over the map. "We'll travel tonight and sleep through the day. We'll try to be on site at the camp at midnight tomorrow night. We'll find our friends, get them out, reverse our steps, and be back here by dawn the next day. Without firing a shot. Then Eloise's thing will get here—Chimp says it will somehow come to us—and we all go home." He glanced at the PDA. "Lewis, can you patch that thing into our helmet eye panels so we can see it better?"

"Affirmative."

Five minutes later the Firebrand team, plus Myong-Chol and Gil-Su, were looking at the high-resolution color photos of what Hoeryong Family Camp Number 22 looked like from space. Jason and Trieu shared a helmet to let Myong-Chol use one. Gil-Su used the PDA and translated Myong-Chol's narration.

At first glance, the satellite photo looked like a vein of silver streaking a brown boulder. A narrow strip of silvery blue and rosy pebbles ran roughly north-south on the right third of the photo. An even thinner silver stripe wound in from the left with a sinuous curve that looked suspiciously like a stream. The rest of the photo was dirt brown and dark green trees. When they zoomed in, however, the silver in the large strip turned out to be irrigated fields in a riverbed, and the rosy pebbles were tightly clustered buildings all made from the same brick-colored material. Camp 22.

"Prisoners with families live here, here, here, here, and in these buildings here." Myong-Chol spoke through Gil-Su and annotated the image with the three-button mouse as Lewis had shown him to do. "The furniture factory is here. The food factory. The pharmaceutical factory."

Little green ticks dotted the image as he spoke. The factories were long buildings arranged around a courtyard or loading area. The prisoners' quarters were uniformly small rectangular buildings clustered together in military-like sequence, like buttons on a phone. The camp was huge. It sprawled over dozens of square miles.

Myong-Chol continued. "Here is the greenhouse. Here, the slaughterhouse. Can we zoom in to this spot over here, Lewis? It is the headquarters."

The image centered on an area just above where the stream came in from the left and joined the riverbed on the right. The images were so clear and they could zoom so close that Jason almost expected to see people walking around directly below him. He could see individual fields now. They were striated and the water in them gleamed silver—they looked like icy parking lots. The buildings to the left of these fields were not so densely packed. They were arranged around two large courtyards that touched at the corner, like a square-sided figure eight. A green diamond appeared atop a wide white building that was the biggest structure Jason had seen in the camp.

"Kim Il-Sung Memorial Hall," Myong-Chol said. "For guard assemblies and propaganda meetings. Below it is the theater, where they show the glorious achievements of Kim Jong-Il. Did you know he invented computers and has cured cancer? Or that he could fly airplanes when he was only five years old? Such is what they tell children in North Korea."

The team exchanged amused looks.

Myong-Chol identified the other buildings of the headquarters compound: armory, administration offices, weapons store, guards' quarters, supply depot, camouflaged antiaircraft gun, propaganda bureau, and, most importantly to the team, the guards' night-duty room and the detention and torture center.

This last, Myong-Chol explained, doubled as the medical facility for the base, and was where Chun-Mi would probably be taken so her pregnancy could be terminated. He guessed that Ki-Won would be held either with her, in family quarters there in the compound, or anywhere else out in the camp where families were housed.

They spoke for two hours more about how the team should approach the camp, what patrols would be in place, when the shifts changed—or at least when they used to change when Myong-Chol was a guard there—and what the guards' response would be to various alarm scenarios. Jason was on the satellite radio to Chimp twice. Jason and Chris stayed over the map with Myong-Chol and Gil-Su to talk strategy, but he released the others to gear up for the journey.

There were still three hours of darkness left when Jason finally left the table. He stretched as he crossed to the corner where Trieu sat reassembling her sniper rifle after cleaning it. The sweet scent of gun oil always took Jason back to SEAL Team Three. He sat beside her and leaned heavily against the slat wall. He put his hand on her left shoulder blade. "How're you holding up?"

She set the gun down and faced him. The almost-spent candles lit her cheeks in a lovely peach glow. "As well as can be expected. We're all fatigued from stress, travel, exertion, and adrenaline letdown. We could each use twelve hours of sleep. Then when we return, I prescribe another week down under on the *Pride of Gippsland.*"

Jason smiled wistfully. "Wasn't that great?" He took her hand and brought it to his knee. "Trieu, I want to tell you something. It won't be easy for you to hear, but I need to say it."

A slight crevice appeared above her nose. "What?"

"What we're about to do is pretty risky. Actually, it's probably pretty dumb. We have no safety net under us, no air strikes to call in if we get in trouble. We're walking into a place where, when there's nothing good happening over at the Kim Il-Sung Memorial Hall, the guards just decide to kill somebody instead." He sighed explosively. "What I'm trying to say is that we may not come out of this one alive. I think it will be a miracle if any of us makes it out, personally. But don't tell the guys I said that. And, well, I just want you to know that even though we've been together like, what, seven days? I love you deeply. In a way it seems like we've always been together. I think my heart connected to yours in that first dance, do you remember?"

She lifted her chin. "I remember you made a pass at me."

"I know," he said, feeling the temperature rise in his immediate vicinity.

Trieu smiled faintly and stroked the stubble on his cheek. "Jason, don't be so certain we will die on this mission. I believe we will come out of it alive. I don't believe these three missions are all God has for the Firebrand team."

"Well, Eloise could always replace us. I'm sure sh—"

"No, I mean *us*. *This* team. These members. Besides," she said, knocking on the vest lying beside her, "you've got us all wearing armor this time."

"Okay, okay," he said. "Shut up a minute." He leaned across and kissed her tenderly. She kissed back more forcefully. He wrapped his arm around her back and drew her close. Then: "Well, I hope you're right," he whispered into her ear. "I do want to take you on a honeymoon. Anywhere you like. But I want to say one more thing, just in case that doesn't happen, okay?"

She pressed her cheek against his and stroked his hair. "All right."

"If you make it out of this but I don't, I. . ." He sighed and started again. Then stopped again. "I want you to. . .to find someone else to marry."

She drew back and looked at him. Jason tried to gauge the expression in her eyes. Was it ridicule? *Of course I'll marry someone else. You think you're irreplaceable?* Was it confusion? *But I thought we were tragic lovers fated to live together or not at all?* What was it? His chest shuddered like it always did when he was feeling intensely vulnerable.

"Jason," she said, and by the tone in that one word she told him he was safe with her. "We will not talk of that. I believe God wills for us to be together. Whether that is for seventy years or just these seven days, I do not know. But whatever happens I know His purposes will be served in you and me because our hearts are truly His." She leaned forward and kissed him passionately.

It took several seconds afterward for Jason to find his voice. And then all he could say was "Whoa."

"Now," she said, slapping him playfully, "go pack or you'll hold us all up."

CHAPTER 28

DETENTION AND TORTURE CENTER

Shin-Hwa, do not come at all. Die inside me. May whatever it was they injected me with kill you quickly, my precious daughter. I feel you writhing, boiling, trying to get away from it. There is only one way you can run—but don't!

Your father lies dead. Killed by your countrymen. Your family burned to death in the accident. Your mother they will kill. Little Ki-Won, your cousin, they have taken away. And you, tiny child, if you come here, you will not live long. Corrupt at birth, they call you. The dogs are ferocious. They pull at their leashes at the sight of me, while the guards they ignore. You are to be fed to them.

I will not allow it. If you still live when you are born, I will kill you myself. Better to die in the hands of love. Better to go ahead of me to the arms of Jesus.

Wait for me there, Shin-Hwa, won't you? Bring Him and wait for me. I will follow soon. Together we will go to the house He has prepared. You and me and your father, Bum-Ji. Will he be there? Oh, I pray he will. We will be so happy. You will never know a day of suffering in this accursed world.

Do not come at all.

* * *

The man they brought in this afternoon is dead. They laid him on the other side of the cement floor from me, beyond the operating table. The two doctor students put me on the table there for the abortion then moved me off here to wait.

Then they put the prisoner on the table. They stuffed his mouth with cotton and taped it shut and strapped him down then proceeded to cut his fingers off one by one. They took turns trying to find the fastest way to cut off a finger. The blood spilled into a metal bucket and sloshed onto their shoes, which made them very angry. When the man passed out, they removed his eyeballs and played with them. Finally they tired of their fun and had soldiers put him against the wall to die. It didn't take long for that to happen.

My water broke this morning. I thought it was perhaps the fluid they had injected into me coming out again, but I felt my body squeezing and cramping. Now it was night and Shin-Hwa was coming. And when she did, I would kill her.

How would I do that? Should I smother my precious newborn with my hands or bash her head on the floor? Perhaps it would be better if I strangled her?

All my life I'd dreamed of being a mother. For nine months I imagined how I would play with my child. I collected wise sayings to teach. When Jesus showed me I would have a girl, my imaginings became as real as if she'd already been born. The sparkle in her eye—I could still see it. What a mischievous, perfect child she would be. When we were escaping China, I allowed myself to imagine the expensive dresses I would buy little Shin-Hwa.

And now I was imagining how to murder her.

Master Jesus, if I killed myself now, before Shin-Hwa was born, would You receive us both into Your arms? Surely You would. You spoke to me once. Do You remember? You said, "Do not fear, dear one. I have plans for you. I will keep you safe." What went wrong? Why have You broken Your promise? Or is this the plan You had in mind? You've kept me safe until now—for this? This was Your plan? Forgive me if I don't thank You.

I got to my feet. My belly ached but I made it to the operating table. The straps they had used to hold down the prisoner were lying loose on the table. I held one and snapped it taut. It would hold. I looked up. Metal girders lined the ceiling. A thick black electric cable ran along the middle one and down to the operating lamp, which was off now. The whole medical chamber was lit only by two purple bug-killing lights at either window. If I stood on the table I could possibly toss one end of this belt over the girder and still have plenty left over.

I climbed onto the table. It creaked terribly under my weight. My right arm couldn't hold me up. An angry black bruise covered that arm. The scab from the piercing had rubbed off again and the wound oozed dark blood.

It didn't matter. None of it mattered. Now that I was here, this would likely be my only chance *ever* to protect my baby, and I was going to take it.

I balanced on the table and rose to my feet. If anyone came in now I would lose my chance. On the third try the buckle threaded over the girder and down to me. I fed the loose end through the buckle and pulled it tight against the girder.

Now for the noose.

* * *

A ghostly green figure pulled back the cutout section of chain-link fence. The perimeter fence was ten feet high and had a triple row of barbed wire extending inward at the top. But a handy pair of wire cutters had made the job a lot easier. The fence shivered and jingled like sleigh bells in Garth's grip. He motioned for the others to go through.

Jason went through first. He went ten feet in and dropped to one knee shield, pointing his CAR-15 across the moon-washed flatlands beyond a line of trees. Nothing. He gave the A-OK sign and the others came through and formed a defensive perimeter.

He looked back to watch Garth come through and noticed that the hole he'd made was in the shape of a cross. He spoke softly into his mic. "Cute shape, Garth. What's that all about?"

Garth knelt behind him and put his wire cutters away. "Maybe a Christian will be assigned to fix it. Maybe it will give him some hope."

It was ten minutes before midnight. Three hours ago they'd crossed into North Korea eight miles to the west, just south of Sanhe, and had slowly made their way here. Myong-Chol moved like the soldier he was, so he was no liability. Jason wondered again about the wisdom of leaving Gil-Su behind, but there was no going back for him.

They were in the streambed west of the camp, in the creek that on the satellite photo looked like a narrow silver ribbon leading toward the river bottom. The stream was more like three streams weaving together in a watery braid, all following the same general track between dirt roads on both sides. The roads were lined by trees no doubt planted by slave laborers. A handful of light points shone in the low valley ahead, but it looked like enough for five or six families, not the twenty thousand prisoners and guards Jason knew were there.

The night seemed unusually silent, as if subdued. The creeks trickled to their right, and Korean crickets chirped. But where were the howling wolves of the Mongolian plain? Where was the flutter of night birds prowling the dark skies? All of North Korea they'd seen appeared bereft of wildlife, especially mammals. Perhaps everything still living knew better than to show itself or be eaten in this famine-stricken land.

Jason cycled through his helmet views until he came to the dot-race electronic schematic. Lewis had used the daytime satellite imagery for the background, so their blue dots appeared to be walking around on a fine summer day instead of the middle of the night. It made Jason feel exposed.

"Okay," he said, shifting the view back to night vision only, "now straight on for half a mile. Keep to the tree line. Patrol column formation. Chris, take us there."

"Roger that."

Chris moved at the base of the trees on the creek side of the road, quietly but swiftly. Jason came next, twenty feet behind, watching the creek side and the second road beyond. Trieu followed, watching left. Lewis came next, watching right and acting as Myong-Chol's "handler." Rachel was next, watching left. Last came Garth, covering their rear.

After ten minutes, Chris went to one knee and lifted his fist. The others knelt, continuing to watch in their assigned directions.

"We're here," Chris said.

"Roger that," Jason said.

He cycled back to the dot race. Their dots were lined up one hundred yards due south of the first large compound, which Jason remembered was the threshing house. The cluster of identical structures to the right of it was the first set of prisoner housing units. With the identical peaked roofs glinting in the moonlight it looked like a sleepy neighborhood in Anytown, America. Was Ki-Won in one of those?

Here the creek bed widened. The place they needed to leave the road was another two hundred yards east, but the trees there were sparse and the left bank took them within fifty yards of some of the structures.

"Chris," Jason said, "I'm not ready to get that close to those buildings. Let's cross to the right bank and follow those trees across that gap in the tree line ahead. Then when we're due south of the detention and torture center, we'll go straight across in bounding overwatch."

"Roger that."

"And everybody," Jason said, "masks on."

"Yes, sir."

They all—Myong-Chol included—pulled the black terrorists' masks over their faces. The team put their helmets on over that.

"All right, move out."

Jason followed Chris across the creeks, which here had merged into a reeking, boot-sucking marsh. When they were all across, he called a halt to listen for signs that they had been heard.

Nothing. Though in the far distance to Jason's right front, he heard dogs barking at each other. Deep, menacing barking from big dogs. For now at least they were far away.

When they reached the spot Jason wanted, he ordered them back across the creek bed and to the line of trees.

It was getting more intense now. They were bordered on three sides by fields or structures used by the death camp. The place where guards like Myong-Chol impaled people on poles and killed Christians for fun. A thick stand of trees on their right would take them across this open field in full concealment, but it would also take them right to the doorstep of the guards' rest room and, just beyond, the night-duty room. It would have to be the open field.

He spoke quietly but clearly into his helmet microphone. "Bounding overwatch in twos. Bravo will take Myong-Chol. Go."

This was a basic combat maneuver they'd practiced so many times they could do it blindfolded. Jason didn't even have to tell them what order to go in because they always went in the same order.

First Chris and Lewis advanced into the wide-open field. The others covered the position they were headed toward and any likely enemy positions. Jason's night-vision gear showed them as distinctly as if they *were* doing it in broad daylight, but to anyone else they would be all but invisible. Twenty yards in, Chris and Lewis took a knee and scanned with their guns the area ahead of them and to their right, where the next team would end up. Chris motioned for the next group to advance.

Jason looked at Trieu, who knelt beside him with Myong-Chol at her shoulder. The mask hid her face, but her delicate eyelashes sparkled in the moonlight. Without a word they rose together and led Myong-Chol across the field, keeping to Chris and Lewis's right. They passed them, went forward another twenty yards, and knelt. Jason checked the position on the left where Garth and Rachel would come, and motioned for them to advance.

In this way they leapfrogged across the rough field in three minutes, moving from covered position to covered position in almost perfect silence and in good tactical order. They reached a double line of trees at the north edge of the field.

Here it got tricky. Jason motioned for the team to halt. Thirty yards to their right, at the end of this tree line, was the guards' rest room. Fifteen yards ahead and to their left, just across the tree line, was a storage shed for farming equipment. Immediately beyond that was an eight-foot wall surrounding a building that looked on the satellite photo like an upside-down 4: the detention and torture center. Through the trees directly in front of them was a wide assembly yard. On the other side of that was the white-roofed theater, which seemed to glow green in their night-vision gear.

Farther across the courtyard, a light was on in the office of the camp director, but it seemed to be a security light more than a work light. Besides that, and what light the moon provided, this portion of the camp was dark. An odd glow coming from the direction of the detention center caught Jason's eye. The light flared briefly just as the sound of an electric shock reached the enhanced sound detectors in his helmet. A bug zapper.

He listened. Bugs made occasional kamikaze dives into the zapper, and from the direction of the theater he heard the low roar of a fan. He devoted five minutes to listening to and watching the guards' restroom and the guards' night-duty room beyond it, but no one seemed to be moving around. Even the dogs appeared to have gone to sleep. There were guards here—awake and on duty—but Jason knew his team had the advantage. The guards had no reason to fear the inmates, having broken them with torture and by rewarding informants in their midst, and no reason to fear attack from the outside. They would be lax, but Jason's team would be sharp. The attacker always had the edge.

Just to be sure, Jason directed the team around the back of the equipment shed to a spot on the wall that was doubly hidden from anyone in the courtyard to the team's right. On their left were two large trees and beyond that a tilled field. In this little corner they were perfectly concealed. He felt a perverse urge to just stay right here for a minute.

Instead, Jason pointed at Garth and interlaced his fingers. Garth nodded and went to the wall. He let his gun retract to his chest, then leaned his back against the wall and joined his hands together to provide a step up. Jason pointed at Chris, himself, and Lewis, then motioned "over the wall." The smell of open sewage and wild onion mixed nauseatingly here.

Chris put his foot in Garth's hands and reached. Garth lifted and Chris pulled himself to the top of the wall. He spent thirty seconds there, scanning the darkness with his CAR-15. Jason watched through the feed on Chris's gun cam. It was cramped inside the walls. Only fifteen feet of open space between the walls of the gray building and the surrounding walls. They were there only to keep people in, after all. Chris disappeared over the top of the wall. Jason heard him drop softly on the other side.

Text appeared in the upper left-hand corner of Jason's screen.

In position. Lewis had programmed in a number of commonly used tactical messages that could be keyed from each person's mouse. In this way important coordinating information could be transmitted without anyone opening his mouth.

Jason went up next. He saw that Chris had moved to the right corner of the wall where he could cover two sides of the building. Jason dropped down and moved beside Chris, allowing Chris to watch the long length of the wall while Jason watched the two doors facing the wall where he'd just jumped over. He keyed the *In position* text command.

Lewis came over next. He dropped nimbly to the dirt and covered the doors with his MP-5.

Jason keyed *Hold position* so that the three of them could assess the situation. One of the bug lights was at the far end of the building, down Chris's way; the other was on the backside. Nothing moved in this place, this little walled area that had seen who knew how much pain inflicted on innocent people. Did the spirits of those killed here remain nearby? Two fabulously healthy fruit trees grew at the far end of the courtyard. They towered over the building, the bug lights, and the wall.

Jason keyed text messages: *All clear. Proceed to next position.*

Trieu dropped over next, followed by Myong-Chol and Rachel. Finally Garth heaved himself up and over, landing with the least sound of any of them.

As they'd rehearsed, Jason and Trieu came to the corner of the wall where Chris had been and assumed overwatch positions. Myong-Chol knelt between them. Jason had a clear view of the wooden gate to the right of the fruit tree and the bug zapper. If anyone came in, they'd be momentarily blinded by the light and then struck by pepperballs and sedative-rich protein bullets.

The other two teams gathered before the doors on the south end of the building. The plan was for them to go down these parallel halls, taking out any opposition they encountered, meet at the crossbar of the 4, find Chun-Mi, and retrace their steps, bringing her to safety across the wall, across the field, and through the cross cut in the fence.

The plan wasn't clear on how they were going to find Ki-Won in all of this. The plan was hoping for a miracle.

On a silent signal, Chris and Garth each pushed through their wooden doors. They lifted their assault rifles and moved swiftly into the room. Lewis and Rachel followed instantly.

Jason wanted to watch through their gun cams but had to be vigilant on the gate. If his team made any sounds, bad guys might come.

The seconds ticked by, each one feeling like ten. No sharp sounds of the CAR-15s launching pepperballs. The MP-5s were silenced, so he didn't know if they were firing or not.

Still the silence prolonged. *Come on. They should be there by now.* Had they been captured? Was this all some kind of ambush?

The nearest door opened. Jason and Trieu both swung their weapons to it. A dark figure stepped through.

It was Lewis. His mask was off. He all but ran over to Trieu. Chris followed more slowly, his mask also gone.

"Trieu," Lewis whispered. "You've got to get in there now!"

"Where are Garth and Rachel?" Jason said. "Are they down?"

"No. We found Chun-Mi! Trieu, you've got to get in there!"

Chris knelt beside Jason. "We'll take over here. You two go in. Don't worry. No black hats inside."

Jason nodded. He led Trieu toward the door.

Chris hissed. "Take Myong-Chol."

Jason gestured for Myong-Chol to follow then led the two of them inside.

A metal shelving grid lined the right wall of the cement hallway. Ancient medical equipment filled the shelves: oxygen tanks, traction braces, bolts of gauze, and rusted surgical utensils designed to do things Jason didn't want to think about. At the junction of the halls a large steel washbasin stood against the wall, mineral-water stains down the center. The sewage smell that permeated the prison was here mixed with the smell of rubbing alcohol. A dirty cloth divider on a rolling steel frame partially blocked the way into the main room. Jason stepped around it.

And saw Chun-Mi.

Garth and Rachel were lowering her to a rusted iron bed in the center of the room. A belt hung down from above, a loop tied in the bottom.

Trieu was past Jason before he knew it. "What happened?" she said, pulling her helmet and mask off. "Did they hang her?"

Garth put Chun-Mi's arm beside her. "What?"

"The noose," Jason said, pulling his own mask off. "Did you bring her down from that?"

Garth saw it. "Oh. No. She was crumpled over on her side."

At that moment, Chun-Mi moaned.

"She's alive!" Jason said.

"Yeah," Rachel said, covering the front door with her MP-5, "but she's in a ton of pain."

Trieu checked her pulse. "Myong-Chol, ask her where it hurts."

Jason looked at Myong-Chol. He'd heard his name but hadn't understood the rest. "Now's when I wish we'd brought Gil-Su," Jason said.

Rachel glanced at him. "What about Lewis's PDA?"

"Great idea, Raych. Lewis," he said into his squad radio, "does your PDA translate English to Korean?"

Lewis answered with a text message. *Affirmative.*

"Rachel," Jason said. "Switch places with Lewis. We need him in here."

"Roger that."

Jason pulled security on the front door while Rachel went out the back. Trieu continued her assessment of Chun-Mi, who seemed to be in great pain, though he could see no fresh blood anywhere. Old blood everywhere, now that he noticed: across the floor, on the sheets, and in a black stain on the floor by the cinder-block wall.

Trieu looked up from her patient. "Jason, she's in labor."

He blinked. "Say what?"

"She's in hard labor. Her water's broken. I don't know how long ago. This baby has to come out now."

"No, Trieu, no. We've got to get her out of here. She can deliver in the bush."

"Listen to me, Jason. She can't be moved. She's fully dilated. I can feel the baby's head in the birth canal. This child could crown at any minute."

Oh, dear Lord, why couldn't this have waited? "Okay," Jason said, his mind racing through ramifications. "Can you make it happen fast? We've got five hours until first light."

"I can't make her hurry up, Jason. It could take ten minutes or it could take all night and into tomorrow."

"Tomorrow! We've got to be out of here in four hours."

Garth looked at Trieu. "What about a C-section?"

"That's major surgery," Trieu said. "And unless a medical team with anesthesia and sterile instruments rolls up sometime soon, this baby's coming out the natural way."

Lewis stepped around the divider. "Is she going to be okay?"

"Lewis," Jason said, "work with Trieu and Myong-Chol on your PDA. English and Korean."

"Ten-four." Lewis powered up the handheld device. "What do you want to say, Trieu?"

"Ask her how long it's been since her water broke."

Lewis began typing it in. "You're going to deliver her baby?"

"If I can."

Jason rubbed his face. This was crazy. An image of a chubby face popped into his mind. Ki-Won. "Lewis," Jason said, "ask Chun-Mi where Ki-Won is. She can tell Myong-Chol and he can lead us there. That's what we'll do while Trieu's helping her."

Lewis punched in a word and pressed a button. Out of the PDA's tiny speaker came a man's voice speaking a Korean word, which Lewis immediately followed with "Ki-Won?" He looked at Jason. "I think it's saying 'Where?' and I'm saying his name. You think she'll get that?"

"I don't know, bro, but it's a good idea."

Chun-Mi lay sweating on the bed. No pillows or sheets. Just a flattened pallet mattress and the corroded bars of the bed rails. She was conscious, but to Jason she appeared delirious. A wave of contractions eased and her body relaxed. She leaned to Myong-Chol and spoke at length. Again Jason wished Gil-Su were here.

The tone of Myong-Chol's answers changed. He sounded more upbeat. He turned to Jason and beckoned for him to follow. He patted Jason's CAR-15 and nodded seriously.

"Okay, buddy," Jason said. "I gotcha."

Then Myong-Chol reached for Lewis's PDA. He handled it like an expert now, calling up the satellite image and showing them first where they were and next where they were going.

Their objective was nearly a mile north, right in the middle of the prison complex. It wasn't the farthest cluster of buildings that housed prisoners with families, but it wasn't the closest, either. And it certainly wasn't the one they would pass on their way out. Jason remembered noticing this group of buildings in the sat photos. It was the one that looked like a telephone number pad, except this phone had more than twenty "buttons."

As he looked at the photo, it appeared to him that they could cross the whole distance by staying in the fields to the west of the prison buildings, which ran north-south in the riverbed. It would take longer to bypass the headquarters compound by dipping south and sweeping way west before turning north, but the direct route meant marching right past the camp administrator's office and the Kim Il-Sung Memorial Hall. No thanks.

Myong-Chol pointed at Chun-Mi, opened his mouth, and motioned something coming out of it.

"Chun-Mi. . . ," Lewis said, as if playing Charades. "Threw up? No, *says*. Chun-Mi says. . ."

Myong-Chol pointed to Chun-Mi's belly.

"Chun-Mi says her baby. . ."

Myong-Chol drew a finger across his neck like a knife.

"Chun-Mi says her baby is dead," Lewis said.

Garth groaned. "They must've done the abortion."

"No!" Lewis said. "No, I don't believe it. We got here in time. Didn't we, Jason? Didn't we get here in time to save her baby?"

Jason felt a heaviness pressing down on him. "I guess not, Lewis."

"She's wrong," Trieu said, unpacking things from her medical kit. "You're going to have to learn some new Korean words, Lewis, because somebody's got to tell her her baby's still alive. She's having a few decelerations, but nothing too severe. The baby's doing great."

The heaviness Jason had felt vanished instantly, and for the first time today he felt a sense of optimism about this mission. "That's amazing! Trieu, you've got to deliver this baby. She's got to make it. We'll buy you whatever time you need. And in the meantime, we're going to go get Ki-Won. We'll be back here just as soon as we can. Lewis, you stay here and do the translating and guard the door. I'll leave Rachel outside watching the gate."

"You know it, baby," Lewis said. "And I'll put a couple motes out watching the courtyard, too. Channel surf to it before you cross it again."

Jason patted Lewis on the back. "Outstanding. Oh, and try to get that strap down. It can't be good to have a noose hanging down over a woman giving birth. Just seems creepy."

"I'm on it."

Jason moved to Trieu and put his mouth next to her ear. "Lord Jesus, guide Trieu's hands. Protect this baby. Protect this mommy.

Protect us all. Help all of us get out of here safely. But. . .Your will be done. Amen."

She nuzzled his cheek. "Amen."

"Do your magic, my love," Jason said. Then he turned to Garth. "You ready to go?"

"Born ready, baby."

"Chris," Jason said into his mic, "you're with us."

Chris answered with a text message. *Roger that.*

"But grab Rachel's MP-5," Jason said. "I want one of us to have tranqs. Then meet us at the gate in sixty seconds."

"Roger that."

"Rachel, if you like the spot you're in, fine, but you can find another one if you want. Be advised that Lewis is going to put some motes outside the wall, so you can keep an eye on the court-yard, but stay inside these walls. Copy that?"

Her answer was in text, too: *Affirmative.* Then a text message in chat group shorthand appeared, typed on her electronic keypad: *b crfl. i want kw back. want u back, 2.*

"Copy that, Rachel," Jason said. "Thanks. All right, Chris, Garth, Myong-Chol; masks on, people. Let's move."

CHAPTER 29

THE NICE MAN

SHIN-HWA WAS ALIVE? My baby still lived inside me? When her thrashing vanished, I thought she was dead. I felt weak movements after that, but I thought it was only the contractions.

The contractions. Like the one that doubled me over when I was trying to reach the noose.

I still couldn't believe Jason-Scott and the Americans had come. When I saw them in their masks, I thought they were North Korean guards here to execute me. When they pulled their masks off, I thought I must have been dreaming. Nobody went to these camps intentionally. And no one ever left. And yet Myong-Chol had left. He'd come back, too. Back to the camp where he had been a terror. Why had he come?

Perhaps I *was* seeing a vision, like the one with the warriors at the river. Perhaps these American soldiers were not real men and women, but angels from God. It was hard to know what was real. The pain. The loss. The fear. Minutes ago I was planning to kill my daughter, now a trained doctor was laying out medical tools and giving me medicine for the pain? And my daughter was still alive?

Was she horribly burned? The trainees had said she would be burned. They said she would boil and swallow the liquid and burn from the inside out. They said she would look like a candied apple. Would she be a horrible freak when she came out?

I lay back, watching the youngest American taking down my noose.

Push, the little machine kept saying to me. When the contractions came, the woman doctor would press a button and the thing would say *Push* in Korean. A talking box that wasn't a radio. This had to be a vision.

Another contraction was coming. The most awful cramps I'd ever felt, as if a motorized clamp were squeezing down across my belly.

Oh, Shin-Hwa, why do you want out so badly? Your whole life will be pain like this. If only you would die.

*   *   *

Five thousand prisoners slept in the little neighborhood of single-floor dwellings arrayed in rows before Jason. Mothers, fathers, children. Perhaps some of them had committed actual crimes, but Jason suspected the court of world opinion would judge most of them innocent. Why couldn't he free all of them? Why couldn't they raid the armory and weapons storage and distribute guns to every adult male? How many guards were there—two hundred maybe? Twenty thousand enraged prisoners would overwhelm them in ten minutes.

But then what? Make a mass run to the border with China? If the North Korean Air Force didn't mow them all down before they got there, the Chinese military would stop them at the Tumen. It would be over as soon as it began. And that's *if* these malnourished and broken people would take up arms against their captors, which they no doubt wouldn't.

Better to find their lone needle and leave the haystack in God's hands.

Jason checked his watch. Two-thirty in the morning. He really wanted to have this camp behind him by four. Myong-Chol was on his right, bellied up to the berm, just as Jason was. Chris was crouched fifteen feet to their right, watching their right flank and rear. Garth watched their left flank and rear.

No lights lit the prison houses, which were forty yards to the east of their position. Jason's night-vision gear showed uniform dirt walkways in front of evenly spaced dwellings, each fronted by a door in the exact middle. Fifteen-foot passageways bisected building from building. The smell of open toilets assaulted Jason's nose. One hundred prisoners slept in each of these "houses," Myong-Chol had said, all lying on the dirt floor like stinking human sardines.

Which one was Ki-Won in?

A flash of light flared in Jason's goggles. They all saw it and sunk lower. As Jason watched, the light swayed and bounced. He whispered into his microphone. "Flashlight."

Thump-thump-thump. Creak.

Silence.

Creak-thud. Thump-thump-thump.

The flashlight moved from the doorway of one building to the doorway of the next. Jason saw the soldier—only one—thump up the stairs of a prisoner billet, open the door and look inside, then let the door slam, and thump down the steps and head to the next door. The man began to whistle casually.

"Inspections," Jason whispered. "One guard. Sidearm. Unsuspecting."

Garth and Chris both keyed text messages: *Roger that.*

Myong-Chol tapped Jason on the shoulder. He pointed to himself, then to the guard, then gripped the lapels of his shirt and pointed back at the guard.

Jason nodded and gave a thumbs-up. "Guys, Myong-Chol

wants to switch clothes with the guard. Then he can make the inspections himself and maybe find Ki-Won."

"Roger that."

"You guys happen to have those chloroform rags with you?"

"Negative."

"Then Chris will shoot him with the tranq and I'll keep him quiet till he passes out. Copy that?"

Two text messages: *Affirmative* and *Roger that.*

The whistling guard slammed a door and walked down the dirt path toward the last dwelling on the row, which was nearest Jason and the others. When he thumped up the steps, they made their move. They crossed the distance with the silence of sharks in water and were twenty feet behind him as he stood in the open doorway, looking into the dark building.

He let the door slam and clomped back down the stairs. He'd just puckered his lips to whistle when Chris's dart hit him in the chest. His hand shot to the spot and he looked down in irritation.

Jason sprang to him. He covered his mouth with one hand and put him in the sleeper hold.

The guard's eyes bulged and he thrashed against Jason's grip. Jason pulled him around the side of the building as Garth and Chris covered the approaches. When the thirteen seconds it took for the sedative to circulate through his body were up, the guard was out.

Jason's heart raced. Despite all the times he'd done that, actually touching and overpowering an enemy was always an excruciating, intoxicating experience.

Myong-Chol trotted to them and changed into the guard's clothes while they pulled security. It turned out Myong-Chol was a few sizes larger than the guard, so he ended up just changing into his uniform jacket, holster, and hat.

Chris retrieved the dart from the guard's body. Then he, Jason, and Garth took up positions watching down the walkways between rows of houses.

Myong-Chol snapped on the guard's flashlight and nodded to Jason. He walked to the nearest door and looked inside.

Jason heard him call Ki-Won's name then speak softly but authoritatively. Sleepy prisoners answered him and he shut the door and moved toward the next one.

* * *

The nice man was here again. Ki-Won was glad to see him.

"Wake up, little Ki-Won."

"I remember you from the river," Ki-Won said.

The man was very tall and strong. He made Ki-Won feel like he was with his mommy and daddy again.

"Come, Ki-Won, we must go. I will take you to men who have come to help you."

He followed the man over the stinky people. He stepped over their legs and heads. He hoped they wouldn't wake up. He was glad to leave them. They were sad and mean—and really stinky. When they were outside Ki-Won saw that it was nighttime. The cool air felt good.

"Are you taking me to Mommy?"

"No, child. Your parents can't come to you right now."

Ki-Won couldn't usually see at night, but this time it wasn't hard. He held the man's hand as they walked. But when they got to the edge of the house, Ki-Won stopped.

"I'm not supposed to go this way. They hit me when I came this way before."

The strong man looked down at him with nice eyes. "No one will hit you now. I am with you, aren't I? Come, we must hurry."

Ki-Won tried to run but he fell. The man picked him up. He hugged the man tightly, because he loved him. They walked right past the mean men. They walked together and laughed. But when Ki-Won and the man passed, they acted like they weren't even there. Maybe they liked the nice man.

"Where are we going?"

"To the men who have come for you, Ki-Won. They don't know you've been moved, so we must take you there. You will be safe with them. And I will watch over you, too. Would you like that?"

Ki-Won hugged the nice man's neck. He smelled like happy things. "Yes. But I miss my Mommy."

"I know, my child. She loved you with all her heart."

That made him feel good and sad at the same time. "I have a question."

"Yes, little one?"

"How come you understand me and no one else does?"

The man didn't answer. He just smiled. That was okay. Ki-Won was just glad to have someone to talk to.

He didn't know how long they walked, but they passed lots of buildings. Finally the man put him down in the middle of a path between some other buildings. Ki-Won saw a light coming and it scared him. But the man pushed him toward it. "Go on, Ki-Won. They are nice. You know them."

* * *

"That was the last one," Jason said softly. Myong-Chol walked back toward them, his flashlight bobbing in front of his steps. "Either the boy's not here or we missed him."

"Great," Chris whispered. "What are we going to do now? It's after three."

"I know. We'll. . .I guess we'll just have to send Myong-Chol back through every—"

Text from Garth flashed onto Jason's view screen: *Enemy unit spotted.*

Jason keyed his response. *Roger that.* He waved Myong-Chol forward and turned off his flashlight. Then the three of them silently approached Garth's position.

Garth knelt at the corner of a house, pointing his CAR-15 up the walkway. Jason knelt five feet to his right. Chris knelt five feet to Jason's right. Myong-Chol knelt behind Garth in perfect darkness.

Somebody was coming. The acoustic amplifiers in their helmets picked up stealthy footsteps, which suddenly stopped, then started again. Whoever it was knew they were there. He was coming down a side passageway. Chris would see him first.

Jason's palms were sweaty. If he or Garth had to fire, it would probably bring more guards. Only Chris's MP-5 was silenced.

Crunch-crunch-crunch. Furtive footfalls. *Crunch-crunch.*

Chris gasped.

What was it? A squad of North Korean commandos who could move in complete silence? An attack dog?

Chris turned wide eyes to Jason and he stood up in surprise. "It's him. It's the kid."

"What?"

Jason stood and moved around the corner. There stood Son Ki-Won, pudgy-cheeked, shape-loving Son Ki-Won. "How in the world?"

Garth grabbed Myong-Chol's flashlight and took off his helmet and mask. He shone the light on his own face. "Ki-Won," he whispered. "It's me, little buddy. It's papa bear."

Ki-Won's face broke into a toothy smile. He said something in his private language and ran to Garth. Garth picked the boy up and held him close. Jason heard what sounded like a sob from the big man's chest.

"I can't believe it," Jason said.

Chris scratched his neck. "Maybe he woke up when Myong-Chol was leaving and followed him out."

"Who cares?" Garth said, handing the flashlight back to Myong-Chol. "We've got him, and I'm getting him out of here."

"Right," Jason said. "Let's go."

* * *

"Oh, that is so nasty. What is that?"

Trieu let the bloody liquid spill onto the operating table and floor. "It's leftover amniotic fluid, Lewis. Keep the light steady, or I'll send you to boil water and tear sheets."

"Yes, ma'am," Lewis said, keeping the hooded flashlight pointed where it needed to be. "But that *is* nasty."

Trieu could feel the baby's head slipping through the cervix. She wished she could express that to Chun-Mi. It might encourage the poor woman. The contractions were hard and steady. Every time Chun-Mi pushed, the baby moved a centimeter closer to fresh air.

The wave passed and Chun-Mi relaxed. Trieu released the woman's knees and let her rest. She moved the scissors and Kelly hemostat that had almost fallen to the bloody floor. She needed those to be as sterile as they could be.

She checked Chun-Mi again and decided it was time to do an episiotomy. She picked up the scissors in her rubber-gloved hands and moved them toward Chun-Mi.

"Wait!" Lewis said. "What are you going to do?"

"I'm going to do some cutting, Lewis. Perhaps it would be best if you put the flashlight down and kept watch outside with Rachel."

"Yeah," Lewis said. "Gladly."

When he was gone Trieu went to do the episiotomy, but another wave of contractions was upon Chun-Mi. Trieu put the scissors down and grasped Chun-Mi's knees. "Gently now, push."

Chun-Mi pushed. She was doing so well. How awful not to be able to tell her so. Trieu smiled and nodded until her cheeks and neck were sore.

Chun-Mi screamed. It wasn't especially loud considering the pain she was in, but it was the loudest sound Trieu had allowed around herself for the last six hours. She just knew it would bring the camp down on them.

"Shh! You have to be quiet. I know it hurts. I know! But shh!"

Chun-Mi nodded, her cheeks pulled back in a grimace of pain. She pushed again, her face going purple and veins in her neck bulging.

"Breathe now, honey," Trieu said. "Baby needs you to breathe."

After two more good pushes the contractions passed. Trieu performed a neat episiotomy and set the scissors aside. She checked the baby's progress.

"Oh, that's so good," she said softly to Chun-Mi. "One more push like that and we'll see the top of your baby's head!"

What will this poor baby look like, dear Lord? Tiny, certainly. Malnourished. But scalded hideously? Poisoned and dying? Please, Lord, let her be all right.

"Trieu." Rachel's voice came from Trieu's helmet, on the floor beside her.

She couldn't do more than look at it.

"Trieu," Rachel said. "Someone's coming."

* * *

The man called in Korean. It was a commanding voice that expected to be obeyed. For a millisecond Jason cherished the hope that it was Myong-Chol playing a joke on them. But he knew it wasn't.

Chris was on point. Garth was next, carrying Ki-Won. Myong-Chol had been next until he'd dropped his flashlight. Jason had passed him but paused beside a tree trunk to cover Myong-Chol until he took his place in line again.

Now that wasn't going to happen. Myong-Chol was illuminated by two flashlights. Two men called to Myong-Chol. For a moment, time seemed to hesitate.

Jason raised his rifle. The flashlight beams overwhelmed his low-light gear, temporarily blinding him. He sensed Chris and Garth coming into position on either side of him.

The men called to Myong-Chol again. He was looking right at Jason, though the soldiers couldn't know this. His face, which had tightened in fear, now seemed to unfold into peace. He faced the lights, shoulders squared, and answered in a tone more authoritative than their own.

The men lowered their flashlights and answered sheepishly. Jason could now see they were uniformed guards. Three more were approaching from the direction of the headquarters compound. Chris had led them west again to skirt these buildings, but some kind of patrol had spotted Myong-Chol.

Myong-Chol issued what sounded like orders to the two men, who snapped into attention. He laid into them about something. The other three neared and Myong-Chol barked at them, too. They ran to fall into line.

"He's bluffing," Jason whispered.

At a command from Myong-Chol, the five guards turned crisply right and marched back toward the headquarters. Myong-Chol walked beside them, sounding cadence.

"He's giving us time to get away," Chris said incredulously. "It won't work. Come back, Myong-Chol. They're going to figure it out."

"Kromer," Garth said, "I admire that man too much to let this go to waste. He's buying us time. I say we use it to get Ki-Won out of here." He jutted his chin toward Myong-Chol. "He's in God's hands now."

"Roger that," Jason said. "Chris, take point."

"No, man," Chris said, still watching Myong-Chol's diminishing figure. "You do it this time."

Jason patted his helmet. "Okay. I'm point. Garth next. Chris last. Let's move."

*　　*　　*

"Two guards with rifles. Two dogs on leash."

Lewis raised his MP-5 to the gate. It didn't bother him to look through the mote camera image superimposed over the green night-vision terrain before him. It was a little freaky to see men and attack dogs walking toward him with one part of his brain and with another to see a solid wall thirty feet away, but he'd always been good at multitasking.

He looked at Rachel, masked and dangerous, kneeling at his right. He hoped she remembered she had the CAR-15, not her MP-5, and didn't fire unless she had to. On the other hand, he liked it better when someone surprised the person with pepper-balls. He preferred popping tranqs into people who were coughing and crying. This was the first time he'd be the main shooter on unpeppered enemies.

And what about the dogs? Would the Versed darts affect them? Would they pass out before or after they ripped his throat out? Lewis wiped his sweaty hands on his legs and prepared for something horrible.

Forty feet from the gate, the guards stopped. They looked at something to their right.

"Wait," he whispered. "They've stopped."

"I know, Lewis," Rachel hissed. "Shut up."

The dogs seemed to sense something in the detention center courtyard. They looked toward the gate and Lewis could hear them growling. They pulled at their leashes—but the guards wanted to go another way. With stern commands and several yanks on the leashes, the dogs and the guards moved off left.

Lewis just about passed out from the relief.

* * *

Trieu had delivered seven babies before this one. Five were naturals. If she did a million, she wondered if she'd ever get used to seeing a baby's head sticking out from its mother's uterus.

Chun-Mi's baby had crowned ten minutes ago. Two good pushes later Trieu had worked its head out. The child was not the candied-apple baby that saline abortions usually produced. This baby had frizzy hair and delicate eyebrows.

She aspirated the baby's throat and nostrils. Her little chin quivered in the cold outside world. "Your baby is so beautiful, Chun-Mi. One more push, Chun-Mi."

Chun-Mi looked confused. But she was fatigued beyond speech.

"Come on, Chun-Mi," Trieu said, making sure the hemostat was handy, "one more push."

* * *

"Squad, halt!"

It was so strange, standing in this courtyard again. Myong-Chol knew every window, every tree, every brick of this place. He'd sworn he'd never return. Yet here he was.

The men beside him were all new. *Truly, Lord, You are good to me. And it is Your doing that I wear the uniform of higher rank than any of these. See me through to the end.*

"Left face."

They turned to face him. They were at the west edge of the headquarters compound. The long building on the north of the courtyard was the guards' quarters. The supply depot formed the eastern side of the compound. The propaganda bureau's offices on the south. The whole area was lit by a tall light post at the center of the assembly yard. Four halogen bulbs gave the night a bluish brightness.

"Men," Myong-Chol said, "in a moment I am going to release you from your duties and return you early to your beds."

This clearly pleased them, though they hardly moved. They were so young. Young and cruel, as Myong-Chol had been once.

"But first I will tell you something you have never heard. You will think me insane for saying it, but I assure you it is the truth. Tomorrow you may report my words to your commanding officers, and they will deny it is true. But it will be up to you to decide."

Myong-Chol swallowed. *Lord, here's my life.*

"Long ago, there was a great ruler named King Yahweh. This king made a law. The punishment for breaking this law was death. Can you imagine such a place?"

CHAPTER 30

TEN THOUSAND CHARMS

SNIP.

With one firm cut, Chun-Mi's physical bond with her daughter was severed. The umbilical cord, held closed by the Kelly hemostat, draped across the baby's wet body. Trieu laid the infant into Chun-Mi's arms.

"She is perfect, Chun-Mi," Trieu said. "There is some mild burning on her shoulder and she is very small, but somehow. . ." Tears blurred Trieu's eyes. She wiped them with her wrist. "Somehow God has protected her. She is perfect."

Chun-Mi didn't understand the words, but she understood Trieu's teary smile. She looked with shock at the squirming, squawking newborn in her arms. "Shin-Hwa?"

Trieu cried and nodded. "Shin-Hwa. God's peace."

Chun-Mi looked all over her baby. Saw the shoulder. Felt her hair. A smile like a blooming rose spread across her face. She held her baby to her and kissed her, tears falling from her eyes. As Trieu delivered the placenta and took care of her patients, Chun-Mi lifted her shirt and gave her daughter her first meal.

* * *

"I'll go up, then you hand me the boy."

Jason waited until Garth put Ki-Won down and formed a step at the base of the wall around the detention and torture center.

"Oh," he said, "better do this first." He spoke into his microphone. "Trieu, Rachel, Lewis, be advised we are coming over the wall. Don't shoot us. Copy?"

Text from Lewis: *Roger that.* Then: *good 2 c u.*

Jason put his foot into Garth's cupped hands. "Chris, you follow me over." He stood and reached for the wall as Garth lifted him up. He lay on the top of the wall a moment, checking the ground. Something was wrong, but it wasn't on the inside of the wall. He looked at the base of the flourishing fruit trees.

"Where's Chris?"

* * *

"Remember," Myong-Chol said to the five guards. "His name is Jesus Christ. He is God. Kim Il-Sung is not, no matter what you have been told. Kim Jong-Il is no god, either. He is insane. The Christians in your keeping will not renounce their faith because they know God is the only true power. Only Jesus Christ can give you peace and forgiveness today. Only Jesus Christ can take you to heaven when—"

"What's going on here?"

Myong-Chol knew the voice instantly. It was Heo Wan-Koo, an especially dark-hearted soldier whom Myong-Chol had groomed.

Wan-Koo had always been thick of body, but now as he stepped down from the barracks and into the light, Myong-Chol saw he was actually overweight. How obscene to carry extra weight while starving every prisoner. Yet it fit with the philosophy Myong-Chol had cultivated in him.

Wan-Koo wore no shirt and his pants were unfastened. His belly quivered when he walked. The other guards grew unsure at his approach. "Why aren't you men enforcing curfew? And who are you?" He said to Myong-Chol. "I don't recognize you. Are you the new officer from Camp 15?"

Myong-Chol lifted his chin and strode toward Wan-Koo. "It is me, old friend. Kim Myong-Chol. Your old master. Don't you remember?"

Wan-Koo's eyes widened. He stepped back nervously. "M– Myong-Chol. But I heard. . ." Then his eyes narrowed. "Wait. I heard you defected. You betrayed your nation."

"I did defect, Wan-Koo. And if finding the truth means betraying a lie, then yes, I betrayed your country. All because of those Christians we tortured, Wan-Koo. Like the ones you torture now. I tested their faith and could not break it, remember? That power is unbreakable. And so I have allied myself to it." He turned to the five guards. "Ask them. You will find I have been poisoning their minds with the truth. The truth that Jesus Christ is the only true God!" Myong-Chol tilted his face to the stars and shouted. *"Jesus Christ is the only true God!"*

"Shut up!" Wan-Koo's hands squeezed into fists. "Be quiet."

Myong-Chol backed away from him. "No, I want them all to know. I want the guards to know why they can't break the Christians. And I want the Christians to have new hope. *Jesus Christ is the only true God! Jesus C—"*

Wan-Koo's punch folded Myong-Chol double. The second punch landed across Myong-Chol's neck and dropped him to the dirt.

Guards leaned out the windows of the barracks. A few staggered down the steps. "What's all the shouting?"

Myong-Chol embraced Wan-Koo's leg as it kicked his ribs. He

swept Wan-Koo's other leg out from under him and staggered to his feet. "Listen to me, all of you! Jesus Christ is the one true God. You can go to Him. He will forgive you. You're not too far gone. Your leaders have lied to you. They are starving you. You torture innocent people. You know it's true. Listen to me. Jesus Christ is the one true—"

The five guards mobbed him, followed by Wan-Koo. They drove him to the ground and pummeled him with kicks and punches, shouting in anger. Ten more guards gathered from the barracks. The night guards ran from their post.

Myong-Chol's cries were shouted down, his outstretched arms twisted and broken.

That was when the flashbang grenade exploded.

* * *

It electrified the team. Jason and Lewis froze in their tracks, Chun-Mi and her baby on the stretcher between them. Garth, Ki-Won strapped to his chest, swung around from point in the middle of the field half a mile west of the headquarters compound. Rachel and Trieu lifted their rifles toward the spot where the flash and the *BOOM* had been.

Rachel went to one knee. "It's Chris."

Jason and Lewis put the stretcher down. "Stupid, stupid, stupid. They'll raise the alarm."

"Shouldn't we help him?" Lewis said.

"No!" Jason said, mashing his fist to his forehead. "We can't help him now. He's made his choice. We have to go or we'll all be caught."

He felt Trieu's eyes on him. Suddenly he remembered a stunt like this of his own, somewhere in the heart of Kazakhstan.

"Okay, look," he said, "here's what we'll do."

* * *

The first flashbang stunned them all into paralysis. The second sent them running for cover.

Chris shot them as they ran. Tranquilizer darts that would drop each one in thirteen seconds.

Nine, ten, eleven hits. But there were twenty more already and now the camp was waking up.

He fell on them like a berserker, shooting, jump kicking, punching, pulling, rifle butting. He hoped his black mask and wired helmet would terrorize them long enough to make his play.

He shouted and ran at the last few guards around Myong-Chol, firing his MP-5 and dropping a smoke grenade.

They shrieked and scattered.

He pulled the pin on a smoke grenade and lobbed it toward the scattered guards. He tossed another one toward the steps of the barracks.

"Come on!" he yelled to Myong-Chol, hoisting him to his feet. Myong-Chol was groaning and limp.

Someone opened up at them with an automatic rifle. Chris hit the dirt and returned fire. He lobbed a flashbang that way and dragged Myong-Chol toward the darkness at the western edge of the compound. Myong-Chol was deadweight.

Chris spotted a soldier in the upper window of the barracks pointing a rifle at him. He shot a dart that way, but then heard the awful *click* of an empty clip.

"Come on!"

He dragged Myong-Chol on, trying to reload clips as he moved. Machine-gun fire erupted from three sides now. Shells snicked by him and pelted the ground all around. Soldiers poured from the barracks. More came from the far edge of the compound. The air-raid siren moaned to life. The guards seemed impervious to the smoke and unfazed by the flashbangs.

Across the yard he saw guards with attack dogs. The dogs sprang from their leashes and sprinted for him, their jaws slavering. He was going to die.

Then his fellow warriors ran up behind him, laying down what sounded exactly like live weapons fire. Two masked soldiers ran by him, launching tear gas, smoke grenades, and flashbangs. The roar of their weapons was deafening. Where had Jason and Garth gotten M-60 machine guns? And since when did they use live ammo?

Chris didn't care. And why not use real ammunition on evil men like this, anyway? He'd thought that all along. He lifted Myong-Chol over his back in the fireman's carry and lumbered west.

He couldn't believe the furor of war those two men had brought. The night was lit by explosions and flashes. The dark sky resounded with heavy weapons' fire. An eerie keening split the night even louder than the air-raid siren. The dogs yelped and ran away faster than they'd come. Way to go, men!

He ran for a quarter of a mile. No sign of pursuit. The battle raged on behind him. But this was too much. He'd turned off his squad radio before, but now he turned it back on. "Garth, Jason, I'm away. You guys get out of there now!"

Myong-Chol was dead. He didn't have to be a doctor to know it. He'd felt the bullets strike him even as he tried to pull him away. But he didn't have it in him to leave the man behind. He hefted Myong-Chol's body and ran on.

Suddenly two more masked figures in uniforms he recognized coalesced in the green distance before him.

"Lewis? Trieu? You guys, tell Jason and Garth to come on."

The figures looked at each other and joined Chris in running away. The larger one lifted Myong-Chol from Chris's back and put it on his own.

"Wait a minute," Chris said. "Is that you, Garth?"

Garth lifted his mask. "Yeah, it's me."

Chris looked on the other side. "Jason?"

"Yep."

Chris stopped and turned around. At the headquarters compound, a five-pronged flare shot up like fireworks. "You mean that's Trieu and Rachel and Lewis you sent? Are you insane?"

Jason turned to face him. "What are you talking about?"

"In there!" Chris said, pointing to the battle. "Who did you send in there? Who's there right now?"

"Nobody!" Jason said. "The team's behind us. The whole team, except for you. Garth and I were coming to see if we could save your backside, but before we could get there you set off the bombs. Did you raid their armory? That's all I could figure. And what's that weird sound? It sounds like a sea monster or something."

"What?" Chris's legs wouldn't move. "No, I. . . The armory? No. But—I saw two guys in our uniforms. They were masked. I thought it was you and Garth." He shook his head in shudders. "They're using live ammo, I think."

"Well, who cares?" Jason said, tugging at his sleeve. "Maybe it's South Korean special forces. Maybe it's our own guys and we just got lucky. Let's get our people out of here and figure it out later."

Chris stumbled backward, watching as a field of darkness on the far side of the riverbank erupted into a rolling yellow fireball.

"It's. . .I. . . Oh, dear Lord, what are You doing?"

He turned and ran. All the way to China.

* * *

Three black limousines idled at the riverbank. A dirt road stretched out behind them. It was dawn.

Jason crouched in the brush at the edge of the Tumen. They were on the China side, but only by inches. The rest of the team, plus their precious cargo, were hidden in the shore brush behind him.

There was an odd seal emblazoned on the side of the limos. It wasn't the Chinese seal or anything from North Korea, South Korea,

Russia, or the United States. He was running out of guesses.

A man who appeared to be a Polynesian islander in a *Hawaii-Five-O* black suit stood out of the lead car and removed dark glasses. He seemed to be able to see Jason despite his concealment.

Jason raised his CAR-15.

"No need for that," the man said in English, though with an Asian accent. "I am a friend."

Jason stayed low. "Okay, friend, what can I do for you?"

"We represent the island nation of Nauru. These cars," he said, indicating the limos, "are official consular cars of the Nauran embassy in Beijing."

"The island nation of. . . ?"

"Nauru."

"Never heard of it."

"We are a very small nation. Only twelve thousand citizens."

Jason looked at him suspiciously. "But you have an embassy in Beijing?"

"Yes," the man said, suddenly beaming. "It is quite new."

"Uh-huh."

The man stepped forward slowly. "The White Lady thought you might be interested in our help."

Jason stood. "The White Lady sent you?"

"Yes." He went to the rear door of his limo and opened it. "The nice thing about our new embassy," he said grandly, "is that we allow North Korean citizens to claim asylum."

A smiled zipped across Jason's face. He chuckled. *Eloise, you sly dog.*

"Tell me, sir," the man said pointedly, "would your team like a ride? And, more importantly, would the people with you like to plead for the nation of Nauru to grant them political asylum?"

Jason shook his head in wonder. "I don't know. I'll ask them."

"Ah, I did not think you spoke Korean. Perhaps I can help with that, too."

"They speak Korean on your island nation?"

"Oh, no! But I have someone here who does."

A tall, handsome Asian man stepped out of the limousine.

"Gil-Su!" Jason said.

"Yes, it's me! And I've got all the others in the cars already. Aunt, Grandmother, Sun-Hye—all of them!" He rushed to Jason and the others, who were rising from their concealment.

"I must urge haste," the Nauran said. "Our moment of privacy is drawing to an end, I fear, and it would be best if you were all out of sight before that happened."

Gil-Su spoke quickly to Chun-Mi, still on her stretcher. Chun-Mi nodded her head so vigorously Jason thought she might throw a disk.

"Yes!" Gil-Su said, "she wants to claim asylum. And she speaks for the children, too." Then Gil-Su looked around frantically. "Where is Myong-Chol?"

Chris waved him to a spot on the white river rocks. Gil-Su went to Myong-Chol's body and knelt over it, instantly in prayer.

"Come," the Nauran said. "We must move now."

Jason and Lewis grabbed the stretcher and got Chun-Mi and her baby in one of the limos. Garth snatched up Ki-Won and bounded to another limo. Ki-Won laughed wildly and clutched Lewis's perfect rectangle. Chris carried Myong-Chol's stiff body to the third limo and put him in the back seat. Finally Jason put Trieu in and sat beside her.

He shut the door, and the cars began to roll just as military trucks tore up on the North Korean side and military Jeeps approached on the Chinese side.

Jason watched through deeply tinted windows as the Nauran official explained the situation. He and Trieu laughed at the looks of horror and consternation on the faces of the soldiers.

Then they watched the soldiers grow smaller and smaller in the rearview mirror.

EPILOGUE

"UH. . .OKAY, Gil-Su, thanks. I, um, I'm kind of new at this, so I. . . Well, I guess that's obvious, huh?"

The small congregation chuckled warmly. The faces out there were predominantly Asian, with a few familiar Caucasian faces and one wonderful black face. Besides the ethnic makeup of the congregation, the church looked like any small church Chris had ever seen. Two columns of wooden pews stretched back along a central aisle. Stained-glass windows lined either wall. The carpet was burgundy and the walls were white. Ceiling fans tried to keep the warm air circulating.

Chris held the wireless microphone to the side and cleared his throat. He shifted his legs, sloshing the water dangerously close to the lip of the baptismal pool at the front of the sanctuary.

"Well, I guess I should just tell you why I'm here." He took a deep breath. "You see, I was brought up in a Christian home. Went to church since I was two weeks old. Knew all the Sunday school verses and all. A leader in my youth group. I thought I had it all figured out. I'd heard every sermon ever preached, it seemed like. Three times!

"But there was always this little tickling in the back of my mind. Something the matter, you know? I'd hear people talk about having a 'personal relationship with Jesus,' and I thought I knew what that was. I thought I had it. Because, you know, I prayed and stuff. But sometimes I'd just meet someone who seemed to kind of have something real, you know? Something I didn't have. They kind of glowed or something. And I'd think, 'Man, I want that. Why don't I have that?'

"But all I ever knew was to do more stuff. Memorize more Bible verses. Join more committees. Go on more mission trips. Sometimes I could get that feeling like, 'Yeah, I know what they're talking about. I've got a personal relationship with Jesus. A friendship.' But then it would fade, you know?

"Anyway, I just kind of floated through life. Doing church stuff when I felt guilty, but most of the time just saying, 'Forget this. I can't maintain it,' you know? I got into the marines and, well, you know the marines." His forehead wrinkled. "Or maybe you don't. Anyway, it's pretty wild. You've got to be really strong in your faith to hang with it, you know? Because marines get pretty crazy in their free time. And I. . .I went pretty crazy with them. All kinds of crazy things. I did get married, but I messed that up.

"Anyway, I was pretty much at the bottom of the barrel when"—he looked at Eloise—"somebody found me. She gave me the chance to find my faith again, to be part of something for God. And I thought, 'Yeah, that's what I want. I'll do all this stuff for God and that'll really make Him want to be my friend, you know?' Dumb, huh? But I didn't know it. I did these things with this group, but I still knew something was missing. It's like I was playing some game or I was on stage. Everybody else was real, but I was a play actor.

"But then I met the guy we're burying today. Kim Myong-Chol.

He was radically saved, you know? Totally sold out to God. He knew he would die if he went back. . .to where he went, but he said he had to. He said he had to go to his home and tell people about Jesus.

"Now I've been around a lot of Christians in my life. I count some of them my dear friends." He found Jason's face in the crowd, and the faces of Rachel, Lewis, Garth, Trieu, Doug and Jamie Bigelow, and Eloise. "But nobody rocked my world like my brother Myong-Chol. He made me understand what real faith is. When I heard him tell his story, God, like, opened my mind and I saw myself. I saw that I'd totally missed the whole thing. I understood what it meant to have that personal relationship with Jesus because I saw it in Myong-Chol. And I knew I didn't have it for myself.

"That was the worst part: knowing I'd been lying to myself and everyone else for all those years. And knowing that if I'd died then I wouldn't go to heaven."

He fell silent. The water was cold around his legs and torso. The crowd was probably getting sick of his droning on and on. This was Los Angeles, after all—not exactly a place known for patience. But it was a Korean-American church, so they probably had better manners than most. And this was important.

"I know exactly when I gave my heart to Jesus Christ. It was a surrender for me. I gave up the game and my pride and the fight, and I surrendered my all to Jesus. It was outside this crazy man's farm over across a big ocean. I ran out through his wheat fields and past his pigs and chickens and found me a place under a big tree. And right there I did my business with the Almighty." He smiled at the congregation. "And now *I* have a friendship with Jesus Christ!"

"Amen!" the crowd answered.

"And I know it's not about what I do and stuff, but what He's already done! And what He's doing in me!"

"Amen!"

"Okay, Gil-Su, bro," Chris said. "I'd better hand this thing to you right now or I'm gonna jump out of this bath and lead us in some old-time religion!"

Eloise lifted her hands. "Glory, hallelujah!"

Gil-Su took the microphone, smiling broadly. "Chris, Myong-Chol was my hero, too. My heart is still weeping over the loss of that great saint. But I can think of no better celebration at his funeral than to baptize a man who came to Christ because of his witness. I *know* he's dancing in heaven right now." He raised his left hand and covered Chris's nose with his right. "And now, because of your profession of faith, in the name of the Father, the Son, and the Holy Spirit, I baptize you my brother. Buried in Christ's likeness. . ."

He plunged Chris under the water, then lifted him out, soaked and dripping.

"Raised to walk in newness of life."

* * *

"I've never been to a baptism-funeral."

Eloise laughed. "Neither have I, baby. But praise God, what a day!"

She and Jason waited together in the receiving line. They were in the fellowship hall-slash-Sunday school room-slash-weekday day care center of Gil-Su's church: Lighthouse Korean Baptist Church. The walls of the room were bright blue. A white column beside the door to the kitchen had a brown tree painted on it. Three women wearing plastic aprons stood at a table by the kitchen, ladling rice, soup, and a spicy smelling meat dish into wide bowls with tulips on the rim. Gil-Su's congregation talked and laughed and eagerly received their steaming bowls. It was a little chilly in here—perhaps compensation for the sanctuary, which had been too hot.

Chris shook hands and greeted people at the head of the line, his hair slicked back. Eloise was tenth in line. Jason was next. Trieu held Jason's hand and walked just behind him. Rachel, Garth, Chimp, Jamie, and Lewis followed. Garth had Ki-Won on his shoulders.

Gil-Su approached from the direction of the punch table. "How do you all like my church?"

"It's a blessed place, Reverend," Eloise said. "I declare I've never felt so welcome in a church."

"You're sweet to say it, sister. Enjoy your lunch." He shook hands with the team members and stopped in front of Lewis. "I know it's rare to find such a delicacy in Los Angeles, Lewis, but I told the ladies of the church how much you like *kimchi,* so they made up a batch just for you!"

Lewis's eyes bulged. "Please, no!"

They laughed.

"I'm only teasing," Gil-Su said. "Enjoy your meal. We go to the graveside in one hour."

The line paused and Eloise gave Jason a mighty hug.

"What was that for?" he asked.

"What's it for? It's for how I love you all. I just thought one more time of how blessed y'all were to get to see God's mighty right arm unleashed. Glory! And I just had to hug someone. Praise Jesus." She patted her hands together. "Didn't I tell you God's power is unveiled in places like this? Lord, I'm so blessed right now I could just bust. Tell me again about the angels, Jason. Pretty please. Tell me what they looked like. And what did Chun-Mi's river angels look like? Hallelujah! I wish I spoke Korean."

Jason looked over to where Chun-Mi sat in a padded chair beneath a painting of an Asian landscape. She looked radiant in her white sundress. Shin-Hwa slept in a white carriage at Chun-Mi's elbow.

"Well, I never saw any angels on this trip," Jason said. "Not that I know of, anyway. Chris saw the commando guys. I'm still not convinced they weren't SpecOps boys from somewhere. But Chris said they looked just like us. He said he thought they were using live ammo, but Chimp's satellite imagery showed no ambulances and no new graves. Radio traffic says nothing of needing lots of new guards. Nothing either about finding strange tranquilizer darts. Stuff really did blow up, but whatever those guys dished out, it didn't kill anybody."

"It's a miracle!" Eloise said. "A pack of miracles. Mercy, how good it is to serve our Savior. Can I get an amen?"

"Amen!" the team—and several bystanders—answered.

"And you'll have to get Gil-Su to ask Chun-Mi about the angels again. She says they looked like tall Asian warriors in her vision. And as for this kid," Jason said, tickling Ki-Won atop Garth's head, "who knows how he found us that night. Like I said, I didn't see any of it myself. But I would not be a bit surprised if this whole thing wasn't something God was up to and we just happened to be in the right place at the right time. I mean, look at us. We didn't even have cause to use that armor you made us lug halfway across China—though we did wear it. Considering what we pulled off, *that's* plenty of evidence that God was on the job."

"Mmm-*mmm*, what a mighty God we serve," Eloise said, shuffling forward with the line. "And don't forget they tried to abort that baby but it didn't work. I don't want to hear that they were medical students and they just flubbed it. I choose to believe that was the hand of the good Lord keeping that baby safe."

"Absolutely," Jason said. "Okay, but here's a miracle, too: the island nation of Nauru? How in the world did you come up with that?"

Eloise chortled. Then she wagged her head coquettishly and winked.

"Okay, keep your secrets. But that's the last time I call you 'the White Lady.' "

"Amen to that, boy! Thought I was going through a Michael Jackson turnaround for awhile, I tell you what."

They were at the front of the line now. Eloise gave Chris a huge hug. "Bless you, child."

Trieu hugged him and kissed his cheek. "Welcome to the family, Chris."

Chris extended his hand to Jason, but Jason went straight for the hug. "Praise God for you, my brother."

The others greeted him, too. Jason watched slyly as Rachel leaned in for her hug. She whispered to him for several seconds, then planted a kiss on his cheek that was something more than polite. It lingered. Chris held her elbows and kissed her cheek back. When Rachel finally turned away, her cheeks were bright red.

Her eyes met Jason's. He lifted an "I caught you" finger at her then gave her a double thumbs-up. She swatted a hand at him, but he could tell she was pleased.

He and Trieu got punch and drifted toward the refugees, who sat together. He greeted each one. Grandmother, the matriarch and sometime prophetess. She had seen so much. Aunt, whose foul demeanor had seemed to fade away with the tuberculosis. And according to Gil-Su, she had prayed to receive Jesus. Uncle, who looked old and small, smiled brightly when Jason shook his hand. Youn-Chul, who never left Sun-Hye's side. She sat very close to him, almost clinging. Gil-Su said they were engaged but had wisely decided not to set a date for at least a year. Joo-Chan sat with them, on loan from South Korea for a few days.

Eloise was providing counseling for them all. With the exception of "Jilin Jade," the prostitute rescued with Sun-Hye, who stayed in Seoul where she had extended family, the entire group had elected to immigrate to America.

Then there was Chun-Mi and her baby. Jason knelt beside her. "I know you don't understand me," he said to Chun-Mi, "but I want you to know how sorry I am for the loss of Bum-Ji. He was a wonderful man."

Her smile mellowed at the mention of her husband's name, but it remained a smile nonetheless.

Jason stroked the baby's scruffy black hair. She was tiny and thin, but her eyes shone like black stars and her hands gripped his finger with strength like her mother's faith. She wore a frilly pink dress. "God's peace," he said softly. "Shin-Hwa."

Now it was Chun-Mi's turn to speak to Jason and Trieu. They couldn't understand her, and yet, they could. She was saying, "Thank you. I have lived a terrible life. But full of joy, too. In a dark place when I had despaired, you brought me hope. Thank God for you."

They hugged and wept.

Finally Jason led Trieu to a couple of metal folding chairs away from the chatting crowd. "Well," he said, "it looks like you and I are going to have a chance, after all. I'm not letting a little thing like a hostile nation let you get away from me, you know."

She smiled coyly. "Just try to lose me."

He took her hand and caressed it. "You're amazing, Trieu. Have I told you that lately? I still can't believe you delivered a baby in a North Korean concentration camp. Talk about life rising out of death. There's a resurrection story for you."

She nodded. "I think you're pretty amazing yourself. How you deal with all the surprises we face and still lead us with such resolve. It's a beautiful thing to watch."

They sat together quietly, watching their friends goof off, watching Ki-Won run around with a whole stack of shapes, watching Eloise laugh with thin Korean women, watching eight North Koreans beginning a new life in the country of people they once thought were savages.

"So," he said, leaning in and kissing Trieu's ear, "have you decided where you want to go for our honeymoon?"

"You mean there's something more than the trip Eloise is sending us on?"

"Yes. St. Moritz is amazing, I'm sure. I can't wait. But when you and I are married, I want to go somewhere alone. Somewhere wonderful. Anywhere you want."

She raised her eyebrows. "Anywhere, Jason?"

He chuckled. "I trust you, Trieu. Anywhere you want."

"All right. Then I'll give it some serious thought. But don't we have a wedding to plan first? You're not getting your honeymoon without my wedding, buddy. Come to think of it, I still don't have an engagement ring from you. You'd better get busy, mister."

Jason smiled. "Oh, Trieu, I knew you'd make an honest man out of me."

Her presence took his breath away. How she sat, what she could do, the depth of her faith. Here was his angel. He didn't know if he could take her into battle again, but one thing was for sure: They were getting married first. He'd already cleared it with Eloise.

The world could wait.

ABOUT THE AUTHOR

Jefferson Scott has written several thriller novels, including *Operation: Firebrand, Operation Firebrand: Crusade, Fatal Defect,* and *Terminal Logic.* A graduate of both seminary and film school, he currently lives in Orlando, Florida. Visit the author's Web site at www.jeffersonscott.com.